When the Moon Met the Sun

The Ashford Saga: Book One

Alaina Hope

When the Moon Met the Sun

The Ashford Saga: Book One

Copyright © 2025 by Alaina Hope

Editing by Hannah G. Scheffer-Wentz, English Proper Editing Services

Cover art, map illustration, and internal illustrations by Kelci Parsell, Kelci2D, https://kelci2d.framer.website

For those whose light has been dimmed.

Burn bright enough to blind.

ANVALI
OCEAN

Jackton

Glaytred
Forest

Neokell

Acrynd

Kyrish

Wittuck
Woods

LEVAST

ISLES

The Haven

Cairnyl

Telawol

Yarpeck
Woods

Breckshyre

Diorum

The Cabin

ECHEN

BAY

Prologue

I sit at my mother's vanity, looking at my reflection in the mirror, Mother standing behind me as she places different tiaras on my head. Today I turn five, which means I'm finally old enough to pick out my tiara for official appearances. Mother took it upon herself to present all the options to me herself, instead of having a servant do it.

So far we've gone through six, and there's only two left.

I hope I like one of them.

The next tiara Mother places on my temples takes my breath away. It's nothing like the ones I tried on before—they were either too heavy, didn't fit appropriately, or simply didn't look perfect upon my head.

But this one? It is most definitely *perfect.*

It's silver, of course, but instead of diamonds, it has rich, purple gems embedded in it, each one so vibrant it reminds me of the soft purple at the center of the moon lilies in the royal gardens. The gems make a pretty swirling pattern, and I know this is the one I want.

"This one, Mother. It's beautiful," I say to her, leaning closer to the mirror for a better look. I can't help but grin from ear to ear at the sight.

I can't help but think about how much I look like my mother.

The straight of my nose. My heart-shaped face. Even the set of my lips. It all resembles her.

"Alright, my sweet. It's a lovely choice," she said, tucking all of the other headpieces back into the boxes they came in. Then, she comes and kneels beside me, taking my small hands in hers.

I look at the scars on her wrists, the ones that look red and puffy, as though they never fully healed. I asked her once what they were from, but she started to cry, so I didn't ask again. Now, I'm unsure if I really want to know.

"You look stunning," she said softly, placing her finger under my chin and tilting my head up, forcing my gaze away from her scars, so our eyes meet.

"Thank you, Mother. I think I look like you," I say with a smile. She smiles in return.

"Now, are you ready to practice? Remember, this is our little secret," she said in a low voice. I notice her eyes shift to check that the door to her chambers is shut.

I nod enthusiastically. This is just another reason, one of countless, why I love my mother so much. She actually lets me practice my zirilium, while Father only wants me to hide it. I don't understand why, but he can be mean and scary, so I don't use it around him. I only feel safe letting them show when I'm with Mother.

She smiles at my excitement, letting go of my hands and cupping hers together in front of her. I mimic her movements, doing the same.

"Great. Now, just like we practiced last time. Envision the flower sprouting from the palm of your hands, and…" she trailed off, having closed her eyes as she spoke. A small, green sprout emerges from her hands, out of thin air. I watch with wide eyes as it grows taller and taller, until a fully mature moon lily sits in her hands.

She opens her eyes and smiles at me, then shifts my hair, placing the flower behind my pointed ear. I return her smile, amazed that she's able to conjure plants from nothing. I don't know anybody else in the North that can do the things that Mother does.

Then again, Mother is special. She's not like the other Northerners—she doesn't have wings like the rest of us.

"Now it's your turn, alright? You've got it this time, my sweet. You were nearly there last time we practiced," she said. "Focus your energy

on the task at hand, and it'll come to you. The zirilium needs an outlet."

I nod, closing my eyes, just as I had seen my mother do countless times before.

I strain, feeling all my zirilium coursing through my small body. I reach for the one I need, the one that has the same softness as a flower petal, and focus all of my energy into the palms of my hands where the plant should sprout from.

But I never get the chance.

I hear Father's voice before I see him. The door to Mother's chambers slams open, rattling the doorframe. He begins yelling at Mother, saying all sorts of things that he's too loud and angry about for me to hear him clearly.

My eyes fly open, startled, and I see Mother is standing between me and Father now. She's... shielding me from him, I realize with a start.

"Elore, I told you what the plan was regarding her, and yet you're still going against my direct orders! This," Father points between me and Mother, "is not happening."

"Horace, just let me explain—" Mother attempts to rationalize, but Father moves faster than either one of us could've anticipated. The back of his hand flies across Mother's cheek, causing her to crumple to the ground, holding her hands over her reddening face.

"Mother!" I gasp.

Time seems to slow in that second. I can feel where I still have harnessed energy resting in the palm of my hands, but suddenly I'm losing control over it. Instead of the softness I felt before, the zirilium feels hot, almost painfully so. I can't seem to stop it as the rest of the energy in my slight form gathers in my hands, beginning to shake from the strain.

The sound of Father's voice grounds me to the moment, a constant string of curses flying from his mouth as he stands over Mother. I watch as Father raises his hand in an attempt to strike Mother again.

She's kneeling now, begging him not to hurt me. A wave of sadness overcomes me, then anger.

With a cry, I use my wings to boost me, to be able to run fast enough to get in between the two of them before Father can strike again.

"No!" I yell, then throw myself into my Mother's arms, trying to shield her body with my own, like she had done for me so many times.

Except this time, when my hands make contact with her skin, there's a flash of blue.

Then she lets out a gut wrenching scream of pain.

Assuming the scream is from the pain of Father hitting her, I hold on tighter, trying to provide her with even an ounce of comfort.

Suddenly, I'm yanked backwards, off of Mother, by strong hands—Father's hands. I squirm, screaming for Mother, but for some reason, she's crumpled on the ground, not moving.

This only causes me to panic more, but for a reason I can't place, I realize I'm suddenly extremely tired.

The fight dies out of me, and I stand with Father holding me by the shoulders as we both stare down at my mother's unmoving form.

I listen, as if from a distance to my father's voice, devoid of all emotion, say, "You did this to her, Aviva. This is all your fault."

I don't see Mother again after that day.

Chapter One

"Come on, Aviva, pick up the sword."

I peered out across the large, cobbled terrace I stood on, watching as dark clouds began gathering to the north. Spring had just begun, but apparently the sky here wasn't aware, as it was ready to continue dropping fresh snow on top of the ice still coating the ground from the storm last week.

I took in a deep breath of fresh mountain air, trying to soak in the rare opportunity to enjoy the outdoors without a downpour of some sort.

As I basked in the sun's unforgiving rays, I leaned down to pick up the sword my *lovely* twin brother had tossed at my feet moments before, like he'd instructed.

"Good. Now remember your stance, and then..." I barely had time to get myself into position before he leapt forward, knocking the sword from my hands—for the third time in a row—in one swift motion.

"I surrender," I groaned before lowering myself to the ground, splaying my wings out on the stone behind me. In the North, wings touching the ground was generally not allowed, especially as royalty, and supposedly reflected poor character—but when it was just me and Dimitri, neither one of us cared all that much. I also didn't care in the moment that my gown would likely become filthy so soon before dinner. "You know swords aren't my specialty, Dimitri. Now, add some daggers into the mix, and then we can have some real fun." I grinned up at my brother, hoping he wasn't too disappointed in my easy defeat today.

Any day Dimitri had to spare, he insisted on dragging me to this terrace to train with me or practice a new maneuver he learned—as though he hadn't trained me enough in our nineteen years of life together.

He shook his head, sighing, but a small smile tugged at the corners of his mouth. "You might be in a position one day where you won't have your daggers, Viva. You're more likely to find a discarded sword on the battlefield, rather than a dagger. I just want you to be prepared for anything."

I wondered to myself what the point was, since females weren't even permitted in our father's army, but decided to keep that thought to myself.

He walked over to where I sat and took up a spot next to me, bumping my shoulder with his affectionately. "I will have to take you up on the offer to fight you on your terms, though. Maybe it'll help convince me you're not completely hopeless after all." He said it as a joke, but to me, I knew there was a layer of truth to it.

Being the cast-aside princess of a kingdom at war wasn't the easiest role to play. It wasn't a role at all, really. Our father resented me, although I couldn't know for sure why due to the fragmented memories that made up my early childhood. From what I gathered, I believed it was due to the fact that I was born fortunate enough to be able to wield all five northern zirilium, while Father's only son, Dimitri, couldn't wield any. What Dimitri lacked in wielding, though, he made up for in swordsmanship. He never needed to be able to wield ice or lightning, water or air, or even the weather.

Although, it wasn't like Dimitri knew I could wield anything, let alone all five Northern zirilium. He didn't know why Father treated me the way he did. In the eyes of my brother, we were both powerless, so we should be on equal ground, right?

Due to Father resenting me for things I couldn't control, he preferred to keep me out of the public's eye. I rarely got permission to leave the castle grounds, but I still snuck into the city often enough to be recognized by the townspeople if I wasn't careful. As Dimitri and I got older, though, he'd been able to sway Father more and more into giving me more freedom. Though it was likely just to please Dimitri, more than anything. I treasured those precious memories, especially on days like today. One time, he convinced Father to allow me to accompany him to The Thousand Stars Festival some years ago, seeing as it only happens once a decade. Father had told us once how much Mother had loved the festival—one of the only positive memories he ever shared about her—and I had been set on going ever since. The night of the festival, Dimitri and I shared a floating lantern, as we shared everything, and wrote as many anxieties and fears on it as we could. So many, in fact, I was surprised it was still able to float while carrying the weight of our burdens—but float it did. And though my problems didn't disappear that night, for just a moment, I had felt lighter.

"I don't want to go to Father's dinner this evening. Can't you make up an excuse to get us both out of it? We could sneak into the city instead," I suggested to my brother, trying not to sound too desperate. I'd do almost anything to avoid such an uncomfortable night. Not only was it a dinner with Father and his advisors, there would also be an ambassador from the South there. The news about the ambassador had come as a surprise to us all. The North and the South of Inphis, our continent, had been fighting since long before I was born. Though, if the rumors were true, there was a new king in the South. Rumor has it he was looking to find peace with us, instead of war. I imagined I was only invited to dinner to play the part of the pretty, obedient princess, but even then, if I could avoid the whole ordeal, I would.

Not only that, but I also wasn't sure I wanted to be anywhere near a Southerner. The thought of sitting at the same table with somebody who has likely committed war crimes against my people made my stomach turn sour.

"Please," I said, turning to face him. "I hate having to put on such a facade for Father's diplomatic purposes. I doubt I'll even talk to anybody the whole night if I were to go. Nobody would miss me if I weren't there, and we both know it."

Dimitri sighed, running a hand through his snow-white hair, the color matching mine perfectly. A Heartshire family trait that had been passed down from our late grandparents, and their parents before them. "I'm sorry, Viva, I can't this time. Father specifically requested your presence for tonight. Aurora will be here any moment to help you get ready." He looked at me with a gleam in his eyes I couldn't quite place, which was unusual for us. Usually, I could read him like an open book.

I should have been excited at the news that my best friend would arrive soon. That was what I *should* have focused on. Yet all I could focus on was the fact that Father actually *wanted* me there tonight, along with the unsettling look Dimitri had in his eyes.

"Are you sure he was talking about *me?* Do you know why?" I questioned, my thoughts beginning to run rampant.

The only time I routinely saw Father was once a day, around midmorning. He and Hugo, our royal trokav, visited my chambers every day to bring me my daily elixir. The one I'd been taking for as long as I could recall. Ever since the accident when I was a small girl, I'd willingly taken it. Father said I was born with a slight defect, which was why the accident happened in the first place, and the elixir helped correct it. Considering he found it important enough to personally see to the task every day without fail, I never pushed for more answers aside from the bits and pieces I remembered myself. After all, one should be able to trust their own father.

Dimitri slowly rose from the ground, offering me his hand. "No, he wouldn't tell me, but I can't shake the feeling he's planning something for tonight. Something big." He sounded worried, the opposite of his usual bravado and confidence. The tone of his voice made my stomach drop.

"Please be careful tonight. Stay with Aurora if she's permitted inside the room," he said as I took his hand and rose to my feet.

"You know I will. But please, if you discover anything before then, find me," I said, watching him as he picked up our discarded swords and placed them back on the racks that covered the stone wall behind us.

Just as Dimitri opened his mouth to speak, another voice called out, "Viva!"

A smile erupted across my face at the sound of her voice. I spun on my heels and caught sight of Aurora descending from the sky, her smokey-gray wings elegantly pumping at just the right pace for a perfect landing. A moment later, I found myself wrapped up in her, squeezing her tight and letting her cinnamon scent wash over me.

"I've missed you!" I said, pulling back after a moment. Dimitri and I met Aurora the night of The Thousand Stars Festival after some older kids had broken the frame of her lantern, so it couldn't fly. We offered to have her light ours and help us send it off, and she'd happily accepted. Together, the three of us watched our lantern soar high above our heads and join the other nine hundred ninety-eight. Since that night, she'd been my best friend. And although I didn't get to see her often growing up, in recent years she had begun studying under Hugo to be the next royal trokav, so she resides in the castle now. I was grateful that she lives so close now, as I used to go months without seeing her.

"I've missed you, too. When Dimitri mentioned the dinner tonight, I figured it would be a good excuse to tell Hugo in order to see you and help you get ready," Aurora said with her usual small, mischievous smile playing on her full lips.

"Can Aurora and I go for a really quick fly before we go get ready? Please Dimi?" I asked, turning back to face my brother. He crossed his arms over his chest, looking ready to say no, before he saw the pleading look on my face. Emotion flashed across his features, then he sighed and shook his head, knowing I had won without saying another word. It seems I would always hold a soft spot in my brother's heart.

I grinned, unfurled my wings, and launched myself into the sky in one quick motion.

My bone white hair whipped across my face as I soared upward in a spiral, then leveled out. I looked down to see Aurora hot on my heels. My smile broadened, and I pumped my wings even harder than before, prepared to out-fly her. Despite being stuck inside the castle the majority of the time, I'd always been able to beat her and Dimitri in a race in the sky.

I took off in a counterclockwise circle around the castle, feeling the chilly wind reach between every silver tipped feather of my white wings like an icy caress. I took the opportunity to look out across the kingdom I called home. Gatlyn Castle was nestled between the western portion of the Salic Mountains, providing natural protection on almost every side. To the south lay Hollis, the largest establishment of citizens in our territory. The city sat at the base of the mountains just below the castle, nestled nicely into the largest valley in the entire mountain range. We often called it the Tower City, as many of the buildings here practically touched the sky and had ledges that us winged fae could fly straight into, with bridges connecting them all. As I glided through the sky, I came to the edge of the mountain range where it suddenly dropped off into Cynth Bay.

I paused, holding myself suspended in the sky with a gentle pumping of my wings. I opened my arms wide and tilted my chin towards the clouds above my head, taking in every second of this moment that I could. I loved being a child of the sky, and the freedom that came with it. I would live up here with the clouds as my neighbors, if it were possible.

The sound of frantic wing beats snapped me out of my thoughts, and I turned around to find Aurora coming to a halt in front of me.

"How do you always manage to leave me behind in the clouds like that?" Aurora exclaimed, slightly out of breath.

"By actually *trying*," I teased.

"When Dimi is here, I can usually use him as an excuse for being left behind like that. But alas, today I have no such excuse. I really need to step up my game. Maybe I'll even beat you home this time," Aurora replied, grinning.

Dimitri's own white, silvery-gray tipped wings—the spitting image of my own—didn't get as much use nowadays with all of the meetings Father has had him attending lately. Six months ago, Father appointed him to be a part of his War Council. Dimitri had been ecstatic, delighted at the opportunity to be of greater help to our people. Unfortunately, he wasn't allowed to share much of what went on in the meetings, but he always assured me most of it was a bore, anyways.

"Speaking of home, we have to get going. Dinner with the Southern ambassador starts at dusk," Aurora said, blowing out a breath.

I sighed. I knew she was right, but I hated it all the same.

Just as I opened my mouth to try to convince her of helping me sneak out of dinner, the snow began. Small snowflakes clung to my eyelashes, hair, and clothing. Aurora squealed and quickly flew to my side. "Zirilium please, Viva! We can't look too horrid for dinner!"

A part of me wanted to relish in the moment and let the snow soak into my bones, but I knew my friend—my sister—was right. Father would be furious if I showed up to dinner soaked and frostbitten from the snow.

Aurora moved closer as I took a second to focus. I focused on the feeling of joy and freedom I had felt in the sky just moments before. Since I wasn't allowed to openly practice my wielding, it doesn't come as easily to me as other Northerners. Tapping into my emotions gave me something to focus on when my surroundings weren't calm like my mind needed to be in order to wield.

Enveloped by that fleeting memory of peace, I waved a hand over our heads, letting a constantly moving air current escape me. The snow, not being able to get through the rapidly spinning disk of air, continued its descent to the ground around us, without another snowflake touching the two of us.

"Let's get back to the castle. Then we can get you all fixed up and ready for what I'm sure will be a great dinner." Aurora spoke loudly so I could hear her over the wind and snow, remaining positive as always. I nodded my head in response, and together we made our way back to the castle under the protection of my air zirilium.

***

The next half hour was a fury of dress picking and hair braiding. Aurora had selected for me a beautiful, lilac-colored, silk gown that grazed the floor with a white, lace accented corset, complete with a floral pattern at the end of the sleeves and on the small train that trailed behind me. She braided my hair into a waterfall type style and wove in small lilac flowers. For the final touch, I clipped my necklace on, resting the five small, pale stones at the end of the chain between my breasts underneath my dress, so they couldn't be seen. Five moon stones, one for each Northern zirilium I was able to wield. I didn't expect to need them tonight, but I always found it comforting to have them on.

I caught a glimpse at myself in the mirror and paused, even though Aurora had just told me to hurry out the door. I looked... pretty—for once. Usually, my royal stylist made me look much older than I am, but this outfit looked as though it had been made for me alone. Aurora knew exactly what I liked, and what I needed tonight. I'd likely never feel completely comfortable in all these priceless dresses Father deemed necessary for me to wear, but tonight was the closest I'd likely ever get.

I turned to my best friend and closed the distance between us, pulling her into a hug.

"Thank you," I whispered into her shimmering blonde hair. I felt her wrap her arms around me, holding me like she may never get another chance to.

"I love you, you know. Now, we really do need to get going," she said, stepping towards the door and opening it for me.

"We forgot something!" I said over my shoulder as I rushed back into the heart of my chambers. My large, wood framed bed sat in the middle of the room against the far wall, colored in the North's signature colors of silver and blue, with wooden bookshelves and silver accents taking up every inch of space they possibly could along the far left wall. The right wall housed the entry to the washroom. Next to that was my vanity where I had sat just moments before as Aurora meticulously put every hair in a specific place atop my head.

Sitting on the left side of the vanity atop a white, velvet pillow sat my mother's tiara. Father had passed it down to me on my thirteenth birthday, and since then, it had been among my most prized possessions. Now, its aquamarine centerpiece shimmered as I reached for it, as if it could sense it was about to be worn again after so long. I rarely had an appropriate opportunity to wear it, seeing as I didn't usually get the chance to represent my nation in front of anybody, let alone somebody from the South. Everybody in the North already knew who I was, as most have watched me grow up—at least from afar—so the tiara more often than not remained on its perch, watching and waiting.

"Here, let me help," Aurora said, striding over and gently taking the tiara from my hands. I turned to face her as she placed the tiara on top of my head, nestling nicely atop the braid she had woven.

"There. *Now* you're ready," she said with a smile tugging on the corners of her mouth. I peered at my reflection in the mirror one more time. A smile crept onto my own lips as I realized how much I looked like the paintings I had seen of my mother, even if only for tonight.

"Alright, let's go," I said to my best friend, linking our arms together. Knowing I could face anything so long as my best friend and twin were present, we walked out of the door and towards the unknown of the evening.

Chapter Two

I took up my place at my father's left side while Dimitri sat to his right, both of us looking out across the long, marble table that Father often used for meetings with his advisors, all of whom were present. The Southerner and I were the only females at the table, as the advisors my father kept were all males. On the tabletop was showcased a variety of traditional Northern treats—a giant roasted hog, candied carrots, spinach and strawberry salad, and some sort of pie I couldn't make out from my position. Then there were other dishes I didn't recognize, which I assumed were dishes native to the South, to make our guest more comfortable.

Father had addressed her as Princess, so not only was she here as an ambassador for the South, she was also royalty. She sat at the other end of the long table, opposite of Father, her dirty blonde hair so rich it was almost a brown color instead. She held her chin high, her shoulders squared back, and a soft smile played on her lips. She was dressed in fitted, brown trousers and a cream-colored tunic, with colorful jewels hanging from her pointed ears, throat, and wrists. A circlet of golden ivy sat upon her temples, curving around the back of her head. The title of "Princess" didn't even need to be spoken aloud for one to know she was important, and it was obvious that she knew it, too.

The thing that stood out the most to me, though, was a curious set of brown markings on the back of her right hand, crawling up the back of her forearm. It was a specifically detailed pattern of swirls and swoops, the darker brown making it stand out against her tan, freckled skin.

Her appearance, while regal, still shocked me and left me stunned. The Princess didn't *look* like somebody who would kill my people in cold blood, or sit back and laugh while she ordered Father's soldiers' wings chopped off. She looked oddly sophisticated—nothing like the cruel beasts that I'd grown up hearing stories about. Beasts who shouldn't even be allowed to call themselves fae.

"Thank you for joining us here in the North tonight, Princess and Ambassador Teagan Thorntier. It's an honor to have you present as our guest, and we're grateful you made the long journey to be here. We hope you make yourself at home throughout the duration of your visit." The voice of my father, King Horace Heartshire, rang out across the room, making all of the chatter that may have been occurring cease instantly. I watched as all heads turned his way, his voice alone commanding attention. That wasn't the only thing about him that demanded attention, though.

The high backed wooden chair he sat upon, which had been custom made specifically for Northerners with large wings, also drew immediate attention. The top of it was crowned with a carving of a wing overlapping a crescent moon—the symbol of the Northern royal house, the Heartshire's family line. This wasn't his throne room, but the chair he sat upon was close enough to a throne that it still drew immediate attention to it, due to its sheer size and the fact that all other chairs around the table were of normal sizing. Another variable was likely his giant, black wings that poked out from above his broad shoulders, even though they were tucked in close to his body. Black wings were a rare sight to see, even among us winged fae of the North.

Something that had always stood out to me personally, though, was Father's graying, black hair. An obvious sign of aging. I spent so much time reading, it was difficult to imagine the era, centuries ago, where us fae were *truly* immortal. When we didn't age as the humans do, when we were known for more than just our zirilium. In today's world, our lifespans didn't exceed that of a normal human—the only humans being those in the Levast Isles—and I felt as though we as a people had simply accepted that fact. Nothing, not even the records, said *exactly* what caused the fae to lose their immortality. And nowadays, nobody seemed to care all that much.

Well, at least nobody in the castle talked much about it. I'd heard rumors of fae making it their life mission to travel our realm in search of answers, but most Northerners were too busy fighting to survive, fighting in war, or fighting to please my father to worry about our lost immortality.

Personally, I'd always wondered what it would be like to know true immortality, as our ancestors did. As a young girl, I used to tell Dimitri that I'd crack the mystery someday. That I'd be an adventurer, somebody brave and courageous, who would finally restore the fae to their previous glory.

I'd since outgrown such silly, unrealistic daydreams.

Continuing to drown out the voice of my father as he began introducing his advisors to Princess Teagan one by one, I gazed around the large meeting room turned dining room instead, my mind still far away. I was rarely permitted inside—on any normal day, it would be used only by Father and his advisors. The gray cobbled stone walls rose high above our heads, with a giant crystal chandelier hanging down above the marble table in the center of the room. Windows lined the long side wall, providing a clear view of the snowy Salic mountain scape that surrounded Gatlyn Castle.

Looking out of the south facing windows, I could see Hollis laying at the base of the mountains in the distance, most windows and buildings lit up by lanterns for the evening. That was the city that Dimitri and I would always sneak out to explore as kids. The city that held The Thousand Stars Festival once a decade, and where we met Aurora. The city that was bursting at the seams with life, food, and music, which held so many of my favorite memories. The only place I felt a sliver of peace at—on the ground at least. There, dressed in commoners clothing, I was just Aviva. Sure, I was recognized sometimes, but when we visited in secret, hood obscuring my features, nobody could tell I was my father's daughter. And that in itself took such a heavy weight off my shoulders.

"And to my left, the Princess of the North and twin to my heir, Prince Dimitri, is Aviva. Princess Aviva, rise." I was snapped back into the present as Father introduced me to the room. I swiftly rose to my feet on command, my heart suddenly racing as every pair of eyes in the room fell on me. My eyes flicked up to meet Aurora's, who stood along the far wall next to Hugo. Instincts kicking in, I curtsied, inclining my head slightly towards Princess Teagan, giving her my respect.

"It's an honor to make your acquaintance, Princess Teagan," I said, doing my best to keep a small smile on my face to mask my growing mix of emotions. I couldn't help the anger bubbling in my stomach as I spoke, but also a small piece of me envied the female before me. She had something I didn't—a *purpose* for her kingdom.

Princess Teagan smiled in return and swiftly nodded before I sat back down.

"Now, I'd love to get down to business if that's alright with you, King Horace," Teagan said, her voice firm and strong as she met Father's gaze.

"Why of course, Princess. Go right ahead," Father said, a small, mischievous grin beginning to play on his mouth.

"As you well know, Your Highness, our two nations have been at war for centuries. My brother, the South's newly appointed King, has recently ascended the throne after the death of our parents. One of his wishes for our nation and our home is to put an end to this war between us. I've come here today to discuss this with you and see if there is anything the South can do to make this happen. For the sake of both of our people," Teagan said, subconsciously sitting taller as she spoke, like she was trying to appear larger than she was.

Her proposition surprised me—she worded it as though she cared for those beyond her borders.

My father took a moment, letting the words sink into the room before he asked, "And what would you propose to make this happen?"

Teagan looked ready for this, responding fluidly. "My king suggested a project both nations could partake in to bring us closer together. We could build a town together, somewhere in the middle of our two lands, where volunteers from both nations who also want peace could move to. A merging of our two people in one place, to start."

The newly appointed king was a bit of a mystery—there wasn't a soul in the North who had met him or even had direct contact with him yet since his coronation.

Father seemed to ponder this a moment, then looked around the room at his advisors. "My dear advisors—do you believe any of your people would be willing to make such a move? To reside in the same town as ones from the South?" he asked them, his demeanor calm but curious.

A choir of responses along the lines of, *no* and *not a chance* rang out from the table of advisors, causing Teagan to inhale a sharp breath.

Father's advisors each had a smaller city than Hollis that they oversaw and cared for in the North, most being scattered around within the mountains somewhere. It didn't surprise me that Father was displaying the situation as leaving the decision up to them, though they all know they'd risk losing everything if they went against him.

"I'm sorry, Princess Teagan, but I don't think that will work for my people. Did your king have any other ideas?" Father asked, swiftly rejecting her proposal and turning his full attention back to her.

"Of course," Teagan said, refocusing. "We'd like to offer to have a portion of our plant wielders visit some of your less privileged towns to provide healing herbs and vegetables. They could teach them how to maintain the plants in their environment, so your people could provide for themselves. We assume after being at war for so long, this would be beneficial for your people. Many of them also serve as our trokavs, and as such, they can teach your people which plants could best serve them based on different illnesses or wounds."

Trokavs—our healers—in the North were often water wielders, but in the South they must be plant wielders. *How convenient it must be to be able to sprout any herb you need*, I couldn't help but think.

Father looked around the table of advisors once again before he asked, "Advisors—are you having any trouble providing for, healing, and feeding your own people?"

Another chorus of *no* rose from the table, but it was noticeably less confident this time.

"It seems we're sufficient on that front as well, Princess Teagan, though it was a swell idea. What else do you have for me?" Father asked, his grin growing slightly.

A muscle in Teagan's jaw ticked in frustration, but she quickly masked it, moving forward. "Truthfully, Your Highness, we were hoping one of those solutions would work for you. But, we also considered asking some of our crystal wielders to come to the

North for a period of time, to help your people find your moon stones easier and more efficiently. Is that something that would interest you instead?" Teagan asked.

The South had their own set of zirilium—earth, fire, plants, crystals, and shadows. Although shadows didn't originate with the South, but rather the Ocrein Isles to the west, their two peoples mixed for centuries in the past, their zirilium melting together in return.

The South's crystal wielders were so in tune with the world around them, they could sense the crystals in the ground that they forged their sun stones from, and those which the North forged our moon stones from. Without crystal wielders, our people dug blindly for these rocks. The sun and moon stones were then fashioned into different pieces that can be worn, the most common in the South being gloves, so the zirilium wielder wearing them could draw strength and power from them. These stones were essential in battle and they helped those still mastering their wielding to have better control and focus over their zirilium.

Father took a moment before turning to one of the advisors sitting across from Teagan. If my memory served correctly, he oversaw Neokell, to the east.

"Advisor Clive. How are things at the mountain dig site and mines? Has our efficiency decreased at all as of late?" Father asked, addressing Clive directly.

Clive, a burly male who looked as though he desperately needed a hair trimming, cleared his throat before responding, "No, Your Majesty."

Nobody addressed his obvious hesitation.

"I thought that was the case, though this is my favorite proposition so far, and can be discussed further in the future. Princess Teagan?" Father said expectantly.

Teagan's pointed ears had turned a bright shade of red, but her face was a perfect mask of control.

"Your Majesty, did you have something specific in mind instead of the propositions I've brought before you?" Teagan asked, her tone clipped and more serious than before.

I turned my head to watch as a full smirk spread across my father's face. For a moment, he looked purely wicked.

"Everybody besides our dear guest and my children, get out of my sight. *Now*."

There was a pause, as if the room itself was holding its breath. Nobody present had been expecting something like this, but to disobey Father was a death wish. I watched the back of Aurora's head as she walked out after a beat of hesitation. A few moments later, the room had been cleared, even of the servants.

Teagan raised an eyebrow and motioned to the now empty room. "So?"

"You were right, Princess. I do have something specific in mind. Aviva, stand." Father commanded.

My stomach plummeted to the floor, but I slowly rose, standing straight with my wings tucked close to my back. My heart began pounding as I turned my head to gaze upon my father in anticipation.

My father held an arm out to me, turning back towards Teagan, before announcing: "To begin finding a way to coexist peacefully, I want your king to marry my daughter, Princess Aviva."

Chapter Three

"**W**hat?" Dimitri exclaimed, suddenly on his feet and slamming his hands onto the table before us. "Father, you can't be serious."

My ears rung as Father and Dimitri argued, and suddenly I couldn't hear a single word they were saying as my thoughts spiraled.

Me. *Marry.* My father wanted to marry me off to the King of the South, to the *enemy.* I knew my father likely resented me, but I didn't know he *loathed* me like this. I'd lived my whole life hearing about the atrocities the South had committed against my people, to the point where I only knew how to feel disgust and fear towards them.

This must have been the *something big* Dimitri had felt our father was planning. We had recently turned nineteen, the age where Northerners were generally allowed to start getting married if they wished to do so. But I always thought I'd marry for love—not as one of Father's power moves.

I'd only ever experienced love from within the pages of a book, never firsthand. I used to dream of finding love as a child, and even as a young teenager, with my books fueling my imagination.

All of those dreams feel as though they had just evaporated into thin air.

I looked down at my blank left forearm—the spot where, once an Inphisian gets married, the other party's family sigil goes. Both female and male received the other's family crest as a tattoo—a permanent mark to serve as a permanent reminder of whose family you belonged to and served.

"That's quite *enough*, Prince Dimitri. This doesn't concern you any longer—I allowed you to stay as a privilege, but obviously you can't be trusted to behave. Therefore, you're dismissed." Father's booming voice overpowered the protests of Dimitri, bringing me back to the scene playing out before me.

Dimitri opened his mouth to continue arguing, but Father held up a hand and said, "Now, Dimitri."

My twin's mouth snapped shut and his jaw clenched together hard. He met my eyes and I knew he could read every emotion and anguished thought on my face in that moment.

I'm so sorry, he mouthed to me, before swiftly walking out of the large room without looking back.

My father ran a hand through his salt and pepper colored hair. "I apologize for my son's outburst. Now that he's been handled, what do you say, Princess Teagan?" Father asked after taking a steadying breath.

Teagan hadn't let her carefully crafted mask of control slip, but it was cracking. Her eyes narrowed as she gazed upon my father, and she lightly worried the inside of her cheek between her teeth. Though the rest of her body language didn't give it away, her eyes showed how she was contemplating all of the ways this could have gone differently—and that she still hadn't been expecting this.

Though I hadn't been permitted off the castle grounds very much throughout my life, I always observed people. The guards and servants around the castle, the instructors and mentors Dimi and I had growing up, and even the people of Hollis when I had the opportunity to sneak out. Reading other's expressions and emotions came as easily to me as flying did.

Teagan inhaled a deep breath before saying, "You can't expect me to make a call like this for my brother. We will consider your offer, if you're sure none of my earlier propositions would work instead. But I must return home to discuss this with my king first."

"Unfortunately your propositions will not work, but I believe this to be a great idea for our two peoples. I would hate for you to make such an important decision on behalf of your dear king. We will await your messenger in the days to come," Father answered her. The same wicked expression from earlier returned to his face once again, and he appeared as though he'd just won the entire war with one conversation.

Teagan nodded stiffly before rising from her chair. She politely tipped her head downward towards my father respectfully before saying, "You'll be hearing from us *very* soon." With that, she dismissed herself from the room without another word, the food on the table left untouched by all.

The second the door shut and I was alone with Father, I rose from my chair, wings spreading high above my form, and exclaimed, "What was *that?*"

Father leaned forward to place his elbows on the table and his head atop his hands, not bothering to look my way as he gazed upon the chair Teagan had been sitting in across the table from him. "Sometimes, Aviva, you have to sacrifice those you love for the greater good of your people."

I couldn't believe what I was hearing. "Greater good?" I asked. "*Those you love?*" I practically yelled. I'd never spoken to him this way before, but my control was fraying. "Father, we both know this isn't much of a *sacrifice* for you. But why? How does this help you? Princess Teagan had multiple good ideas that would actually *benefit* our people, yet you kept turning them down. Why is this the only option that works for you?" Tears welled in my eyes, threatening to spill onto my cheeks as I spoke.

My father and I had never been particularly close, but I never thought he'd do something like this. Even if we'd never had a typical father-daughter relationship, he was still the male who taught Dimitri and I to fly. He was still the one who taught us to wield a sword and daggers and bows. He was still the father who told us stories of our late mother before bed anytime we begged as children. So how could he do this to me now?

Father sighed and ran a hand through his hair, turning to finally meet my eyes. "Aviva, I don't have to explain my plans or strategies to you. There's more at play here than you know about. If the messenger from the South returns and they agree to my terms, you will do as you're told. There will be no debates about this, understood?"

A single tear escaped and rolled down my face as I tried, one final time. "But Father—"

I was quickly cut off as he raised a hand to silence me, just as he had done to Dimitri, and ground out between clenched teeth, "*Understood?*"

My bottom lip quivered before I ran a hand down my face, pulled my wings back in close, and lifted my chin. There was no room for emotions here; he'd only become more agitated.

I knew from experience.

"Yes, Father," I said, not allowing my voice to shake as that indifferent mask of mine slid back into place. If he was going to pull this card, the least I could do was not make a fool of myself in front of him.

"Good. You're dismissed. Stay on the castle grounds in case you're needed," Father said, already turning away from me again.

I forced one foot in front of the other until I made it outside the room, where I found Dimitri waiting.

"I heard everything, Viva. I'm so sorry. I promise I had no idea this is what he was planning," he said, taking me into his arms and wrapping his wings around me in a tight embrace.

The moment his wings closed around us, I loosened the grip I had on all of my emotions I had been holding back. Tears freely flowed down my face and my chest shook from the pressure as I held on tightly to my twin.

Dimitri's wings around us gave me enough privacy to feel like it was alright to be vulnerable for a moment. Being raised as Northern royalty, we were taught that emotion was solely a weakness. Anytime I cried as a child, Father would simply ignore me until I stopped—then carry on as if nothing had happened. Father always said that emotions were what would get you killed if you weren't careful.

After a handful of moments, my tears ran dry and I released my brother, raising my hands to my face and wiping the tear tracks away. I squared my shoulders back, putting the emotionally disconnected mask I wore every day of my life back on, and nodded to Dimitri to let him know to lower his wings.

He raised an eyebrow, but didn't object. He tucked his white, silvery-gray tipped wings back against his body and motioned for me to lead the way.

***

I found Aurora waiting in my chambers, reading one of my books about the different zirilium, with another book about the Northern ritual of the veltik khan next to her—a fight to the death. The one in her hands was one of the few volumes I owned that actually mentioned something about the South and what they could wield. Usually information on the South was limited, but being royalty did have some perks.

The moment I walked in, she tossed the book onto the bed next to her and hopped up. "So, how did it—" Aurora stopped mid-sentence when she saw the look on my face. I saw her eyes shift over my shoulder to Dimitri, who I imagined was shaking his head, silently signaling for her not to ask.

"I need to clear my head, so I'm going for a fly. Can you fetch Eden for me and meet me at the back exit? I don't think I'll make it to the stables without being caught. Father ordered me to stay on the grounds," I said to Aurora, clenching my fists in an effort to keep my hands from shaking.

When my emotions were as intense as they were right now, my zirilium became much more difficult to control, and that much harder to hide from my twin. They had been closely tied to my emotions for as long as I could remember. Holding it all in like this, it made me feel like there was an eternal static crawling under my skin. Most Northerners my age had full control over their zirilium by now, but Father had never taken the time to properly train me, despite being able to wield both the weather and water himself. Most of his time was spent preparing Dimitri to rule someday.

"Yes of course, I'll meet you there," Aurora said, turning to leave, then turning back.

"Dimitri, care to join?" she asked, to which Dimitri nodded, his jaw clenched again. I knew he was still wrestling with himself and his thoughts over what just happened. I was confident Aurora had only asked Dimitri to join her just now so he could fill her in on how the meeting had gone. Though, I didn't mind. That just meant Dimitri would also get a chance to release some of the pent up emotions I knew he must be feeling.

"Don't get caught, Aviva. I mean it. After what just went down, be extra careful sneaking out tonight," Dimitri warned, his voice firm but quiet, since we were still standing close to the doors.

"I will, I promise. I'll see you both soon," I said, waving them out.

Once they had departed, I let out a shaky breath, then quickly stripped off the lacey lilac dress and my mother's tiara I had donned earlier in the evening. I replaced the gown with a dark gray tunic and pair of black trousers, and I quickly braided my hair into a long, simple plait down my spine. If I could, I'd dress like this all the time, but Father always said it wasn't appropriate for a princess. Nonetheless, I hoped the dark clothing would help me to blend better, seeing as the sun had long since set.

I was grateful to have Dimitri and Aurora in my life, people who truly cared and knew what I needed with no questions asked. Aurora had been there when I'd been gifted Eden by my father. Father had wanted Dimitri and I to both receive our griffins at the same time, so he adopted two females from the same litter and gifted them to us on our fourteenth birthday. He had been away for a couple weeks at the time, and found them just in time to bring them back to the castle for our birthday ball. I took one look at Eden and knew that would be her name, and that she was the only griffin for me. She was white and gray all over, which had reminded me of my wings. Dimitri had a harder time bonding with Ziana, who was a dark charcoal gray. She was smaller than Eden when we first met them, but within the first year of having them, Ziana almost doubled the size of Eden. She was built like a fighter, which had always been perfect for Dimitri. I like to imagine they were made for each other, like Eden and I were.

Many of the people in the North have a special bonded griffin to call their own. Most are trained for battle, but some—like Eden—are just bonded to fly on, or with. They're intelligent creatures, and are generally in tune with their owner's emotions. Though if given the chance, I'd gladly train Eden for battle, seeing as she's already very speedy and agile.

I finished lacing up my black boots and donned a thick wool coat, then took a moment to double check that the wooden, dark chocolate doors to my chambers were locked. It wouldn't slow the guards down much if Father realized my absence, but sometimes every moment counted.

After ensuring the doors were indeed locked, I turned to the bookshelf housing all of my favorite pieces. Books had always been an escape for me, a way to leave the grasp of my father's fury and neglect, so I had obtained a vast collection of rare books, some not even the royal library knew existed. They were some of my most prized possessions, aside from my mother's tiara and my sword, Elaera.

Reaching a hand out, I gazed upon the green and gold book at my eye level, pulled the top of it towards me, then let go. A second later, a soft *click* sounded throughout the room, and the bookshelf swung open, revealing the hidden passageways I'd used since I was a child. The passageways were like the silk of a spiderweb, the tunnels connecting the castle together. They tied my room to Dimitri's, to the library, to the kitchens, to multiple different meeting and lounge rooms, and to various exits, some of which the servants didn't even know existed.

After swinging the bookshelf back into place behind me, I ran a hand over the stone wall as I walked, the cracks and grooves I knew by heart leading the way. Dimitri once claimed he heard Father talk about how often our mother used to roam these tunnels, but I was not convinced. From what I'd heard about her from a mix of townspeople and servants, she seemed like she was an open book. I couldn't imagine she'd need to sneak around like this at all.

I continued my silent walk in the dark without lighting any of the torches hung on the walls, the soft fall of my feet with every step the only echoing sound. My fingertips were wet with condensation; somehow these tunnels were always warm and wet despite the frigid environment just outside. The passageway descended and twisted, branching off in different directions, but I let my feet lead the way.

My zirilium scratched and clawed under my skin, begging to be released, becoming more and more agitated the longer they were held back. *Soon*, I thought, silently pleading with them not to surface just yet.

A painful moment later, I finally arrived at the end of the tunnel. I ran my hands over the stone until I felt a small notch, then swiftly pushed it in on itself. Another small *click* sounded, and the stone wall cracked open to reveal the darkness of night.

This exit led directly out into the trees behind the castle, where there were sparsely any guards. I pulled a small mirror out of my pocket, using it to reflect the surrounding area outside the hidden door. After ensuring I wouldn't be caught, I pushed the hidden door open further until I could slip out and shut it firmly back into place behind me. If you didn't know what to look for, you'd never even notice it was there.

Walking straight into the line of trees, I didn't look back. I continued to let my feet carry me, having walked this path countless times before. I walked until I reached the small, icy clearing where I found Aurora waiting for me with Eden.

"Please don't be gone long. We can't let your father know you're not at the castle. Dimi is staying near him in case he goes looking for you for any reason," Aurora said by way of greeting. I took a quick moment to appreciate the sight of my friend. Her loose, sun kissed hair was tucked into the hood of the fur-lined cloak she had donned. Her deep, blue eyes were shining with worry as she bit the edge of her lip. A pang of guilt shot through me.

I closed the distance between us and embraced her tightly. "I'm alright, I promise. I'll be back before you even notice I'm gone, then we can talk about where to go from here, alright?" I spoke softly, trying my best to sound reassuring.

"I know, I know. Go. I'll be here when you get back to return Eden," Aurora replied, letting go and handing me Eden's reins. I smiled at my best friend, putting all the warmth I didn't feel into it, before turning to Eden. I tried not to notice how my smile instantly dropped again the moment I turned away.

I could tell Eden picked up on my turbulent emotions and needs immediately. She chirped at me quietly before lowering herself to the ground so I'd have an easier time mounting her. She knew better than anyone how much I hurt when my zirilium was pent up.

I gently scratched the top of her head in thanks before swinging a leg over her back and settling into the saddle. "Let's go," I said softly to her, and she chirped in reply before jumping up into the sky.

Within moments, we were flying high above the kingdom, just below the clouds and heading toward the bay. The snow was unrelenting, but it provided the perfect coverage—from below, Eden's snowy coat and feathers would blend in perfectly with the clouds neighboring us.

Suddenly, my skin started to burn from the inside and I felt hot all over. Wincing, I leaned my head closer to Eden's and spoke in a strained voice, "Faster."

In response, her wings began beating even quicker than before, until we cleared the surrounding mountain range where I'd spent my entire life. Another handful of wing beats later, and the mountains dropped off abruptly into Cynth Bay.

I let out a pained breath as I set my eyes upon the midnight blue water that lapped at the shore below. Once we were positioned over the middle of the bay, I unfurled my own wings and lifted myself off Eden with gentle strokes.

"Thank you," I said to Eden, scratching under her chin. "I couldn't have made it without you."

Eden softly head-butted my upper arm, then shot straight up into the clouds, where she would stay until I called for her to return. She knew this routine as well as I did.

I held out my hands in front of me, watching how much they had begun to shake as I felt sweat forming on my brow, despite the frigid temperature. The storm around me continued on, seeming to only grow more relentless, as if it could sense how restless my own emotions were. The moon stones tucked into my top were now glowing brighter, as if they, too, could feel all of the energy I was holding in.

Suspended in the same spot Eden left me, I closed my eyes and took a deep breath. Pushing away the pain I felt physically and emotionally, I called to the pent up energy I felt flowing through my very veins. Focusing on the sensation crawling beneath my skin, I slowly lifted my hands above my head. Suddenly, I sliced my hands through the air as if striking down an opponent. In the same moment, two lightning bolts shot out of the black clouds above, roughly following where my hands had directed them, then branching out on their own accord, striking the water down below. Never perfect, even now.

The moment the lightning faded, my skin ceased its burning and the energy I had felt pent up in my veins before seemed to ease. Just to be safe, I adjusted my wings and took a nosedive toward the ocean below, which had also become much more restless since my arrival.

While jerking to a stop just before I hit the surface, I called to the water below, causing it to spray up all around me without having been physically touched. I stretched my arms out before the water had a chance to fall and in a swift motion, froze the circle around me into jagged icicles.

Only Northerners who wielded both water and ice could manipulate its form, whether fluid or frozen, and I was thankful for my abilities in that moment.

My breath came out in a gasp when I realized I had indeed called water to me and managed to freeze the full circle around me, not just a portion of it like I had done during the few times I allowed myself to practice my zirilium in the past. A sudden swell of pride surged up in my chest, pushing aside the swirl of negative emotions I had felt there before.

Not being able to hold the ice for more than a few wing beats, I quickly let them drop back into the ocean, where some of them splintered upon impact. It was like all my energy left my body the moment the icicles hit the water, and suddenly exhaustion took over my being. All at once, the storm became loud in my ears and goosebumps erupted over my skin. My teeth began chattering as the cold set in, freezing the sweat on my skin, making my clothes feel heavy.

After a final look at where my icicles had been swallowed up by the bay below, I pumped my wings upwards while I brought a hand to my mouth and whistled a single note, long and loud. A moment later, Eden broke through the clouds in a swift motion, coming straight for me. She leveled out just below me, and I gently positioned myself on her back, slumping forward against her.

"Back to the castle, please. I can't fly alongside you this time, girl," I said to her, exhaustion beginning to tug on my bones. *At least I will be able to think clearly now*, I thought as my heavy lids slid shut and the darkness captured my senses.

Chapter Four

After the long, tiring walk back to my rooms, all I wanted to do was curl up in bed and sleep the remainder of the evening away. *Maybe I'll wake up from this nightmare*, I thought, almost hopefully.

Yet the moment I carefully slid the bookshelf back into place behind me, Dimitri stormed in looking as frustrated as ever. His hair was disheveled, as if he'd been running his hands through it often—a nervous tell of his since we were kids—and his clothes were wrinkled, which Father never allowed.

"You look as rough as I feel, twin," I said to him, trying to lighten the dark mood I could feel looming over him like a shadow as I began crossing the room toward him.

"You have to go along with it, Viva," he blurted out abruptly.

I stopped dead in my tracks the instant his words hit my ears. I met his stare from where I now stood, my breathing starting to quicken as I asked, "What did you just say?"

"I'm so sorry, but I've spent this whole time trying to think of a way out of this, and I can't find one. Even if you were to run away, Father would hunt you to the ends of the continent and even beyond it. You *know* this to be true. I even tried talking to him again, but he's dead set on this. I don't know what he's planning, but whatever it is depends on this," Dimitri explained, taking a step forward.

Dimitri had spent years unofficially assisting Father with war plans—if he couldn't come up with a way out of this, nobody could.

I took a step backwards in response, making Dimitri pause in shock. Even though my body was betraying me, my voice didn't waver as I said, "Dimi, I don't *care* what Father wants anymore. I've always done what he's wanted of me, and where did it get me? In an arranged marriage to our *enemy!*"

Dimitri's emotions were plainly painted on his face—pain, frustration, guilt, sadness. He was always an open book with me, which I generally appreciated, but not this time as his voice softened and he spoke gently, "Viva, this is bigger than just you now. If this works and Father's intentions are true, our people could finally know *peace*. Our males would no longer have to die in a nonsense war, our females would no longer have to learn how to provide for their families as widows, and so many of our children would no longer have to be raised as orphans. Aviva, if this works, it would change *history*." As he spoke, he slowly walked towards me, hands raised and palms facing me—as if I were a wild animal. Maybe a part of me was, the part I kept locked away, deep inside my chest, hidden away from him. The part that wanted to run free, the part that wanted to take what was mine, the part that wanted *power*—but that also simply wanted justice for all the wrong that had been done to me and what had been taken from me.

This time I didn't back up, feeling myself slowly giving in as I retorted, "What about what *I* want?" I tried, and failed, to ignore the way my voice cracked as I spoke.

His face fell, and for just a moment, it was like he was already grieving me.

He quickly covered it up, looking remorseful instead as he said softly, "I'm sorry, Viva."

My bottom lip quivered as I realized what this meant. I truly didn't have a choice in the matter. Father would make me go by force even if I tried to refuse, and if I attempted to run away, he'd just drag me back by the wings. Either way, the end result was the same.

Yet, in the back of my mind, a small sliver of me held onto the hope that maybe, just maybe, I'd be able to get away from the South and escape back to the North after the marriage. I'd have to be thoughtful and play it safe, but just *maybe*.

That small hope was the only thing that kept me from breaking completely as I slowly dropped to the floor, the physical and emotional exhaustion hitting me all at once. Dimitri was there in a wing-beat, sliding his arm under my legs and behind my back. He carried me to my bed where I curled up and quietly sobbed, grieving the life I thought I'd have. The one where I got to be with Dimitri and Aurora every day, where I got to spend dawn to dusk helping my people, and where I got to eventually master my own zirilium in public. Now, I might never see my brother and best friend again, nor my people. Not to mention, nobody in the South is to have information on Northern zirilium or how to control it. All of the elementary pleasures I had envisioned for my life were gone, just like that.

Simply so I could fulfill my purpose as a pawn in Father's game.

I don't know when, but at some point Dimitri departed. In his place I found Aurora stroking my hair and murmuring comforting, yet empty, words until my tears ran dry and exhaustion overcame me.

***

The next morning I woke up alone, the sun slipping through the drapes and landing directly across my pillow. I used a hand to shield my eyes and sat up, realizing it looked to be about mid-morning. Father and Hugo would be here soon for my daily elixir.

I quickly scrambled out of bed, aiming straight for the washroom. After washing up in my in-ground bath, I headed for the closet with the intent of picking out my clothing like armor. Father always wanted me to look the part of a princess, but considering he was about to sell me out to be a queen instead, I figured I could start dressing how I wanted for a change.

Standing in front of the mirror of my vanity, I looked upon the clothing I had donned. I wore a white corset top that hugged my torso nicely, and which had small pearls sewn into it in swirling patterns. When the sun hit the pearls just right, a small rainbow sheen was visible in each one. Soft, gray trousers that flowed at the bottom hugged my hips, and white heels with the same pattern of pearls adorned my feet. I slid my arms into a long, dark gray fur cloak that matched the color of Aurora's wings, in order to shield the cold air of the crisp morning away. I tugged on my moon stone necklace, settling it beneath my top, and added a white leather belt, which held a total of six of my daggers—perfectly crafted for my hands. I had a total of a dozen on me today, the other six tucked away in hidden pockets along my clothing. Dimitri and I had gotten a handful of these sets of clothing made for me in secret, just in case I ever needed it.

For the final touch, I wove my snow white hair into a circlet around my head, placing my mother's tiara perfectly on top.

As I put on each piece of clothing and braided each lock of hair, I added a mental wall in my mind to block out my anxieties, emotions, and irrational thoughts. I built each wall brick by brick, minute by minute. I could see the walls of dark stones in my mind, making ivy and vines grow over the walls, fortifying them with thorns. *I will not let my father get the best of me today.*

Without even a chance to second guess my decision to not wear one of my normal dresses, a series of four timid knocks on the door to my chambers let me know that Hugo had arrived. Letting out a small sigh and pushing my nerves back behind those mental walls, I walked across the room and allowed him in.

The moment Hugo saw me, his eyes widened as he took in my change of appearance. He didn't stumble long, though, and quickly dropped into a bow before straightening again.

He was a short man, barely taller than me, with a wild, white beard and long, gray hair pulled back into a low ponytail. He wore the usual royal trokav attire—a long, black coat with the Heartshire family symbol on the back, along with black pants and a plain, gray shirt. They weren't meant to stand out, but the outfit always looked professional. Plus, the black coat hid any blood or gore they got on it.

Hugo had always been skilled and respectful, and he did his job well. He'd been a great trokav throughout the years to me and Dimitri anytime we got hurt, always patching us up with his gross yet efficient elixirs and potions. Aside from that, he was also Aurora's mentor. Usually trokavs in the North didn't wield zirilium, but despite the fact that Aurora can wield water, Hugo saw great promise in her and decided to make her his protégé when she was sixteen. She'd been learning from him ever since, and although I never mentioned these daily visits to her, she'd quickly figured out something was off after studying with Hugo. Now, nobody but her, Hugo, and Father knew about these visits. Or what, exactly, they meant.

Not even Dimitri.

"Good morning, Princess. I've brought you your elixir this morning. I added peppermint to it this time, to try to mask the taste a bit," Hugo said, looking slightly sheepish. I'd been complaining of the taste for as long as I could remember, but no matter what he added, it only made it worse. I never told him, though, because I appreciate that he thought to add anything in the first place.

My face must give me away each time, unfortunately, because he kept trying new things.

"Thank you, Hugo. I appreciate your efforts," I said, taking the glass bottle from him and popping the cork off. I took a small sniff of the liquid inside and was surprised to find that it didn't smell quite as horrible as usual.

I put the bottle to my lips and took the liquid in one great swig, barely registering the taste on my tongue. I felt myself grimace behind my mental walls, but put extra care into making sure the disgust I felt didn't show on my face.

Hugo smiled, as if he were proud of himself for finally finding a combination of added ingredients that didn't make me gag.

I handed the now empty bottle back to him, then cocked my head to one side as the liquid sat heavily in my stomach. "Where is Father?" I asked. Father only misses elixir time if something very important was happening.

Hugo's smile instantly dropped, and he suddenly looked nervous. Although he refused to meet my eyes, he responded, "Ah yes, well, about that... he's requested your presence immediately in the throne room, Princess. And before you ask, no, I was not informed as to why." Before I could respond, he quickly leaned in and grabbed my hand, whispering, "I saw a messenger bird with the Southern symbol on it fly in not too long ago. I'd assume it has something to do with that."

I gaped at the small male, realizing how much he just risked to tell me that. If Father didn't want me to know, Hugo shouldn't have told me. Though, I suppose I've always held a soft spot in the old male's heart, as he's watched me grow up since I was a babe. I shouldn't be this shocked that he'd go out of his way to warn me, and yet I was. Not being completely, totally loyal to Father could cost you your life in the North.

Before I could even respond he took a step back, bowed, and said, "Good day, Princess." Then he excused himself from my chambers, leaving me alone with my raging thoughts.

Why—and how—was there a Southern messenger hawk here already, when the dinner was just last night? What was Father planning? What does the message say? How long did I have until I had to leave everything I'd ever known behind?

I braced my hands on the tabletop of my vanity and took in a shaky breath. *You can't spiral. Get it together, Aviva.*

Looking into my own eyes in the mirror, I took one moment to allow myself to be frightened. To worry about my future, to be anxious about what I was about to face. Then I cleared my throat, the sound bouncing around my quiet chambers. Straightening my spine, I rolled my shoulders back and pushed all of my nerves back behind those fortified walls in my mind. Envisioning those walls once again, I imagined a large lock sliding into place at the very front wall, holding those gates together as a final piece of defense against the outside world. Then, I headed for the throne room.

My heels clicked against the smooth, black stone floor as the throne room doors shut behind me and I walked towards my father. My jaw hurt from the effort it took to keep my mouth shut.

"Ah, daughter. I'm glad you made haste. I have great news for you," Father said as I stopped in front of his throne. Oddly enough, I noticed that it was only us in the great room made of smooth cobblestone, black tiles, and crystal chandeliers. No guards, no advisors, no servants—not even Dimitri.

I knew relaying this information in the throne room was intentional—to remind me that he was not only my father, but my king. That he held all the power here. Well, in every way except one, but he'd never acknowledge the fact that I could potentially be a greater zirilium wielder than him someday if I only had the practice. And free reign to even admit that I *was* a wielder in the first place.

I bowed before him, giving him the submission I knew he wanted, while in the same breath defying his wishes with my attire.

"Good morning, Father. What news could be so great?" I asked innocently, not even bothering to point out my state of dress. Under normal circumstances, he'd have reprimanded me immediately, but today was bigger than that. And surprisingly, it seemed we both understood I knew what this was about.

"The King of the South, family head of the esteemed Thorntier line, has agreed to the conditions laid out to Princess Teagan. An entourage from the South will be arriving shortly to collect you and a single chest of your things," Father said, his usual amused look having faded from his clean shaven face.

Only one chest? I asked myself.

Even though I was confident this would be the result of his demands, I still felt his words like a physical blow. My chest ached, but I simply dipped my head in response. I wouldn't let him have the satisfaction of seeing how hurt I truly was.

"And when am I scheduled to leave?" I asked, making an effort to keep my voice light despite the heaviness weighing in my gut.

An unsettling smile slowly crept over my father's expression as he said, "Oh, did I forget to mention? You're to leave within the hour."

Chapter Five

Less than an hour later, I was closing the doors to my chambers behind me, for what I thought might be the last time. Despite my raging emotions, I held my chin up high and kept my spine straight, forcing my emotions back behind that wall.

Father never mentioned anything about my choice of clothing, but that was the least of my worries now.

I spotted the Southern royal procession out of the windows of the castle's foyer before we were even outside, my father talking with Princess Teagan. There was one main carriage surrounded by multiple horses with males—as well as females, something that would never be seen in the North—atop them. The strangest things in the procession, though, were the *giant* wolves in the lead and taking up the rear. From where I stood, I could see two of them—one with an ashy gray and white coat, the other with an almost pitch-black coat and slightly larger than the first one.

Why in the Stars are those beasts so large?

"Princess Aviva!" The sound of my name from Hugo's lips made me pause before I could reach the front doors of the castle.

Spinning on my heel, I saw Hugo and Aurora rushing towards me, faces flushed and both looking more tired than usual. My curiosity spiked when I noticed they were each holding one side of a wooden crate.

Once in front of me, they set the crate on the ground between us. Hugo bowed low and cleared his throat, which seemed to be a signal between him and Aurora, as she quickly followed his lead, bowing at the waist.

"I'm so glad we caught you in time, Princess. We were just barely able to fulfill the King's request before you left," Hugo stated, slightly out of breath.

"And what request would that be?" I asked.

"He asked us to make as many of your...*elixirs* as possible and as fast as we could. I even had to get Aurora to help me, so at least she can say she learned something new lately. This crate is all we could make with the time restraints and ingredients I had left. These should last you a long while, though! Not to worry," he said, as though he were proud. And why wouldn't he be? He was just doing my father's bidding. Yet, it still rubbed me the wrong way. The fact that everybody in my life is somehow *alright* with me being shipped off to the South.

Taking a deep breath, I shoved my frustration behind those fortified walls in my mind before speaking. "Thank you, Hugo. That wasn't even something I had stopped to think about. Your efforts, both of yours," I nodded toward Aurora, "are greatly appreciated."

Hugo nodded, then started ringing his hands together in front of him nervously. I could tell by his stiff, hesitant body language that he didn't know how to say goodbye. In reality, I didn't, either. I'd known Hugo for as long as I can remember. He'd always been there when I'd needed him, and he'd always thought about the things I hadn't even dreamed of. He'd always been one step ahead, always prepared, such as right now. How do you say goodbye to somebody who had been like a grandfather to you? Somebody you're not sure you'll ever see again?

Loosening a breath, I closed the distance between us and embraced the older male in a firm hug.

"Thank you for always looking out for me, Hugo," I said thickly. I felt his arms come around me and return my embrace, his plain, white wings tightening against his body.

"Always, my princess," Hugo responded, his voice cracking just slightly.

He pulled away, cleared his throat, and bowed once more before turning and walking outside. I assumed he was going to update my father about the elixirs, as he lugged the chest behind him, leaving me and Aurora alone.

I turned to my best friend next, who already had tears shining in her eyes. Aurora, who had always done her best to crack a joke in order to cheer me up, suddenly had no more jokes to tell.

Well, this is going to hurt, I thought to myself.

"Aurora, I—" Before I could even speak another word, her arms and wings were thrown around me in a tight embrace.

At a loss for words, I simply returned her embrace just as firmly. My chest heaved as I felt a tear fall from her face and onto my shoulder, but I shoved those emotions deeper down and lightly stroked her hair instead.

"It's going to be fine. This isn't goodbye, alright? Take care of Eden for me. I'll see you both again. In this life, or the next," I said, biting my lip so it wouldn't quiver. I didn't even get to say goodbye to my griffin, and I wouldn't be surprised if Father had done that on purpose. At least I'd had one final fly with her last night. That would have to be good enough. And I knew Aurora would take good care of her in my stead.

"I *will* see you again, Viva. I promise," she said through her tears. I wasn't sure if I could force myself to believe her, so I simply nodded my head instead of voicing my doubts.

After another moment, we both let go, and I gently wiped the tears from her cheek with the back of my hand. "Thank you. For everything," I said, then turned around and headed for the front doors.

Before I could even take a step, a hand came down on my arm and pulled. I was suddenly face to face with a fierce looking Aurora, despite the tear tracks staining her other cheek.

"Listen to me, Aviva. Whatever you do, *do not* drink those elixirs anymore. I don't know exactly what's in them, but something is off about them. The ingredients Hugo used don't make sense together, and there were some ingredients I'd never even heard of in all my training. Something isn't right, I swear to you," she said abruptly and very quietly, looking around the foyer as she spoke, as if to make sure there was nobody listening.

"What are you—" I began to question her, but was quickly cut off by the sound of the doors opening, and Dimitri waiting just beyond them.

I looked back at my best friend and met her eyes. I desperately hoped all the unspoken words between us were conveyed in my eyes as I stared at her. She nodded slightly, and I did the same. I decided right then and there to not take any more of the elixirs from then on. I trusted Aurora with my life, and I had no reason to suspect her of lying to me. But if that's the case, what had Hugo and my father been giving me all these years?

And why?

Heading outside, I came face to face with my twin. He looked even worse than when I saw him the night before, with purple circles under his eyes and his hair still disheveled. Though at least he had changed into fresh, crisp clothes.

Dimitri turned towards me as I approached him, holding his hands behind his back.

"Aviva, I... I'm sorry I couldn't stop this," he said, then hung his head.

In truth, part of me wanted to be angry. I wanted somebody to blame, and Dimitri was an easy target—plus, I knew he would take it. But I also knew that wasn't fair. He didn't control the schemes our father puts together, and blaming him for it in what could be our last moments together wouldn't be fair. So instead, I simply stepped closer, flared my wings into a circle around us, and pulled him into a fierce embrace.

"I love you, brother. I appreciate you trying, I really do. This wasn't your fault. Don't blame yourself after I'm gone," I said, desperately trying not to choke on my own words.

He wrapped his arms around me firmly, squeezing me to him like if he held on tight enough, I wouldn't have to go. "I love you too, twin. When you look to the moon at night, remember that we're looking up at the same one, and maybe you won't feel so far away. And don't forget, you'll always belong to the sky," he said, his voice shaking slightly as he spoke.

Just as I was about to pull my wings in, Dimitri quickly pulled out a small, rectangular box from inside his cloak and shoved it towards me. "Here, a parting gift. Viva, there's more at play here than you know. I found this in a box of Mother's things. Don't open this until you're alone, alright?" he said, sliding it into my own inner cloak pocket, close to my heart. The box was thin and went unnoticed, neatly tucked away.

I looked up at him, confused, but nodded nonetheless. "Thank you, I think," I said, drawing my brows together in confusion.

The moment was over as quickly as it started as I pulled my wings back, and in the same motion, Dimitri and I both tilted our chins up and squared our shoulders back. Just like we'd both had ingrained in us since we were children.

Suddenly, I realized there were no Northern guards outside, or in the foyer of the castle.

Weird.

Walking towards the procession, I came upon my father and Princess Teagan speaking in hushed voices that abruptly stopped as I grew nearer.

"Hello again, Princess Teagan," I said, dipping my head in respect to the strong female standing in front of me. I was inclined not to trust her, but I didn't want her to know that. So playing it neutrally and with respect would be key in our interactions, especially as she'd soon be my sister-in-law.

Today, she was in brown leather gear that looked like what the North wears when riding our griffins. A stab of pain went through my chest at the thought of not being able to ride Eden again, but I kept a small smile playing on my face, not letting it show.

"Please, just Teagan. We are to be sisters soon enough, after all," she said, and though she was smiling, it all seemed very forced.

I nodded, though I had to suppress a scoff.

"Can I have a moment alone with my father please, Teagan?" I asked, keeping my voice light.

"Of course. King Horace, we'll be staying in touch," she said with a nod towards my father, then headed towards the carriage.

"Aviva, I know you must have mixed feelings about this whole ordeal, but you're doing the right thing. Your compliance in this has made things much easier for me," Father said, with next to no emotion in his voice.

I spun on my heel to face him fully, my wings flaring slightly as I spoke. "I'm not doing this for you, *Father*, but for my people. They more than deserve a chance at peace. *Don't* mess this up for them. They've sacrificed enough," I said in a hushed yet fierce voice. Now that I knew I likely wouldn't see my father at least for a long while, I couldn't find it in me to fear him.

Father's eyes widened slightly and his nostrils flared—the only sign that he was angry—but before he could even open his mouth to speak, I turned and walked away, heading in the direction I saw Teagan go.

Within a few strides, I found Teagan waiting outside the door of the carriage. Now that I was closer up, I realized just how detailed it was. It was a rich, forest green with countless gold accents. There were gilded vines covering the entirety of the carriage, with small thorns and flower buds sprinkled throughout. There was a wolf's head in place of a handle, and the Southern Thorntier family crest—a wolf's head with a silhouette of the sun behind it—on each of the wheels.

Teagan placed a hand on the wolf head handle and opened the door for me.

"You'll be riding in here until we get to The Haven, Princess Aviva. Hopefully we'll be there before nightfall tomorrow," she said, seeming slightly uncomfortable with my presence. "Our group will split into two, with the wolves leading the faster one. That way we can get back to the South quickly, so we can make preparations."

From what I understood, it took roughly three days or so to make it from Hollis to Cairnyl. The fact that the giant beasts could shave off an entire day was astounding.

"You can call me Aviva, I really don't mind. I'd prefer it, actually," I said, trying my best to sound friendly, though I felt differently. If I were to ever have any chance at escaping the South someday, I'd have to start with gaining their trust.

Teagan shook her head slightly. "You're to be my queen, Princess," she said in explanation, then nodded towards the open door to the carriage, silently motioning me to get in.

I held back a sigh, then turned towards the carriage. Just as I went to step up into it, a hand shot out, offering assistance.

"Please, let me help."

The tan, toned hand belonged to the most handsome male I think I'd ever seen. His eyes were such a rich green, they reminded me of the dense forests I'd read about the South having. The sun hit his chestnut hair just right, making it glow with red undertones, and his cheeks were splattered with freckles. The smile playing softly on his lips made my breath hitch ever so slightly. This revealed a single dimple on the right side of his face and a small scar that marred his jaw to the left. The scar did nothing to take away from the rest of his features though, such as his strong cheekbones and straight nose. He was... *gorgeous.*

"My lady?" he asked, still holding out his hand. That was when I finally noticed that he, like Teagan, had a winding, swirling brown pattern on the back of his hand that was climbing up his arm. Where Teagan's marking had seemed sharper and more angled, his was all soft swoops, though his seemed to cover less of the length of his arm than Teagan's did.

I cleared my throat then reached for his hand, figuring if I refused it wouldn't reflect well on my intentions or my character. Yet the moment my hand touched his, I had to hold back a gasp—it had felt like lightning had ignited under my skin.

I quickly brushed it off as being my zirilium starting to build up. There was no way it could be anything other than that. Especially since this male was Southern.

Not to mention I was to get married to the King of the South soon.

Teagan shut the door to the carriage once I sat in the seat across from the male, who I assumed couldn't be more than a couple years older than I was.

Shortly after the door had shut, I heard the reins of the horses snap, and we jerked forward into motion. I quickly moved closer to the window and shoved the curtain out of the way, watching my father, Hugo, Dimitri, and Aurora grow smaller and smaller the further we rode away, all but my father waving.

I watched out the window for what felt like hours as we traveled further away from everything I'd ever known. I watched as the only people I cared about in the entire world disappeared from view, then stared at Gatlyn Castle until the Northern flag flying high on top also disappeared from my line of sight.

It seemed we were going the long way around Hollis, not through it, but I could still see it far off—the tall towers with balconies and ledges that us winged fae flew into, as well as the bridges connecting all of the tallest buildings together for easier access. The city where I'd been raised, where I met my best friend, and where I'd gone to study the people who lived there and made connections. Tears threatened to fill my eyes as I watched that city built in the sky slowly vanish across the horizon. And all too soon, I was farther from home than I had ever been, and I wasn't sure I'd ever see it again.

Sighing, I let the curtain fall closed and wiped a single tear from my cheek that had somehow managed to escape, despite my fortified mental walls. I shifted uncomfortably in the small space, tucking my wings in tight to my body, but I still felt squished. Though, I also wasn't willing to move any closer to the stranger I was sharing air with, so I remained close to the window.

This carriage was obviously not built for fae with wings, I thought.

"Uncomfortable?" the male asked, and that's when I realized he had been observing me this entire time.

Suddenly embarrassed, I felt my cheeks and the pointed tips of my ears flush with color as I slightly flared my wings, then tucked them back in. "*In more ways than one*," I mumbled to myself in the long dead Northern language, Nolvym.

I had found books written in the dead language around age ten, hidden away in the royal library, and decided to teach it to myself. Dimitri had never understood why I cared enough, nobody alive spoke it anymore—not after the entire continent agreed to only use the common language. Though, that was shortly before this war began, all those centuries ago.

Dimitri didn't seem to understand that speaking Nolvym made me feel closer to our immortal ancestors, made me feel closer to the time of peace they had gotten to experience. It made it easier to imagine myself there.

I didn't let myself think too hard about the expression that passed across the male's face at my quiet remark.

For the next few minutes we rode in a peaceful, yet slightly tense silence. I made sure to keep my expression flat, passive.

"So, who all was present in telling you goodbye? If I'm not mistaken, I counted a total of only four fae, and no guards," the male asked abruptly, interrupting the moment of quiet.

It was an effort not to roll my eyes at the question. There couldn't be a good reason for him to be inquiring about me personally.

Ignoring him, I turned back to the window. Although I could barely see out of the window with the sheer curtains in the way, I stared on.

Shifting to face me more fully, he tried again. "What was it like being raised in the North, Princess?" he asked, his voice staying calm and level, even though I imagine my silence wasn't the answer he had been wanting. But if he thought I was going to start trusting Southerners now, he was sorely mistaken.

I remained silent. I wasn't sure what he was trying to get at, but I needed time to think in order to forge a plan. I'd be mild and respectful when necessary, but that doesn't include small talk with a stranger that I'd probably never see again after we arrived in the South.

He sighed, then spoke again, still staring at me. "Listen, I understand you have no reason to trust me, but I will be a great ally to you in the South, so we might as well start working together sooner rather than later."

I cleared my throat to hide the laugh that threatened to erupt from my throat. *The audacity.*

I ignored him.

Though his voice never grew louder, the slight shift in his tone gave away his frustration as he said, "If you won't tell me about yourself, then I'll do it for you, based on what I've observed in our short time together," he declared. "You keep your circle small—whether that's been an active choice or not, I do not know. You love the city you grew up in, and probably feel sick leaving it like this. You don't trust anybody but yourself right now, which I understand—from what I've heard, you were just as blindsided by this ordeal as the Southern royals were. And lastly, you're terrible at hiding daggers."

I snapped my eyes to his, shocked at the accuracy of his words. I met his eyes head on for the first time, and suddenly I felt like he could see straight into my soul with just one look.

Before I could open my mouth to speak, he held up one of my twelve daggers and dangled it in front of me, before pulling it back and inspecting it.

"Your right sleeve hung slightly lower than your left, so spotting it was simple. Lifting it off of you when I offered you a hand, even more so. You definitely have a lot to learn, Princess."

I felt the surge of emotions in the same moment as my zirilium began to sing under my skin, asking to be released. Anger, frustration, grief—all of it swirled around in my heart and head until I couldn't think clearly.

In the next breath, I unsheathed the dagger I had stashed in my left boot and pointed the tip of it right at the hollow of the male's throat. To my shock, one side of his mouth lifted up in an ungodly, handsome smirk, flashing that dimple.

"You have some nerve," I ground out between clenched teeth, pressing the dagger slightly harder against him.

To my astonishment, the male didn't even flinch, or move an inch. He remained perfectly still, not breaking eye contact as he said, "You have no idea."

"Who are you, anyways?" I asked, holding the dagger firmly in place.

"You can call me Byn. And like I said, I will be a great ally for you, Princess. Let's skip the pleasantries and get right to working together, why don't we?" he suggested, still wearing that obnoxious smirk on his full lips.

"If you think for a moment that I'd trust anybody from the South, you're going to be very disappointed," I stated, matter-of-factly.

Just then, the carriage hit a small bump in the road, disrupting the careful hold I had on the dagger. Byn winced slightly as the dagger pulled a small drop of blood from his soft skin.

I quickly pulled the dagger back before I could do anymore damage, and replaced it to its holder in the side of my boot.

His hand went to where the dagger had previously been, and his eyes only left me for a moment to look down at his hand, which drew back with a splotch of bright red blood on it.

"You win this round, Princess. Don't get used to it," he said, wiping the blood on the brown leathers he wore that reflected Teagan's perfectly, then handing the dagger he stole back to me.

I was careful not to let our hands touch again.

My heart hammered in my chest for a long while after our interaction, but his eyes never left me again for the remainder of the ride. I could feel his gaze upon me as if he were actually running a finger along my skin. I was used to studying people, but it seemed I was being outdone in my own skill set by the way Byn seemed to study every slight movement I made.

I did my best to block it out, and I didn't bother looking over at him again. I wouldn't give him the satisfaction of letting him know how easily he had gotten under my skin. How easily he knocked down the mental walls I had built brick by brick to keep my emotions in check.

I watched the icy blue sky turn orange and pink, then a deep blue as night fell. We still carried on for hours, all in silence. Sleep beckoned me, but I refused it, hating the idea of letting my guard down when surrounded by the enemy.

We carried on, neither myself or the male I shared the carriage with allowing ourselves to sleep. We made minimal stops, and though they prompted me to eat, I refused. My stomach was still in knots, thinking about everything I had left behind, and the uncertain future I would soon be facing.

Just as my eyelids had begun to droop the second night of travel and I could practically hear sleep calling my name, the carriage came to an abrupt stop. I quickly sat up straight, heart pounding with the realization that I had nearly fallen asleep so close to the enemy.

"Where are we?" I asked, turning to Byn for the first time since I'd held my dagger to his throat the day before.

A small, thoughtful smile made its way onto his lips as he said, "Princess Aviva, let me be the first to welcome you to The Haven."

Chapter Six

Teagan led me through the front doors of the castle. At least, that's what I imagined this structure was. It was crafted of wood and stone, with intricate arches and tall watchtowers. Though, I couldn't stop to scout out hardly any of it as Teagan ushered me straight from the carriage to inside. I did not see Byn again after leaving the carriage, and a tiny piece of me was disappointed. Though he frustrated me, I also felt like he saw me, picking up on things nobody has ever bothered to observe about me.

The first thing I noticed after stepping inside the walls was that Southerners did not keep high ceilings. In the North, our ceilings were so widely open—especially in Gatlyn Castle—that you could fly a small circle around the room. Here, I immediately felt squished, though fortunately it was not nearly as cramped as the carriage.

I wonder if they realize I could've flown here on my own.

Without saying a word, I continued to follow Teagan through the maze they called The Haven. I noticed there were guards stationed outside, but not as many inside. Within the walls of the castle, I mostly saw civilians. Mothers with their children, young adults, and the elderly. Not very many seemed to be awake at such a late hour, but each one stopped to look at us. Everybody we passed either bowed or dipped their head towards Teagan, then stopped dead in their tracks when their eyes landed on me.

Then the murmuring began.

I wasn't surprised—if the books I had read were correct, the South had only ever truly mixed and mingled with the Ocrein Isles. Ever since the Islanders closed their borders a little less than two decades ago, it had just been the Southerners and those from the Isles who decided to stay behind. The ones who chose to remain here risked never being able to see their homeland again.

The humans, unlike the Ocrein Isles, didn't give their people an option when they, too, closed their borders. According to records, the humans of the Levast Isles had supported my ancestors and my father's ancestors for generations. Trade routes flowed freely between them, and the humans were always a shout away from helping us in any conflicts.

They haven't been seen or heard from in ages, though—ever since the fae's immortality was stripped away. Some even say the Stars were punishing us. But not a whisper has been heard from the Levast Isles, and my ancestors gave up generations ago on trying to reestablish relations.

No—the fae here definitely weren't accustomed to seeing those outside of their borders, let alone a child of the sky.

The only thing that kept me from faltering as I listened to those murmurs was years of training myself not to react to those around me, which was a necessity as my father's daughter and Princess of the North. Instincts took over as I squared my shoulders, flared my wings slightly then tucked them back in, and raised my chin high. I didn't spare a glance at a single soul as I followed in Teagan's footsteps, and Teagan never looked back to see if I followed.

After a few twists and turns, the people thinned out until it was only Teagan and I approaching a long hallway with multiple doors on either side. A small wave of relief overcame me when we were finally out of the public's eye. I hadn't realized what it would be like to be surrounded by Southerners—fae who had the blood of my Northern brothers and sisters on their hands.

"This is my family's private wing of the castle. You won't find any civilians here. Most of them are staying for your wedding," Teagan explained as we walked past a set of guards posted at the mouth of the hallway.

I was led all the way to the second-to-last door on the right, Teagan motioning to it. "This will be your room, at least for the next couple of nights. Or if you get tired of my brother," she tried to joke.

"Why only a couple of nights?" I asked.

Teagan paused, pursing her lips together, then said, "Your wedding is in two days' time—in the early afternoon, Princess. My brother and I thought it best to not put it off."

I sucked in a sharp breath and held it in my chest for a moment, thinking and trying not to panic. *I'll be married in just a couple days.*

"I guess I should get some beauty rest, then," I finally said with a calm I didn't feel after a couple of quiet seconds. Teagan nodded, then opened the door for me to lead the way inside.

The inside of the room was modest yet elegant, and my trunk of belongings had already been placed at the foot of the bed, along with the wooden crate from Hugo. The room was decorated in soft shades of blue, from the plush rug to the curtains over the windows, to the quilt on the four-poster bed. Hidden under the blue, though, were traces of the green and gold of the South. The sheets were a pine green, and all the hardware in the room was gold, down to the doorknob leading into the washroom. Though, a small part of me was moved that they even tried to make this more comfortable for me by adding my nation's colors. It's not like they had much time to prepare.

None of us did.

Although I was touched, I reminded myself they were the enemy. Nothing more than heartless killers—despite their attempts to sway me otherwise.

"I'll be back in the morning to bring you breakfast," Teagan said from where she stood in the doorway.

I nodded, and she inclined her head before shutting the door behind her, though I noticed she didn't lock it as she left. I listened to her footsteps retreat down the hall until I could no longer hear them before getting to work collecting materials.

Walking over to the small table next to the bed, I picked up a vase full of blue and white flowers I'd never seen before. Taking it to the washroom, I dumped out the water and left the flowers in a heap on the table.

Unfortunately, I couldn't find a rope, but I did find a tattered blanket hidden away in the closet. I cut it into strips with a dagger, then set off to work with what I'd gathered.

Within ten minutes, my contraption was complete. Now, if anybody were to open the door without me disarming the suspended vase, it would fall and shatter, alarming me of the person's arrival.

Sighing and finally feeling somewhat comfortable, I collapsed onto the bed. That's when I suddenly remembered the box my twin had given me early yesterday morning.

Sitting up, I pulled the rectangular box from my cloak and slid the lid off. My breath caught as I peered in.

Inside the box sat a small dagger with a family crest I didn't recognize, detailed with a bright blue gem that I believed to be some variety of sapphire.

Hands shaking slightly, I lifted the sheathed dagger, dropping the box onto the bed. On the back side of the dagger was another unknown insignia, but instead of a blue gem, it had a deep green gem that I didn't recognize.

The workmanship of the dagger was unlike anything I'd ever seen back home, despite all the time spent training with various makes and models of blades alongside Dimitri. Most daggers nowadays in the North are basic, with little detail to make them special, unless you decide to commission a local to craft you a specific design or pattern. It was highly unlikely the dagger in my hands now was of Northern origin.

My mind reeled with questions. Dimitri said what was in this box he'd found in our mother's things, but where did he even find some of her things after so long? And what was a likely Southern-crafted dagger—or possibly Ocrein Isle crafted—doing with her belongings? Where did she get this from in the first place?

Frustrated, my eyes burned with tears that I frantically tried to blink back.

What does this all mean?

Shaking my head, I took a few deep breaths to help clear my mind. I slid the dagger into my top, nestling it in place, then walked to the washroom and splashed cold water onto my face.

For a moment, I simply stared into the mirror above the sink. I was beginning to get purple smudges under my eyes from the stress, and the braid I'd put my hair into that morning was falling down in places. I was careful in taking it down, and took extra precaution in setting my mother's tiara next to the blue and white flowers on the bedside table.

Sighing, I returned to the bedroom and threw myself onto the bed. Exhaustion hit me heavy and fast, and before I could even care about changing clothes, sleep overcame me.

***

The sound of glass shattering had my heart pounding, bolting up from sleep, and reaching for the nearest dagger—the one still resting in my sleeve.

I'd set my little trap every night since arriving a couple days ago, and so far, I'd run into zero issues. Until now, that is.

After a couple seconds of blinking the sleep from my eyes, as well as the morning light, I slowly lowered the dagger back down as I took in the sight before me.

While focusing my eyes forward, I did my best not to think about what today's rising sun meant for me. How this would be the day my fate was sealed, forever.

My wedding day.

A small, unkempt child stood just inside the entrance to the room with the doors cracked behind her and my trap in pieces at her feet. She had a bewildered look on her face, like breaking a vase was the last thing she expected when sneaking into somebody's room.

Her eyes widened when she saw me move and, realizing I was awake, she immediately began apologizing. "I'm sorry!" she said, one of her front teeth missing. She couldn't have been older than eight-years-old.

Sleep still hovering around my brain, I slowly sheathed the dagger and asked her, "What are you doing in here?"

I hadn't left this room since I arrived. I'd been reading the books I haphazardly threw into my chest when packing at the last minute. I had made sure to pack my favorites, along with ones about the South to try to prepare myself. I'd read them all twice over the past two days. Teagan offered to show me around, but I politely declined. She had even resorted to bringing food to me three times a day, but the more of it I ate, the worse I began to feel.

The small child placed her gloved hands behind her back, looking at me innocently with big, caramel-colored eyes. "I just wanted to meet the female who's about to marry my brother. Teagan kept telling me not to, but I wanted to anyways. I've been trying to sneak in since the night you arrived, but my sister can be hard to slip away from," she admitted sheepishly, then looked down at the pieces of broken translucent glass. "Sorry about the vase..." she mumbled.

I swiped a hand down my face, as if I could physically remove the sleep from me. *She's just a child*, I thought to myself, then realized what she'd said. *No, she's a princess. I didn't realize there were any other princesses in the South besides Teagan.*

Thinking only of gaining her trust, I slid out of bed and said, "That's fine. Just don't tell anybody about this next part, alright?"

She nodded enthusiastically in response, eyes still wide.

I walked towards her, careful to still keep distance between us. I motioned for her to back up, and she stepped to the side, away from the broken shards. Fortunately she was wearing shoes, though I couldn't help but notice the colorful paint splatters on them.

I took a deep breath to help center myself, as I always had to do before wielding any of my zirilium. *Being self-taught has its downfalls.*

A moment later, I felt it. A slight prickling sensation under my skin. I could feel the air moving around me in a different way than before. Like I could will it to carry out my every desire.

Using the air around me, I used circular motions to surround the area where the vase shattered. Slowly with my air current, I pushed every little piece towards one another, until they sat in a neat pile in the middle of the floor.

Wielding air had always been one of the easiest zirilium to learn for me. It felt like an extension of my surroundings, and it was the simplest to control in my experience. Air had always been my favorite zirilium because of it.

Quickly before I could lose my focus, I grabbed the small waste bin in the corner of the room and sat it on its side next to the pile. Concentrating again, I used one last air current to shove all of the pieces of glass into the bin. Then I stood the bin back up, and waved a hand towards it, looking back at the young female. "See? No big deal," I said, trying my best to sound nonchalant. Though sweat had begun to bead at my temples from the effort, I did my best not to let it show. I couldn't show any weakness to the Southerners, even to a child.

"That was *so* cool, miss! I've never seen anything like that before! How did you do that? Do you have mind powers?" the child asked, drawing closer and holding her little hands in fists of excitement.

To my surprise, I found my lips tilting up into a smile.

"No, I don't have mind powers. I wielded the air around us," I explained, looking down into her doe eyes. I took this moment to get a better look at her.

She had chocolate brown hair that only went down to her chin, but it was wavy and disheveled, as if she'd just rolled out of bed. She had pointed ears like I did, and a small string of green beads hanging from her hair framed the left side of her face. One of her suspenders had slipped off of her shoulder, and a pine green shirt lay underneath. Gold bracelets hung from her wrists, clinking together every time she moved her arms. Brown, leather gloves adorned her little hands, though they had no stones on the knuckles like I'd seen some of the civilians had when I arrived. Her skin was about the same shade as Teagan's, which adds up, since if she's also a princess, this must be Teagan's little sister.

Just as I had opened my mouth to speak, the doors to the room swung open and a loud voice yelled, "*Margo!*"

Teagan slapped a hand over her mouth once she saw me standing there with who I now know as Margo. "Apologies, my lady. I've been looking for this one for the better part of half an hour, and this just isn't where I was expecting to find her." Teagan looked down at the remaining scraps of blanket I'd used to set my vase alarm and tilted her head, but seemed to think better of asking any questions.

"Margo, go find Quinn so she can help you get ready. I'm going to help our new family member here prepare for the ceremony. We don't have a ton of time left," she said, though she seemed stiff, which wasn't unusual in my presence.

Margo opened her mouth, probably to object by the look on her face, but Teagan met her eyes and raised an eyebrow, and that was that. Margo sighed loudly, then turned to me and smiled, revealing dimples on both cheeks I hadn't noticed before.

"It was great meeting you, miss! I suppose I'll see you out there!" she said, then scurried out of the bedroom.

Teagan looked like she wanted to strangle her sister as she watched her leave the room, then turned to me and plastered a smile on her face that didn't reach her eyes. "Alright—let's get you ready!"

Roughly two hours later, I was dressed in a flowy, white gown with a long, lacey train and sleeves stopping at the elbow. The dress by itself seemed a little simple to be a wedding dress for the South's future queen, but I was sort of grateful since I'd always hated drawing too much attention to myself. The gown was pretty regardless, though I felt a small pang of guilt when Teagan had to cut slits in the back to let my wings slip through.

The outfit change also made it a challenge to hide any daggers, but I made sure to put the Southern dagger Dimi had given me in my corset top, close to my heart, when Teagan had turned away.

Teagan had pulled and teased my hair into a beautiful updo of elegant swoops, natural waves, and braids, and had done my makeup so I sparkled the same way the moon reflected on the ocean at night.

I was adorned in gold cuffs and anklets, which felt so foreign on my body compared to the silver jewelry Northern royals always wore. On the bright side, I got to keep my silver earrings and the necklace holding my moon stones, just tucked into my top so only the silver chain was visible.

Lastly, Teagan had crowned me with a golden circlet similar to what she wore which wrapped around the back of her head and disconnected in the front. I noticed it looked like the branches of a tree woven together around my head. Somehow, I didn't mind it too much—though part of me longed for my mother's tiara, which was now tucked away safely in my trunk of belongings.

Teagan explained that at the end of the ceremony, the circlet would be replaced with a crown, but that in a couple days I'd be outfitted for my own casual circlet to wear on the regular, like the one adorning her head.

"What do you think?" Teagan asked, and this time the soft smile on her face seemed genuine as she backed up and settled her gaze on me, proud of her work, no doubt. I turned to the side and looked at myself across the room in the floor to ceiling mirror.

The dress hadn't been crafted for wings, so we'd had to make cuts in it to allow them out. I had them tucked in, like I seemed to a lot recently, and they peaked over my shoulders. I longed to stretch them and soar in the sky again, but I pushed those thoughts away and focused on what I saw instead.

I looked pretty, even if I wasn't used to any of these customs with the slit gown and gold adornments. Teagan had styled me to look like a queen, and she was successful. But I didn't feel as though I looked like *me*, and something in my chest ached at the sight.

"It looks great. Thank you for all your help," I lied easily, turning back to face her.

Teagan smiled, and then in the same moment, both of our heads snapped towards the doors leading out to the hallway at what we heard. In the distance, somber music began playing on what I believed was piano.

"We're late!" Teagan gasped, then grabbed my hand and pulled me towards the door.

Acting on instinct, I ripped my hand back to my body, startling Teagan.

"I'm sorry—" Teagan began, but I quickly interrupted her.

"Let's get this over with," I said, the tone between us shifting from smiles back to being tense and stressed.

Teagan nodded, then headed out the doors and down the hallway. I followed behind, not exactly knowing what to expect from this point on.

Chapter Seven

After a confusing bout of twists and turns through the unfamiliar hallways of The Haven, Teagan and I finally arrived in front of a pair of tall, honey-colored doors with large golden handles. There were two guards beside each door, all of them at attention and not moving a muscle, even to look at us as we walked up. The music had gotten increasingly louder the closer we got to our destination, and now I could tell it was playing just beyond these doors.

"You ready, Princess?" Teagan asked as she motioned for me to stand right in front of the doors, facing them.

"As ready as I'll ever be," I stated, not knowing how else to reply. She didn't answer, just moved to stand behind me and lifted my lace train off of the ground so it wouldn't snag as I walked down the aisle.

I'm actually about to do this, I thought suddenly, and had to suppress the surge of emotions back behind that mental barricade in my mind.

I'd been doing that a lot these past couple of days.

Teagan must have nodded to the guards, because before I could even be warned, the two closest guards moved and pulled open both doors, standing to hold them open with their bodies.

Spine straight as a rod, I took a step into the room, and slowly began walking. The soft music of a harp swept over me, and it sounded like whoever was playing had constructed this song just for this moment. They likely had, as royal weddings were generally quite the event. The room I stepped into was huge, and I realized this was what I believed to be their throne room. It doubled as a spacious courtyard in what I imagined was the middle of the castle.

There was a large wooden platform in the middle of the room where I could see a large throne made out of a tree. The throne looked like it had been crafted while the tree was still alive, the branches bent and shaped into perfection. It had a high back, and some vines had begun to grow on it.

It wasn't until I walked through the arch above that I realized only half of the space was filled with fae, specifically the right side. *The groom's side*, I realized. My side of the audience was completely empty. A pang of sadness and bitter surprise rang through my chest.

I had never imagined my own wedding being like this. I had always imagined having Father walk me down the aisle, not having to walk myself. I'd imagined Aurora and Dimitri by my side, supporting and encouraging me. I imagined my people attending, those who have seen me grow up from afar.

Never did I imagine this *emptiness* on my side of the aisle, and in my heart.

Caught up in my own thoughts, I didn't see the small dip in the ground in front of me until I'd already stumbled into it. I didn't fall, and quickly recovered, but with every pair of eyes in the room on me, my pale cheeks flushed, embarrassed.

For the first time since entering the room, I dared to look towards the altar in the middle of the platform ahead of me, towards the groom. Suddenly, I stopped dead in my tracks, right in the middle of the aisle.

Up at the front of the room, standing in a forest green suit with gold accents and wearing a similar circlet to Teagan's, stood Byn.

There was a tiny pink line on his throat, likely new skin and mostly healed by now, where my dagger had been just a few nights before.

My eyes locked with his and my breathing started to increase as I began to panic.

I'd held a dagger to the throat of the King of the South. He was the one that rode with me all the way from Gatlyn Castle. He was the only Southerner to ever see me shed a tear. He was the one who warned me he'd be a powerful ally here in the South.

I guess he was right.

Behind me, I heard Teagan clear her throat, signaling for me to continue walking, but my feet were frozen in place. Suddenly, I didn't feel like I could go through with this, didn't know if I was strong enough.

Slowly, Byn nodded towards the platform, silently encouraging me to keep walking. I could hear the crowd murmuring, but his eyes never left mine. As if I was the only person in the room that mattered to him in this moment.

I knew I couldn't trust him, and I hardly knew him, but somehow he was the only one getting me through this right now.

Without taking my eyes from his, I slowly placed one foot in front of the other again. My steps began to gain confidence the more of them I took, and soon I was stepping up the few stairs that led to the top of the wooden platform.

In the span of a few heartbeats, I stood in front of him, staring into his deep, green eyes, which only looked brighter when he was dressed in forest green. He wore a soft smile on his face as he continued to make eye contact, never breaking it.

What is he playing at? Is this all just for show?

I could feel Teagan carefully laying out the lace train of my dress behind me, then from the corner of my eye, I noticed her sit in the front row of Byn's side of the aisle, next to Margo and four other people I didn't recognize.

I could hear the officiant asking everybody to please be seated and began speaking, but my heartbeat was pounding so loud in my ears I couldn't make out much of what he said.

My eyes drifted to stare at a spot behind Byn, trying to focus on the words being said and failing. I could feel the mental walls in my mind starting to crumble. I shifted my hands to be in front of me and started moving them in a fidgety way, my mind filled with anxieties and needing an outlet. I rung them out and picked at my cuticles, and likely would have made them bleed if Byn hadn't reached out to grab my hands.

My instinct was to rip them out of his grip, as I had to Teagan, but when I attempted to move, he held firm and gave a gentle squeeze.

My eyes snapped to his, and so quiet I knew only I could hear him, he murmured, "Just keep your eyes on me."

If we weren't in front of what was probably hundreds of people, I'd have gaped at him. I still didn't trust him, but his expression was so open. That's when I felt like I was really seeing him for the first time.

He was likely not many years older than I was, maybe twenty-two-years-old or so. If what I'd heard around Gatlyn Castle was correct, then both of his parents had recently passed away, I believe in battle. He must still be grieving, and yet here he is, marrying a stranger. The daughter of the male likely responsible for the death of his parents. He probably hadn't even had time to grieve before being thrown into becoming a king and taking on all the responsibilities of an entire kingdom.

I can't even begin to imagine...

I wondered how long he'd known he'd become king. Some children are late bloomers when it comes to their zirilium, like I assumed Margo was since I didn't see any sun stones on her, unlike

Teagan who wore a bracelet with two stones on it. Sun stones, the equivalent of a Northerner's moon stones, helped to shape and control the Southerner's zirilium. The long sleeves Byn wore blocked my view of any bracelets he could be wearing, and none of his gold earrings had any stones that looked like Teagan's. I couldn't guess how many zirilium he could wield, but it had to at least be more than two, since obviously Teagan wasn't the heir.

In Inphis, the way an heir was decided was by which child could wield the most zirilium. If the children couldn't wield any, then the male was automatically picked, and if there was no male, then the oldest of them was chosen. But royals often breed for the sole purpose of having children with multiple zirilium, so I imagine Byn could wield quite a few.

This was also, I believed, why my father had hidden me away—so nobody in the North would know that *I* was my father's true heir, and not Dimitri.

"My lady?" I suddenly realized somebody was talking to me, and snapped back into the present moment.

The moment of my *wedding*.

"Repeat after me, please," the officiant said.

Looking back into Byn's eyes, I nodded, taking an ounce of comfort in his openness. I might not trust him or any of his people, but right now I had a role to play.

"I vow it," I said, repeating after the officiant. What he had said I was vowing to, exactly, I wasn't sure.

"Now you, King Thorntier. Repeat after me: 'I vow it.'"

"I vow it," Byn responded, not a bit of hesitation in his voice.

"By word and deed, you are now husband and wife," the officiant said, making my heart race all over again. "But there is one more step: action and law. Now, the ceremony will conclude with both King Robyn and Princess Aviva receiving the other's family crest on their inner left forearm. If you both would..." he said, trailing off as he motioned to the small table and chairs set off to the side, placed directly in front of *Robyn's* side of the room.

Together, we moved to the side and sat across from each other, Teagan standing only to position my dress train just so, then returning to her seat. Robyn didn't let go of my hand as we sat, and only let go once he moved to shrug off his green jacket and roll up the sleeve covering his left arm.

A young male dressed in various shades of brown and yellow walked onto the platform from the second row of the audience, carrying a box of supplies. Within moments, he was set up, and looking at me expectantly.

"Actually, Kent, I'd prefer to go first," Robyn said, cutting in.

I looked from Kent back to Robyn in shock. Usually in these types of things, the female would get tattooed first. But by offering to go first, Robyn was putting his trust in me. If I wanted, I could fly out of the open ceiling after he got his tattoo and never look back, leaving him branded forever.

But where would you go? a quiet voice from deep inside of me asked.

"Alright, Your Majesty," Kent said hesitantly, then turned his attention to Robyn.

I watched intensely for the next half hour or so as Robyn sat through getting tattooed with my family's insignia and the symbol of the North: a flared wing with a crescent moon behind it. The tattoo was done in plain black ink, no color, and simply looked like a branding—to me at least. Robyn didn't flinch once, not even when the needles first touched his skin.

Then, it was my turn. I was feeling extremely warm, but I tried not to think about it. I laid my arm out on the table as Kent placed the pre-drawn stencil on my inner forearm and got ready to tattoo.

I was about to be tied to the South for the remainder of my existence. It was about to be permanently inked on my pale skin for the rest of my life. Even if I were to escape now, I could never truly know peace. I'd be wanted in both the North and South.

I watched the needles puncture my skin and felt my hope die along with it.

After another half hour, Kent was done. I had stared at pieces of Robyn the whole time, and I noticed he watched intensely as his family's insignia was inked onto my skin. I looked at his shoes, which were brown combat boots that were somewhat scuffed—as if he thought he might have to hop into battle at any moment. The sun shining through the canopy of leaves above us made his brown hair glow with hues of red. The small scar on his jaw looked somewhat fresh, as though it had only been fully healed for a little while now.

Fortunately, he was so focused on the tattooing process he didn't seem to notice me watching him. His eyebrows were furrowed together as he watched the needle puncture my skin repeatedly, and his smile had dropped.

I couldn't help but wonder what he was thinking about.

I looked down at my arm as Kent announced he had finished and stared at the fresh ink there. It was a wolf's head with a sun behind it. The Southern royal family's insignia. On my skin.

Forever.

I was now, officially, tied to them.

"In action and law, the tattooing has been completed. I now present to you for the first time as a wedded couple: King Robyn Thorntier and his wife, *Queen* Aviva Heartshire Thorntier!" the officiant announced, his voice booming throughout the room as the crowd rose from their seats and began clapping.

Robyn and I were led to the middle of the platform, where he lightly grabbed my sweaty hand in his and raised both his arms up, taking my arm into the air with his. He positioned our arms so both of our fresh tattoos faced the crowd full of faces displaying disgust, excitement, hope, and disappointment, then said in a loud voice: "My people, meet your new ruler, Queen Aviva!"

Chapter Eight

Robyn didn't let go of my hand after he announced me as his queen and we were each ordained with the thick cloaks and crowns, both headpieces made of pure gold set with various gems—and heavy.

Robyn led me back down the aisle as the crowd continued to clap while we exited. Not knowing what else to do, I simply allowed myself to be led. At least we were moving away from all the people and their mixed reactions.

I didn't know what to think of Robyn, or *Byn*. Who was he really, at his core? All I knew was that he was now my husband, he was the King of the South, and he was a liar, apparently.

I could feel my zirilium starting to become restless under my skin.

He ushered me out into the hall and around the corner, into a small room that looked like it could've been a bridal suite of some sort. Likely where the royals got ready to make appearances before their people.

The second the door shut behind us, I spun on my heel to face him and said, "So the King of the South is a liar on top of everything else. Great to know!"

Robyn's lips parted in shock, but he quickly recovered. "Aviva, I've never lied to you, and I don't plan to—*ever*."

I scoffed. "Yeah right, *Byn*. You could've told me who you really were back in the carriage, but you didn't. What do you call that?"

Robyn leaned against the door behind him, suddenly looking much more tired than before as he said, "Robyn or Byn, either way I didn't lie. I told you I'd be a powerful ally, didn't I? Just because I didn't tell you why or how that was true doesn't mean I lied."

"Right, you just tell selective truths. Because that's *so* much better than lying," I retorted.

Robyn sighed and responded, "Listen, I understand you don't trust me. I wouldn't either if I were in your shoes. But you *don't* know the whole story—or at least not my people's version of it. Please, just let me prove myself and my people to you. You're on the wrong side of this war, Aviva."

Before I could respond with another sarcastic response, there was a knock on the door Robyn was leaning against.

Robyn, seeming to understand the knock to be a sort of signal, straightened up and narrowed his gaze at me.

"I understand we don't trust each other. You have no reason to work with me. But just... *try*. Please," he said. The emotion in his voice sounded genuine. Raw.

He was right—I didn't trust him, or anybody else here in the South. I'd grown up hearing how they were cold blooded murderers on the battlefield, that their war crimes are too horrible to be spoken aloud. I should have been scared for my life. But... the King of the South just said *please* to me, in an attempt to try to get me to work with him.

I looked down at the tattoo now adorning my left arm. If I was truly stuck with him for the rest of my too-short, mortal life, I guess it couldn't hurt to try. Even if I did manage to escape someday, I'd never truly be free. It had been a fool's hope to begin with.

My resolve solidifying, I met his gaze again and nodded once.

Seeming just slightly more at ease, he turned without another word and opened the door behind him, then motioned for me to follow him.

The moment I stepped out of the door, though, I nearly slammed right into a wall of flesh. I looked up slightly, meeting the light green eyes of the female in front of me, then cocked my head to the side. I looked over her shoulder as Robyn turned back, having noticed I wasn't following him, and his eyes widened slightly at the sight before him.

What's this all about?

I shifted my eyes back to the female, ready to get a better look. The girl seemed to be roughly my age, maybe a little older, but she had a fierceness about her—like she'd seen things I couldn't fathom. She had a mass of wavy, bright, ginger hair, and a scar that ran down the right side of her face, cutting through her eyebrow and over her eye, straight down her cheek.

She took a half step closer to me, so close I could smell the scent of rosemary as her hair slid over her shoulder.

"*Quinn,*" Robyn said, as if warning her.

"Listen closely," she said. "You may be my queen, and I'd lay down my life for you, but Robyn is a good person. He doesn't deserve any of this. You may not trust us, but we don't trust *you*, either. Trust is *earned*, understand?"

Suddenly feeling attacked, and by a stranger nonetheless, I raised my lip in a silent snarl. "That goes both ways," I snapped in response. My skin buzzed with pent up energy.

Quinn's eyes lit up ever so slightly, as if surprised and somewhat satisfied by my response. She took a step back, then turned around to look at Robyn. A look passed between them, one I imagined would lead to a talk later, before she dipped her head to him and walked away swiftly in the opposite direction.

I looked to Robyn, tossing him a confused yet curious look, but he simply shook his head and sighed. I couldn't help but notice the way his hair shifted, showing off the tips of his pointed ears that were adorned with small gold hoops chained together. Truly fit for a king.

He led me back the way we came, through the same tall doors I had stood at before with Teagan. Although, this time when I paused, it was because I could hardly believe I was walking into the same courtyard as what felt like just moments before.

The rows upon rows of chairs had been done away with and were now nowhere to be seen. Instead, there were two long rows of tables with all types of foods and beverages on them, most of which I didn't recognize, and a makeshift, checkered dance floor in the middle. On the outskirts of the open space were tables and chairs, decorated in green table cloths and some type of gold centerpieces. They matched the long buffet tables flawlessly.

Robyn looked back at me when he realized I had ceased following. A soft, handsome smile overcame his face as he noticed my awe-filled expression, flashing that dimple that had my stomach feeling like it was doing a flip.

"If everybody helps, it makes the load lighter and work gets done faster," he said, still smiling.

As if that explained everything, he carried on, heading straight for the platform again. The platform now had a long, rectangular table on it with eight chairs on one side, all facing the rest of the open room and the people filling it.

Before we could walk around to the other side of the table to sit, two tall males stepped into Robyn's path.

"Byn!" the blond one said.

"How are you feeling, brother?" the other asked, the one with a white streak in the front of his hair, slightly falling into his face.

"Fine. Good. Great, actually," Robyn replied, seemingly flustered all of a sudden. He cleared his throat, then stepped out of the way to expose me standing behind him to the two males.

"Oh! My apologies, my queen," White Streak said.

"It's an honor to meet you, Queen Aviva," the blond one said as they both bowed at the waist.

Robyn seemed like he was holding back another sigh, but his eyes had lit up since these two had shown up. They must mean something to him.

"Aviva, this is Chester, but we all call him Chess," Robyn said, motioning towards the blond one. He was shorter than the other two males, but still far taller than me, and had a softer face. He was probably younger than them both. He had brown eyes that were as dark as chocolate, and his hair was barely long enough to fit into the small tie he held it back with. I noticed he had a belt on with various bottles and pouches.

I dipped my head towards him politely in response.

"And this," Robyn said, "is my oldest friend, Ezra. We've known each other since we were both very small children."

He motioned towards White Streak, which I realized then wasn't due to age—it must have been a birthmark of some sort. His face and eyes were still youthful, and the remainder of his hair was all a dark brown. His eyes were the color of fresh honey, and he wore an orange sweater vest on top of his creamy, long sleeve shirt, even though we were exposed to the warmer elements.

"It's nice to meet you both," I said, an automatic response.

"Chess is my royal trokav, though he's just recently been appointed as such. And Ezra is the most knowledgeable in probably all of the South. We rely on him quite often," Robyn said, providing me with further context, which I realized I greatly appreciated. Back home in the North, both Father and Dimi would rarely fill me in on such details. They always said they were unimportant or unnecessary for me to know.

Against my will, I could feel myself beginning to warm towards the South, just slightly. Nothing I had seen so far screamed *beasts,* despite what I'd been taught my entire life.

"We know this whole arrangement probably isn't what you wanted, but we *are* happy to have you here, my queen. I'm confident you'll fit in nicely," Ezra said, a soft, genuine smile on his face.

I smiled back, but timidly. Logically, I knew I couldn't trust any of these people, no matter how genuine they might seem. Yet, my heart desperately *wanted* to trust them.

Maybe coming here was a way for me to start over, to have a fresh start, I thought hopefully.

Robyn and the two other males shared a few more words before the pair broke off towards one of the buffet tables, Robyn leading me around the table before us on the platform towards the chairs. He led me to the two in the center, where he then pulled out a chair for me and signaled for me to sit.

I hesitated, then realized I didn't exactly have anything else to do. After all, this *was* my wedding afterparty.

I sat, pooling the train of my dress at my feet. Robyn adjusted the chair so I'd be closer to the table, and in doing so his hand grazed my shoulder. Even through the thin cloth of the wedding dress, I could feel the warmth radiating from his fingertips into my skin.

I took a moment to focus on keeping my breathing steady.

"I'm going to grab us both some food, if that's alright with you," he said, removing his hands from my chair and stepping to my side. I nodded, not trusting myself to speak. The next moment, he turned and walked off the platform, moving in the direction that Chess and Ezra had gone.

Once he was far enough away, I let out a shaky breath.

Stop letting him get to you, Viva. He's the enemy, I scolded myself.

Then why didn't he feel like it?

I shifted awkwardly in the chair, trying to not squish my wings against the backing.

It was a fruitless effort, I soon realized. The South wasn't built with fae like myself in mind.

A few moments later, I saw Margo running from Teagan's grip and up to the platform. She climbed into the chair to the right of me, gaps in her crooked smile.

"You look so pretty, Miss Aviva! And now you're part of our family!" Margo exclaimed, excitement oozing from her every pore. Teagan, who had been chasing after her, now stood behind Margo's chair.

"Thank you, Margo. And please, just Aviva. Or Viva, if you'd prefer," I said, meeting Margo's gaze, while moving my hands to my lap as I began to pick at my cuticles.

"Viva is such a pretty name," Margo swooned, placing her elbow on the table and her head in her gloved hand. *Curious*, I thought, *that even for formal events she doesn't remove her gloves.*

Part of me was shocked that a princess could have such a lack of manners, but another part of me still wasn't sure exactly what to expect from the South.

I opened my mouth to compliment Margo's dress—which wasn't covered in paint—when her mood drastically shifted. She was now openly staring at the crown sitting upon my head, her brown eyes slowly pooling with tears.

"Margo?" I asked softly after a moment.

Teagan looked at me, confused, then looked at Margo and followed her gaze. Understanding seemed to flash across her features.

"Come here, Margo. It's alright," Teagan said gently, guiding Margo into her arms as a tear escaped Margo's eyes, scooping her up with ease.

"Did-Did I do something wrong?" I asked, puzzled.

Teagan's eyes tore into my own as she said, "She's only ever seen our mother wear that crown."

Before I could even think of a response, Teagan held Margo closer to her chest, then swiftly walked away.

Guilt hit me like a wave hits the rocks in Cynth Bay, and suddenly I felt light-headed.

Robyn, Margo, Teagan—their parents are gone forever, because of the actions of my people.

I had never really thought about it before, how much the war had affected so many people on such a deep level. It had always felt so far away from my life up in Gatlyn Castle.

Light-headed, I gazed at the ground my feet rested upon for a long moment, trying to center myself. I didn't want all of the Southern guests milling about to notice my turbulent emotions. My nails dug into the wood of the chair I sat in, knuckles turning white. My wings dug uncomfortably into the chair, which only added to everything else overwhelming my senses.

I don't know how long I sat there like that, but soon enough Robyn walked back up the stairs of the platform holding two full plates and a wide smile on his face.

When he saw my expression, which I suddenly didn't have the energy to guard anymore, his face dropped, eyebrows furrowing together. I could feel the walls I had built up slowly falling.

"Aviva?" he asked, setting the plates on the table next to us. I shook my head silently in response and slowly looked up at him, but even that took more energy than I had.

What was happening to me?

The second our eyes met, something passed between the two of us. It was like I could feel his worry in my own chest as he gazed upon me, and his... guilt?

What could he be feeling guilty for?

He looked paler all of a sudden, as I imagined I looked right now.

He crouched down next to me, breaking our eye contact, and that weight of anxiety in my chest lightened.

"What's wrong? Can I do anything?" he questioned.

"I-I think I need to lay down. Is there any way you can get me out of this afterparty?" I responded.

Robyn looked around the crowded room, at the couples who were already dancing in the middle of the space, at the people on the outskirts trying different foods. He looked back at me and nodded. "Whatever you need," he said, and part of me ached to believe him.

Robyn stood up and offered me his hand, but the moment I went to stand up, another wave of dizziness hit me, causing me to slump back into the chair.

"I don't think I can walk," I said in a small, shaky voice. My face flushed in embarrassment.

Robyn, ever quick on his feet, responded, "That's alright, I have an idea. Do you trust me?"

"Do I have a choice?" I retorted, but my heart wasn't in it this time, the response sounding weak.

In the next heartbeat, Robyn slid his arm behind my back and under my legs, careful not to crush my wings, then lifted me and held me close to his chest. He was thoughtful enough not to let the train of my dress drag as he stood, then walked straight for the main doors.

I had to do my best not to squeal at the sudden close contact between us. I'd never been this close to a male outside of my family, and definitely not one as attractive as Robyn. I could feel my zirilium responding to the surge in my emotions, pumping like the lightning I wield throughout every vein in my body.

Robyn kept his head held high while I tucked mine closer into his chest, as if I could hide from the world while inside his arms. I instinctually had wrapped my arms around his neck, and couldn't help peeking up at him as he smiled at everybody he passed, and even winked at one elderly female, who smiled kindly in response.

Everybody in the room watched as we left, the crowd parting for us. They clapped and cheered, some even shouting their congratulations.

As soon as the door shut behind us, I could hear myself think again in the quiet hallway. Robyn's smile slowly faded as the doors slid to a close behind us.

His steps became quicker, but he never faltered, ever light on his feet.

This close to him, I finally noticed how pleasant he smelled—like fresh rain and magnolia tree blossoms. A very soft sigh escaped my lips.

Once I realized that I had just *smelled* him, I could feel my cheeks and ears flush bright pink. I cleared my throat awkwardly, hoping he hadn't noticed.

I could almost feel the pride radiating off of him. As a fae male, even without our immortality, males were known for being possessive and proud of their females. Whether Robyn had wanted this union between the two of us or not, I could *feel* that ancient instinct kicking in inside of him as he held me close.

After many twists and turns through the never-ending hallways that I still didn't recognize, I finally mustered up enough energy to lift my head, and I realized we had made it back to the royal's private wing of The Haven.

Yet, as we came nearer to the end of the hallway, we didn't stop in front of the room I had been assigned to for the past couple of days. No, we continued walking all the way to the end, the very last room behind the center doors of the hall. He used his elbow to push the handle down, then stepped inside, leaning against the door to shut it behind us. He shifted so two of his fingers were free of supporting my legs, and snapped once.

Suddenly, soft orange light filled the dark room. Through my foggy feeling mind, it took me a moment to realize he must be a fire wielder, and another moment to comprehend that he had just lit every candle in the room with a single snap.

I inhaled sharply, the realization of who exactly he was settling upon me all over again. I quickly shoved at his chest, causing him to let go, and I just barely got my feet under me before I could fall to the ground.

"Woah," he said, raising his hands up as if he were surrendering.

"This isn't the room Teagan put me in," I said accusingly, though it took all my remaining strength to stay on my feet without swaying.

"You're right. Now that we're married, you'll have to stay in here. This is my—*our*—room. I'll sleep on the couch so you can have the bed," he explained.

My mouth parted in shock at his words, and for the first time, I looked around at the room. My jaw fell open fully at the sight before me.

Unlike the room I had been in before, there was nothing Southern about this room. There was no green or gold, or even any wood paneling. The walls were stone, as though it had been an addition to the main part of the castle. Every little detail, down to the door handle and pillow cases, were either silver or a shade of blue. Not every shade of blue matched, but it was all blue nonetheless. There was even a white fur blanket laid out across the bed, like the kind I had back home on my own bed. I noticed even my trunk had been moved to be sitting at the foot of the bed.

Lastly, I noticed that this room had a large balcony in the back, off to the side, facing the forest behind The Haven and open to the sky. My heart ached to soar through the clouds again.

I turned to look up at Robyn, who I then realized had been staring at me this whole time.

Snapping my jaw shut, I cleared my throat and said softly, "Thank you."

He smiled, obviously satisfied with my response, then gently led me to the bed. I insisted on changing first, which I retreated to his washroom to do. After I emerged in more comfortable clothing, I followed him as he once again led me by hand to the bed. I curled up alone in the middle of the feather soft mattress, pulling the fur blanket up to my chin.

Beads of sweat had begun to pool on my forehead, even though chill bumps were erupting across my skin. My head was still spinning, now even worse than before. I even thought I saw Robyn reach out to stroke my hair as my blinking became slower and I finally closed my eyes for the evening.

Chapter Nine

I sat up suddenly, my temples throbbing. In a moment of blind panic, I frantically threw the fur blanket off of me, looking around the unfamiliar room.

It took a heartbeat, but the memories from the day before eventually came crashing down like a bucket of cold water being poured over my head. I gasped, then snapped my head toward Robyn, who was fast asleep on the couch looking fairly uncomfortable, his long legs hanging over the edge and the blanket not fully covering him.

I assumed from the way the room was just barely beginning to light up that dawn wasn't too far off. Looking toward the balcony only confirmed my thoughts. But why was I up at this time?

A wave of nausea overcame me, and for a moment I simply sat there, in the middle of my now husband's bed, my head in my hands.

When the next wave hit, I scrambled out of bed, heading for the door that led to the hallway. I made sure to keep my steps light, like I always did when sneaking around Gatlyn Castle, so as not to wake up Robyn. I knew his quarters housed its own washroom, but since I wasn't sure what was overcoming me, I wanted to be alone. I didn't want him waking up and trying to fret over me, or berate me—whatever it was that the Southern King would do.

I softly clicked the door shut behind me and walked to the neighboring room, the space Teagan had originally assigned me to. Funny, how I was so close to my future husband when I arrived and didn't know it. More funny still that I had met him before knowing who he was.

Funny? More like aggravating, I corrected myself.

Shutting the door firmly behind me, I grabbed the chair from the vanity and slid it in place under the door handle so it wouldn't open unless I moved it. I didn't want any visitors, but I also didn't have time to set a trap like I had in the past.

Before I could even be proud of myself, my stomach suddenly did a flip, and I slapped a hand over my mouth, then made a run for the washroom.

I fell to the floor in front of the chamber pot, barely making it in time to dry heave over the side. A few more of those, then the bile of my stomach burned its way up my throat.

I sat there for what felt like hours, retching over and over, but still trying to be as quiet as possible; I wasn't sure who was nearby, who could be listening.

Only bile ever came up from my stomach, and suddenly I realized I couldn't place the last time I had eaten. Robyn had brought me a plate last night at the party, but I had started to feel even worse than before and had asked to leave. And before the wedding, I thought the food had been making me sick, so I'd been eating less and less of it.

After another moment, I sat with my back against the wall, my stomach calm again for the time being. I put a hand to the cold stone floor and let it ground me.

I took this time to reflect on yesterday. I didn't know what overcame me, but being that close to Robyn *cannot* happen again. And what was I thinking, to even be considering putting my trust in him?

I let out a groan, frustrated with myself.

My head was still pounding, and a layer of sweat coated my skin—even though I felt as cold as the ice I wield.

When a few heartbeats had passed, I hauled myself to my feet, placing my hands on the rim of the sink and finally allowing myself to look in the mirror.

Then, I screamed.

The scream ripped itself from my throat like the bile I had just expelled. Nothing I did could have stopped it.

Looking in the mirror, I had made eye contact with my reflection, but something wasn't right.

My eyes. They were... wrong.

Well, one of them was, anyways.

I blinked rapidly, thinking this was some kind of trick, but my reflection didn't falter.

My right eye, which for my entire life had been as blue as the water in Cynth Bay, and more importantly *matched my left*, now shone as green as fresh moss on the side of a tree.

My breathing started coming faster, and I wrapped my wings around myself, beginning to panic.

Think. Think. Think.

In the distance, I heard the door to the room being knocked on, the handle being rattled. The chair must have held firm, though, because nobody came to stop me as I walked out of the washroom, scanning the chambers.

Aurora had warned me about the elixirs. I never knew exactly what was in them. I only knew they helped balance me after the accident when I was but a small girl. Father always said they helped, that they were good for me. But then why did Aurora say the exact opposite? Why did I listen to her, if at least part of me didn't believe her? Hadn't I always believed something wasn't right?

Retracing my actions, I realized one of the last things I had ingested was one of my elixirs. That was also when I realized I hadn't eaten a complete meal in what was likely days.

I had abruptly stopped taking my elixirs a couple days ago, when I left the North. Since then, I'd felt sick most of the time, in one way or another. Are these the side effects from not taking them?

Or were the elixirs blocking parts of me even I didn't know about?

My ears were ringing so loud, I could barely hear Robyn on the other side of the door, begging and bargaining to be let in as I searched the room. Things had been moved since I had last been in here, but I knew I hadn't seen it in Robyn's room.

Sliding to my knees, I lifted up the blanket that hung off the side of the bed and peered underneath.

There you are.

Reaching out, I grabbed the box and tugged until it sat in front of me. Opening the lid, I scanned the contents.

Inside sat more vials of elixirs than I could count in the moment.

I stood, picking the box of elixirs up and walking back to the washroom with determination set in my bones, even though my hands shook. Sweat still gleamed against my forehead, and my head still throbbed. But hiding under all of that was something else.

Something new.

Something... *powerful*.

I took one final look in the mirror, as if to reassure myself once again that I wasn't seeing things, then used all the strength in my body to hurl the box and all of its contents at the mirror.

The sound of glass and bottles shattering snapped me back to the present moment, and tears sprouted to my eyes instantly as I watched the remains fall, chest heaving.

In a moment where it felt like time slowed, I caught my own reflection one last time before all the shards fell to the ground.

I looked... hollow. My skin was even more icy than usual, and dark bags hung under my eyes. My hair was horribly unkempt, and my cheeks appeared sunken in ever so slightly. Even the color of my white hair, which usually shone in the moonlight, looked dull.

I watched as every piece fell and broke, listening to the chaos. The sound had drawn me back to reality, and once all the pieces settled into a heap on the washroom floor, I finally heard Robyn's warning.

"Stand clear of the door!" he yelled, and the second I looked up at the door, it burst into flames.

The doorframe didn't catch fire, but the wood of the door quickly crumbled, until Robyn seemed to get impatient and threw himself through the remains of it, embers sticking to his clothes. He snapped, and they were put out, then our eyes locked. I wanted to hide from his gaze, but it was like the pull of a magnet, and I couldn't look away.

His eyes widened with the realization of what had changed as our eyes met, and once again I felt like I could feel the swirl of his emotions in my chest. Fear, panic, confusion. I wondered for a moment if he could feel mine, too.

Suddenly, I didn't have it in me to fight anymore. I was frustrated, and sick, and so, *so* tired. A sob clawed its way up my throat—a broken, strangled sob, which led to another, until I was sinking to the floor, chest heaving with cries. Robyn was there in an instant, catching me before I hit the floor.

I didn't have the strength to push him away, even though I knew I should have. He was supposed to be the enemy. But if that were true, then why didn't he feel like it anymore?

I folded myself into his chest, clutching onto his shirt like my life depended on it. He murmured sweet, calm nothings as I wrapped my wings around the both of us instinctually—my safe place.

He was the only thing grounding me as my chest wracked with sobs, so much so that it felt like my heart was going to split down the middle. In an attempt to calm myself, I shifted closer and leaned my ear against his chest, listening to his heartbeat.

Seeming to understand what I was doing, he began stroking my hair and, to my surprise, humming. It was a sweet melody, almost sad in a way, but beautiful. His husky voice carried it well as he continued to hum the tune and run his hand through my tangled hair until the sobs slowly ceased, and just a few tears were rolling down my face instead of gushing like a broken dam.

After I caught my breath, I slowly retracted my wings, tucking them in against my back. I couldn't meet his eyes as I said quietly, "I'm sorry."

I could practically feel his shock as he said, "Why are you sorry?"

"You were likely promised a noble, mature, strong queen to help you rule, and I've only been rude, accusatory, and a total mess since I got here," I answered honestly, throat raw.

Realizing we were still holding each other, embarrassment flooded me and I quickly shoved at his chest, standing up swiftly but then swaying slightly. I leaned against the washroom doorframe and closed my eyes as lightheadedness overcame me.

"Aviva, look," he said, wonder lighting up his voice.

I peeled my eyes open reluctantly and followed his hand to where he was pointing.

There, where all my tears had fallen onto the floor, I watched as small, white flowers began to sprout from the cracks. They grew at an alarming rate, going from small sprouts to full grown flowers as high as my calf in just a couple of heartbeats.

A gasp escaped my lips, and I looked up at Robyn as I asked, "What does all of this mean?"

He looked like he had to physically force himself to look away from the flowers as his eyes met mine. Without a word, he closed the gap I had created between us, and gently gripped my chin.

My eyebrows furrowed together in confusion, and I tried to rip myself from his grip, but I was caught between the doorframe and his tall figure as he held firm on my chin and tilted my face up to meet his eyes, making my breath catch.

His eyes bored into mine, and I once again felt like he could see straight into my soul.

But if he was going to examine me, I was going to do the same. I stared into his eyes as the seconds stretched on, and in that moment I realized green might be my new favorite color.

His eyes flickered to my lips, then back up to my eyes. I felt my cheeks and ears turning red. I cleared my throat, interrupting whatever his train of thought might have been, and he seemed to understand as he took a step back, then another.

"This is going to sound crazy, but... I think you're at least *part* Southern," Robyn said abruptly.

I almost wanted to laugh, but when I thought about it, nothing else made sense. Only the Southerners have green eyes, along with brown, while everybody in the North has solely shades of blue and gray. And how else would the flowers have sprouted from my tears, if there wasn't something more going on?

But I didn't have to admit that to him.

"You're crazy," I said, crossing my arms over my chest defensively.

"You know I'm right, I can feel it. If you have Southern zirilium, I can train you, Aviva. It would be my honor," he said, and I could feel my frustration boiling up along with my zirilium. It made my skin itch.

"What are you going on about? I can't wield anything. Weren't you told that before you agreed to marry me?" I asked sarcastically, though the lie didn't sound as convincing as I wanted it to.

"Like it or not, you're my wife now. You and I are tied together. The ink they use for royal marriage tattoos in the South is one of a kind. It makes it so we can... sense each other. Feel each other's emotions. And right now, I can feel you're lying. Just as I can sense the power of your zirilium," he said matter-of-factly.

I forced myself to keep my expression schooled, but panic threatened to overrule. He could sense my zirilium? And is this why I'd been able to feel what he had been feeling since the ceremony?

I took a step closer to him, crushing the white flowers under my feet as I kept my expression flat and said, "Listen, Robyn. I do not want, nor need, your help. I never will. We are husband and wife, but that is all. We are *not* friends."

He seemed to deflate at my words, and he looked as though he wanted to push more, but decided against it. I could feel his disappointment in my own chest as he nodded once, then made for the door.

"I'll... get this fixed," he said awkwardly, motioning towards the door, then stepping through the remains of it, the fire of which had long been put out, and walked down the hall.

When I could no longer hear his footsteps, I found myself once again leaning on the doorframe of the washroom. Slowly, I slid to the floor until I was level with the fragments of mirror, bottles, and elixir that had spread over the floor and splattered on the walls, running down like rain on a window.

Ever so slowly, I tore my mental wall down. I had been too sick and uncomfortable yesterday to utilize it, but now it just seemed useless. Just as I had built it, I ripped it down, brick by brick, thought by thought. When I built it, it had been built with thoughts of who I was at the time. The Princess of the North. My father's daughter. A twin. A wielder. Someone who was strong, and loyal, and sometimes reckless. But now, I couldn't place who I was if I had to pick myself out from a crowd. I hadn't even recognized myself in the mirror.

What use was a mental wall built with things that seemed a world away? Like they belonged to an entirely different person?

As I tore down those walls, the tears began to fall once again. It was like the reality of my situation was finally sinking in.

Maybe the wall had been a protection in that sense.

I watched as my tears became one with the puddles of elixir on the floor, and I watched until the tears made it impossible to see. Breathing became more and more difficult, until my chest hurt so badly I thought it might burst.

There I sat, sobbing uncontrollably with my wings wrapped around me and my arms around my knees, for who knows how long.

Who am I?

Chapter Ten

It'd been nearly a week since I'd seen Robyn last, and I continuously had to remind myself not to care.

The last time I saw him was the day I ruined all of the elixirs. After he had left the room, I didn't know where he went. Teagan, who seemed to know what happened that day but had yet to say anything to neither confirm nor deny, had been bringing me some sort of breakfast every morning. She mentioned once that he was out on a routine mission, but she didn't specify any more than that, and I didn't have the heart to ask. She checked in daily, but she didn't stay long. Sometimes she offered to help do my hair, and the one time I agreed, I realized she's a complete master at it. I had been so out of it on my wedding day that I hadn't taken the time to appreciate her talents, but after she braided my hair into a beautiful crown around my head today and adorned it with small purple flowers, I made sure to let her know I appreciated her efforts. I had been rewarded with one of the few genuine smiles of hers I had seen.

She had also gifted me with a special kind of eye patch, one that sat on my cheek bone and nose just so, and somehow balanced so well, that it didn't slip or fall off. Teagan advised me that if I was going to be seen by the people, then I needed to hide the change until we decided how to handle it, along with figuring out what it all meant.

I had a feeling she was simply handling the situation the best she could until Robyn got back. It felt odd to cover one of my eyes, but I understood her concern, and obliged.

I was dressed in a lilac purple top that was even softer than my white, fur blanket, along with a pair of gray, leather pants Teagan had let me borrow. The lilac top matched the flowers in my hair perfectly.

I still only had my boots from back home, so I slid those onto my feet and padded out of the room and down the hallway, towards the main section of The Haven.

I'd been staying in my original room since Robyn disappeared. The mess of broken glass and bubbly elixir had been cleaned up and the door replaced the same day it had been burned, which I suspected Robyn had a hand in, maybe even Teagan. The two seemed closer than I had originally thought.

It had felt too odd to stay in Robyn's room without him, even though his room felt more like home than anywhere else in the castle.

Since I didn't know what to do with myself the day after Robyn vanished, I decided to start doing research of my own about what was happening to me. I'd been going to The Haven's royal library every day since. It wasn't quite as grand as the library in Gatlyn Castle, which had spires and bookshelves that went up countless levels, but it still felt comfortable. It made me feel normal again, being surrounded by leather, paper, and ink.

The library back home had classified knowledge that we obtained through the humans of the Levast Isles. Centuries ago, the humans were allies with my ancestors in the North. The humans had always been known for their expanse of knowledge, and when they closed their borders, they allowed their previous allies to keep what tomes had been gifted to them. But since those tomes were centuries old at that point, they were kept away from the main part of the library, classified and unread. The thought always left a bad taste in my mouth. Shouldn't knowledge be accessible to all?

I allowed my feet to guide me toward The Haven's library, knowing the route by heart now. It was one of the only places in the castle I knew how to get to, after having asked a guard the day after Robyn's departure to lead me there. He had seemed hesitant, nervous even, but I do suppose being queen had some perks, as he quickly gave in and showed me the way.

Being a Northerner did, too, because almost everybody in the library left me to my own business.

Almost.

"Is Laurence here today?" I asked the female named Maya sitting at the entryway. She was here every day like clockwork, from sunrise to sunset. She had curly, dark hair to match her chocolate skin, though her eyes were the most striking, as they were the color of a sunset—a brown so full of color it took your breath away. With her dark skin, I assumed she hailed from the Ocrein Isles, but I never asked to confirm.

Maya shook her head and gave me an apologetic look from underneath the hood of her forest green cloak. That was one thing I still didn't quite understand—a good amount of the library's servants simply didn't talk, or talked only when absolutely necessary.

The only one who had said more than a few words to me so far was Laurence. He seemed to be about Father's age, likely a little younger, and had gray sprinkled throughout his brown hair, also like my father. But unlike Father, Laurence seemed to be kind and helpful. He's been showing me around the library all week long, helping me without even knowing the origins of my curiosities.

He had shown up out of nowhere after I spent an hour wandering the library, trying to figure out how things had been categorized, and where to find the information I wanted. Since then, he'd been nearby to help whenever I needed it, green cloak and all.

"Thank you, anyways. If he shows up, tell him he knows where to find me," I said to Maya, then walked through the entryway and into the main part of the library.

Stepping into the massive space, I wondered if I'd ever tire of coming here. The main part of the structure was made of different shades of deep brown wood, while the floor was made up of a beautiful, vibrant red granite, speckled with dark crystals that seemed to match the walls. The pillars that lined all the rows of bookshelves matched the floor, but seemed to be carved with images of different creatures or plants you'd find in the South. One showcased a family of foxes, while another seemed to be entirely encased in what I believed to be some type of poisonous plant.

The next pillar I passed as I walked deeper inside resembled a creature I instantly recognized. It was like one of the giant wolves I had seen in the Southern procession that had led me to The Haven, and who had made our trip so much quicker.

I reached out as I passed and lightly touched the tip of the creature's nose, almost affectionately.

My feet continued to carry me deeper into the library until I found the small area I had been utilizing for the past week. There was a long, leather couch with a matching reclining chair, both facing a low table. The bookshelves surrounded the area in a way where there was just enough privacy that I could lay out all the books I collected on the table without fear of being watched or stared at.

The books I had been studying yesterday were still on the table, in a neat stack on one end. I sighed, remembering how unhelpful they were. Gathering them all up, I placed them on a return cart resting around the corner.

Padding back to the table, I sat down in the leather chair and dug my fingers into my temples.

I had already tried to look into eyes changing colors, and had come up empty handed there. When I looked into Southern powers, I found that tears could indeed sprout flowers. It has something to do with how zirilium can often be tied to the wielder's emotions. I had always known that my Northern zirilium were closely intertwined with my feelings, but I didn't know many other wielders growing up, so I didn't know all zirilium could work that way at times. Apparently, learning to wield outside of your emotions was a difficult feat.

I tried not to let it bother me too much, the fact that Robyn had been there to witness that. Now I was confident he knew I could wield—though I was sure he didn't know exactly *what* I could wield.

Even I wasn't confident in the full extent of that one.

While scouring the library, I had also looked into natural ingredients and combinations in elixirs that could nullify or suppress specific zirilium, but only found partial answers. There had been accounts of some trokavs using different concoctions to somewhat suppress the entirety of a wielder's zirilium, but never just part of somebody's zirilium. And these accounts said nothing about eyes changing color.

My working theory was that somehow, Hugo and my father had created a brand new elixir with unheard of strength. It seemed to have suppressed just my Southern genetics—if it was true that I had any to begin with.

Which brings us to today—I wanted to search the genealogical records of the South. Despite how little I knew of my mother, I knew her name and maiden name—Elore Ashford—and if I was lucky, I would find her name in the records somewhere. Then, I'd have to accept that maybe there was more to my mother than met the eye.

If only she were still around to ask her.

A pang of heartache and guilt shot through my chest at the thought.

"Your Majesty!" a familiar voice called out, interrupting my thoughts.

My head snapped up at the sound of Laurence's voice, my hands dropping from my head as I quickly got to my feet.

"Laurence?" I asked curiously. "Maya said you weren't here today, but—" I paused, suddenly stunned into silence as I took the male in.

Usually, Laurence was dressed in the thick, green cloak all of the library's keepers wore. He even kept his hood up, so his face had always been cast in at least partial shadows. Until today.

Today, he was dressed in a simple outfit—a gray, cotton shirt and black slacks. But what stood out the most were his piercing, icy blue eyes.

"You're... Laurence, are you Northern?" I asked in a hushed voice, my wings flaring slightly in surprise.

His eyes tracked the movement, and a flash of pain crossed his face for less than a heartbeat before it was gone again.

If he was Northern, why was he not trying to hide it at all?

Laurence, ever the kind male he was, smiled at me, and there was something almost like pity hidden within it.

"Let us sit, Your Majesty," he said softly.

Suddenly feeling on edge, I hesitated, but slowly returned to the chair behind me while Laurence turned to pull the curtain that blocked the entrance to the area we were in closed, so we'd have complete privacy.

It wasn't until that moment as he pulled the curtains closed that I noticed the two large bumps on his back, right at the base of his shoulder blades.

Right where my own wings sprouted from my back.

I gasped at the sight, realizing his thick cloak had hidden more than just his eye color.

Laurence turned back to me, seeing my expression, and a troubled look flashed across his features. He moved across the space and sunk into the couch across from me.

"What happened to you? How are you here?" I asked him quietly.

"If King Robyn hasn't told you yet, I'm not sure it's my place... but you were my princess before you were the South's queen, and that alone means I have a duty to tell you the truth," he said, taking a deep breath. I noticed his hands had begun to shake ever so slightly.

"The truth? What are you talking about? Why won't anybody just tell me what's *really* going on?" I questioned, suddenly feeling very small.

"Well, let's start at the beginning. Your observations are correct—I am originally from the North, just like you. While our circumstances of arrival differ, we are the same in that way.

"Many years ago, I joined the Northern army to serve my kingdom. I truly thought I was doing the right thing. I had been born and raised in a family of soldiers, and I wanted to make my parents proud. I worked hard as a young male, using my zirilium of air, water, and ice to serve King Horace to the best of my abilities. I spent years as a lieutenant, and had been freshly appointed to captain at this time. There was a battle five years ago, my last one ever—though there've been so many since then, it doesn't hold a light to the entirety of the war. My family was proud, but the higher into the ranks I climbed, the more horrendous things I saw, all from the North's hands. The cruelty, the war crimes, how some of the soldiers treated the female Southern trokavs they captured... it was all too much. I didn't realize what was going on behind the scenes until it was too late. At the time of my last battle, I had already said my oath to King Horace personally when I had been appointed as a captain in his army. So when it all became too much, and I defected, it didn't take long for me to be caught. I had no idea where I was going to go, all I knew was that I couldn't take it all anymore. Just because the Southerners were our enemy, didn't mean they weren't worth being treated without an ounce of respect." I watched as Laurence took a steading breath, then carried on, calm once again, though his eyes shone with sadness.

"Apologies, Your Majesty, it still makes my blood boil. Once I was caught, I was brought to the far side of the battlefield, before your father. He laughed, thinking I was a fool for trying to escape him and my duty to his army. But there had been others who had begun to disagree with his thinking, and he had heard those whispers. He decided to use me as an example of what happens to those who went against him, or tried to avoid their duties. Two of his personal guards pushed me to my knees before him, with my back to him. He stood behind me as I listened to him unsheathe his sword. I was convinced my time had come as he pressed the side of it to the left of my neck. He could have had my head in his hand in one fell swoop. Instead, he said death was too easy a punishment for me. What happened next... it still haunts me to this day. I remember screaming until my voice no longer worked like it should. It took four of his guards to hold me still as he used that sword to cut through every bone, tendon, and muscle at the base of my wings." He choked out the last part, like he could still feel the pain. Tears sprang to my eyes and my hand covered my gaping mouth as I listened. Guilt shot through my heart like an arrow.

"After... after it was done, his men dragged me to the outskirts of King Horace's encampment. As they were hauling me away, I can still recall watching him throw my wings into the fire in the middle of the camp, further proving his point to any others who were considering defecting. My wings, such a large part of my identity... reduced to ashes, just like that.

"Once they dropped me at the outskirts, they took turns kicking and spitting on me. None of them expected me to survive—I still don't know where I drew the strength from. But once they departed, I clawed my way to the edge of the battlefield, trying to make my way to the green trees. I knew if I could make it to the edge of the forest, the South could find me. I imagined they couldn't be any worse than the North—maybe they'd have the decency to put me out of my misery. Instead, Sir Chess found me. He was just a boy then, a freshly appointed trokav for the Southern army. He took one look at me and vowed to help in any and every way he could. From then on, he personally oversaw my healing. Once I was brought to The Haven, he checked in on me multiple times a day, using his plant wielding to aid in his potion, elixir, and salve making. He made things to take the pain away, bandaged me up, and added ointments to my bruises, cuts, and stumps. It took weeks for me to heal physically, even with his help. I'll forever be grateful to him for how kindly he treated me when I needed it most."

Laurence spoke with such purpose, it was impossible not to be deeply enveloped in his story. His voice shook at times, and his hands began to shake even more violently the longer he spoke.

Reaching across the table between us, I gently placed a hand over his shaking ones, trying to steady him.

"Laurence, I know it likely means nothing, but I am so, *so* sorry you went through all of that. I'm so sorry for my father's actions. I... I had no idea," I said, fumbling for words.

A troubled smile crossed his face before he said, "It isn't your fault, Your Majesty. You were just a girl at the time—you couldn't have done a thing even if you were aware of what your father had been doing. But if it hadn't happened, I wouldn't have been taken in by the South. King Robyn—he had only been Prince Robyn at this point—gave me a place here, at The Haven, in this very library. I serve him now through working in the library as a head servant, and he gives me housing and a place to call home. Many of the servants that stay here have some type of troubling past—it's why some refuse to speak. For me, the quiet of the library helps quiet my mind and its voices. It's given me a sense of purpose and helped me to heal."

I offered him a small, sad smile in response to his own, before a thought crossed my mind.

"Laurence, I'm honored you've told me all of this but... why now? Why are you telling me all of this?" I asked in a quiet voice, though I feared I already knew the answer.

"Queen Aviva, you forget—I've been where you are. I was raised with all of the same stories and propaganda that you were. But all the cruel stories you heard about the South? The Southerners didn't do any of those things, the *North* did. The Northerners only switch up the narrative to keep their people in line and terrified. It's all manipulation, a scare tactic. The South... they're good people, Your Majesty. I know you've only been here a short time, and you have no reason to trust them. But if you can't trust them, trust *me*, Northerner to Northerner, when I tell you—you're on the wrong side of things if you're still envisioning the South as your enemy." He spoke in his usual kind voice, but his words struck like a blow to the chest.

I let out a deep breath slowly before speaking. "So, let me get this straight. You're pretty much saying everything I've ever known... it was all a lie. I hadn't even known my father was capable of such horrific acts. And while I've been fighting Robyn tooth and nail thinking he's the evil one here, in reality, it was my own father?"

Laurence met my eyes as he said with a steady voice, "That's exactly what I'm saying, Your Majesty."

I sucked in a sharp breath, even though I had expected that response from him.

"I'm inclined to believe you, considering how pretty much everything I've seen of the Southerners so far has been genuine and of pure intent," I said, then took a moment to ponder.

"Laurence, since you were raised in the North, can I ask you something?" I asked him.

"Anything, my queen," he said without hesitation.

"My mother... was she Northern? All the portraits I'd seen of her back home were in black and white, and my memory of her is foggy, to say the least," I admitted. "Though I don't remember her having any wings."

Laurence's eyes widened slightly, letting me know this wasn't the question he had been expecting, though he answered anyways.

"There were rumors your mother was of Southern origins, though I have no idea if that was true or not. Your father kept her out of the public's eye as much as he could, and she was only around a handful of years before she disappeared as mysteriously as she arrived. I don't know where she and your father met. All I know is one day we suddenly had a new queen, and a few years later, we didn't. Your father made a public statement, claiming she had passed, but not everybody believed him. I do remember, though, that everybody who had the honor to meet her, adored her and spoke of how kind-natured she was. You take after her in that sense, I believe." He spoke in a tone that felt very affirming, though I didn't realize how much I needed to hear about her.

I nodded, taking in this information, while being slightly disappointed at not getting a straight answer.

Another shot of guilt rang through me as I realized I very well might be one of the only people alive who knew the truth about what happened to my mother.

And, accident or not, it was all my fault.

After a moment, I looked back up at the male before me and met his eyes.

"Can I trust you?" I asked, seemingly out of nowhere.

Laurence nodded firmly once and said, "Always, Your Majesty."

"I need to find out more about my mother. I know her maiden name, and if she was from the South, I was hoping you could help me find her genealogical records to confirm. Think you're up for it?" I questioned, trying to lighten the heavy mood that hung around us like a storm cloud my father had conjured.

His spine straightened and his face lit up at being given a task. "I knew you had to have been searching for something specific this past week, but it wasn't my place to question you. I vow to help in any way I can," he promised.

"Thank you, Laurence," I said, the corners of my mouth tugging up into a small smile.

He nodded, returning my smile with one of his own.

In a way, he reminded me of the father I'd always wished I'd had.

"Her name was Elore Ashford," I said, standing up as I spoke, ready to search through the shelves and shelves of books. It wasn't until I looked back at Laurence that I saw just how his face had blanched.

"Did you say Ashford, Your Majesty?" he asked slowly.

My eyes narrowed as I turned back to him and said, "Yes, I did."

Carefully, he spoke with the softness of a griffin feather, as if he was trying not to frighten me as he said, "That's the name of one of the highest ranking noble families in the entire South."

Chapter Eleven

"Pardon?" I stammered. "You're confident?" I pressed Laurence further, who was still sitting on the couch before me as I placed both of my hands on the table to steady myself.

The male nodded stiffly. "I'm confident, my queen. They've been among the other noble families invited to the castle for meetings with the king and his advisors on multiple occasions." He paused. "Your Majesty, you even have a set of grandparents," he said in his usual, soft voice. As if that made any of it less painful.

My eyes snapped up to meet his as my jaw dropped slightly open.

I hadn't even considered that looking into my mother's origins would lead me to finding any family. In my mind, where she came from was always a mystery, something I'd never truly have an answer to. But this... I couldn't have come up with this in any scenario I'd made up in my head.

I shook my head to clear my thoughts, slamming my teeth together harshly.

"Did you know?" I asked with much more calm in my voice than I felt. I could feel my zirilium beneath my skin simmering.

Each morning while I took a bath, I created different objects or shapes with the water, or used the air to float some of the bubbles high above my head. I did this each day, hoping to keep my zirilium at bay, but I knew as I felt it crawling through my veins that I couldn't hold it off for too much longer. Bubble baths wouldn't suffice forever.

Laurence looked stunned momentarily, but quickly recovered and shook his head side to side before saying, "No, Your Majesty, I hadn't a clue. I don't know much about the noble families of the South—most of my time is spent here in the library. I much prefer books over people these days. I wasn't even aware that the Ashford's had any children, let alone a daughter. But now that you mention it... well, I've only seen them in passing, but I can see small pieces of them in you. You even share Lady Billie's face shape."

I inhaled sharply at hearing this, but nodded despite the churning in my chest.

I realized in that moment that I'd decided to trust Laurence.

After a moment of silence, I cleared my throat and reached for the Southern-crafted dagger I now kept on me at all times. It made me feel closer to my mother somehow, even if it didn't change the fact that she was gone for good.

Pulling it out, I placed it on the table before Laurence.

"Dimitri, my twin, found this among our mother's belongings. It was my first hint that my mother might have Southern origins," I said, sliding the knife closer to his side of the table.

Laurence gently picked up the blade, flipping it over in his hands. He murmured, "Interesting," as he did so.

"What is it?" I prodded.

"Well, both sides of the dagger have a small family insignia etched into the weaving pattern on the hilt. This one," he motioned to one side, "is the Ashford family's insignia. But this one," he flipped the dagger over, "I have never seen before. It's unlike any of the Southern ones I've come across in my time here."

I groaned, sinking back into the leather chair behind me.

"Why was my mother such a complicated female?" I asked, exasperated.

Laurence frowned slightly, then slid the dagger back across the table for me and stood up.

"I'll return momentarily," he said, then slipped through the curtain back out into the main sector of the library.

I took the blade into my hands and studied it, wondering how I hadn't recognized my own mother's family insignia before now. The insignia that Laurence had pointed out as being the Ashford's was the perfect image of a willow tree, one that looked like it would sway in the wind with the slightest breeze, but had deep, strong roots. I turned it over, observing the other side. The image of a wave was etched into it, with small stars overhead as if depicting the ocean at night.

Interesting, I thought.

Shortly after, Laurence returned with a large book, forcing him to hold it with both hands as he stepped through the curtain, letting it fall closed behind him. He rounded my side of the table and placed the book between us.

"This book lists every noble family that's been in the South in the past few centuries, all the way up to modern times. Let's see..." he trailed off as he opened the book with a soft *thump*, then began thumbing through it until he found the *A*s portion of the book.

Together, we flipped through the pages until we came across one that had the name *Ashford* scrawled at the top in loopy handwriting. Below the family name was that same family crest, the one with the willow tree, except this time, with more room for details. I noticed a small bird perched on one of the branches.

"Here we are," Laurence said as we reached the page. My eyes widened in surprise as I took in the large family tree, full of so many members it took up two pages side by side.

It seemed that for many generations, there had been solely large families, with a minimum of three children each, spanning all the way up to nine children in some generations. Almost every name had a small symbol underneath it, indicating whether that person had been a wielder or not, and if so, what kind. There was a leaf for plant wielding, a flame for fire, a rock for earth, a gem for crystal, and a plain black circle with loopy lines swirling from it for shadows.

Lightly running a finger over the lines tying the families together, I followed the flow of the generations down and watched as the number of Ashfords slowly dwindled down to almost nothing over the course of a few centuries. Down towards the bottom of the second page were two names—the only two that hadn't yet been crossed out unlike all the others, indicating these people were still alive.

The names read: Billie and Geoff.

My fingers paused on their names as I released a breath I hadn't realized I was holding in.

"These are my grandparents?" I asked quietly.

Laurence, next to me, nodded in confirmation.

Below the names of my maternal grandparents, there was one name remaining, though it too had been crossed out.

Elore.

I sucked in a sharp breath, as if reading it had physically pained me. My fingertips hovered in the air above her name before I gently stroked the page, as if I could feel her through it.

"The Ashford line ended with her," I said, suddenly feeling bitter, though I think it was simply to cover my own guilt.

"No, my queen. She lives on in *you.* You uphold the Ashford line now, along with your brother," he said to me.

I loosened a breath, trying to let go of the tightness in my chest at the thought of Dimitri. I hadn't realized just how much I missed my twin until that moment.

I wonder what he would have to say about all of this.

"You're right, Laurence. Thank you for showing me this," I responded, hoping I sounded genuine.

He flashed me an encouraging smile, then aligned his spine as he stood back up to his full height, nearly a head taller than me.

"Unfortunately, I have to take my leave now, Your Majesty. You were right when you said I wasn't supposed to be here today. It's my day of leave, and I have some things to tend to," Laurence said, then bowed deeply.

"Laurence, you can just call me Aviva. I truly don't mind. And thank you for helping me today. I greatly appreciate it. Let me know if you ever need anything, alright?" I said as I watched him straighten back up.

"I think I'll stick with Your Majesty. And it's been my pleasure, I assure you." He smiled as he dipped his head once towards me, then left through the curtain.

I sat there for a long while after his departure, simply staring after him and wondering what the Stars I had just uncovered.

***

I remained in my small, private portion of the library with the same book Laurence had retrieved for the next few hours, until the high windows up above revealed it was already late in the afternoon.

I had already flipped through the giant book twice, looking at each and every family crest, trying to match one to the insignia carved onto the backside of the dagger. After the first time going through each page of the hefty tome, I thought maybe I had over-looked it. After the second, I simply gave up, concluding that it wasn't in this book. Obviously, the mystery crest didn't belong to any of the noble families of the South.

Once I'd accepted my defeat regarding that book, I stared at the dagger for a long while, flipping it over and over again in my hands.

It was one of the last ties I had to my mother, and yet part of it was etched with a stranger's family insignia.

What does it mean?

Lost in thought, I barely had time to conceal my dagger again as the curtain parted and a tall figure stepped inside.

For a moment, I thought Laurence had returned, but looking up, I caught a glimpse of a white streak of hair, shining like a beacon against the rest of his messy, deep brown hair.

"I thought I might find you here," he said, stepping into the small space.

White Streak! I thought to myself as I recognized his face from the wedding afterparty. *Please don't call him that to his face, Viva. Stars, what was his name again?*

"It was Ezra, right?" I asked, getting to my feet from where I had sat comfortably in the low chair.

He smiled, then nodded. "The one and the same."

I took just a handful of seconds to study the male. He stood just as tall as Robyn, maybe an inch taller even, his pointed ears unadorned aside from a single golden hoop at the top of his left ear. Today he wore a golden yellow sweater vest over a cream shirt, along with dark brown pants and boots to match. He carried a small satchel on his hip that looked worn with lots of use. Overall, besides his obvious birthmark, he looked almost... ordinary.

For some reason, this made me wary.

"So, can I help you with something?" I asked him, not exactly sure why he was here.

"Oh, right. Well, Teagan had said you had been here all week, and somebody needs to check in on you while Robyn is away," he said. I tried to ignore the way my breath caught when I heard Ezra speak his name. Then, I watched as his eyes slowly drifted down to the book I had left open.

The top of the page which clearly displayed the Ashford family name.

Quickly, I slammed the book shut and pulled it closer to my body, but left it flat on the table.

Ezra, not put off in the slightest, smiled.

Does anything make this male uncomfortable?

"Southern nobility and their lineage. Interesting choice of subject to study," he said after glancing at the cover of the leather bound tome.

When I made no effort to respond, he motioned to the couch across from me and asked if he could sit. I hesitated, but nodded after a heartbeat, slowly lowering myself back into my own chair as he took his place at the table across from me, where Laurence had sat just hours before.

"I came here to talk to you on behalf of all of the Valwain," Ezra stated, sinking into the couch further, as if he couldn't be more comfortable.

I arched an eyebrow as I questioned, "Valwain?"

Ezra looked at me in muted surprise. "Robyn hasn't told you about us yet?"

"Seems there's a lot he doesn't tell me," I mumbled.

"The Valwain were a sect of highly skilled warriors of the South that lived many centuries ago, at the beginning of the war. There weren't very many of them, but just one of those warriors made up for a dozen regular soldiers on the battlefield," he said before carrying on. "Years ago, when Robyn, Quinn, Teagan and I were just learning to properly wield a sword, one of our instructors told us about the Valwain. We decided we'd be the new Valwain for the people of the South, just in a slightly different way. Pretty much, it's Robyn and his close circle—at least nowadays. You're part of that, now, too. Well, if you'd like to be, that is."

Ignoring his offer, I asked, "Who all is in your little group?"

"Well, there's Robyn, who is, of course, our king and leader. Then there's Teagan, a skilled warrior and our main diplomatic fae. Quinn, who I believe you've had the pleasure of meeting, is the general of all our Southern armies. There's also Chess, who is our royal trokav, and a great one at that. Drayven, or Rayven, who is our top spy and a fantastic shadow wielder, though I don't think you've met him yet. Then there's me—the male with too much knowledge in here." He tapped his temple, smiling, then shrugged when he saw my quizzical look. "Swords didn't suit me, and I never developed any zirilium, so I found my strength in a vast, deep well of knowledge. Aside from that, there's Margo, but she's an unofficial member," he said with a wink.

I nodded in understanding. I'd always found books to be an escape, a comfort, and a constant within a world full of chaos.

Before I could respond, he made an *oh!* sound and turned, reaching into his satchel. A second later, he pulled out a small leather book tied shut with a piece of twine. He slid it across the table to me.

"A book, for you. It's about the history of the Valwain, in case you were curious," he said, sounding excited to be sharing this with a fellow book lover.

Slightly stunned at his generosity, I replied, "Thanks..." then, not exactly knowing what to say and feeling awkward, I said, "Anyways, sounds like you have a well-rounded group. Where has Robyn gone, anyways? Run off with his mistress already?" I jabbed, though I immediately regretted it.

I knew I shouldn't be so harsh, but I couldn't help it. I thought we'd had a moment, and then he was just *gone*. How could I trust, or let alone *like*, a male who was never around and only gave me vague answers to my questions?

Ezra's smile faltered slightly, his calm composure slipping just a bit, though I didn't think it was a mask like Robyn and I seemed to wear. It appeared like Ezra genuinely was a laid back kind of person, not letting much bother him.

And I just got under his skin.

"Despite what you seem to believe about us Southerners, *my queen*, Robyn is the most loyal person you'll ever have the pleasure of meeting. He is devout to a fault, and would never betray your trust like that. You're his *wife*. He's yours as much as you are his. Plus, you're the reason he decided to head the mission he's currently on." As he spoke, I could clearly see all of his emotions—frustration and hurt, mostly—written across his features.

"What mission?" I pressed, ignoring the rest of what he said, and suddenly feeling a pang of worry as my stomach did a small flip. "Is he alright?"

Ezra, seeming to find my reaction satisfactory, forced a smile as he said, "I'm sure he's fine. It was a stealth mission, not combative. But you should ask him yourself. You two have to learn how to talk to each other for any of this to work."

I made a small *huff* sound, then leaned back in my chair, careful not to press against my wings.

Ezra sighed, his white hair falling into his face, then placed his elbows on the table, resting his chin on his hands.

"Listen. The Valwain and I are all heading to Robyn's family's secluded cabin at Echen Bay to relax and recharge. Since you two are married now, we shouldn't be needed quite as much here, seeing as we should, in theory, have peace with your father from here on out. We all talked, and we want you to come with us. What do you say?" Ezra's voice was back to normal, no hint of the frustration he had harbored moments ago, and a small smile played on his lips.

I looked up into his soft, honey brown eyes, searching them, as if this was some kind of trick.

Why would they want me to come?

"Am I required to? Am I the Valwain's prisoner?" I asked, my tone snarky.

Ezra shook his head as he said, "Not in the slightest. We're *requesting* your presence, if you'd be so kind as to grace us with it."

For a moment, I pondered. It wasn't like I had anything more important to do here at The Haven. There were only so many books I could find to study. Plus, if everything Laurence said earlier was true, the Southerners aren't the villains of this war. At some point, I was going to have to learn to trust them.

So what was I waiting for?

Additionally, I realized, a small part of me has missed Robyn this week, although I couldn't place why.

Maybe it was the way he carried himself, with the confidence of a great ruler. Or the way his slightly too long hair fell across his forehead just so. Or maybe it was the light that shone in his eyes that made me want to keep fighting, even when everything in me screamed to give up.

"So?" Ezra said, snapping me out of my haze. "Will you come with us?"

I hesitated a moment, but slowly nodded as I said, "Yes. I'll join you all."

He jumped up from the couch, a smile beaming across his face. "She said yes!" he exclaimed, resulting in a few voices in other parts of the library to hush him. He had the decency to look sheepish, obviously having forgotten where we were.

I couldn't help but smile.

"Pack what you can, my queen. We leave in the morning."

Chapter Twelve

A series of sharp knocks on the door had me stumbling over my untied shoe laces to reach it.

"One moment!" I shouted through the door, reaching down to tie up the laces of my black boots. They matched the rest of my black, leather outfit perfectly for traveling, besides the giant slits and holes I had to make in all the clothing I had been given here in the South so that my wings could fit through the backside of the tops. I had also made sure to braid my hair into two plaits down the sides of my head and down my back as soon as I woke up this morning so I wouldn't have to bother with it. The only part of my hair not perfectly tamed were the bangs that fell across my forehead.

I took a quick look at myself in the mirror and fussed over my bangs for a moment. I made sure the fitted eye patch was in place—I still wasn't sure I wanted to display my recent change to the world—and went to open the door.

If I hadn't been in such a rush to fling the door open, maybe I would have noticed that I had heard that specific knock before.

I stopped dead in my tracks, the slight smile I had given my reflection falling off of my face as I looked up into the green eyes of Robyn.

It had only been a week since I'd seen him last, but he already looked different. His skin was a half shade darker, as if he'd spent the entire week outside and the sun had shone solely on him. The time outside made his freckles pop, too—his cheeks and the bridge of his nose covered in them, like somebody had splattered a spray of paint on him. His eyes, though, I recognized, and feared I always would. I knew I'd be able to pick his eyes out of a crowd anytime, the perfect shade of forest green. They matched his deep green, cotton shirt perfectly, complimenting his brown, leather pants.

I imagined I should be upset with him for leaving and not telling me anything about it, but I couldn't think past the relief of seeing him in one piece in front of me.

It wasn't until I heard my name being said, for what I assumed wasn't the first time, that I snapped back to the present moment.

"Pardon?" I asked, not having been listening in the slightest.

A knowing smirk overtook his plump lips as he said, "I was just saying I came to fetch you. Everybody else is outside, getting ready to depart. Where is your bag?"

I opened the door further, the smell of freshly carved wood coming off of it still strong from being replaced, and allowed him to step inside. I rounded the side of the bed and went to reach for my bag, but Robyn beat me to it, grabbing it and slinging it over his shoulder in one smooth motion.

It took everything in me not to stare at his toned muscles moving beneath the skin of his arms.

It wasn't until he turned his back on me to walk out of the door that I realized the bag I had packed with my few belongings matched his, which was hanging from his other hand, perfectly.

"Ezra gave me that bag yesterday. It wasn't a spare though, was it? It's yours?" I asked as I ceased walking before I exited the room.

He turned his head to look over his shoulder and simply nodded, still wearing that stupidly handsome smirk of his. Then he walked out of the room, forcing me to follow after him.

Fae males.

It took a few paces, but I caught up with him. If I hadn't known better, I could've sworn he was taking smaller strides than normal just for me.

Not having anything to carry or put my focus into, I held my hands together in front of me and began picking at my cuticles without thinking much about it. Truthfully, I was nervous about this trip. We were venturing even farther into the South, farther than most Northerners had ever gone, yet here I was. I also didn't know the Valwain all that well yet, and I didn't know what to make of them. I knew I wanted to learn to trust Robyn and the rest of them, but how do you start letting people in when your whole life you had a wall built around your heart?

Seeming to sense my worry—probably literally—Robyn shifted the bags to one hand and reached across the space between us, gently brushing his knuckles across my hands, causing me to drop them back down to my sides. The moment our skin touched, I could feel the zirilium pumping in my veins sing.

"About my Valwain, you have nothing to fear. Each member is a good fae, sworn to protect and serve the citizens of the South—which includes you now. Some might be a little rough around the edges, but I assure you, we all only want the best for our people," he spoke quietly, "especially you."

The last part he said so softly, I thought I'd misheard him.

I took a deep breath and nodded, loosening the breath again a moment later, willing my racing heartbeat to calm down. "*Thanks*," I murmured in Nolvym, too anxious to be outright in my appreciation.

I caught his surprised look out of the corner of my eye, but thought nothing of it when he failed to carry on the conversation.

After a few more minutes of walking through the mostly empty castle—I imagined not many were awake this early in the morning, for it was just shortly after dawn—we stepped outside into one of the side gardens. Just beyond it was the rest of the Valwain, three horses, and some unexpected visitors.

Even from where I paused on the castle steps, I could clearly see the *giant* wolves huddled with the rest of the Valwain. From the looks of it, they were the same two from when I was brought to the South—one almost entirely pitch black with brown eyes, and the other gray and white with green eyes. The gray and white one was crouched down, flat on its belly, allowing Teagan to strap a large leather saddle to the creature, along with some of the group's luggage.

Robyn, who hadn't noticed I'd ceased walking until he got down the handful of steps, followed my gaze to the pair of wolves.

"Sometimes I forget having Titan Wolves isn't an ordinary thing for most fae," he mumbled, then motioned for me to continue following him.

Once I reached his side, I looked up to meet his eyes and parroted him, "Titan Wolves?" I'd never heard about them in any of the books I had read on the South.

He nodded. "A dying breed of especially large wolves. They can run faster and jump higher than any other mammal on the continent. What's left of them are only ever bonded to Southern royalty."

He pointed to the wolf that was being loaded up with luggage, then said, "That's Lychen, Teagan's wolf. She bonded with him when she was eleven." He pointed to the black wolf next. "And that, is Atlas. He's one of my best friends. I bonded with him when I was thirteen, and we've been together ever since."

Slowly, we started walking toward the group again. I was so lost in thought and anxiety ridden I barely noticed the beautiful garden we were floating through—full of all kinds of varieties of Southern wildflowers, each sector a different color.

"You said you and Teagan were *bonded* to them. What's that mean, exactly?" I asked him as we drew closer to the group.

"It means our lives are intertwined. Atlas and I know each other well from years of being together, but because we're bonded, he's also able to pick up on my moods—kind of like how you and I are able to feel each other's emotions—and therefore he can predict my actions better during battle. Also, he shared his markings with me once he decided I was the one he wanted to bond with. I didn't just pick him, he had to pick me, too." Robyn stretched his marked right arm out and motioned to it. "These markings are the same as the ones Atlas has. Watch this," he said, a small mischievous smile playing on his mouth.

He whistled a double, high pitched note and Atlas' head immediately snapped in our direction. He came bounding over after catching sight of Robyn.

As the large creature walked over, I noticed he had the same swirling pattern on his head that Robyn had on his arm in a deep brown color, almost blending in to the black surrounding it. Starting right between his eyes, it traveled up between his ears and down his spine. Though, I noticed, Atlas' marking was longer than Robyn's was.

Likely sensing my curiosity and following my gaze, Robyn said, "The stronger the bond grows between a rider and their Titan Wolf, the more of the wolf's markings they'll gain. That's why Teagan's markings covers more of her arm than mine does, because her and Lychen have been bonded for years longer than Atlas and me."

I had to suppress a sigh as I thought of Eden. I hadn't had much time to think about her recently, and the ache of being separated hit me all at once as I gazed at Atlas.

"Interesting," I murmured, then took a step back, slightly behind Robyn as Atlas drew close. Only then did I realize exactly how huge the Titan Wolves were.

Atlas stood at least twice my height, forcing him to crouch down in order to meet Robyn face to face. I seemed to only be as tall as one of his legs.

When Atlas was finally face to face with Robyn, he let out a *huff* of hot air, blowing Robyn's hair out of his face. I noticed his tail had begun swishing back and forth, too. It was clear that Atlas was extremely fond of Robyn, allowing him to reach up and scratch under his jaw, and Atlas simply leaned into Robyn's hand.

If he were a cat, I was sure he would've begun purring.

"Atlas, there's somebody I want you to meet. I told you about her, remember?" Robyn said, then stepped aside so I was no longer cowering behind him. "Atlas, meet Aviva. Aviva, Atlas."

Atlas's ears perked up as he looked at me, his tail gone still.

Suddenly I felt lightheaded with nervousness.

"It's alright," Robyn cooed. "Here, give me your hand."

When I hesitated, he added, "Just trust me, Avi."

My eyes snapped up to meet his, shocked by the new nickname I'd just heard come from his lips. He had the decency to blush slightly, but his hand remained outstretched, waiting.

I wondered for a moment if he knew *avi* meant *love* in Nolvym—a term of endearment.

Slowly, I put my hand in his, and together he guided our hands toward Atlas.

The wolf lowered his head even more, meeting us halfway, our hands falling directly between his eyes. I gasped softly as I felt how soft Atlas' fur was, and gently stroked the markings that were there after Robyn lifted his hand away.

Atlas, seemingly content with my presence now, moved quickly as he reached out and licked the side of my face, leaving behind a trail of wetness.

I squealed in disgust and surprise, while Atlas' tail had once again began wagging.

Robyn laughed—a deep, rich sound. "That's his way of saying he likes you."

"Tell him to keep it to himself next time," I grumbled, desperately trying and failing to wipe my face dry.

"Here, let me," Robyn said, still chuckling, and stepped in front of me. I lowered my hands, daring to look up into his eyes, only to find he was already staring into mine. There was a sparkle in his eyes I hadn't noticed before now.

Likely just the sunlight.

With movements gentler than I thought possible from him, he gripped my chin, tilting my head to the side to expose where Atlas had licked. He lifted the hem of his soft shirt up and used it to wipe the remnants off my face, painfully slow.

My gaze, betraying me for just a split second, flickered down to where his toned stomach was now exposed, then back up to his eyes. Though his gaze was focused on my face, I knew by the smirk he now wore, with that dimple on full display, that he hadn't missed what I'd done. Despite my best efforts to control my embarrassment, heat crept up into my face and ears.

A moment later, he dropped his hands from my face, allowing his shirt to fall back into place. It wasn't until he took a step back and said, "There we go," that I realized I had been holding my breath.

I cleared my throat, murmuring my thanks, as Atlas rose to his full height and led the way towards the rest of the Valwain.

Everybody in the group seemed to work together like a machine—Ezra was verbally listing everything they needed and making sure everybody had placed their luggage on a wolf or horse. Quinn was saddling all of the horses. Teagan and Margo were preparing Lychen, who was still lying flat on the ground. Robyn had begun preparing Atlas, equipping him with a saddle and our bags. Chester was bringing the last of the bags outside. And helping him, I spotted a new face.

He was unlike any male I'd come across before. His deep, rich olive skin showed just how much time he spent in the sun, and his curly, dark hair fell into his face. His pointed ears were longer than anybody else's I'd ever seen, and he had a scar running horizontally across his face, over his nose and covering parts of his cheeks, slicing through the scruff on his jaw. His eyes were so dark they looked like they absorbed the sunlight, and his full black leather gear and cloak matched perfectly.

Obviously having seen me staring, Ezra said something to Quinn, then came to stand next to me.

"That's Drayven, but we all call him Rayven. He's from the Ocrein Isles, over to the west. They mostly keep to themselves nowadays, but over the centuries their people have slowly mixed with ours here in the South, and they've always been a powerful ally. Well, they were before they sealed their borders. The Isles is actually where shadow wielding originated from—the South was only able to obtain it by breeding and passing it down to their children. A lot of the noble families have shadow wielding in their bloodlines. It's strategic, I believe," Ezra explained as we both watched Rayven cross the small clearing to help Robyn and Chess load the last of the bags onto Atlas.

I nodded, then tilted my head to look at Ezra. "I appreciate you always making the effort to fill in the gaps for me. It's been... quite a learning curve, coming here," I admitted, making an effort to be honest for once instead of guarded.

A small smile fell upon his face as he said, "It's my pleasure. I love sharing knowledge, and we all want you to feel welcome."

Before I knew it, Robyn had come over and led me to where Rayven was strapping bags onto Atlas, who was now laying down like Lychen.

"Rayven, I want you to officially meet Aviva. Aviva, this is my top spy, most loyal companion, and one of my closest friends, Rayven. Rayven, this is our new queen and my wife, Aviva,"

Robyn said, motioning between Rayven and I as he introduced us.

I couldn't stop the pink blush that crept up my neck and face as I listened to him call me his wife. Obviously, I knew what we were to each other, but this was the first time I was hearing him actually call me his *wife*. It just made it that much more real, but instead of feeling dread like before, it almost felt... *right*.

"It's great to finally meet you." I smiled at Rayven.

Rayven nodded, and said with a deep, rough voice that sounded like it didn't get used much, "Same to you, my queen."

Out of nowhere, a bird squawked above us, and Rayven lifted his arm up so his elbow was facing away from him. Suddenly, a large black bird landed before us on Rayven's upper arm.

I took a step back, startled, but Robyn was there in an instant, lightly gripping my upper arm to keep me from stumbling.

Rayven looked at the bird and lightly pet the top of its head before saying, "This is Lark."

He offered no further explanation.

Robyn, picking up where Rayven lacked, said, "Lark is Rayven's personal corvid. Him and I are the only ones who are allowed access to our corvid perch, besides their caretakers, here in Cairnyl. We've helped to raise and train them to be messenger birds for all corners of the South and even beyond. They're much more intelligent than people give them credit for, I assure you."

I stared at the bird for another moment, then simply responded, "We *definitely* don't have those in the North."

Rayven and Robyn both let out a hearty chuckle, then Robyn and I headed back over to Atlas.

"Ready to go?" Robyn asked, offering me a hand, as if to assist me in hopping onto Atlas' back.

I stilled, not having thought to talk with him about this before. The tips of my ears flushed pink.

"Actually, Robyn... if it's alright with you, I'd really prefer to fly," I said lowly.

His eyes widened slightly, and I could feel his surprise in my own chest.

Feeling the need to over-explain, I rambled on, "I mean, truly, if it's alright with you. It's just, I've been cooped up in The Haven like a bird in a cage, and I *dearly* miss feeling the wind in my hair and wings. I miss the sky."

Robyn shook his head slightly, then let out an awkward laugh. "Yes, yes, of course that's alright. Truthfully, I'm not sure why I hadn't thought of that before now. That's no problem at all. I apologize for not considering how cramped The Haven must've felt for you. I hope you enjoy yourself up there," he said, though I couldn't help but notice the slight look of disappointment in his eyes, matching the feeling radiating from him into my own chest.

I nodded, feeling a tad embarrassed.

Robyn turned to face the rest of the group, then smiled. "Alright, my Valwain. Let's get going!"

***

Turns out, traveling to Diorum was much more enjoyable than I had thought it would be.

The sky was clear of clouds and endless, as if I could fly forever. The wind pulled stray hair from my braids that whipped across my face, but I didn't mind. The feeling of freedom that flying gave me was euphoric. More than once, I paused mid-air, wings pumping, and simply tilted my head skyward towards the sun, feeling the air currents slide between the feathers of my wings and wrapping around me like a hug from an old friend.

I observed the group from above the entire day. I noted how Rayven stayed close to Robyn, how Lark stayed close to Rayven, how Teagan and Robyn led the way on their wolves' backs, and how Chess brought up the rear. I noticed how Ezra had decided to ride with Quinn together on one horse, him holding onto her waist from behind. And I couldn't help but notice how Margo often looked up at me, awestruck.

At one point, I watched as Margo seemed to get increasingly more upset. I lowered my height in the sky, flying close enough to hear her as she begged Teagan to let her fly with me. When I vouched for her to Teagan, promising to be careful, she gave me a wide, toothy grin.

Teagan had been hesitant, but I learned Margo had a secret weapon in her arsenal—puppy dog eyes. Teagan had folded in an instant.

When I'd neatly tucked Margo's small frame into my arms, I shot up into the sky in a spiral, causing her to let out a series of giggles. I couldn't help but smile as we leveled out and I heard her gasp. She hadn't been able to believe the sight of her kingdom from that angle, how the forests and hills were so vast they disappeared into the horizons.

We only remained a few moments, as I could see Teagan was visibly anxious, before I placed Margo back in her spot upon Lychen's saddle.

Besides that, I made sure to use as much air zirilium as I could without tiring myself out too much. I only used it when I was high enough I knew nobody could make out what I was doing, and I didn't use any other zirilium for fear of being spotted by the group below.

Why I was so fearful, I couldn't place. It was just instinct, to hide that part of myself.

We had stopped for lunch earlier in the afternoon, the wolves leading the way forcing us to keep a fast pace. Now, my stomach growled as I watched the sun dip lower into the sky, changing from a bright blue to different shades of orange and pink. The sight brought a small grin to my face.

Not only was I hungry at this point in the day, I was also tired. My wings were beginning to ache, and my shoulder blades strained from the effort of flying for an entire day. I'd never trained as Dimitri had, learning to fly for such long distances.

Maybe I should have.

I looked down just in time to see Rayven pointing towards our left, and following his direction, I could make out a small town in the distance, not too far off. I took the liberty of assuming this was Diorum, where they had told me at lunch we'd be resting for the night. Ezra had also mentioned it was completely out of our way, but that this is the route that the late king and queen had taken to get to their family cabin, so it was tradition to pass through.

I tilted my head back down towards the group, having felt a tug of something I couldn't place in my chest. I realized Robyn was waving for me to descend.

I took my time, relishing in the freedom I always felt in the arms of the vast openness before me.

Stars, I love being a child of the sky.

Eventually, I came to fly next to Robyn, who had a small smile of his own on his lips. I realized in that moment that I hadn't been feeling just my own joy, but his as well.

"It's incredible, how different you appear when you're in your element." He tilted his head skyward, as if he were still searching for me up there.

I paused, not knowing how to respond. I had been watching the group most of the day, yet had failed to notice just how much my own husband seemed to have been watching me.

I cleared my throat, then decided to change the topic. "So, this is Diorum?" I motioned to the small town that was now just moments away from us.

Robyn nodded, looking ahead at the group of wooden and stone buildings. "If you can, be patient with them. Everybody in the South knows who you are by now, and they're wary, from what Rayven tells me. But once they get to know you, I'm sure they'll love you."

I nodded in understanding. If the roles had been reversed, I'd be wary, too.

"Also, I have a request, if you will," he said, his voice lowering just a tad.

Still softly flying next to him and Atlas, I looked at him and cocked an eyebrow, encouraging him to go on.

"Well, I want to minimize the shock that goes through the townspeople when we get there, and I want us—you and me—to appear as a strong, united front. Would you be willing to ride with me on Atlas for the last few moments?" he asked.

I studied him for a moment, contemplating. This wasn't exactly a shock—he was the freshly appointed king who took a Northerner as his queen. His people could be wary of not only me, but of him, too. In all honesty, it was probably the right move on his part.

No wonder he wants to display a united front.

"Alright," I said after a moment, "I'll do it."

Robyn let out a small sigh of relief before thanking me. He shifted backwards in Atlas' saddle, making room for me to sit in front of him.

My eyes widened slightly and I could feel the tips of my ears heating up. I hadn't thought about just how *close* I'd have to sit to him for this scheme to work.

Robyn, likely feeling my confusing swirl of emotions—embarrassment, nervousness, and a dash of excitement—smiled up at me and promised, "I don't bite." Leaning towards me and lowering his voice so only I could hear him, he added, "Not until you give me the all clear, that is."

I scoffed and rolled my eyes, replying, "In your dreams, Thorn-tier."

Nothing could stop the flush that crawled up my neck and cheeks, though, and from the smirk now upon his lips, I knew he'd noticed, too.

Settling into the front of the saddle, I pushed myself all the way forward and tucked my wings behind me, trying to keep some distance between the two of us. I didn't know why he got under my skin so easily, but a little distance would do us some good.

Atlas seemed to have other ideas, though, as shortly after I settled in, he stretched his back like a cat, lowering his front half and raising his back half. Robyn, having nothing to hold onto, came crashing into my back and my wings.

A small hiss escaped my lips at the sudden pressure, but when Atlas leveled back out, Robyn didn't remove himself. I could feel his solid form against my back, pressing against my wings and pinning them in place. I could feel every ragged breath he took, like it took a considerable amount of effort to be this close to me.

It took everything in me not to focus on *his* swirl of conflicting emotions in my chest.

I forced my breathing to level out, only for it to hitch when Robyn slowly wrapped his arms around my waist. I could feel his breath on the shell of my ear as he murmured, "Just a little pretending, right?"

I swallowed, trying to push down the knot in my throat as I replied, "Right."

That same powerful thing I had felt over a week ago returned, and I could feel it singing in my veins as the King of the South held me close to him, whispering in my ear about the town we were entering. Pulse pounding with more than nerves, he explained how he and the rest of the Valwain had been stopping in this town—Diorum—for as long as he could remember, anytime they went to stay at his family's cabin. It was roughly halfway between

Cairnyl and Echen Bay, if you took the long way as we were, so it was ideal. They always stay at the same inn, and the innkeeper had been good friends with his parents.

I felt a pang of his sadness shoot through my chest at the mention of his parents, but he didn't address it, so neither did I. We were already on thin ice as it was.

Snapping Robyn and I out of our own little world was the sound of people clapping and cheering. I realized soon enough that we were passing through the town's gates, right into the heart of the place.

The crowd parted as we walked, some giving their congratulations, others welcoming the Valwain back once again, while some I noticed stood a bit detached, a bit guarded. And most of those guarded ones were staring right at me and Robyn.

That's why Robyn wanted to show us as united.

Soon, we all stood in front of a three story building made of mostly different types of stones, some dark, some light, some speckled. There was a sign out front that read *Dorothy's Inn*, with a sweet looking middle aged female standing in the doorway, waving at our party.

The group dismounted our wolves and horses before the inn, Robyn having to catch me as I slid off of Atlas' flank. His hands lingered on my waist just a moment too long, and when he did finally remove them, it was as though he had to force himself to.

Robyn left my side to approach who I assumed was Dorothy, the innkeeper, and I watched as she embraced him tightly, almost as a mother would. Upon closer inspection, I could see her medium brown hair beginning to gray at the roots, and the slight wrinkles she had from years of smiling and laughing.

My smile faltered as I gazed upon her. I suddenly found myself wishing to the Stars that my people could know what it was like to laugh and smile so freely, without any of the restraint they feel now. Like it seemed so many in the South had the freedom to do.

I rounded to Atlas' front and gently raised a hand to his nose. When he didn't immediately snap at me, I lightly pressed against his nose and thanked him for the ride.

"Here, give him this. He'll love you forever," a voice said from behind me. I turned around swiftly to see Ezra walking over, holding a small leather bag. He reached inside and pulled out a large chunk of some type of dried meat, and handed it to me.

It did not smell appetizing.

Ignoring the stench, I held it up to Atlas. In a flash, he ripped it from my hand and began devouring it.

After he finished a few heartbeats later, he gently bumped his head against mine, then walked over to where Lychen was sitting near Teagan and Margo, who were unloading luggage.

It wasn't until Atlas walked away that I realized the luggage that had been strapped to his saddle had already been unloaded. I looked around and found that Robyn was nowhere to be seen, nor the innkeeper. I spotted Rayven standing near the luggage Atlas had held, and headed over to him.

Rayven, having seen me coming, picked up my bag and held it out to me without saying a word. I slipped it onto my shoulder, thanked the male, then allowed Ezra to lead me into the inn.

The inn wasn't anything extravagant, but it had a homey feel to it—all the furniture was worn in from lots of use, but still in good health. There were vases full of native Southern flowers in every hallway and on every table top. The stone floor had been rubbed smooth from years of footfall. It even smelled faintly of fresh bread, coming from somewhere deeper inside.

Ezra led me up two flights of stairs until we reached the third and final floor, then down the end of the hall to the last door on the left.

"You'll be staying in here, feel free to freshen up. I'm sure Robyn will come to gather you for the festivities soon enough."

"Festivities?" I asked him.

"Oh, right. Well, since the people of Diorum haven't seen Robyn since he was crowned, they'll be wanting to celebrate their new king. They'll prepare food, drink some wine, and have lots of music and dancing. It'll be fun, I promise," Ezra said, flashing a reassuring grin.

"And... where did Robyn go?" I asked, curiosity gnawing at me. He always seemed to disappear.

"Ah... he went to talk to Annie, the innkeeper. This place was named after her mother, Dorothy. She just kept the name the same after she passed," Ezra said, obviously trying to change the subject.

I pressed two fingers to the bridge of my nose. "What is Robyn talking to her about?"

Ezra shifted on his feet, but he couldn't hold a poker face to save his life. "Annie always insists on letting us stay for free and providing for us however she can, but Robyn never lets her. He always makes sure he pays her extra for her hospitality, even if he has to hide the coins in one of her aprons so she finds it later. I'm sure that's what they're talking about now," Ezra explained.

I raised one eyebrow, suspicious. "That isn't a bad thing at all. Why wouldn't you want to tell me that?"

"Well, I don't want it to seem like I'm only displaying Robyn's great qualities to you. I want you to form your own opinions on him, and the rest of the group, without any outside input. You know?" he asked.

I nodded after a moment. It was true—if he only ever talked good about Robyn and the group, I'd be much more suspicious.

I thanked Ezra for showing me the way, then turned into the room, shutting the door behind me.

The room wasn't much to behold. The ceiling was sloped from the shape of the roof above, with a good sized bed pressed up under the sloped ceiling. There was a dresser and a full sized mirror next to it, and a window next to the bed.

Setting my bag next to the dresser, I quickly changed into one of the simple yet stunning dresses I had brought—since apparently there was to be a party—a silky-smooth material made up the black gown with silver accents. There were small chains holding it together at the chest, crossing over one another in an easy but beautiful pattern. After changing, I walked over to the window and peered out.

The sky had grown dark, and the moon was climbing higher into the sky. Gazing upon the moon, I couldn't help but recall what my twin had said to me before I left. I wondered if he, too, was staring up at the moon in that moment and thinking of me, as I was him.

Tears welled in my eyes, but before they could fall, the door was suddenly shoved open. I turned on my heels, reaching for the Southern dagger I now kept hidden in my top at all times, when I realized it was just Robyn.

"Stars, you scared me. Maybe knock next time?" I said, sniffling and wiping my eyes with the back of my hand. I noticed he, too, had changed—now in a more regal outfit, he wore black pants with a silky white, button-up shirt with golden accents and buttons.

I also didn't miss how he had rolled his sleeves up, showing off his markings from Atlas, but also showing off his fresh tattoo on the inside of his other arm.

If I were representing the moon tonight, he was my sun.

Robyn stood in the threshold, staring for a moment. I could feel his confusion in my chest, but I offered no explanation as to why I had been crying, and he didn't ask. Though I couldn't help noticing the way his eyes dragged up and down my form, the small smile that formed on his lips.

"I didn't know I needed to knock on my own door, *wife*. Apologies."

He tossed his bag next to mine, then stepped farther into the room, the door falling shut behind him.

"Wait," I said, "your room? Ezra said I was staying in here, but if you—" realization washed over me. "I see. Still pretending, are we, *husband?*" I asked, placing my hands on my hips.

That obnoxiously handsome smirk crossed his lips once again, dimple flashing. "We can pretend all you want, Aviva. Doesn't make this," he motioned between the two of us, "any less real."

I flushed, but didn't answer, hands still on my hips.

His smirk softened into a smile. "You look beautiful. Only one thing..." he trailed off as he reached out for the bottom of my messy braids. Gently, he freed my waist long hair of their plaits, fluffing them out, my waves now on full display.

After, he took a step back and simply took me in. I could feel his warm emotions in my chest, but I deliberately didn't focus on them.

"Come with me." He held out a hand. "I want you to experience the festivities firsthand tonight. With me."

I hesitated. "I don't know, I'm pretty tired and—"

"Just an hour. Please?" he asked once again, hand still extended.

A moment later I gave in, my hand slipping into his. Our fingers intertwined on instinct, and I couldn't *not* notice how perfectly our hands fit into each other's.

Then we walked out of our room and out of the inn together, hand in hand.

Chapter Thirteen

Before I knew it, I was outside, sitting on a tree stump at the edge of a crowd surrounding one of many campfires. The townspeople had been more than gracious, having prepared the equivalent of a feast in our honor—in *Robyn's* honor. They had just finished telling an elaborate campfire story about one of the ancient Southern kings with some fancy stones that I hadn't quite understood. I made a mental note to ask Ezra about it later.

Robyn had introduced me to so many people during and after dinner, I couldn't keep them all straight at this point in the night. Somehow, though, he always knew. I imagine he'd probably spent more time here than he let on, with how well he seemed to know everybody in Diorum.

It made me question things. I'd now known the two kings of this continent personally, but their ruling styles were on opposite ends of a scale. My father had never associated with who he would consider *peasants* unless it was necessary, while Robyn was here, in the middle of all of them and greeting them each by name. It was so strange. So different. So much *better*.

The Valwain had split up a while ago, all tending to different things and catching up with townspeople. Chess was not too far off, talking with a group of other trokavs, likely sharing recipes and ingredients, if I were to guess.

Rayven was standing outside the group Robyn was surrounded by, observing. I got the sense he did that a lot—watched Robyn's back.

Teagan had taken Margo to dance the moment the music had started, which had only been a few minutes ago.

I hadn't been able to keep track of Ezra or Quinn, despite my Northern-gifted ability to see better than Southerners in the dark.

"Aviva!" Robyn called out over the music as he struggled to depart from the group he was in, telling them he'd be back.

I shifted over on the stump, giving him room to sit by me. Instead, he held out his hand.

Always holding out his hand for me. Patiently.

"Dance with me," he said, though he seemed eager. It hadn't been a command, but a request.

He looked down at my feet, which I hadn't realized I had begun tapping in time with the music.

"I... I only know ballroom dances, traditional Northern stuff. I couldn't possibly dance in a place like this." I spoke loud enough so he could hear, but only him, since he had taken a step closer.

"It's just like flying, I'd imagine. You just let yourself move to the music. Feel it, become it, let it fill you to the brim and overflow. It's... freeing!" he exclaimed.

When he saw I was about to raise another argument, he spoke again. "I'll take the lead. It'll be easy, I promise. Do you trust me?" he asked, his eyes practically glowing, though I knew he'd only had one cup of wine during dinner. His eyes were bright with something else.

Without responding, I slowly stood, taking his hand once again.

Every time our skin touched, the zirilium in my veins sang.

I wonder if he feels it, too.

Before I knew it, he was leading me between countless dancing couples, young and old alike. We weaved between them until we found a spot close to the fire that was a bit more open.

A new song began, and I felt a small wave of panic overcome me.

Before I could completely give in to the panic, I felt Robyn gently cup my cheek and turn my face to look up into his eyes.

"It's just you and me," he said reassuringly.

I flashed a quick smile towards him, not breaking eye contact as he removed his hand and placed it on my waist. He guided my hand to his shoulder, then interlaced our spare hands together.

At first, I seemed to block the music out and tried hard to focus on anticipating Robyn's next move—which I could never get right. He tried to spin me, but I was so stiff I barely budged. I was completely out of my element, and I knew it. I felt awkward, embarrassed, still.

After another failed spin attempt, he leaned down so close to me I felt his lips brush the shell of my ear as he spoke. "Try to relax. Feel the music in your veins like you feel your zirilium."

I jerked my head back, ready to question just how much he knew about any zirilium I had, but he just gave me a lazy smile as the tune of the song began to shift into the next. I knew he was aware at least of the plant zirilium due to our encounter over a week ago, but did he know anything beyond that?

Though, I knew this wasn't the time to question him. For once, I decided I wanted to enjoy myself. Even if it was in the arms of my supposed enemy.

I took a deep breath and closed my eyes. Instead of focusing on every move I *thought* Robyn might make, I let myself focus on what moves I actually *felt* him making.

After a few moments, I felt the music sinking into me. My feet began moving on their own accord, and I was able to feel the small shifts in Robyn's body language that helped me to anticipate any spins or fancy moves.

Together, we danced around the open field, all around the fire and back again. He had been right—it was easy to follow his lead. He spun me often, but not enough to make me feel sick. I couldn't help but notice how easily our bodies moved together. We were like two trees swaying in the breeze, like two birds flying through the sky together.

We worked together in perfect harmony.

Soon, I realized I had gotten the hang of it—I had just needed to relax, like he said. I opened my eyes and beamed up at the male holding me, letting an unrestrained smile cross my lips as I peered into his eyes.

I watched as his breathing hitched when I looked up at him, my expression fully open to him for the first time, my emotions laid bare. I could feel our joy intertwining in my chest, along with something warm.

The songs didn't stop, and neither did we. I looked around us, and noticed a handful of people were watching us, but suddenly it dawned on me that I didn't care. For the first time in my life, I didn't care what those around me thought of me. I just wanted that feeling to last.

That was the only time I had ever felt truly free with both feet on the ground.

The tempo of the song sped up, causing Robyn to challenge us as he began moving us faster, swaying and stepping and spinning. As the world spun around us, I could've sworn I saw a flash of ginger and white dancing together on the outskirts of the field.

Soon, we were going so fast I was sure we'd fall over or step on each other's feet, but we somehow managed not to. I felt exhilarated, *alive*.

Caught up in the moment, I tilted my head up towards the stars above and let loose a hearty, joyous laugh.

I felt Robyn's surprise, causing me to meet his eyes once more. He was *beaming*.

He was obviously proud of himself, but there was something else there, something deeper I couldn't place.

I smiled up at him, not holding back in the moment, and was met with a genuine smile of his own. The tempo rose, and soon we were both spinning and moving perfectly in time with one another and *laughing*.

We laughed together so much my sides hurt, and for the first time in my life, I wondered if this was what pure joy felt like.

Maybe home isn't a place after all.

***

Hours later, well past midnight, Robyn and I slipped back into our room, both still giggling as if we were schoolchildren.

Once the door was shut behind us, I doubled over and took a deep breath, trying to calm myself. I stood back up after a few breaths to see Robyn leaning against the door, still smiling. This time, I smiled back.

We both went our separate ways to freshen up and change into more comfortable clothes, then met back up in the room. Once it was just us, I gently removed the eyepatch and placed it on the bedside table, but didn't acknowledge it.

Turning back to Robyn, I tried not to focus on all his exposed, tan, toned skin, as I realized he didn't sleep with a shirt on.

It wasn't until that moment that I realized we were both to sleep in here. With one bed. *Together.*

Seeming to have my same line of thought, Robyn awkwardly offered to sleep on the floor, grabbing a spare pillow and blanket.

I reached out for him and lightly placed my hand on his arm. "You... you don't have to sleep on the floor."

I felt my face turning pink as I spoke.

Robyn turned to me, jaw slightly ajar in surprise.

Before he could speak, I said, "Just keep your hands to yourself, *husband*."

Closing his mouth, he nodded and swore he would, but I watched as his tan cheeks and ears turned a bright shade of red.

I tucked myself into the side of the bed that was closer to the slanted ceiling, figuring he'd appreciate having more room, despite my wings pressing against the ceiling. I tried not to think about how much harder it would be to escape if I needed to because of this decision.

Soon, we were both settled into the dark, with only a few candles scattered throughout the room.

I peered up above us, out of the window once again. I tried searching for the moon, but couldn't find it. It had gotten too late into the night to see it from this angle. I tried not to focus on the disappointment I felt bubbling in my heart.

"What are you thinking about? It feels... sad. Hurt," Robyn said quietly into the dark. Sometimes I forgot that he could feel all of my emotions, just as I felt his.

If only I had known what I was signing up for with those tattoos.

I let out a small sigh, then turned onto my side to look at him, letting my wings breath slightly behind me.

Avoiding the subject he had brought up, I spoke back into the barely illuminated darkness. "I *want* to trust you, Robyn."

Shifting onto his side to look at me, he replied, "I want that, too, Avi."

The nickname made my stomach flutter in a way I knew it shouldn't.

"Then let's start right now. From here on out, just open and honest communication between us." I paused. "Do you think we're capable of that?"

"We can, I know it. I'd love nothing more than that," he said, and I could hear in his voice how genuine he was about it, how eager.

For a moment, we were both silent, pondering over what we just promised to each other. Then, I broke it. "Where were you when you disappeared for a week?"

Though the room was dark, the candles lightly cast a glow over his figure and his face. I saw his eyes widen and saw him contemplating.

After a moment, he finally asked, "Honestly?"

"Honestly," I responded.

He sighed. "I went to Hollis, to Gatlyn Castle and anywhere else in between that I thought would have answers. Rayven and I snuck in, stuck to the shadows. I wanted to get answers for you—for us. About what was happening to you. About what had been in the elixirs. About what... what they had been suppressing in you."

That was right—a shadow wielder could cause one other person to turn to shadow, too, if they had skin to skin contact.

My breath caught in my throat at his confession. Of all the places I had imagined he had gone, sneaking across the border, into the North, was not even on my list. And he did it... for *me*. When he had barely even known me.

"And?" I asked softly.

He sighed again, though this time I felt his own disappointment in my chest. "Nothing. Whatever they have going on up there, it's tightly locked and sealed away. It was a waste, and I'm sorry."

I nodded, trying not to let the tears in my eyes spill over onto my cheeks. I couldn't even place why I was crying.

Maybe I was surprised a near stranger had cared that much.

He gently reached up and brushed a stray tear from my cheek that had escaped. I tried not to, but I leaned into his touch, soaking up his warmth.

We stayed like that for a heartbeat, then two, with him gently stroking my cheek. I felt so relaxed in his touch, I could feel sleep creeping up on me.

"Sleep well," Robyn said softly, so close I could feel his body heat seeping into me. I heard him snap his fingers, and all at once the room was shrouded in darkness.

And for once, after living an entire life surrounded by ice that had made its way into my heart, I could feel the cold in my chest beginning to thaw.

Chapter Fourteen

I'm flying, soaring through the sky feeling so light I barely register
that my wings are beating behind me. The sky is littered with
clouds, and I float in and out of them like a feather falling to the
ground.

I tilt my head upwards, feeling the warmth of the sun on my skin.
There's a small moment of confusion—usually it's colder up in the
sky, with all the wind pockets and breezes and mist from the clouds.
But instead, I just feel warm. It's oddly comforting, I realize with a
start.

Besides the unusual warmth, something feels wrong. It's too quiet,
too still. Even the clouds appear to have ceased their trek across the
sky.

"Aviva," I hear a voice call out. It's male, and familiar.

When the voice calls my name out again, this time with more
urgency, I realize who it is I'm hearing.

Dimitri.

I call out his name, trying to find the source of his voice. I fly in
circles, through the clouds, attempting over and over again to find
my brother, to find my twin, but he's nowhere to be found.

"*I'm sorry, Viva. I never meant for it to happen like this,*" *he says,*
his voice sounding like it's coming from multiple directions. But I
notice he also sounds cold, detached.

"*Aviva!*" *A second voice comes cascading through the clouds, hit-*
ting me from every angle.

"*Aurora?*" *I cry out, panic beginning to set in.*

Where are they?

What's happening?

"*Viva, I'm so sorry. I just wanted to help,*" *she says, but her voice*
sounds so tired, so sad, compared to the usual brightness she carries
within her.

"*It's alright, I promise I'm alright!*" *I say to her, spinning in a*
circle mid-air, still searching for my best friends.

Their voices grow louder now, so loud I have to slam my hands over
my ears to try to block out some of the sound. They're apologizing, over
and over again. Aurora is louder than Dimi now—he seems to be
fading away. Realizing this scares me, I don't know what it means
other than that I'm losing him.

"*Please!*" *I cry out to them.* "*Stop this!*"

My hands are still over my head, wings holding me in the air as
I double over, folding in on myself, my breathing heavy and rapid.
I can feel my heart slamming against my chest as I listen to the two
people I thought I loved most in the world apologize to me repeatedly,
and I don't even know what for.

Out of seemingly nowhere, I hear a series of chirps—chirps that
sound like Eden, and then everything slowly disappears.

I gasped lightly as the sunlight through the curtains hit my eyes,
squinting against it. The first thing I noticed this morning was
the sound of birdsong outside the inn window, which I assumed
inspired the chirping of Eden I had heard in my dream, and was
what I believed woke me up.

The second thing I noticed was the warmth. Intense, constant warmth radiating into my skin through my back and wings.

Confused and only half awake, I tried to sit up in bed, only to be pulled back down so swiftly I almost squealed in surprise. It was in that moment that I realized what situation I'd woken up to.

Now that I was more awake, I felt it. His warm, firm chest was pressed against my back, skin to skin, as the cut open slits of the shirt I fell asleep in were hanging wide open. His breath tickled my ear, and I was attuned to the gentle rise and fall of his chest. His arm was draped over my waist, holding me in place.

At first, I was frozen, heart still racing from my dream. I didn't exactly know what I was supposed to do. Should I wake him? Should I try to slip away? Should I stay as still as possible and hope this, too, is just a dream?

In the end, I did none of those things. I thought back on our conversation last night, how we wanted to be able to trust each other. I reminded myself that I *did* want to learn to trust this male, and I couldn't keep denying the way he made me feel. I *wanted* to feel safe with him. The warmth I was feeling wasn't just from his body heat, but some kind of emotion, hidden deep in my chest.

One I wasn't ready to face yet.

Moving as little as possible, I turned over so I was facing him, letting my wings drape across the rest of the small space behind me. But when I caught sight of him, I almost couldn't catch my breath.

He looked so at *peace.* I took this opportunity to calm my racing heart by studying his handsome features.

I'd never seen him look so tranquil before. His sun-kissed skin was glowing in the early morning light, his freckles making a bold appearance. He had smile lines next to his eyes, and a few gold hoops and chains adorn the tips of his ears. His eyelashes were so long they grazed his high cheekbones, and he had a strong, lean nose. In an effort not to stare at his full lips, I noticed, not for the first time, the small scar along the side of his jaw.

Gently, I reached up to touch it. I lightly ran my finger along the smooth, pale slice of skin, and realized my breathing had gone erratic, along with my heartbeat, which had only just been tamed. Not only was my heart hammering in my chest, but I could feel my zirilium thrumming in my veins, begging to be let out.

I ignored it.

Still sleeping, he leaned into my touch, as if I contained the last bit of warmth this cold world had to offer.

I gasped, surprised at his affection, even if he was still sleeping.

At the sound, his eyes cracked open, then they widened, seeing how close together our faces were. Our noses were nearly touching, and I was practically breathing in the air he exhaled. His brow creased, and I could feel his confusion and confliction in my chest. His forest green eyes bore into mine, searching for something, though I wasn't sure what. I stared back, feeling myself getting lost in his gaze.

As if nothing else mattered outside of this simple moment.

A heartbeat later, a shuffle out in the hallway broke our connection, and I awkwardly cleared my throat, shifting my gaze to look down at his arm pinning me in place.

"Right. I'm-I'm so sorry. My apologies," he said, retracting his arm from around my waist and slipping out of bed. The warmth fled from my body the second he left, and I surprised myself when I realized I missed it.

I watched his bare back as he ran a hand through his silky hair and focused on his breathing. But most of all, I tuned into the emotions I felt in my chest that I knew were radiating from him. Disappointment seemed to be the heaviest one at the moment, but there were other things there, too. Desire, longing, embarrassment, and that warm feeling I decided I was going to continue to ignore.

Power was pounding in my veins nonstop now, a constant, dull pain, but I schooled my features and decided to keep ignoring that, too.

I sighed.

It was going to be a long, long day. I flexed my wings, realizing I'd never been more grateful to have my own means of travel.

***

Traveling to Echen Bay took the entirety of the day. We rode—or in my case, flew—at a consistent pace until almost sunset, slower than the day before, when we finally reached our destination.

The whole way there, I played around with my air wielding, but it barely scratched the surface of power I felt thrumming through my entire body. I didn't know *exactly* what changed, but ever since I stopped taking my elixirs, my zirilium was more potent, more powerful.

I was starting to worry how much longer I could keep it hidden.

Once we reached Echen Bay, I realized *the cabin* was more of a glorified miniature castle. Built from the surrounding trees, the entire thing was made from varying shades of dark, chocolate wood with rich stone and golden accents. It had multiple different sectors and wings, but on a smaller scale compared to The Haven. Somehow despite its grand architecture, it appeared to be more of a *home* than anything else.

Not to mention the surrounding area was jaw dropping. The lush trees were so tall they seemed to scrape the sky, which reminded me of Hollis, and sent a small pang of homesickness through me. There were multiple small meadows hidden within the forest around us, full of those colorful, Southern wild flowers. The bay might be my favorite part, though. Cynth Bay back home was so blue it looked black—you couldn't see through the choppy, rough waters at all due to how dark it was. But here, the water was a soft, calm teal green. The sun punctured the water just-so, and you could see little creatures in it, swimming around peacefully.

I had been so in awe of the beauty around me, I *might* have flown off when we arrived to go take a sneak peek before the sun set for the day. And I *might* have made Robyn panic just a little bit.

Oops.

After we arrived yesterday, Robyn took it upon himself to show me around. Because the layout of this building was smaller than The Haven, I was able to actually remember how to get around. He showed me the kitchen, formal dining room, library, training rooms, and more. The last place he took me was a small wing towards the back of the cabin, which he told me was where he usually stayed, and where I could stay, too.

He offered me my own room next door to his, which I all too eagerly accepted. In reality, I realized now, too late, that I would have rather stayed in a room with him. I realized after waking up in his arms that I was beginning to feel safe with him. But I fear I let embarrassment overtake me, resulting in cold feet.

Letting people in was proving harder than I thought it would be.

Not to mention how his disappointment had been palpable when I accepted my own quarters with such enthusiasm.

Now, it was the morning after our travels, and I was stiff from how badly I slept on my own. I had felt so refreshed after sleeping next to Robyn—despite the odd dream—that I didn't think about how I might react to sleeping on my own again. Though, I had nobody to blame but myself.

On another note, I learned something new about the Valwain. Their version of *relaxing* and *recharging*, in reality, meant training.

Looking up and out across the small clearing I sat in, I took in the sight of the Valwain.

Teagan was training with Quinn, currently circling each other like vultures, waiting to strike. Chess was doing his own thing, seeing how fast he could make different plants sprout from the earth with his zirilium and collecting vital parts of each stalk to make various concoctions. Ezra was sitting with Margo not too far from me on a small blanket, along with a picnic basket of books to study. And Robyn was training in hand-to-hand combat with Drayven.

And somehow, though everybody else was dressed in training leathers, both Robyn and Rayven lost their shirts along the way.

My eyes were glued to him—my husband. I watched as he threw a flawless punch towards Rayven's jaw, but he knocked Robyn's arm away as if it was no more than an inconvenient bug flying around his face.

They're evenly matched, I realized.

It was in that moment I noticed the tattoo snaking up Rayven's right arm—meant to look like the shadows he wielded. If my limited knowledge on the Islanders was correct, this was a traditional tattoo, only given to those who had mastered their shadow wielding. It was an honor to possess.

I tried my best to focus on their actual training, how they seemed to ebb and flow with one another and perfectly anticipated the other's move, but I couldn't seem to. It was obvious they'd been training with one another for years. Yet all I could focus on now was Robyn.

Sweat has started to bead across his skin, making his golden tan glow even more than usual, especially in the early morning light. I could make out small scars littering his otherwise flawless skin, all over his torso, back, arms, and chest. I tried not to stare at his toned abs, and failed, observing his skin stretch over the muscles there. I watched as he shifted forward and how his hair fell across his forehead, the sunlight hitting it perfectly and lighting it up, showing off the red hues that were usually hidden.

If the sun were a person, it would be him.

My mouth was practically watering.

I heard a throat clear nearby, snapping me out of my careful observations. I could feel the way my face immediately turned bright red, but I tried to ignore it as I looked up at Quinn and Teagan, one of which was the source of the sound.

Quinn was scowling at me. The sound most definitely came from her.

"Having fun?" she asked, though there was an edge to her tone, letting me know she didn't actually care. I wasn't sure what her problem was with me, but I obviously must have done something to offend her.

"Um, sure. I suppose so," I responded, unsure of what else to say.

"You know you were drooling, right?"

My hand flew to my mouth so fast I barely registered it. Even though I knew she was lying, my embarrassment was clear in the flush covering my face and ears.

"*Quinn.*" I heard Teagan say, a warning, but she couldn't wipe off the small smile from her lips fast enough for me not to catch it.

Quinn sighed and placed her hands on her hips. "Listen, we all know there's more to you than meets the eye, yet you keep turning us down when we ask you to train. You even turned down *Byn*, for Stars' sake."

Quinn, Teagan, and Robyn had each offered early this morning on our way out to this meadow, but I had swiftly declined. Although now I was beginning to regret it, with my zirilium growing stronger each moment, causing random pains to shoot through me.

I could feel my expression darken. "You're mistaken. There's nothing special going on with me," I said sharply, then reined myself back in. "I'd prefer to be left alone now."

Quinn opened her mouth to argue but paused when Ezra, who was sitting nearby, dramatically cleared his throat, in a way you knew was meant to be overly obvious. Quinn's cheeks flushed a bright pink, and she turned on her heels to resume her training without another word.

Teagan scratched the back of her neck awkwardly. "I swear, she's an awesome person once she warms up to you," she offered meekly, then followed after Quinn.

I sighed, dropping my head into my hands, and without thinking, reached for the necklace chained around my throat, tucked under my shirt. The chain I kept all my Northern moon stones on. The ones I never let anybody see, because I almost never took them off. It was a silent comfort, having them so close. It helped me feel more in control, when I knew I must be spiraling with how out of control my power felt.

I startled when I felt a sudden weight on my shoulder, dropping my hand swiftly.

Looking up, I found Ezra standing by me.

"Come sit with me and Margo. If you don't want to train, you can at least help me study with Margo. Plus, she'd love to get to know you better." He offered a kind smile.

I nodded, thanking him as I stood up and followed him back to their checkered blanket, the three of us now sitting in a triangle, their current book in the middle.

I sat with my legs crossed in front of me, nodding to Margo and giving her a small wave. She looked sheepishly at me, then picked the book back up in constantly gloved hands, placing it in her lap.

It never occurred to me before how small she was for her age, but sitting next to her now, I could see it. She was likely a late bloomer, and I couldn't help but wonder if she'd developed any zirilium yet. She was already eight, so if she hadn't yet, she hopefully would soon. I was barely four when I began to discover mine.

I cringed at the memory, and a wave of nauseating guilt overcame me.

I took a deep breath, trying to clear my mind, when I felt a tug of worry and curiosity.

My head snapped up, just to see Robyn already staring at me.

Right, I reminded myself, *he can feel what I feel.*

Robyn maintained eye contact, and I saw so many unanswered questions in his gaze.

Rayven seemed to notice this and took advantage of it, swiftly sweeping Robyn's feet out from under him, landing him flat on his back.

I couldn't help but flinch, but I was grateful to not have to answer any questions as the two of them got back to it, Rayven teasing Robyn for letting something like a female get to him.

"She's not just some female," I heard Robyn respond in a frustrated tone, "that's my *wife*, you jerk."

I took another deep breath, trying to control the pink creeping up my neck.

"So why don't we have the star stones today, Ezra?" I heard Margo ask, and at that, I whipped my head back around to pay attention to the conversation unfolding before me.

"What are star stones?" I asked, dumbfounded.

"You don't know the legend?" Margo asked, confused, then looked at Ezra. "Tell her the story! Tell her the story!" She cheered.

"Alright, alright, I will." Ezra laughed, clearly pleased by Margo's enthusiasm. "Get ready. It's quite the story.

"Over four hundred years ago, just before the war began, there was a Southern king named Baron. One day, King Baron Thorntier was alerted of an unusual phenomenon—they claimed the Stars had sent him a gift, for it was shortly after his coronation. His people had discovered a huge rock that had fallen from the sky in a great ball of fire, and landed near the chasm we have our mines at today. Upon further investigation, he found that the rock contained what he named star stones. He was able to harvest and forge five of them to perfection. He realized they were more powerful than any sun or moon stone he'd ever come across. *And* they could be endowed with either sun or moon energy, making them an incredible weapon.

"As a sign of their continued peace, Baron met with the king of the North at that time—I forget his name—and offered them to him, as a gift. After that, the history accounts vary. We know the war began shortly after, but we don't know where the star stones are today; if the Northern king accepted the gift and turned against King Baron. That's one theory, but it happened so long ago, we have no firsthand accounts." Ezra shrugged. "Just one of the many things lost to history over time."

Ezra made a small bowing gesture after he concluded, and Margo clapped, giggling.

"Wait," I said, "is that real? Did all of that actually happen?"

"Well, of course. I mean, small details are lost over time and sometimes the story is exaggerated, but the core facts are the same. It's been recorded for generations," Ezra responded, upbeat as always.

"I heard, back in Diorum, they were talking around the campfire about one of the ancient Southern kings, that he had been the most powerful the South had ever known. Is that King Baron?"

"The one and only," Ezra responded, nodding.

"Huh," I said simply, my mind reeling, wondering how I had never heard of King Baron or the star stones in my entire life in the North.

I guess Laurence nor Robyn lied—we really were kept in the dark back in the North.

Chapter Fifteen

Our group had been at the cabin for a week now, though I'd mostly kept to myself. I sat in on Ezra's studies with Margo, interested in learning about the history of the South, including its different rulers. In this time, I realized Margo reminded me of her brother—she knew exactly how to get you to smile when you weren't feeling your best.

And I'd definitely not been feeling my best lately.

The energy in my veins grew stronger with each day that passed, demanding to be let out. My sleep was restless, and being awake had grown painful. It wasn't just thrumming through my bloodstream anymore—I could feel it in every inch of my muscles, my nerves, my bones. It was as if it had its own life force, taken root in my body. It felt so separate from me, I didn't know what to do about it.

So I tried to ignore it. Along with the people around me who might ask questions.

I hadn't let Robyn too close, because I feared he would be able to see the pain in my eyes. I only sat with Margo and Ezra for short periods of time, for as long as I could control my facial expressions well enough to not give anything away.

I don't exactly know why I wasn't asking for help. It was like second nature—to try to handle issues on my own. I used to have Dimitri and Aurora to depend on, but the Valwain... I didn't know them like I knew my own brother and best friend. Not from a lack of trying on their part—they'd invited me to their nightly group dinners every day for the past week, but I kept turning them down, to Robyn's disappointment. I knew we wanted to be open and honest with our communication, but I hardly even knew where to begin. How did I tell him his bride that he thought was powerless, could actually wield all five northern zirilium? And that there might be more to her than even *she* knew, that hadn't been fully uncovered yet?

That morning when I woke up, something had changed. I knew when I crumpled to the floor the moment I stepped out of bed that I needed to tell Robyn. In reality, I shouldn't have waited that long in the first place. Once I had collected myself, I peeked into his room to try to talk to him, but he wasn't there. Now, I had to try to find him.

I let out a sigh as I stepped outside. One of the first things I figured out how to access from the cabin was the roof. Sometimes I lay out here for hours at night, watching the moon make its way across the sky and the stars dance. It was peaceful—nobody seemed to come up here. It was an open space, with what looked like an abandoned training ring. The Valwain seemed to prefer being around nature, as they always trained down in one of the meadows of the forest. But I liked it up here, where I could see everything around for what felt like miles. I could even see Echen Bay from up here.

I left my hair lose today, and I was already regretting it. I could feel its weight on the nape of my neck, and combined with the warm weather, I could tell I was going to overheat fast in the South's warm climate. Fortunately, I was wearing a cream, frameless corset top today, so that leveled out some of the heat. The top was form fitting but not in a way that was suffocating. It was one of the pieces I had found while rummaging around in my quarters back at The Haven, and I claimed it as my own. I also found some brown, cotton pants, which I slipped on this morning for the sake of comfort. Today was all about trying to remain comfortable, despite my aching body.

Since I planned on coming clean, I opted out of wearing the eye patch today.

I figured going for a fly would not only help me locate Robyn, but also help loosen my stiff muscles. He'd been trying to pull me aside all week to talk, but I kept shutting him out, practically running in the opposite direction. I imagined he knew something was wrong, but I hadn't confirmed anything.

If I thought about it too much, I started to feel guilty. I knew I didn't choose this course for my life, but neither did he. And I hadn't exactly made it any easier on him.

Maybe I really should be looking to lean on him in these situations. Isn't that what we agreed upon?

Sighing, I shook my head to clear away the looming thoughts in my head. If I was lucky, flying would help ease my mind along with my muscles.

I flexed my wings, stretching them and bringing them back in a few times in a row. I closed my eyes, focusing on the muscles I felt rippling in my back and shoulders as my wings moved.

I couldn't imagine not being a child of the sky. I couldn't fathom what it must be like to forever be grounded, to never taste the freedom the sky had to offer.

In a series of powerful beats, my feet left the roof I had been standing on, my wings carrying me up and away.

For a handful of moments, it was just me and the cloud speckled sky. I weaved in and out of the clouds, my muscles relaxing by just a fraction. I let out a sigh of relief and lowered myself below the clouds, searching for the Valwain.

I spotted them a heartbeat later, almost directly below me in one of their usual training spots. In a meadow full of wildflowers, surrounded by the forest.

Everybody is up and at it earlier than usual today, I thought casually.

That's when it hit.

The pain was so excruciating I couldn't even open my mouth to scream. It wracked my entire body in violent waves, one right after the other. I could feel my muscles beginning to lock up, my wings barely able to beat as I started to fall.

My barely flapping wings helped to slow my fall by a fraction, but soon I was spinning out of control, unable to keep myself up right.

And I was heading straight for the Valwain.

The panic in my chest was palpable. Then, time seemed to slow mid-air, and I found myself closing my eyes, giving in.

I couldn't help but wonder if this was what it felt like to be a shooting star.

I didn't expect it to be so terrifying.

I was flung back into the present moment by the sound of Robyn's voice. At first I couldn't register what he was saying, as he was too far away. But the further I fell, the clearer his voice rang out in my ears.

"*Aviva!*" he yelled out my name, over and over, though I knew there was nothing he could do until I landed.

The other's voices were becoming louder now too, filled with panic, and I forced my eyes open just in time to see how close I'd gotten to the ground.

In an effort to not hurt anybody else, I used all the energy I could muster up to strain against my locked muscles and forced myself upright, my wings acting as a parachute to soften my descent as I landed with both feet on the ground.

The moment my feet touched the ground below, the earth *rippled*.

As if I were a stone tossed into a pond, the earth created a circular crater under my feet and stretched outward, shooting up in jagged shards all around me. The moment that happened, I could feel the energy I'd been holding back finally release, bit by bit.

The pain from the fall was nothing compared to the waves of painful power I felt coursing through every inch of my body. The impact from the fall, along with the earth rumbling under me, caused me to drop to my knees on the now uneven ground.

Once my knees hit the ground, the earth rumbled again. In the blink of an eye, various crystals began jutting out of the ground, taking their place right alongside the rows of jagged earth.

I heard thunder erupting overhead, and I barely registered that it had begun to rain. My heart was beating so fast I thought it might explode from my ribcage.

I could no longer tell the difference between the rain on my face and my own tears.

I realized with a start that there was a newfound weight on my legs and thighs, pinning me to the spot.

Straining against my own muscles, I looked down and saw thick, vibrantly green vines wrapping themselves around my body, slowly circling me as though it planned on encasing me and keeping me forever.

I pulled against the plants, trying to stand, but they grew even more rapidly, tightening their hold on my body like a snake wrapping around its prey. The pain increased with every move I made, and suddenly I was outright panicking. My breath was coming in fast and hard, unable to be stabilized.

Soon, my vision went spotty, and my hands started to tingle. The pain was nearly unbearable, and I could still feel the tears making their way down my face. Distantly, I could hear Robyn yelling for everybody to take cover, but they all sounded so far away in the midst of my panic.

My hands tingled until they start to itch, then they started to burn. It wasn't until bright, blue flames erupted from my fingertips and palms that I realized the tingling was the least of my worries.

I gasped, holding my hands out in front of me and staring at them as the winds began to pick up, moving faster and faster. My hair was whipping in my face, the rain soaking every inch of my skin. Then I heard it, the rain as it landed. Only it wasn't just rain now, but tiny spheres of ice, too.

It had begun to hail.

Lightning struck a tree in the distance, and I suddenly couldn't hold it in anymore.

I screamed.

I didn't realize it at first, but I was screaming a name.

His name.

"*Robyn!*" I cried out.

I looked up from my hands to see him struggling to get to his feet against the insane winds tearing at him. It looked as though the upended earth below us knocked him down, but he was still fighting against all of this.

For me.

My chest was heaving and I felt like I was going to vomit, but the pain from the pent up energy was slowly subsiding.

The issue now was that I didn't know how to stop.

Still panicking, I looked down as the shadows from the jagged earth and crystals started to *move*.

They danced and wiggled until they disconnected themselves from the base of the rocks and crystals, then they all flung themselves at me.

I screamed again, hysterical, unsure of what was happening. The shadows moved in circles against my skin, like they were exploring a new land that they planned to call home. They felt like everything and nothing all at the same time. Wet and dry, quiet and loud. I could hear their whispers reaching my ears, and the tears wouldn't stop falling from my eyes.

Not until I felt a new type of sensation against my wrists. I snapped my head back up, just to meet Robyn eye to eye, him kneeling right in front of me.

I jerked back, terrified I was going to hurt him, but he held firm. Gentle, but firm.

I never realized the two things could coexist.

"You won't hurt me," he said, speaking loud enough to be heard over the wind. His words stung, because I wasn't sure they were true.

I wasn't really sure of anything anymore.

"Listen, Aviva. I want you to focus on what emotions you feel coming from me. Try to pull them to you, and release the panic that's taken root in your chest."

I looked down at where our skin was touching, the blue flames so close to burning him, and the panic only solidified, my breathing still coming in short bursts.

"My love, look at me." My eyes snapped back up to meet his. "You're not going to hurt me. Just focus for me, alright?"

I nodded once, realizing the pain in my muscles wasn't as profound now that I wasn't holding back so much energy. I let out a shaky breath, holding it for a moment then releasing it again.

Closing my eyes, I reached out. Not physically, but emotionally. I searched in my own chest, pushing aside the panic and horror until I found that small handful of calm that I recognized as Robyn's. His emotions emitted a green color in my mind, the shade matching his eyes perfectly. But they also *felt* like him—warm and strong and kind.

Once I found that piece of him in my own body, I clung to it. I threw myself at it, then tried to yank at it. I wanted this feeling to engulf me, I wanted to get lost in it.

"Tug at it gently, then let it unravel in your chest until it's all you feel." I heard him talking, and though I knew he was right in front of me, he sounded further away as I threw what was left of my energy into focusing.

I reached for the green light again, but this time instead of demanding and pulling, I gently brushed against it, willing it to unfurl.

And this time, it did.

It was like an animal being coaxed out of hibernation. It moved slowly, taking its time, but eventually it grew and expanded. As it did, the panic in my body became smaller, less significant, until I was able to take a full breath for the first time in what felt like ages.

"There you go, Avi, you've got this," Robyn said quietly, but he still sounded far off.

I took another breath, making sure to fill every inch of my lungs. I continued to coax the calmness in my chest until that was all I felt.

One by one, my control on the zirilium around me came crashing down. First, the rain stopped, the thunder and lightning and rain and ice and wind all ceasing at once.

Then, without opening my eyes, I could feel as the rocks and crystals sank back down into the earth, buried into the same places they originated from.

I continued focusing on Robyn—his emotions in my chest, his skin on my skin, his presence in front of me.

The weight of the plants slowly slinked off of the lower half of my body, returning to the ground where they sprouted from. The shadows dispersed, and I felt them dissipate like smoke as they became absorbed by the shadows around us, of trees and brush.

The last thing I couldn't seem to let go of was the vibrant, blue fire coming out of my hands.

I opened my eyes, tears having ceased, and stared at the fire. I realized it wasn't hurting me, though I could feel the heat radiating off of it.

"Imagine blowing out a candle. Envision the flames getting smaller, then turning to smoke," Robyn said gently, still staring at my eyes. I could feel the panic trying to bubble its way back into my chest, and instinctively I looked back up into his eyes, trying to hold onto the calm he was giving me.

He offered a small smile, one full of reassurance.

I took a deep breath, and did exactly as he said. I closed my eyes, envisioning the flames growing smaller and smaller, as if losing their source of oxygen. I imagined the flame on every single finger slowly going out, one by one, the larger flames sitting in my palms going out last.

I opened my eyes as soon as I felt the last flames subside, and watched as the smoke from my flames disappeared into the air around us.

I met Robyn's eyes and was shocked to find him smiling, dimple and all.

I tried to smile back, but the amount of energy I just exerted was too much on my body. I felt my aching muscles start to shake, and soon I couldn't hold myself up anymore.

I fell all over again.

Except this time, Robyn caught me, cradling me against his chest. Oddly enough, his heart was pounding just as fast as mine had been just moments ago.

He stood swiftly and started walking in what I assumed was the direction of the cabin. That was when I realized he'd been speaking.

"—but you have to train. You need to be able to control your zirilium, so things like this don't happen." He sighed. "I can't believe you didn't tell me," he said quietly, and I could feel his disappointment.

I coughed, then nodded. "I'll train. I promise," I said, though my mouth suddenly was dry and it came out more like a croak than words.

My vision started to darken, and I murmured a quiet, "I'm sorry," before I allowed the darkness to take me.

Chapter Sixteen

W hen sleep finally released its hold on me, I found that I was much warmer than usual.

Forcing my eyes open, I looked up to see Robyn cradling me against his chest, being held in his lap. It was as though he never let me go after he picked me up—like he'd been holding me this entire time.

I shifted my eyes over to look out the window—the sun was beginning to set now—and realized we were in Robyn's room, on his bed, his back against the headboard. I recognized the small space from when I peeked in, searching for him early this morning. It had a bed in the center of the room, two windows in the corner, a door leading to a washroom, a wardrobe, and a small table and chairs, but that was it. Nothing that screamed royalty, let alone *king*. It struck me as odd, how modest he was as a ruler.

Without thinking, I moved my head closer to him, soaking in his warmth. I heard him take a sharp breath, and finally he looked down at me, our eyes meeting.

The relief I felt coming from him was instant, the moment our eyes locked.

I offered him a small smile, and he returned it with one of his own.

"Hi," I said quietly, feeling slightly sheepish.

"Hey," he murmured in response.

He seemed to notice our position suddenly, and made to set me down and move away. I quickly reached out and placed my hand on his chest, causing him to pause.

"Stay?" I asked softly, shifting my gaze to meet his eyes again.

I could feel the surprise radiating from him like the warmth his body emitted. He searched my eyes, probably wondering if this was some kind of trick. But I held his gaze, letting him search all he wanted.

A heartbeat later, he relaxed against me. He nodded, then pulled me closer to him, our bodies flushed with one another. I noticed a small smile playing on his lips.

We stayed like that for a few moments, simply enjoying each other's presence. I rested my head against his chest, relishing in his warmth and his scent—magnolia blossoms and fresh spring rain.

"Aviva?" Robyn called my name softly. I realized in that moment just how much I enjoyed the way my name sounded on his tongue.

"Hm?" I mumbled, content to stay here forever.

"My love, we need to talk," he said, still speaking quietly, as though he didn't want to scare me.

At that, my muscles stiffened. I knew he could feel the shift in my body language from the look in his eyes.

"You're alright, I promise," he reassured me. "We agreed on open communication, right? This is me finally holding true to that," he explained, still holding me. His grip on me tightened, like I might fade away.

Nonetheless, I could feel myself starting to worry. I gently detangled myself from him and moved to sit beside him—though my body screamed at me not to—until my back rested against the headboard next to him. Though, I didn't have it in me to move myself further, our shoulders and sides flushed with each other.

"Alright," I said after a silent moment. Though my heart had started to pick up its pace in my chest.

He reached over and gently grabbed my hand, holding it in both of his. From there, I could see both of our tattoos—where we took on each other's family crest. The symbols for two different nations. It still felt surreal, to see the ink on our arms.

"Why didn't you just tell me you could wield? Especially so many zirilium?" he asked quietly, and I could hear the hurt in his voice as he spoke. My heart ached at the sound.

I let out a sigh. "You don't understand. Father forced me to hide what I was for my entire life—even from Dimitri, my twin. The only one who knew was Aurora, my best friend. Father wanted Dimi to be his heir, not me. But the laws state whoever can wield more zirilium is to be the heir, so Father had me hide that part of me away so the title would revert to Dimitri. I... never had a choice," I said the last part softly, remorsefully.

Robyn ran his thumb thoughtlessly over my hand, and my skin ignited from the innocent contact. "That explains why you never told me about the Northern zirilium. Good job on hiding it, by the way." A small swell of pride overcame him, surprising me. "But what about the Southern zirilium?"

"That, I had no inkling of until that day the flowers sprouted from my tears. From what I've gathered, the elixirs my father had me take every day nullified any part of that. I didn't know I had any Southerner in me at all until after I smashed the remaining elixirs and the flowers sprouted. When you left to go to Hollis, I did as much research as I could in the library. I met another Northerner there, Laurence. He said Chess saved his life years ago, and he's been helping in the library ever since. Anyway, he said he remembers when Father and Mother got married. And he, along with records, helped confirm it—that my mother was originally from the South."

Robyn's idle strokes on my hand came to a pause. "You trust Laurence to know this kind of stuff about you?" he asked.

I nodded. "I trust him."

Robyn seemed to think on this for a moment, then nodded. "I remember him. If you'd like, and if he agrees to it, we could appoint him as your personal guard. He's definitely still got the qualifications for it. I hadn't appointed you one yet because I didn't want to scare you, but it will be necessary when we return."

For a moment, I was stunned. I was surprised he was allowing me to have a say in any of this.

"I'll ask him about it when we get back. If I must have one, I'd like for it to be him," I said, though the idea of a personal guard made me wary.

For a wing-beat, we sat in silence, his thumb rubbing the skin along my hand once again.

"Training is going to be necessary. You understand that, right?" he asked, but there was no venom in it. Just pure concern.

"Definitely. I'll start first thing tomorrow morning," I said, nodding in agreement.

Suddenly I felt a wave of nerves overcome me, and I remembered he must feel it too when he asked, "You're nervous?"

I nodded again, forcing myself to be open and honest for one of the first times in my life. "I don't know the Valwain all that well yet. And... I'm scared of hurting people. I've never had any official zirilium training," I admitted sheepishly.

I saw a smile cross his face out of the corner of my eye. "We can fix that."

Suddenly he hopped out of bed, staring right at me. My hand was still warm from where he had been holding it.

"Join us for dinner tonight. They want to help, Avi," he said. This idea obviously brought him much joy, as he was *glowing*.

I couldn't help but smile back, and I agreed, stating that it was a good idea.

"When is it?" I asked.

"Sunset," he responded, still grinning like I'd offered him the moon in the palm of my hand.

"What? That's any minute!" I said, scrambling to get out of bed. I double checked the window and saw the sky painted different shades of orange, the sun sitting on the horizon.

I heard Robyn laugh as he watched me stress, obviously not at all pressed.

"They'll wait for us, it'll be fine," he reassured me, but I was already heading for the door.

"Give me five minutes! I need to change!" I said, after having looked down at my still damp and dirty clothes from this morning.

A few moments later, I was standing in front of the full length mirror in my room, quickly braiding my hair into a single plait down my spine and fluffing out my bangs. I opted for black, cotton pants and a silk, silver shirt, two things I found at the top of my luggage.

The North was rich in silver, which is why I seemed to have grown so fond of it. Meanwhile, Robyn seemed to feel the same about gold, which was the South's most valued ore.

Instead of tucking my necklace into my shirt, like I'd done for years, I let it hang loose, openly adorning my neck. I looked into the mirror one last time, taking in my simple yet modest appearance, then headed out of the room.

I found Robyn waiting for me in the hallway, leaning against the wall behind him.

When I stepped out, I watched as his eyes roamed my body, drinking the sight of me as though it was all that mattered to him.

It didn't take me long to do the same to him. He had on a pair of deep green pants so dark they were nearly black, with a white shirt adorned with gold detailing and buttons. These types of shirts, I noted, seemed to be among his favorite. His long sleeves were rolled up to his elbows, showing off the different markings on his arms. His top two buttons were loose, showing off a sliver of his smooth, muscled chest.

I found myself thinking once again about how he was the sun to my moon. He lit up my dark world anytime he was around, and he didn't even have to try. Just existing near him made my stomach do flips.

And while it was terrifying to think about my feelings about him, I was also starting to accept it.

I was falling for my own husband.

I shook my head at the sound of Robyn clearing his throat, a small smirk on his face displaying his dimple.

I felt myself turning pink and stood up straighter, focused once again.

He reached across the space between us, holding out his hand.

I looked up into his face, still worried this all might be some extensive mind game. Part of me was still waiting for the other shoe to drop.

But when I saw the genuine, open look on his face, my worries melted away. I found my lips tugging into a small smile as I placed my hand in his. Our fingers intertwined, and I listened as our footsteps softly sounded against the wooden floor below us as he led us to the dining room.

"There's no servants here," I said suddenly as we walked, "who's doing the cooking?" I asked.

"Teagan and I both know how to cook, as well as Chess. He's great with spices and herbs. I think it's the trokav in him," he responded as we turned down a corridor.

"Really?" I asked, surprised.

He nodded. "Our mother wanted to make sure we'd be able to take care of ourselves in every aspect. That included cooking. Teagan and I have even taken to teaching Margo, when we find ourselves with a spare moment."

A strong pang of sadness shot through my chest, and I could tell he was thinking about his parents. Sometimes I forgot he'd lost loved ones, too.

"As for Chess, if I remember correctly, his late sister taught him. He's kind of a jack of all trades, but plants are his specialty. After his sister passed in the war, he joined our army as a trokav, just as his sister had been. He was always one of our top performers, and my family and I have worked with him for years. Once I started ruling, I offered him the royal trokav position. He was so shocked I think he almost cried," Robyn explained.

I listened intently, genuinely interested in learning more about his friends. I opened my mouth to respond, but then I heard the sound of multiple voices at the end of the hall, and my nerves hit me all over again.

Robyn and I came to a stop right before we reached the open door, and I could already smell the aroma of fresh bread and herbs and something sweet I couldn't place wafting out into the hallway.

I took a shaky breath, attempting to calm my nerves, when Robyn gently placed a finger under my chin and lifted my face to meet his eyes.

"There's nothing to be worried about, my love, I promise. They just want to get to know you," he said softly.

I nodded, taking another deep breath, finding comfort in his gaze. I watched as his eyes flicked down to my lips, then back up to my eyes.

That warm feeling returned in my chest, and the air between us suddenly felt electrified.

Quickly, he dropped his hand from my face and took a step back. He ran a hand through his hair, mussing it, and I couldn't help but imagine how soft it must feel.

He smiled uncertainly at me, then quietly reassured me everything was going to go perfectly. He placed a hand on my lower back, leading me as we walked into the dining room together.

A piece of me melted inside from that small gesture.

I made sure my spine was straight, my shoulders were set, and my wings were tucked in before walking into the room.

Conversations quieted as we approached the table, and I noticed they made sure to prepare a basic meal—slices of some type of meat sat in the middle, with an array of different vegetables on the side, as well as the fresh bread I had smelled earlier, and some type of pudding for dessert.

I smiled at the effort they put into the food. Most of the food I'd been presented with in the South had been strange and unfamiliar, but all of this food appeared to be simple, staple foods from the North.

"Sorry it isn't anything fancy—we weren't sure what you liked, so we went with the basics," Teagan said, the first to break the silence. I could see a small bit of flour still clinging to the hem of her gray shirt.

"We're glad you could join us," Ezra said, grinning from his spot next to Quinn.

"Took you both long enough," Quinn mumbled, and I watched with fascination as Ezra lightly elbowed her in the side.

"The guest of honor has arrived! Can we eat now?" Margo asked, obviously excited to get this dinner started. I noticed that her little hands were still bound in the same brown leather, despite it being time for a meal.

Maybe there's more to her than meets the eye.

My smile widened, and I took a moment to glance at the different people surrounding me. People who cared enough to take into consideration what I might prefer to eat. People who weren't scared of me, despite what they saw this morning.

It was almost enough to bring a tear to my eye.

"Thank you. All of you," I said, looking between each of them. My eyes landed on Drayven last, and he dipped his head slightly in a show of respect.

Robyn walked closer to the table, and for the first time, I noticed that while everybody else had an ordinary high backed chair, the chair at the middle of the table—where I presumed Robyn wanted me to sit—wasn't a chair at all, but a wooden stool. One without a backing.

"I noticed how uncomfortable you were that first day I met you, in the carriage. I'll make sure to get some custom made chairs just for you in order to accommodate your wings when we return to Cairnyl," Robyn said, his voice soft. "I hope this is alright for now."

My mouth fell open slightly, stunned into silence that he would even think about something as small as the space my wings take up, or even remember my discomfort that first day.

This time, I had to make an effort not to allow the tears to well in my eyes.

Not knowing what to say, I reached for Robyn's hand and gave it a small squeeze. I looked up into his eyes, and hoped that he could see in them how much I appreciated this small gesture.

He smiled in response, and I could see some of the tension leave his body, as though he was worried I wouldn't appreciate his efforts.

I squeezed again.

He pulled the stool out for me, and though I was continuously shocked at his actions, I sat, realizing the red cushion on top made it much more comfortable than it had appeared.

Robyn sat next to me, the rest of the Valwain following suit. Rayven sat on the other side of Robyn, and Teagan on the other side of me. Margo sat across from Teagan, next to Quinn, and Ezra sat across from Robyn, leaving Chess to sit across from Rayven.

We filled up the eight person table perfectly.

Teagan made an effort to try to serve everybody individually, but soon enough the formalities dropped, and everybody was helping themselves. I waited until almost everybody had gotten their fair share, but Robyn insisted I get my servings before he did.

I gathered a small amount of every dish onto my plate, and dug in.

I listened as they all talked about how their training had been going so far, and how Chess pranked Ezra by discretely placing a caterpillar on his shoulder in passing—just to hear Ezra start screaming a moment later. Apparently, Ezra was not fond of bugs, despite his seemingly infinite knowledge.

I listened to Margo as she explained to Ezra exactly why bugs weren't scary, and how most of them were actually quite friendly. Though, Ezra didn't seem all that convinced.

I watched as Chess animatedly explained how he almost set fire to the vegetables as he and Teagan were cooking, and listened as Robyn let out a hearty laugh that brought a smile to my face.

I learned that besides training with Robyn, Rayven had been in daily contact with the officials back in Cairnyl via Lark, and everything was going as smoothly as expected back at The Haven—at least for now.

It seemed long-lasting peace might be achievable, after all.

"Aviva," Margo said, catching my attention. "You were scary awesome this morning. I've never seen anything like that before! Could you do it again sometime?"

I nearly choked on my food, coughing so it didn't go down wrong.

I heard Teagan shush her little sister, then cleared her throat. "I think what Margo is trying to say is, does this mean you're finally ready to train with us?"

I took a sip of water, then nodded. "Definitely."

"Why didn't you tell us you had zirilium in the first place?" Ezra asked, though his voice carried a tone of genuine curiosity, no sense of foul play.

At his question, I gently set my fork down. I felt Robyn shift his leg closer to mine until our legs touched, and I knew he was offering me silent encouragement. I used the feeling to ground myself, and took a deep breath.

"From the moment my father realized I could wield, he kept me hidden away. I was kept out of the public's eye, and didn't even have my own set of servants or guards. He wanted to keep my abilities a secret, because he wanted Dimitri, my twin, to be crowned his heir. The only other person who knew was my best friend," I explained, keeping my eyes downcast.

"Why didn't you tell anybody your zirilium was getting backed up? This morning could have been avoided all together," Quinn stated, her voice holding an edge to it.

"I'm not used to depending on other people or working in a group. I've always had to handle things on my own, and I thought I could handle this, too," I sighed. "But this morning was a turning point for me. I won't make the same mistake again."

"Stars, you're complicated." Quinn said, pinching the bridge of her nose. "Good try. Now tell us the *real* reason."

I snapped my head up and gaped at her, taken aback at her bluntness, but a small part of me knew she was right.

"Quinn," Rayven, of all people, said her name as a warning. But Quinn didn't break eye contact with me, waiting for an answer.

I realized then that she was challenging me. And I refused to keep hiding.

"I've hurt people in the past with my zirilium, and I was worried if I let it out, I might hurt one of you. I realize now that was a flawed way of thinking, but the pain was so intense at the time, I wasn't thinking rationally." I paused, looking around the table now instead of solely at Quinn. "I apologize for putting you all in danger."

The table was quiet for a moment, but all eyes were on me. Then, in a quiet voice I heard Margo asked, "Who got hurt?"

In an instant, Robyn jumped in. "You don't have to answer that—" he started, but I held up a hand to stop him.

"It's alright, Robyn. Things have to change, starting now."

I slowly got to my feet, and I could feel the emotions welling up in my chest as I thought back. Guilt, sadness, and grief choked me, but I swallowed it down and looked around the table once again as I spoke, making sure to meet everybody in the eye.

"When I was young, even younger than Margo, I-I... had an accident." I took a deep breath. "My zirilium had just recently surfaced, and I was practicing in secret with my mother. Father discovered us, and things got heated fast and... in a freak accident, I mistakenly took my own mother's life with my abilities." I said the last part with less confidence than before, tears threatening to well in my eyes, but I rapidly blinked them away.

I cleared my throat as the table was shocked into silence, and I continued. "In my memory, I only recall a bright blue light when I touched my mother that day. I always thought I had used lightning to kill her, but after this morning, I wonder if maybe it had been fire, instead. Though, I suppose I'll never know. After that day, Father had me start trying different elixirs until we found one he settled on. I didn't know what it was in the beginning, I just knew I felt weaker. Now I know they were nullifying anything about me that was Southern, anything like my mother."

I saw Quinn glance at my right eye, and hoped she realized I meant that change, too, was hidden until recently.

I stood there after I finished speaking for what felt like ages, before Rayven finally met my eyes. He suddenly stood up, placed a fist over his heart, and said, "I wield shadows, and I vow to help train you in the ways of shadow zirilium, my queen."

I gasped at the sudden act of faith, especially from him. He was generally very quiet, and not somebody I'd spent much time with. I nodded my head slightly in his direction, a silent thanks. He dipped his head in an act of respect.

Teagan stood up next, following Rayven's lead, placing a fist over her heart. "I wield earth and plants, and I vow to help train you in the ways of earth and plant zirilium, my queen."

Chess shot up out of his chair, fist over his chest. "I wield plants, and I vow to help, too, my queen!"

A smile broke out across my face, and I couldn't believe what was unraveling before me.

Robyn stood up next to me, following suit. "I wield crystal, earth, plants, and fire, and I vow to help train you in the ways of all of the above, but especially fire, *my wife*."

I gasped at his last words, at his claim in that moment. I couldn't help but notice the way he looked around the table, clearly proud of the people he called his closest friends. His Valwain.

There was a beat of silence before Quinn's chair scraped against the wooden floor as she stood. She slowly raised her fist to her heart. "I wield fire and crystal, and I command armies. I vow to help train you in the ways of crystals and war, my queen." She looked around, then met my gaze. "Don't make me regret this."

I dipped my head to her slightly, a show of respect and acknowledgement.

Ezra and Margo hopped out of their chairs, placing their fists over their hearts, and vowed to help in any way they possibly could.

Finally, I couldn't hold it back anymore. Tears welled in my eyes, and I looked at each of them with awe.

"I can't thank you all enough. I vow to do my best to be worthy of all of your efforts," I said, my voice full of emotion as my eyes flickered around to each of them as I spoke.

I think I might have just made some new friends.

***

Robyn and I turned down the dimly lit hallway that led to our rooms, my hand in his once again.

The rest of dinner was full of chatter and laughter, everybody seeming to be less tense now that all of my issues had been aired out.

I had been worried about drawing close to the Valwain, when in reality, it simply made me feel lighter. It felt *freeing* to let these people in—people I now knew just wanted the best for me and genuinely wanted to help.

I'd been smiling all evening, to the point where my cheeks had begun to ache. And feeling Robyn lightly run his thumb along the side of my hand was only making me smile more.

We came to a stop in front of my door, and I murmured a small thank you to him before turning to enter the room.

I placed my hand on the door handle, but couldn't seem to actually turn it to enter the room.

After a moment of hesitation, I turned back to Robyn. Suddenly my heart was speeding up.

"Listen, alright, this might sound odd, but I promise I'm not trying to be. I just have realized lately that I sleep better when I'm around you, and I've gotten kind of lonely in here by myself. I could really use a good night's sleep, because I haven't really been sleeping the past week, but-but if you'd rather not, that's alright too because—" Robyn lifted a hand and gently cupped the side of my face, forcing me to meet his gaze.

"What are you asking me?" he asked, though I could tell by the smile playing on his lips that he already knew.

"Can I come sleep in your room with you?" I asked quietly. I could feel my face turning pink the more I spoke. My heart was beating so fast I was surprised he couldn't hear it.

"Oh, my love, I thought you'd never ask," he responded just as quietly. He dropped his hand from my face and took my hand in his again, leading me into his room.

We took turns sharing the washroom to get ready for bed, and when I stepped back into the bedroom, he was already laying down, waiting for me.

My face flushed again at the sight of him, remembering suddenly that he enjoyed sleeping shirtless.

He had given me a pair of matching pajamas to wear—an over-sized, brown shirt with brown shorts that were so large on me they hung down to my knees. I had to slice a giant hole in the back of the shirt for my wings, then left my mother's dagger—along with all my other ones—in the washroom with my clothes.

I groaned as I realized how silly I looked in comparison to him. His head snapped up at the sound of me in the room, then froze as he took in the sight of me. His eyes roamed up and down my body, from the shorts to my loose hair hanging down to my waist. I could feel his pride welling in my own chest at the sight of me in his clothing.

"This isn't fair. You look like... like *that*, while I look like a complete dork." I crossed my arms over my chest.

Robyn was still staring at me, seemingly unable to respond, when I felt that warm sensation in my chest again. This time, I didn't ignore it—I just let it be.

He shook his head slightly, knocking himself out of his trance, then lifted up the blanket. "Come over here." His voice was lower than usual, and it took me a moment to register that the fae male in him must be foaming at the mouth at the sight of his wife in his clothes, covered in his scent.

I bit the inside of my cheek, but slowly crossed the room, re-minding myself it was alright to be vulnerable with him. That I was safe.

Once I reached the side of the high bed, his arms wrapped around my waist and tugged me towards him, until I was standing between his legs. I rested my hands on his shoulders, our faces almost level, with me looking up into his eyes ever so slightly.

As our eyes met, I could see the war raging within them. The emotions swirling in my chest from him were as strong as they came—desire, yearning, longing. But with the way his muscles stiffened when my hands rested upon his bare skin, I could tell he was fighting his usual self-control.

As though a war truly was being fought within him, he slowly lifted his right hand from my waist and tangled his fingers into the hair at the nape of my neck. He moved as though it pained him, excruciatingly slow. My heart was pounding against my ribs, and I watched as his eyes flickered down to the long column of my neck, his gaze locking there. I watched as his throat worked, his fingers tightening in my hair. Just the sight of him so easily undone like this was causing my zirilium to sing in my veins.

Deciding to test the waters, I tilted my head to the side slightly, exposing more of my neck to him.

Deep in his throat, a sound similar to a growl ripped loose from his lips. "You have no idea what you do to me, love," he said, his breathing heavy.

Before I could respond, he pulled me the rest of the way into bed. I let out a small squeal, surprised at the sudden break in whatever had just passed between us, but I found myself relaxing rather quickly.

"Another time," he murmured, though it almost sounded as though he was reassuring himself rather than promising me.

He shifted, tucking me against his chest, and after a beat of hesitation, I rested my forehead against him. He wrapped his arms around me like I might vanish into thin air, and our legs intertwined on instinct. My wings spread out behind me, and I draped my arm over his torso, idly drawing circles on his lower back.

At first, I felt him tense up at the sudden contact, but after a heartbeat, he relaxed against my touch. I looked up into his face, and found that there was a slight pink tint spreading across his cheeks.

I couldn't help but smile to myself.

The King of the South, *blushing*.

We lay like this, silently, for a while, until he saw me looking out of the window to the side of the bed.

"What are you looking for when you look out of the window at night?" he asked, his voice soft and gentle. It seemed he'd calmed down compared to earlier.

A sad smile crossed my lips. "*Et lyrm,*" I responded in Nolvym. "The moon. Before I left, my twin brother said as long as we were both looking to the moon at night, we'd be connected. It helps me feel like he's not so far away sometimes," I explained quietly, my voice full of sorrow.

Robyn sighed lightly, then placed his chin atop my head. "*Ve thyrem, Avi,*" *I'm sorry, love,* he responded in the old Northern tongue, surprising me. "I'm sorry. I know what it's like to miss somebody."

"You speak Nolvym?" I asked, my eyes searching his.

He nodded. "I learned it as a child and continued to study it as a teenager. Inphis adopted the common language shortly before the war, so I thought maybe the North would revert back to what they knew best. I always knew I wanted to be the one to bring peace to my people, my family. So I taught it to myself, just in case it was necessary to communicate with the North," he explained, staring back into my eyes as he spoke.

I nodded in understanding, and tried to push the embarrassment I felt rising back down. I'd spoken Nolvym in his presence more than once.

I could feel sleep creeping up on me, so I broke our eye contact, resting my head against his chest once again.

Without lifting my head, I spoke without thinking, simply voicing the thoughts that popped into my tired mind.

"You know, you're the first person to call me that. Avi. People usually shorten my name to Viva as a nickname," I said to him after a moment, slowly closing my eyes. "I like it."

He didn't respond, but I could feel his emotions—warm, and overjoyed, and excited, and relaxed, and content. He was obviously very happy with our current arrangement, and I found that I was, too.

I leaned into his touch as his hand reached behind my head and gently twirled my hair around his fingers.

I was half aware that the idle circles I was drawing on his back with my fingertips became slower, but I felt so at peace in this moment, I couldn't be bothered to care anymore about ignoring how I feel.

"Sweet dreams, Avi," Robyn whispered into the darkness. I distantly felt his lips touch my forehead before I allowed sleep to conquer me.

Chapter Seventeen

I t'd been four long, exhausting days since my first dinner with the Valwain, and I finally felt confident enough in my earth and plant wielding to say I had it under control.

I'd been training with Teagan and Chess from dawn to dusk every day, taking advantage of every moment we could since we had to start heading back to Cairnyl in a few days.

Apparently the officials back at The Haven were not very happy with the Valwain at that point in our stay. Robyn let it slip that we were all supposed to be back by now, but he extended our time here for over an extra week in order to let me have time to train in peace. At first I'd felt guilty, knowing that I messed up their plans. But Robyn reassured me that my training was of the utmost importance—not only so I could defend myself if need be, but so that I didn't accidentally hurt anybody when we did return to Cairnyl.

For the past four days after training, I had attended dinner with the Valwain, then headed to bed, falling asleep soundly in the arms of my husband. Honestly, it'd been the best sleep of my life. I finally felt comfortable and safe with him, and I could tell he felt the same with me. I could *feel* it. I didn't know if I was worthy of him, but I was trying my best to be.

We decided to take things slow, but I'd been enjoying every spare moment I could get with him.

In terms of progress, I was able to call to the earth and plants at will now—sprouting different plants from the palm of my hand and pulling chunks of earth out of the ground, moving them around as I pleased. Earth and plants came easy to me, as they felt like an extension of the Northern zirilium I already had some control over. I found that it felt extremely satisfying to have this power over my abilities. For so long, my zirilium had ruled over me. It was comforting to be able to rule over them for a change.

It was difficult at first, having to disconnect my emotions from my zirilium. I'd been able to call to air with ease, but even lightning was still tied to my feelings. Teagan worked with me patiently until I could focus solely on the zirilium pumping through my veins, instead of getting distracted by my own emotions.

Once I was able to practice getting past those hurdles, I was able to apply them to my other zirilium. I even made it storm, thunder and lightning included, on command yesterday.

I pulled the front doors of the cabin open and stepped into the early morning light. The sun had just risen, and I couldn't help but let out a yawn. I was definitely still not used to being awake this early, but Quinn insisted on getting as much out of the day as we could. She was positive that crystal wielding wouldn't come as easy to me as earth or plants, and I'd be lying if I said that didn't concern me to a degree.

I pushed away the worries trying to take over my mind, pulling my long hair into a ponytail. I flexed my hands afterwards, still not quite used to this new weight on them.

After this morning, I wasn't sure anything could rattle my good mood. Even Quinn.

I slide gently out of bed, trying my best not to wake Robyn. He's usually up with me by this time, but today he seems extra tired, so I try to let him rest.

Ultimately, I'm unsuccessful. I feel his hand wrap around mine, trying to tug me back into his arms.

"Come back," he groans without opening his eyes.

I can't stop the smile that lights up my face.

I squeeze his hand affectionately, then let go. "If I miss my first day of training with Quinn, I think she'd march right in here and drag me out by the ear. Please, let me keep my dignity." I chuckle.

Robyn simply groans again in response, and I can tell he knows I'm right.

I head to the washroom, quickly getting dressed in dark gray training leathers that Quinn gave me, insisting I wear them today. They're somewhat thicker than the usual leathers, but I'm not complaining.

It's only while I'm getting dressed that I realize the necklace housing my moon stones is missing from my throat.

Trying not to panic, I pad back into the main room to ask Robyn. "Have you seen my necklace? I think it might have slipped off while I was sleeping and—"

I pause mid-sentence as I stare at Robyn, still shirtless from sleep and sitting on the edge of the bed facing me. His hair is unruly and sticking up in random places, and my heart lurches at the sight.

That's when I notice the small, brown box he's holding in his hands. It even has a small bow on top.

I stop in my tracks, standing just inside the room, and stare at the box a moment longer before meeting his eyes. I know he sees the question there, and feels my confusion in his chest. He stands up after a heartbeat and crosses the room to stand before me, then holds it out, offering it to me.

"I know Quinn is going to be tough on you these next few days, and I figured these would come in handy. Think of it as a training gift," he says, and I can feel him beginning to get nervous.

His nervousness spreads throughout my chest, reflecting my own. "Are you sure? I mean, you didn't have to. I really don't deserve anything—" Robyn reaches a hand out, grabbing one of my own in his, eyes meeting mine.

"My love, if I could, I would capture the moon for you in a heartbeat. You deserve the world. And until I can get the moon down from the sky, these will have to do," he says. I can hear in his voice how genuine he is. It's in this moment the warm feeling returns in my chest.

Tears spring to my eyes as he speaks, and I nod, not trusting myself to speak as I slowly take the box from him. When I finally lift the cover off, I gasp as I realize where my necklace has gone.

Inside lays a pair of leather gloves, a shade of gray so dark they're almost black. They're fingerless, just covering the main part of the hand, knuckles, and wrist. And on each of the ten knuckles sits a different stone.

On the left glove sits five moon stones, each gleaming their usual silver-blue sheen. I recognize the varying shapes of them as the same stones from my necklace. The right glove, though, holds five sun stones—stones I've only seen on other people, like the bracelet with four stones Robyn wears, which matches Teagan's. They have a golden-yellow gleam to them, like tiny suns captured inside each one.

Robyn begins to get nervous as I stare at the gloves, taking in their beauty, and starts trying to explain himself. "Teagan helped, and we both stayed up super late last night trying to make sure they were perfect for you. I actually picked out the sun stones myself, the same day those flowers sprouted from your tears. I'd been holding onto them ever since. I wasn't sure about taking the moon stones without your permission, but Teagan and I made sure we could make them back into your necklace again if you decide you don't like them. I considered making the gloves with new moon stones, but you've already adapted to these stones' energy, and I didn't want to—"

"Robyn," I say softly.

I hear him inhale sharply. "Yes?" he asks, his voice just as gentle as mine. I can tell he's anxious and worried, waiting for my approval.

"I love them," I say finally and look up to meet his gaze, a smile stretching across my face. He searches my eyes, as though he'll find me lying, but I know he can feel how genuine my words are. His relief when he realizes I truly do love them is palpable in my chest.

"Help me put them on?" I ask. Finally, his face breaks out into a smile matching my own, his dimple on full display. I can feel how proud of himself he is, and how excited he is that I accepted his gift. It makes my heart clench with so much emotion, I'm unsure if I can handle it all.

I clenched and unclenched my fists over and over, stretching out the fresh leather on my hands. The weight of the gloves would take some getting used to, but they were so comfortable they were already starting to feel like a second skin. Somehow, Teagan and Robyn were able to get my hand size exactly right.

It was odd, not feeling the weight of my necklace against my chest. I'd always been conditioned to hide what I am, so having my stones on full display for the world to see was almost... terrifying. Yet in another way, it was also freeing. I even stopped wearing my eye patch after the first dinner with the Valwain. They all knew what I was anyways—there was no point in trying to hide it from them.

This whole trip had come with so many changes, I wasn't sure what to do with it all.

I could still feel the warmth of Robyn's fingers on my skin from where he clasped the gloves closed. He had been more than happy to help me put them on. I ran a finger over the same spots his skin touched mine. I was so focused on thoughts of my husband I didn't hear Quinn approach until she cleared her throat, making me jump.

In an instant, I was standing straighter, lifting my chin slightly and tucking my wings closer to my body. "Good morning," I said after a beat of silence.

Quinn didn't answer at first—she just observed. She looked me up and down intensely, like she was deliberately looking for flaws of some sort. When she didn't find anything to critique me on, she simply nodded once, then said, "Let's go."

At that, she turned on her heel and walked away without another word.

I was so dumbfounded by the interaction, I had to jog to catch up to Quinn, who hadn't stopped walking. I followed her as we walked off the cabin grounds and toward the forest, and I took this time to observe her, too.

The scar cutting down her face and over her eye was a perfectly clean slice, though the wound must have been intense, because the scar was still slightly raised and lacked her normal coloring. Quinn walked in a military manner—her chin held high, shoulders rolled back, and every step filled with confidence. That didn't surprise me, though, since from what I understood, she'd been raised to be general of the Southern armies for her entire life.

Falling asleep in Robyn's arms the past few days had led to lots of talks about the different members of the Valwain, and ourselves. From him, I learned that Quinn's late father was the previous general, and his father before him was general before that. Quinn was an only child, and apparently has no family left since her father died two years ago. She'd been general since then, with great difficulty. She was the first female general in over two centuries in the South, and she was not kindly welcomed by her soldiers. In the beginning, she had their respect because she was her father's daughter only—not because of her own abilities. It'd taken her the full two years since her father died in battle to gain enough respect that her soldiers didn't openly object her now, but she was constantly having to prove herself to them.

Honestly, it sounded exhausting.

According to Robyn, she was the most disciplined crystal wielder he knew—and extremely skilled because of it. He trusted her enough to leave me alone with her to train, though he did warn me she wouldn't go easy on me just because I was her queen. If anything, he said she'd push me even harder.

I'd be lying if I claimed I wasn't at least a little anxious.

I looked to Quinn again as we passed yet another of our usual training meadows, and finally gathered the courage to speak. "So, where are we headed?"

"You'll see," Quinn said, not bothering to glance my way.

I sighed, though I knew there was no use in trying to ask her again. She very well might be the most stubborn person I'd ever met.

A chill erupted over my skin as the wind picked up, blowing my bangs into my face. I blew them out of my eyes and wrapped my arms around myself.

It sure is windy today, I thought to myself.

I continued to follow Quinn as we walked through the forest until we reached the other side, coming out of the brush to be greeted by the vast ocean that made up Echen Bay.

I paused in my tracks and stared out at the water, watching as the wind and water forced powerful waves to come crashing onto the shore time and time again. Almost every other day I'd visited the bay, the water had been calm and tranquil. But today it seemed almost angry, like it was trying to punish the land for something.

I realized I'd fallen behind as I saw Quinn reach the shore, and I sprinted to catch up, stopping at her side.

Just as I opened my mouth to ask Quinn what we were doing here, she spoke.

"Get in."

Stunned, I spun around to face her. "What?"

"I said, *get in,*" she said, obviously beginning to get annoyed. "You're wasting daylight."

Flabbergasted, I threw my hands into the air, wings flaring in unison. "I don't even know what we're doing down here! I know I don't know how to communicate very well, but apparently neither do you," I said, exasperated.

Quinn's nostrils flared, and just when I thought she was about to pounce on me, she sighed instead. She pinched the bridge of her nose, closing her eyes as she explained.

"When you're in battle, you never know what kind of opponents you'll come up against, what kind of zirilium they have, or how strong they are. You have to be able to adapt at a moment's notice. When fighting Northerners specifically, they like to play dirty. They'll slip ice under your foot to throw you off balance before attacking. They'll make whips out of water, sometimes even ice, and some of the strongest wind wielders will throw you up into the air to disorient you. You have to be prepared to face anything, while also maintaining a constant connection to your zirilium and surroundings." She paused, turning her head to look out across the bay. "So to practice, you'll be learning to crystal wield while being pummeled by waves."

My jaw dropped open in shock. "Isn't there an easier way to accomplish that? Is this," I threw an arm towards the water, "really necessary?"

Quinn gave a stern look, and I clenched my jaw shut.

A heartbeat later, I went to ask another question, but Quinn beat me to it. "And no—you're only permitted to wield crystals during this exercise."

I didn't ask any more questions after that.

A couple moments later, Quinn and I were both standing out in the water, and I was fighting back a chill. The water was cooler than it looked—I didn't realize until now just how accustomed to being warm I'd become.

I was standing farther away from the shore than Quinn, per her instructions, both of us fully clothed as I turned to face her. The water was up to my collar bones, while on Quinn, it was only up to her chest.

I silently cursed her for the inches she had on me.

While walking out, I noticed the sand was hiding quite a lot of rocks underneath, and suddenly I was finding myself annoyed that I wasn't allowed access to any other zirilium during this training session.

"Alright. Everything has an energy it emits—especially living people. Focus on the energy of the things around you and underfoot," Quinn said, speaking loud enough to be heard over the water.

But even staying in place was proving harder than it seemed. I couldn't find my footing as the waves continuously crashed into me from behind, sometimes forcing my head under the water. I blinked the salt out of my eyes and stumbled forward, instinctually trying to get out of the path of the waves, when I felt something stopping me.

I looked up to see I'd been pushed forward so much I reached Quinn, who had both of her hands firmly gripping my shoulders. She walked forward, forcing me backwards, until the water was once again up to my collar bones. Then she returned to her spot.

I felt my frustration boil as she pushed me, and I wanted to snap at her. But for once, I found Quinn with a smooth expression, no ill intent behind her eyes.

"This exercise is *supposed* to be frustrating, Aviva, that's what makes it realistic," she said. "Try again. Find your footing, then really focus this time."

I sighed, fighting back a groan. Taking in a deep breath, I nodded to Quinn, then closed my eyes and focused on the sound of her voice.

"Bend your knees slightly, and try to dig your feet into the sand and rocks some to help ground you in place. Then, *focus*. Focus on the energy under and around you, and block out all the rest," Quinn spoke, her voice calm and neutral.

I did as she said, digging my feet into the ground below and finally finding solid footing, no longer stumbling forward with each wave that passed. But when I tried to focus, I couldn't feel anything—the waves, and water, and fish swimming between my feet were all too distracting.

Quinn was silent for a moment, then she asked quietly, "Do you feel them?"

"Feel what?" I responded, slightly annoyed.

"The sand is hiding a pocket of crystals not but a couple feet from us. Reach out your energy as though you're reaching out a hand. The same way you call to the earth or to the plants when you use their zirilium. Focus on the energy the crystals emit, and feel them. Reach for them," she said, her eyes closed.

I suppressed a sigh as another wave crashed into me, but I stood firm, my resolve growing stronger. I wasn't sure I'd ever get this, but Quinn didn't seem to be giving up on me, so I wouldn't either.

I closed my eyes again and *reached*.

As though my energy was a third arm, I reached out, scanning the area around us for different energies. I searched the ground below, feeling lots of rocks through my earth zirilium as well as small sea plants. I cast my reach farther, like a fishing net in a circle around us, and finally felt the cluster of crystals. Their energy felt almost like a prickling sensation at first as I adjusted to the new zirilium, then I dropped the connection.

"I felt them!" I cried out, eyes flying open.

For the first time since I'd known her, Quinn *smiled*. I couldn't help but return her smile with one of my own.

"I knew you could do it after your freak out a few days ago. You just needed to be pushed," she said, still smiling slightly. "Like I said, everything has an energy—you just have to learn what they all are. Now, reach out again. But this time, draw the crystals towards you. The energy of crystals is important in wielding them, but they're also complex. They almost have a mind of their own. Pull the energy of the crystals towards you, and the crystals should come, too."

I nodded enthusiastically, suddenly feeling reinvigorated in my efforts.

I closed my eyes again, casting my net of energy towards the left where I felt the group of crystals before. I found them easier this time, but when I tried to tug at them, they didn't budge.

"Remember, they don't like being told what to do. Pull at their energy with your own, not on the crystals themselves," Quinn said, her voice calm and tranquil once again as she instructed me.

I took a deep breath, letting it out slowly. The waves crashing into my back barely bothered me anymore, the water simply ebbing and flowing around me. I felt like a rock standing tall in the water, taking every hit without budging. I felt pride swell in my chest, and I used that positive energy, feeding it into the connection I felt with the crystals. I used my energy and imagined wrapping a giant hand around the bundle's small circle of energy. Gently, I pulled on the crystal's energy with my own, but nothing happened.

I breathed slowly and deeply, then tried again. I tugged softly a second time, and this time, I felt the crystals give. I continued to pull on their energy until I'd placed them between Quinn and me, letting the connection break off.

As soon as I dropped the connection, my eyes flew open and I beamed up at the redhead before me.

She smiled in return.

"Nice job, my queen," Quinn said, and I could almost hear a hint of affection and pride in her voice.

On the inside, I could tell this was a huge turning point in our relationship. She'd finally just accepted me not only as her queen, but as her friend. I didn't realize I cared what she thought of me so much until that moment.

I didn't let any of that show on my face, though. I simply smiled wide, and let my pride surge for a moment.

"Now, that was just the warm up. Are you ready for more?" Quinn asked, a mischievous smirk replacing her beautiful smile.

Chapter Eighteen

"Aviva," a voice whispered, drawing me from sleep.

I'd spent the last four days of our trip training with Quinn, and it'd been exhausting, to say the least. Not only did she teach me how to find and move crystals, but how to sprout them into different shapes that I could use as weapons. She also taught me basic fighting moves I could use in battle, though a lot of the basics were ones Dimitri had taught me. Instead, I asked her to show me how to take somebody down without killing them.

I decided that if war ever broke out again, and I was forced to fight my own people, I wanted to give them the opportunity to survive, at least.

She showed me where different pressure points were on the body, and how to effectively knock somebody on the side of the head to render them unconscious. In return, I showed her where to snap the bones on Northerner's wings in order to ground them, but not kill or cause permanent damage.

I was proud to say that for all Quinn taught me, I taught her something new, too.

"*Aviva*," the voice came again, and this time I recognized it as Robyn.

I groaned, turning my head away from the sound of his voice. I simply wanted to rot in bed, but I knew that wasn't an option.

Today, we headed back to Cairnyl. I didn't get to spend much time there before we left for the cabin, and now, things would be different when we returned.

Before we came here, I still viewed the Valwain as my enemies, but now I'd accepted them all as my friends.

Not only that, but I wanted to find out more about my mother's family after our return. Knowing that there were pieces of her still out there, and I could get to know them, was almost too much to process. I had to get to know them, but something was holding me back.

I planned on talking to Robyn about it soon, and asking for his help. If anybody would know more about the noble families of the South, it'd be him. I'd been so busy with Quinn the past few days, I hadn't gotten the chance.

"Get up, my love," Robyn said quietly, and I felt him run a hand over my hair in gentle strokes. I turned back around to face him, forcing my eyes open to look at him. He was already fully dressed in his brown riding leathers, and I realized a second later that the sun hadn't even risen yet.

"What's going on?" I asked, sitting up. I immediately began to worry, thinking something was wrong.

"Everything is perfectly fine," he said, likely sensing my bubbling anxiety. "I want to take you somewhere before we leave."

I rubbed the sleep from my eyes. "Where?"

"Well, if I told you, it wouldn't be a surprise anymore, would it?" He stood up from the bed. "Get dressed. I'll go grab us some snacks to tide us over until breakfast before departure."

And with those parting words, he slipped out of the room.

I got dressed and washed up quickly, not knowing how long I had until he'd be back. I dressed in my own leathers, dark gray to match my gloves, and my black boots. It'd be a long day of travel, and I wanted to be comfortable.

I slid all of my daggers into place, hidden in different sheaths all over my body, my mother's dagger sitting close to my heart. I didn't imagine needing them as much anymore, now that I didn't view the Southerners as my enemy, but I still drew a sense of comfort from having them near.

I had just finished brushing my loose, white waves when I heard a familiar knock on the door. Robyn entered the room once again, arms full of different fruits.

He set the fruits on the small table in the corner. "I wasn't sure exactly what you liked, so I got some of everything," he said, and I could see the tip of his ears flush lightly.

Walking over, I saw he not only got fruit, but also an array of small pastries Chess had made the day before for our travels.

I smiled at his genuine efforts. "Thank you." I grabbed one of the bright green apples from the pile.

He held out his hand. "Ready to go?" he asked.

I placed my hand in his and nodded. "Ready."

As we walked, I thought about how comfortable I'd become in my husband's presence. I found peace in his company, and I'd even grown used to falling asleep in his arms. I'd become accustomed to our open talks as we fell asleep, about what we both liked, and what life was like before we met each other. I felt genuine relief when my eyes landed on him after a long day of training, like I could finally relax as long as he was nearby.

I realized with a start that I felt completely safe with him; like together, we could take on the entire world.

The only other fae I'd ever felt peaceful around was Dimitri, and even with my brother, it was never to this level. But the more I reflected back on it, the more I realized how tiring it was becoming to keep such a big secret from him—that he wasn't the rightful heir. It was weighing on my heart, and I wasn't sure how much longer I would've lasted without combusting if I hadn't been sent away.

I knew Dimitri loved me, but sometimes I also felt as though I were a burden, or an extra weight on him. If he were here, I knew he'd tell me that wasn't true, but deep down, I was confident we both knew it was.

But with Robyn, things were different. He didn't allow me to spend so much time around him, talking and falling asleep in his arms, out of a sense of obligation or because he felt a need to protect me, as I imagined Dimitri likely felt. Robyn did those things because he cared for me—and I could actually *feel* how deep those emotions went. We may not have known each other for long at this point, but his feelings towards me had always been clear— I saw that now. I'd been the one holding us back.

But not anymore.

I felt the ground below my feet change, and I realized we were now on the beach, down at the bay. Robyn veered left, taking us on a walk along the shoreline. The sky was slowly beginning to lighten, the stars blinking out one by one.

He explained as we walked that the reason we were leaving so much earlier than the first time we journeyed is because of the communication Rayven had with Cairnyl the past couple of days. Apparently, Robyn's officials and nobles were not happy with him for being gone so long, especially after such an uncertain peace agreement. They were not convinced of the peace between the South and the North, and were kind of freaking out since the entire Valwain was on this trip. As a result, we were not stopping in Diorum on our way back to The Haven—we were traveling nonstop all day and into the night, until we reached Cairnyl.

Part of me was stunned that he was telling me all of this so openly. I was so accustomed to being told next to nothing, the open communication still took me by surprise.

He looked at me curiously, and I could tell by his expression he was wondering why I felt surprised.

"I'm... not used to being kept so in the loop about things," I said after a moment. "It's a good change, and I appreciate you telling me. I simply have to adjust."

Robyn nodded in understanding, likely recalling one of our previous nightly conversations.

He looked up at the sky suddenly, watching as more stars blinked out, and a crease appeared between his brows. "We have to hurry," he said, quickening our pace.

Soon, we came across a rocky part of the beach and approached an ivy-covered wall of stone. From the looks of it, this part of the beach was usually a couple inches under water. I looked around and could note nothing special, until Robyn, with a flick of his wrist, shifted some of the thick vines out of the way with his zirilium, revealing a hidden tunnel in the surface of the rock.

I gasped, shocked that something so large could be hidden so thoroughly. Robyn, still holding my hand, smiled at me.

"After you, m'lady."

I didn't hesitate, knowing that he wouldn't tell me to venture somewhere unsafe. I plunged ahead into the darkness, tucking my wings close to my body. The space was too small for us to walk side by side, though Robyn's hand on my shoulder was a constant comfort.

After a couple seconds of walking blindly, I could see the end of the tunnel, and I realized it was a rather short passageway. Before I could step out of the tunnel, Robyn gently tugged on my hand.

"Do you trust me?" he asked quietly, close to my ear. I could hear him holding his breath as he waited for my reply.

"Yes," I said with no hesitation, "I trust you."

I didn't have time to think about the significance of what I just declared before his hand gently took its place over my eyes, obscuring my vision. His other hand landed on the small of my back, and gently led me forward out of the tunnel.

Once we were out, I could hear the sound of the waves softly crashing onto the shore not too far off. He turned me slightly to the side, then slowly lifted his hand away from my eyes as he said, "We made it just in time."

I blinked a couple times, but considering the sun wasn't up yet, my eyes adjusted easily to the soft light—Northerners could see better than Southerners in the dark. I was facing the ocean, watching as the waves kissed the shore. The sun should be rising any moment.

"Turn around, Avi," he called to me softly.

Turning on my heel, I realized we were in a small, hidden cove. There were the same cliff faces surrounding us, blocking off this part of the beach from everything else. When I turned around, my eyes landed on Robyn, then jumped to what was behind him.

And suddenly it dawned on me why he wanted to bring me here so badly.

Moon lilies.

Behind Robyn, there was a small waterfall cascading down from the cliff face and landing in a small pond. And surrounding the pond were dozens of moon lilies.

A piece of home.

I gasped and covered my mouth with a gloved hand. Tears sprung to my eyes as I walked over to them, falling to my knees. I gently cupped one of the white and gray flowers, their centers a vibrant purple, bowing my head to inhale their soft, sweet scent.

Now I understood why we had to rush here—moon lilies closed up for the day once the sun rose. And we likely couldn't have gotten through the tunnel during high tide, which I assumed would come soon.

I laughed suddenly, a tear escaping and falling down my cheek. My emotions were jumbled, and I couldn't tell them apart. These flowers meant so much more than home to me—they remind me of my mother.

Of the last time I saw her.

"Are you alright?" Robyn asked, kneeling next to me.

I nodded. "These flowers. I didn't realize they grew anywhere else besides the North. They're called moon lilies." I paused, a sad smile taking over my lips. "They were my mother's favorite. Anytime I was sick or feeling down, she'd bring me a bundle of them from the royal gardens. They remind me of her, and of her kindness. After she... passed, Father got rid of all of them from the gardens. I haven't seen one since."

I could feel Robyn's guilt for bringing me here, for inflicting these memories on me, so I spoke quickly, trying to reassure him. "Don't feel guilty, these aren't tears of pain. It's joyous, to know my father couldn't completely erase her. Thank you for bringing me here," I said, making sure to look him in the eye as I spoke so he knew how genuine I was.

He nodded, and I felt his guilt ease. We both stood up, brushing ourselves free of dirt and sand. Robyn leaned down and gently picked one of the flowers, then walked a few paces away, closer to the beach. I followed a step behind.

He turned towards me and motioned to my hair with the flower. "May I?" he asked.

I was caught off guard, but nodded, the tips of my ears turning pink. I held my breath as he drew close, tucking the flower into my hair so it sat on my ear just so.

Like Mother had once done, all those years ago.

Overwhelmed with gratitude, and without much thought, I stepped even closer to Robyn and embraced him in a tight hug.

I could feel his surprise, but also his joy. His happiness was so bright it almost hurt as he wrapped his arms around my waist, returning my hug, tucking me into his chest. I wrapped my wings around us on instinct, fully embracing him. Everywhere his body touched mine, it sent tiny lightning bolts along my nerves. I felt warm and safe, and I never wanted to leave.

He pulled back slightly, enough for us to look at each other face to face.

The sun was finally rising, and it was making him glow like one of the Stars. His forest green eyes were peering into my own mismatched ones, and I felt my breathing hitch as his eyes flickered to my lips, then returned to my eyes.

"Please don't pull a dagger on me for this," he said quietly, then he did it.

He kissed me.

I froze, and he felt the shift. He broke away quickly, but before he could apologize, I fisted my hands in his shirt and pulled him back to me, crashing my lips onto his with a need I didn't realize I had.

He melted against me, kissing me back with a desperation I didn't know could run so deep. His hand came up to tangle in the hair at the nape of my neck, tilting my head upwards towards his. Our lips moved against each other with curiosity, exploring, feeling.

The warm sensation had officially returned in my chest, but also in his. And for once, I let myself accept what it truly was.

Love.

I'd fallen in love with the male I once saw as my enemy. The male who was supposed to be a horrible person, who I wasn't supposed to trust.

Now, he might be the only person in the world I truly, fully trusted.

And loved.

The feeling overwhelmed me, and suddenly I couldn't get enough of him.

He must have felt the shift in my emotions, because his hand fisted in my hair and his grip on my waist tightened, pulling me closer as he deepened our kiss, and I happily complied.

I felt a change in his energy then, something I could only describe as him overflowing with so much emotion, it forced itself out of him in the only way it knew how.

In that moment, as his energy shifted, a ring of fire burst to life around us. I gasped, breaking our kiss as I looked at the flames surrounding us. For a moment, I thought *I* did this, until I looked up into Robyn's eyes. There were so many different emotions swimming around in his gaze, and I realized it came from him.

"*I* burn *for you*," he said to me in Nolvym, and I could hear the desperation in his voice, the love, and joy, and relief, and raw need. I smiled so wide my cheeks hurt, and when he returned my smile with one just as genuine, dimple flashing, I couldn't help but reach up on my tiptoes and kiss him all over again.

He sighed against my lips, pulling me close once again.

The flames grew even stronger, and I realized they might be an issue. I tried to focus on the moon stone on my first finger, and funneled a portion of my energy into it. A moment later, the clouds overheard started to band together, growing dark and heavy.

I gently nipped at Robyn's bottom lip, and he gladly granted me access, our kiss deepening as I explored and claimed what was mine.

A moment later, the clouds overhead our little cove finally let loose all of their tears, morning rain falling down upon us and helping to put out his flames safely, before any flowers—or we—got burned.

We broke apart as the rain drenched us, staring into each other's eyes. He didn't even appear to notice the rain, and if he did, he certainly didn't mind it. He rested his forehead against mine, cupping my cheek and stroking my face with his thumb. We were both out of breath, but he spoke anyways.

"I want you to be my wife and queen in more than law. I want you to be my partner in all things, my equal," he said breathlessly. I could feel a hint of fear in my chest, as though he was worried I'd reject him.

My smile broadened as I said, "I would love nothing more than that."

He smiled, relief flooding his emotions.

I stared into his eyes for a moment, then said, "Byn?"

I could see the surprise in his eyes as I spoke his nickname, but he didn't stumble.

"Yes?"

"I think... no, I know it. I love you. I'm *in* love with you," I said, and I felt my entire face flush pink the second the words left my mouth. I held my breath as I waited for his response.

As he listened to me speak, I felt his joy—which I didn't think could grow anymore—expand in my chest, as though there wasn't enough room in his own. He was practically overflowing with it.

"I've loved you since the moment you put that dagger to my throat, Aviva," he said, and my surprise must have shown on my face, because he let out a hearty laugh.

"Sorry it took me so long," I said sheepishly, looking up at him through my eyelashes, blinking rain from my eyes.

"For you, my love, I'd wait an eternity."

Chapter Nineteen

A series of unfamiliar knocks on the door stirred me from sleep. I turned my head to look out of the window and noticed that it was barely past dawn.

I stifled a groan.

It'd been two days since the rest of the Valwain and I got back to The Haven. We arrived at nearly dawn, as we had traveled through the night to make it back in a timely manner, straight through the heart of Yarpeck Woods. The moment the officials saw Byn had returned, they practically ambushed him, wanting him and various members of the Valwain to jump into meetings right away.

To my surprise, Byn made them wait even longer. He asked them to give him two days to settle in before he attended any meetings. He said he had something of the utmost importance to take care of right away, but that in two days' time he was all theirs for any and all meetings. Giles, his head advisor and assistant in pretty much all things, from what I understood, was not happy with him, but begrudgingly agreed to push all his meetings off until he was ready.

When I asked him what he needed to handle so urgently, he looked dumbfounded that I had asked. "You," he had said. Then went on to explain how he needed to teach me fire wielding before Quinn got ahold of me again and decided to teach me herself.

I couldn't really argue with that reasoning.

Today, we had to deal with all of the meetings. But for the past couple of days, Byn had been teaching me how to control and use my fire zirilium. We went far outside the city limits, close to a nearby river, so if anything went wrong we had a backup option.

We also weren't ready at the time for anybody outside of the Valwain to know about my abilities.

In my training with Byn, I realized fire zirilium acted a lot like air zirilium. They both had a desire to run free, and they were difficult to give shape to. They practically had a mind of their own. Other zirilium, such as crystal and ice, were easily moldable, but fire just wanted to spread and take over everything in its path. I realized quickly that the hardest part of learning to control it was trying to only set fire to certain things, or only parts of an object. It took a good amount of concentration, but I was successfully able to burn our props appropriately, after some practice.

Byn had brought multiple objects from around The Haven that nobody would miss—a random stool that didn't have a place, an unused comb, an empty leather notebook, and a very unpleasant looking hat.

I was able to set fire to them according to Byn's instructions *almost* completely successfully. Though, when he asked me to set fire to only the rim of the hat, I ended up burning the entire thing to ashes. But his way of instructing was calm, patient, and thorough—since he could feel what I was feeling, he was able to help talk me through guiding my energy past my emotions. The next three objects, thanks to his help, I set fire to perfectly.

Beyond learning to control the fire, he showed me how to bend the flames into different shapes and arcs, and how to create dagger and sword like shapes. He showed me how to make fireballs, and how to control how large they were.

I figured that already knowing how to wield air helped a lot in my ability to pick up so easily on fire, and I'd never been more grateful for all the times I snuck out of Gatlyn Castle as a child to practice my abilities.

Byn was still stunned that my fire burned so hot it was almost completely blue, but I could feel that he was proud, too.

The knocks came against the bedroom door again, and this time Byn rolled out of bed, stumbling blurry eyed to the door.

I hadn't slept in my own room since we got back. I'd grown too accustomed to falling asleep in my husband's arms.

"Giles. It's barely dawn," Byn said, his shirtless form filling the crack in the door, not opening it all the way.

I couldn't hear the stuttering reply Giles gave, but I could tell by the set in Byn's shoulders that he was already annoyed.

And today's meetings hadn't even started yet.

"Alright, alright, I understand," he said in reply to something else Giles said, then shut the door and rested against it before he leaned his head back and stared at the ceiling.

"It's going to be an extremely long day, isn't it?" he asked, not breaking eye contact with the ceiling.

I climbed out of bed and padded across the room toward him. I wrapped my arms around his waist and rested my chin on his chest, staring up at him as I replied.

"I fear so. But at least we'll be together, no?" I asked.

His lips lifted into a small smile as he looked down at me, wrapping me up in his arms and holding me tightly as he placed a kiss on the top of my head.

"Yes, at least there's that. You remember the plan?" he questioned, and I nodded.

Supposedly, there had been a lot of talk about me being crowned as queen. A lot of the nobles and advisors weren't fond of having a *purebred* Northerner as queen, so Byn and I came up with a plan, just in case things got out of hand.

We wouldn't show our hand unless forced, though.

"I won't have them disrespecting what's mine," he said lowly, placing his chin atop my head, and I could feel his anger and possessiveness beginning to bubble up in my chest. When he heard what the people were saying about me, he went completely silent. It was odd, seeing somebody so upset that they went silent. Father always lashed out—you always knew when he was angry. But Byn had masked all emotion from his face, and if I weren't able to feel his emotions, I never would've known the fact had made him so upset and frustrated. That was when we hatched our idea as backup, just in case things got out of hand today.

In all honesty, part of me wanted things to get out of hand during the meetings, just so I could show off and put an end to all the talk.

"Come," I said softly, "let's go get ready."

I pulled away and turned toward the washroom, but before I could take more than two steps, Byn's hand was lightly collaring my throat.

I forgot how to breathe in that moment.

With him lightly pulling, I stepped backward until I was flush with Byn's chest. Then his other hand was there, shifting my hair to expose the side of my neck.

"I did say *another time*, and that was days ago..." he trailed off as his head dipped, his lips barely grazing my skin as he spoke. The contact felt like lightning sizzling along my skin.

I inhaled sharply as he lightly scraped his teeth against the soft spot just under my ear, and my hand flew up to tangle in his sleep-mussed hair.

Seemingly encouraged, his kisses became more purposeful as he placed a trail of them down the column of my neck. My zirilium felt like miniature explosions inside my veins as a small, breathy sound escaped my lips. Byn's grip on my throat tightened before it was gone all together, replaced with his hand at my waist. He swiftly turned me around to face him, tangling his hand in my hair and tugging, forcing me to look up at him.

The sudden switch up caused me to gasp, but before the sound could even completely leave my mouth, Byn's lips crashed into mine, as if he could devour the sounds I was making.

This kiss was hungry, possessive. He nipped at my bottom lip, and I granted him the access he was seeking. Our tongues fought for dominance, but he eventually won, sweeping in and claiming what was his.

We broke apart a moment later, both panting lightly. My chest felt warm from all of the love and desire we were both feeling.

Staring into my eyes, he asked, "I want to test something. Do you trust me?"

"Always," I responded, no hesitation to be found in my voice.

A mischievous smirk overcame his handsome face, flexing his dimple. I watched curiously as he reached a hand out towards my left wing, which was flared slightly, and lightly ran his fingers over one of the most sensitive parts.

I couldn't stop the soft, pleased sound that escaped my lips.

My hand flew up, covering my mouth, and I could tell by the heat in my ears and face that I was bright pink.

"I thought so," Byn said quietly. I tilted my head up to meet his eyes, and couldn't help but notice how proud of himself he looked. As if he had just uncovered a great mystery. I shuddered as he reached out and repeated the movement, biting the inside of my cheek to keep from embarrassing myself again.

Just that simple movement had my blood singing for him, my heart pounding. But before he could reach for me once again, I forced myself to take a step backwards.

"We have meetings to attend today," I said, shaking my head, as though I could clear the fog looming there anytime Byn came too close.

"I could attend to *you* today, instead," Byn suggested, though with the look in his eyes, I knew he was aware I was right. I raised an eyebrow at him, almost in a challenge.

"Let's go get ready," he said after he took a few deep breaths, holding his hand out towards me. I gladly slid my hand into his, and together we headed for the washroom.

The sun had fully risen and was blessing Cairnyl with its light by the time we were ready to make our appearance.

We coordinated our outfits for today—silver and gold, black and white, moon and sun. Opposites in almost every way, yet working together in perfect harmony.

I picked out a long, frilly, black dress with silver lace accents on the sleeves, chest, and hem. There was a long slit down the side that showed my leg as I walked, and I was wearing a pair of black heels. I thought wearing black would wash out my features, but surprisingly, it brought them out more—the white of my hair, my pale skin, my blue eye.

The whole outfit was thanks to Teagan, who would be joining us for the meetings today. Apparently, a minimum of two members of the Valwain had to be present.

I left my hair down today, hanging in long waves down my back and fluffed up my bangs. I placed the black eyepatch over my green eye, sliding it perfectly in place so it wouldn't budge until I wanted it to.

Exiting the washroom, I stumbled upon Byn slipping the last button on his vest in place.

He was wearing a pair of white pants and one of his favorite white shirts, both with golden details. Though what made him truly look regal was a golden vest with white accents on it, swooping in detailed patterns across his chest and back.

Atop his head was his golden circlet, one that was open in the front, looping around his head and each end, stopping at his temples. Both ends had a small sun on them, and the rest was crafted to look like vines.

He caught my eye, and I could see his breath hitch as he took in my appearance.

"Sometimes, I truly can't fathom that you're my wife," he said breathlessly, crossing the room in a few long strides and taking my face gently in his hands—none of the possessiveness present from before. He kissed me passionately, and I had to force myself to hold back a groan of pleasure.

"Byn," I gasped, breaking off the kiss. "We have to get going."

He sighed, then seemed to remember something suddenly. "I have a gift for you!" he said, then rushed to the wardrobe.

He came back out with a small square box with yet another bow on top.

"Byn, you really don't have to—"

"Please, just open it. I definitely had to," he said, gently pushing the box into my hands.

I shot him a playful glare, which earned me a wink that made me blush just a bit.

I tugged the lid of the box off and gasped as I peered inside.

It was a silver circlet that complimented his perfectly. Instead of two suns on the ends that rested on the temples, there were two crescent moons facing inward. The part that looped around the back of the head was made up of different zirilium—one was vines like his, while another looked like waves, and the last one reminded me of lightning bolts. All three were intertwined and sort of loosely braided together, connecting together again at each moon at the front.

"I wanted to incorporate each zirilium somehow, but with ten, it's harder to accomplish than I thought it would be. I hope this is good enough," he said, rubbing the back of his neck nervously.

"I love it. I absolutely love it. Thank you so much," I said, taking the circlet from the box and holding it, examining the details.

"Here, let me help you put it on," he offered, and after another moment of admiring it, I handed it over to him.

He led me to stand in front of the full length mirror in the corner of the room. Standing behind me, he gently adorned me with the circlet, making sure it held my loose hair in place out of my face.

I couldn't help but smile.

I never in my life thought I'd have a love like this.

Tears sprung to my eyes, and Byn felt the shift in my emotions instantly. He came to stand in front of me and gently gripped my chin, forcing me to look at him. I could see the question in his eyes and concern on his face without him even speaking a word.

"I just... I never thought I could be loved like this. I'm so, *so* grateful for you," I explained, blinking back my tears.

He smiled sadly and pressed a light kiss to my lips.

"Avi, you're worthy of everything you never thought you deserved. Everything, and so much more," he said softly.

I took in a shuddering breath, nodding, and he embraced me tightly. I returned his hug, clinging to him as though he might slip through my fingers like fine sand.

***

Giles led us from the private wing to what I referred to as the business side of The Haven. That was where all the main meeting rooms, royal library, and formal dining halls were. Giles and Byn were discussing the topics at hand for today, and I should probably have listened in, but I found my mind wandering.

Speaking of the library, I made a mental note to check in on Laurence at the next possible opportunity. I wasn't even sure if he knew I'd returned.

I readjusted the eyepatch on my face, my nerves starting to overcome me. Back home, Father never had me attend any meetings with his advisors or nobles—only Dimitri, as his heir, was permitted. I'd never had to sit in front of so many people I was aware disliked me before.

We were just down the hallway from what must have been the meeting room we were attending today when Giles said something that caught my ear. My attention zoned back in to the conversation at hand when I heard the name *Ashford* pass Giles' lips.

"I'm sorry, can you say that last part again?" I asked the stout male.

He wasn't much to look at—he wore a pair of crooked spectacles, had graying, brown hair the color of packed earth, and was barely taller than I was.

"I said that Lord and Lady Ashford won't be in attendance at today's meetings—they're home caring for a sick loved one, from what I hear," Giles explained for the second time.

I stopped dead in my tracks, my mind reeling.

I might have even more family.

There was nobody else listed on the lineage lines in the royal library. Maybe it was a family friend? Because another relative would have to be registered in the records, right? Who else was out there that I knew nothing about?

I could feel myself starting to panic, my lungs constricting, when Byn placed a steading hand on the small of my back, leading me a few paces away from where Giles stood.

In a hushed voice, Byn asked, "What can I do? What is it?" Concern was written all over his face, his brow creased.

"The Ashford family—that's the family my mother descends from. Byn, if their reasoning for not attending holds true, and it's a relative they're taking care of, I could have even more family out there," I said quietly, wringing my hands together to keep them from shaking.

What kind of experiences had I missed out on, not knowing I had more family than just Dimitri out in the world? What relationships could I have cultivated? Did they even know I existed?

Byn visibly reeled back in shock at my revelation.

"Really?" he asked. When I nodded, he said, "It's just... I've grown up around the Ashfords. Everybody knows—or believes—their daughter died during the war, but I would have never made the connection..." he said, trailing off.

He looked at me for a moment, and took a second to analyze me. As though finally accepting this news, he said softly, "I've seen portraits of your mother when she was young, hung up in the Ashford house. You have her eye under there." He cupped the right side of my face and ran a thumb over the edge of my eyepatch.

I set my lips in a firm line to keep them from quivering, and I shook my head as if I could physically clear the fog of questions building up in my mind.

"We can deal with this later. Right now, we have more important matters to attend to," I said, squaring my shoulders and wings back.

Byn began to open his mouth to object, but I held out my hand before he could utter a word.

"Together," I said.

He smiled softly as he slid his hand into mine. "Together," he agreed.

Soon we arrived at the tall, delicately carved wooden doors, hand in hand. Giles opened them, announcing us as we entered.

Everybody in the room stood as we made our entrance, my heels clicking against the marble floor. I stared straight ahead, chin held high, at the high backed wooden chairs that were obviously meant for royalty. The Thorntier family crest was engraved on the high backs, and it wasn't until Byn and I walked closer that I realized the one to the left had been carved specifically to accommodate wings.

My eyes flickered to Byn's as he walked over to the chair and pulled it out for me to sit in. I knew he could feel the swell of emotion in my chest, the gratitude and joy and thankfulness. His eyes softened when his gaze met mine, and he dipped his head slightly in acknowledgment.

I sat, my dress pooling around me, and I allowed my wings to flare out slightly, taking up extra space in the altered chair.

Byn sat to my right, crossing one ankle over his knee. He waved a hand halfheartedly, and everybody in the room took this as a sign to be seated. For the first time since we stepped foot into the room, I allowed myself to subtly look around.

Like most rooms in The Haven, the room was crafted from different stones and a soft, honey colored wood. There were giant wooden pillars holding the ceiling up, carved to look like vines were climbing them. In the middle of the room hung a giant chandelier, ordained with pure, transparent crystals that I imagined were dug from the very earth we stood on. The round table before us was made of one solid piece of dark stone, but had countless small, clear crystals mixed into the stone. The crystals in the table reminded me of the chandelier.

Taking a look around the table, I couldn't help but notice how many people were present. Most were males, some with their wives, but there were a few solo females present. With that, I was impressed. From what I understood, my father only allowed the males of the Northern families to represent themselves before him.

I noticed Teagan sitting on the other side of Byn, our three chairs the only ones with high backs and family crests on them. I dipped my chin ever so slightly in her direction, a sign of respect, and she bowed her head in return. Finally, after the room had been silent for what felt like ages, Byn spoke.

"I apologize for the delay of this meeting. I had other matters to attend to. Now, I have heard the talks of the people, and I can say simply that I am not pleased with what I've heard. I will give you all one opportunity to speak your mind, then I expect these matters to be put to rest, am I understood?"

The room murmured their understandings.

"Now, who would like to represent you all in voicing your concerns?" Byn asked.

I stole a look at my husband. His spine was as straight as a sword, shoulders rolled back, and chin held high. He reflected my own body language almost perfectly. If it weren't for the tension I could see in the set of his shoulders, I would almost think he was comfortable leading meetings like this.

I admired him, really. I knew he had been trained for all of this since he was a small child, but he truly did make it look easy. He was practically a natural.

The only thing giving him away was the anxiety I felt in my chest that I recognized as his.

"Well?" Byn asked again.

This time, a handful of people turned their heads to look at one male sitting directly across the table from me. He had a shaved head, but the small hairs you could see were distinctly gray. His skin was a few shades darker than Byn's, as though he worked outside his entire life and was permanently colored by the sun. He wore an outfit of teal and black, and I could tell by the way he held himself that he saw himself in high regards.

Acknowledging the looks tossed his way, he cleared his throat and slowly stood.

"Your Majesty, I mean no disrespect, but a lot of us, including myself, are not fond of this... *union* between yourself and the Heartshire family. We understand it has brought peace—but at what cost?" the male said.

"Do go on, Farrowtide," Byn said, leaning forward in his chair.

I saw the male's throat bob before he seemed to double down.

"King Thorntier, do you really expect us to be alright with you willingly tainting the bloodline of your family? The name your parents died to uphold?"

Byn seemed to seethe at the mention of his parents. His anger was palpable as he said, "Do not dare to speak about my parents in such a manner, Thomas."

For some reason, Thomas Farrowtide continued on, despite the clear warning.

"All I'm saying is, you can't expect all of us to simply accept the fact that for the first time in Southern history, we have a full blooded *Northerner* as our queen. Not only a Northerner, but a non-wielder at that! All the signs to reject her were there, as clear as signs from the Stars come. I mean, she's a *crid* for crying out loud!"

At that, I felt Byn's anger ignite in my chest, as though there was so much of it, it overflowed into my own body.

A crid, or cridual, was a common slur for Northerners, meaning worthless, dirty, talentless, or useless. I only knew this from books—I never thought I'd actually be called one to my face.

Before Byn could set the male on fire, I stood swiftly. Thinking only of our plan, I slammed my palm face down on the top of the table, making direct eye contact with Farrowtide and focusing all of my energy.

My hands, which were adorned with my gloves that nobody noticed before now, were presently on full display as the ground began to shake. The stone and crystal table beneath my hand began to crack, the sound ear-splitting. The crack went from directly under my hand, toward Farrowtide and reaching him in the span of just a couple heartbeats.

Then, the table broke in half completely before us.

The people screamed and scrambled, moving out of the way as the pieces of the table landed on the ground with a heavy *thud*.

Byn was unphased, still seated, but even Teagan was now standing a few paces away.

I didn't look away from Farrowtide, though. Not even as I walked between the pieces of broken stone and crystal, heading straight for him.

I focused my energy again, conjuring a fireball to the palm of my left hand. Farrowtide's eyes widened so far I thought they might pop out of his head. He started trying to retreat, so with my other hand, I forced plants up through the marble floor. Focusing through my sun stones, I called to the plants, making them wrap around the male's ankles and up his legs until he was rooted in place.

I stood before him now, ball of blue fire in hand, calmly seething.

"I may be Northern, but make no mistake, I am no crid. I belong here just as much as you do," I said firmly, loud enough so the whole room heard.

With that, I yanked the eyepatch from my face and stuffed it in the pocket of my dress, staring Farrowtide in the eyes.

The male gasped as he noticed my eye, which had been hidden up until now from the people, as well as my gloves and the fireballs I'd made. He tried to free himself, but only stumbled and fell to the ground. He cowered, covering his head with his arms.

"I-I'm so sorry, my queen! I meant no harm!" he said, his body shaking.

I scoffed, and turned on my heel to face the rest of the crowd.

"I may not be a full-blooded Southerner, but make no mistake, I *am* Southern," I said, looking around the room at the different expressions on the people's faces. Fear, shock, worry.

"I *am* your queen. And while this male," I pointed behind me to Farrowtide, "claims the Stars warned you all of me, I object. The Stars have *blessed* me, as I wield all ten zirilium—both Northern and Southern," I said, my voice loud and steady. "If anything, I'm *assisting* the Thorntier bloodline."

I waved a hand toward the broken table, and though I made it look effortless, I was focusing like I'd never focused before. Thanks to my zirilium, the table slowly pieced itself back together. I used earth to break it, and I used crystal to fix it. Mending the gap between the two broken pieces by forcing the crystals to grow and fuse together, I focused until all that showed that the table had once been broken was the shock of clear crystals running down the middle of it, once again a perfect circle.

With that, I took a page out of Byn's book and raised my hand, snapping towards the ceiling. With that, I conjured up a small storm of gray clouds inside of the room. The people retreated, standing along the walls and cowering, but I carried on. I forced the wind to pick up, ruffling the hair and clothes of everybody in the room.

"Now," I said loud enough to be heard over the air ripping at me, "can we all carry on with these meetings in peace, or are there more objections to my presence here?" I asked, looking around the room at the different males and females.

When nobody spoke out against me, I flicked a wrist towards the ceiling, and the clouds slowly dispersed before they let loose any rain, taking the violent winds with them.

I smoothed down my dress and hair, and as an afterthought, released Farrowtide of the plants holding him in place. I calmly walked around the table and sat back down in my chair. I maintained a calm, neutral mask, one without much emotion on my face.

The chandelier was still shaking from the winds as Byn said, "If that's all, I'd like to discuss more important matters now."

Chapter Twenty

It'd been weeks since my display at that first meeting, and since then, almost every day has been full of meeting after meeting. We discussed crop distribution, taxes, building new roads between towns, the profits from the mines at the ravine, and a ton of other topics I would have never even thought about.

Byn took the lead during the meetings majority of the time, but sometimes another Valwain member did instead, depending on the subject at hand. Quinn always took the lead when it came to any topic regarding the South's soldiers, and Teagan and Rayven were always on top of communication with the North, which seemed to be growing sparse.

Today was the first day in weeks that we had a break—a moment to breathe. Byn insisted on taking me into town, down into the heart of Cairnyl. He wanted to show me the place he grew up—and he also wanted to find a thank you gift for Teagan, who had been present at almost every meeting alongside us. She didn't have to be, but she endured with us, and I know Byn was secretly relieved to have his sister to rely on.

First thing on the agenda this morning was to head to the dens to check up on Atlas and Lychen, along with Lychen's mate, Gaia. Apparently, there were a couple different dens throughout

Cairnyl, but Atlas and Lychen were the only Titan Wolves on active duty, so they were kept the closest.

After giving the wolves their breakfast and belly rubs, we met up with Quinn and Rayven at the perch. That was where all of the corvids in Cairnyl stayed, and were bred and trained. Rayven had just finished checking the latest letters when we arrived, and offered to show me around.

He explained how they tied the vials to the birds legs and slid small notes inside that they then transported across the continent. He told me how the birds were divided into sectors, each one taught how to go to a specific location or town. Then he showed me where the corvids favorite spot to be pet was, and I got to apply this knowledge to Lark, who wasn't quite as intimidating as he was before.

In an effort to also relax, Rayven and Quinn offered to walk around town with us. Though, truthfully, I didn't think either of them knew what the word *relax* really meant.

They now walked a few paces behind Byn and me, their bodies stiff and mechanical. It seemed neither one of them could turn off the soldier or spy in them.

A few paces behind them, though, walked Laurence.

After my outburst at the first meeting, I went to go find him and offered him the job of being my personal guard. There was nobody I knew that I trusted more for the task, and now he was always within a few paces of me.

The male almost cried at the offer I gave him. I made sure he'd be paid handsomely, but it was the honor and care I put into asking that had him emotional. I may not have known him very long, but he reminded me of the father I always wished I could have had. He accepted the assignment with glee, happy to be of service to the royals of the South, who had saved him all those years ago. He'd even become friendly with Byn now, who was happy I now had extra security.

In the beginning, I thought I would hate having a constant shadow, but I'd grown quite comfortable with his presence. I made sure he took a day to himself every week, whatever day I spent with one of the Valwain, and that he was only with me during the day time. I'd hate to overwork him, but he was devout and stubborn.

Now, my hand rested on the inside of Byn's elbow as we walked into the heart of Cairnyl. It almost took my breath away, how cozy and warm it was here during late-spring. So different from the Salic Mountains I hailed from.

Every storefront was painted a bright shade, each color of the rainbow appearing at least once. There were large windows at the front of every building, giving a sneak peek of what that store was offering. The cobbled road was worn down from years of use, and there was a small yet beautiful fountain in the middle of the square, the centerpiece displaying one of the Southern kings of old that I didn't know the name of.

Though all of us were dressed in casual-wear today, we all got recognized every time we turned onto a new street. I thought my features were the most noticeable—white plait down my back, pale skin, wings. But I tried my best to blend in today. I had a simple, form framing lavender shirt on and gray cotton pants that flared out as they went down my legs. I wasn't accustomed to all of the attention we were receiving, but Byn paused and talked to each person who stopped him, greeting most of them by name. Suddenly, it reminded me of how he treated the people back in Diorum.

After saying his farewells to the latest person who came to say hello, Byn gasped at something he saw in the storefront of a bright yellow building, and tugged me into the store with him, the rest of our party ducking inside behind us.

Byn gently let go of my hand and gave me a quick kiss on the cheek before walking to the back of the store to talk to who I assumed was the owner and craftsman of the shop.

Rayven and Quinn followed Byn, stopping to look at different art pieces hung up on the walls as they went. Laurence stayed nearby, always within earshot of me. I turned towards the display in the front of the shop's window and admired the different art pieces they had presented. Beautifully crafted leather sheaths for swords and daggers of all sizes, banners showing off the Thorntier family crest, and a stunning art piece that depicted the market square right outside in all of its beauty.

I looked out through the window as a mother and her young daughter stopped and stared into the shop, pointing at the paintings and banners, smiling. The mother leaned down and said something that made the little girl laugh, and I felt a pang of envy and sadness strike through me at the sight.

The two females carried on in their walk, and I continued to watch the people come and go, until one person in particular caught my eye as she approached, glancing at the sheaths on display.

The female on the other side of the glass couldn't have been more than two or three years older than I was. She had short, wavy hair, such a dark brown it was practically black. Her skin was olive toned—not as dark as Rayven's, but not as light as Byn's, either. Her eyes, though, were striking—a brown center surrounded by a ring of moss-colored green—the perfect hazel.

It was only when she looked up from beneath the black hood obscuring her features and met my eyes that I realized why I found her face so interesting.

The firm set of her lips, the straight of her nose, the crease between her brows—even the shape of her face resembling a heart.

She looked almost identical to Mother.

My jaw went slack, and the girl seemed to have a similar reaction to my own appearance. She stumbled back, as though physically struck.

Then, she made a run for it.

I busted out of the shop, not bothering to tell Byn or Laurence what I was doing. My mission was simple—catch up to her and talk to her.

Ask her why she looked so much like my mother.

"Wait!" I called out to her, but she was already weaving her way through the crowd at full speed.

"*Stars,*" I cursed under my breath, then set off in a sprint, in the direction I last saw her.

The buildings and clothes of the people were mostly colorful, so the female's black cloak stood out like a sore thumb as I gently yet firmly pushed my way through the crowds of other fae who were simply out shopping for the day.

I decided to run instead of startling the people around me by flying, and I listened for the sound of the female's soft footfall over the sound of my own. The boots she was wearing had a small heel on them, clicking against the cobblestone ground with every step she took.

Soon, we cleared the crowds in the square and made it down a side road. I heard Laurence telling me to wait up from somewhere behind me, but the female just turned down another street and I feared I was close to losing her. The thought carried my feet even faster than before.

"Please! Wait!" I yelled out to her as I rounded the corner, and suddenly we were running down a straight, narrow street with nobody else on it.

The female never bothered to look back, but my words seemed to frighten her as she picked up the pace and raced ahead even farther.

She made a swift, sharp turn down a dark alleyway. I caught up a few heartbeats later, rounding the corner and saying, "Please—" when I realized the alleyway was empty, and led to a dead end.

There was no female present. Nothing but a couple trash cans, boxes, and some litter. The alleyway was drenched in shadows, so

I walked the length of it, thinking maybe she'd hidden behind one of the trash cans, but she was simply gone.

I returned to the mouth of the alley when Laurence finally caught up, out of breath. I was panting myself, my heart pounding from the chase, but I was more confused and frustrated than anything.

"What," he panted, "was that?"

"I... I saw somebody. She-she looked like—" I was cut off by the sound of a blood curdling scream in the distance.

From this part of town, we were closer to the forest now—I could see the tree line in the distance. I realized with a start that it was the sound of a female screaming, but then I heard it.

Chirps.

Distressed chirps.

I knew without a doubt those were the sounds of a griffin—not any sort of normal bird or beast. I'd grown up in a place with far too many griffins for me not to be able to recognize them.

Just then, I saw Byn round the corner, along with Quinn and Rayven, coming from the direction of the town square.

I took one heartbeat to meet Byn's eyes, and I knew he heard the noises, too. He dipped his head once, then jerked his chin towards the sky. I could feel his anxiety in my chest, but I pushed it down, not letting it overpower me.

Trying to keep my mind clear, I began to flap my wings forcefully, launching into the sky.

I heard Laurence curse as he watched me take off.

I didn't know who was in trouble, where they were, or what they did, but I needed to find out. And somehow, I knew Byn understood.

I loved him all the more for it.

I flew up and over the buildings of Cairnyl, flying in a wide circle until I pinpointed where the screams were coming from.

They sounded closer to the forest than to the town, so I quickly readjusted my course to head that way.

The closer to the forest I got, the louder the voice and chirps became.

"There's been a huge misunderstanding!" the female voice called out, and I spotted her in the same moment, right on the outskirts of the forest, thankfully outside of town.

I realized as I listened to her cry out that I knew that voice.

I'd heard it most recently in my dreams.

I saw the small group then—the numerous guards that had ropes over both captives—a Northerner and a griffin.

Aurora and Eden.

I recognized the smokey gray wings of Aurora and her shock of light blonde hair, along with the white and gray feathers of Eden. I narrowed my wings, dipping down to get closer.

"I need to see her! You don't understand!" Aurora cried out, fighting against the ropes wrapped around her torso, holding her arms in place by her sides.

Eden snapped at one of the guards who came too close, but there was two on each side of her, all holding ropes they'd thrown across her back to keep her in place.

I landed forcefully, the ground beneath my feet rippling like water a couple feet around me, the earth shooting up in small, jagged spikes. I hadn't even felt the energy leave my body, my heart pounding in my chest.

"Release them," I said sternly, staring down the guards, my face void of emotion.

When they hesitated, I stepped forward out of my ring of jagged earth. "*Now*," I said, venom dripping from my voice.

To my surprise, I wasn't panicked like I previously would have been. I simply wanted to get to my best friend and griffin, and I didn't like that *my* guards weren't following orders.

After I said that, they shared glances with one another, then dropped the ropes and backed up quickly, as though fearful.

I rushed forward, reaching for Aurora, who was now knelt on the ground, struggling against the ropes tied tightly around her, her arms, and her wings.

"Here, let me," I said gently, making quick work of the ropes and throwing them to the side. From the corner of my eye, I saw Eden shaking off her ropes, too.

"Aviva." Aurora sounded exhausted yet relieved as she fell into my arms, and for the first time, I got a truly good look at her.

She was dirty from head to toe, like she'd been traveling for a while. Her light blue dress was ripped near her shoulder, and her hair was hanging down in a tangled mess. Eden didn't look much better, I realized, both of them sharing matching purple eye bags.

I hugged her tightly to my body, then pulled back and brushed the hair from her face.

"Aurora, not that I'm unhappy you're here, but this was reckless. What happened? What brought you here?" I said softly to the female who was once my closest friend in the world, not wanting the guards to overhear.

Finally, Aurora picked her head up and looked me in the eyes. To my surprise, she didn't even acknowledge the change in my appearance since the last time I saw her, or the way the earth just moved beneath my feet a moment ago.

But what she said next knocked the breath out of my lungs.

"I came to warn you," she said breathlessly. "Aviva, you don't have much time. A battle is coming."

Chapter Twenty-One

I t took us longer than I'd like to admit to make it back to The Haven. Aurora was exhausted and leaned on me the entire way, slowing us down, but I didn't mind.

Shortly after Aurora relayed her message to me, Byn and the rest of the group found us. Once I explained who Aurora and Eden were, Byn simply asked what I needed.

Byn took Eden for me, after I introduced him to her and showed her that he was trustworthy. He mentioned taking her to the den where Atlas and Lychen stay, since they didn't exactly have a place to keep griffins, to feed her and clean her up.

Seeing my husband care for my griffin was a sight I never thought I'd see, and it pulled at my heart strings to watch.

Rayven went with Byn, while Laurence and Quinn trailed behind Aurora and me as we all hiked back to The Haven. Quinn tried to object to taking her into our home, but I reassured her that Aurora was like a sister to me. Quinn mumbled something about that not meaning much nowadays, but I didn't take the bait, ignoring her and taking Aurora down the private wing, to the room I had originally stayed in. The room still had some of my old clothes—dresses and such that I knew Aurora would feel more comfortable in.

Teagan and I had been redoing my wardrobe the past few weeks, adding in regal dresses for formalities, as well as things I've found *I'm* comfortable in. Things that made me feel more like myself, such as trousers and vests. For once, I was in a place in my life where I could dress for myself instead of for everybody else, and I'd been taking advantage of that.

That was why I was still so surprised that Aurora hadn't said anything about my appearance yet. Not only the change in eye color or display of power, but also the way I dressed and held myself.

I was chalking it up to the shock and exhaustion, but this still didn't seem like the same female I knew.

Something had changed.

Or maybe it was simply that *I'd* changed.

Once we made it into my old chambers, I leaned Aurora against the bed and gathered up some clean clothes, then set off towards the washroom. I started her a hot bath, using some fancy soaps that smelled like eucalyptus to create lots of bubbles in it for her.

Barely speaking any words to each other, I did for her what she used to do for me countless times after exhausting myself using my zirilium—I helped bathe her.

I turned my head while she undressed, then turned back after I heard her settle into the bubbly water. She let out a long sigh of relief, and I could see some of the tension in her shoulders melt away, the same way the dirt slid off of her pale skin.

"So," I said as I used my zirilium to pour some water from the bath onto her head, drenching only her hair, "would you rather talk to me about things now, or would you rather us continue this in silence, and you explain everything afterward to not only myself, but my husband, as well?"

Aurora shot me a look I couldn't quite place, and that stunned me momentarily. Usually I could zone in on her expressions and the emotions they held—I'd known her for so long, it was like second nature.

Maybe I've just been away too long, I thought.

"Just you, Viva," she said finally, and I nodded.

I reached over and handed her some soap, then made a motion, encouraging her to talk as she cleaned off.

As she began to talk, I started to shampoo her long, bright blonde hair, massaging her scalp with care. After her hair, I moved onto her wings, delicately washing them free of dirt and sweat. They hung over the sides of the tub, which was obviously not meant for Northerners.

Despite everything, she had still always been there for me. The least I could do was return the favor.

"It all started when I overheard your father and Dimi talking in one of the lounge rooms. I had just been walking by, but I heard my name and stopped to listen. I thought maybe they were talking about me and my progress with Hugo as far as my trokav training went, but I was sorely mistaken."

Aurora took a shuddering breath before continuing on. "They were going to try to kill me. Well, King Heartshire was, anyways. When Dimi asked why, all the king said was that I *had information I shouldn't,* and that I had to be *taken care of.* I don't know what he thinks I know—the only thing I can think of is that he finally caught on to me knowing about your zirilium, but I can't know for sure now. Anyways, Dimi must have panicked, because he suggested instead of killing me, they simply throw me into the dungeons to *rot,*" she said the last part with anger, but I could see the tears that glistened in her eyes that told me she was hurting.

"Dimitri really suggested that?" I asked, stunned. The brother I knew wouldn't let anything like that happen to an innocent, especially Aurora.

Aurora nodded. "He's not the same since you left, Viva. He's cold, distant, and sometimes outright cruel. Your father has really started to depend on him, giving him bigger tasks and keeping him on a tight leash—nearby at all times. He's kept him under his wing like never before, and Dimi is suffering because of it. Your father is rubbing off on him in the worst ways possible. You would hardly recognize him now, after the past three months."

This information came like a punch to the gut. My twin was always so kind, so unbreakable in spirit, despite everything our father put him through. Hearing that Father had finally crushed his will... it must be much worse than I thought.

Before I could ask any questions about Dimitri, Aurora carried on. "That snippet of their conversation was enough for me to want to run by itself, but I was so scared, I was frozen in place. I stayed rooted to the spot, but now I'm grateful I did. The next thing Dimitri said was that they shouldn't worry about how to handle me until after the attack on Cairnyl. That the attack, which was happening so soon, should take priority over everything else. Your father, albeit begrudgingly, agreed."

Aurora took another deep breath, setting the soap on the rim of the porcelain tub.

"After I heard that bit, I snapped back to reality. I got out of there as fast as my wings could carry me. After I snuck Eden out, we didn't look back. You trained her well. I don't know how she knew, but she knew we needed to go right then and there. She's quite a trooper."

I took a moment to digest this information, forcing myself to remain calm, before asking, "When are they coming?"

Aurora looked down at the bubbles before her as she murmured, "Tomorrow night. They want to attack when the moon is out and strong so their moon stones have a constant charge as they fight."

I opened my mouth to talk, but was interrupted as Aurora turned her head to truly look at me for the first time since we entered The Haven.

"Your father used you as a ploy. He's claiming the South kidnapped you and forced you into marriage. That's why there was nobody there besides us during your send-off, and we were not even permitted at your wedding. He didn't want anybody to know his true plans. Aviva, he wants to rule the entire continent. And he's not afraid to kill everybody and *anybody* standing in his way."

My hands went still from where they were cleaning Aurora's wings as I listened to her speak. I wasn't *entirely* surprised at my father's lies and deceit, but I was surprised Aurora was able to make it here without much trouble to tell me all of this.

"Aurora, how exactly did you escape? How were you not caught?" I asked slowly, resuming my gentle strokes along her smokey gray wings, carefully keeping my expression neutral.

"I knew I couldn't leave Eden, nobody would have cared for her if I had left her. So I snuck her out like old times, then we took to the skies. The snow hasn't completely stopped yet in the mountains, despite us being far into spring now. So we used the clouds as coverage until we couldn't fly anymore, but I knew we weren't in the North anymore when we landed. Then, we walked through that forest for what felt like forever, until those guards found us," she explained. "I told Hugo before I left that I wasn't feeling well, and that I was going to stay with my parents down in Hollis for a few days. He didn't have any issues with that and accepted my leave on the spot."

Aurora surged forward suddenly, water sloshing over the sides slightly at the movement. Grabbing hold of my hands, her voice was dripping with concern as she said, "I had to make it to you—you had to know. You have to save yourself. You have to flee, get as far away as you can. Viva, your father will stop at nothing—he will strike you down the moment he sees you simply to cover his tracks."

I reeled back as if she had physically slapped me.

"You want me to do *what*? Aurora, I'm not going anywhere," I said, visibly shaken.

Aurora's brows furrowed and she shook her head, dropping my hands. "I don't understand. I came all this way to warn you—so you could *flee*. So you could *survive*."

"I'm not going to go into hiding while these fae stay behind and get slaughtered. I'm going to fight, to do my part. It's the least I can do," I said confidently.

To my surprise, Aurora let out a sharp laugh.

Once she caught her breath, she blurted out, "Let's be real—you can hardly even wield a sword!"

Offended and bristled, I let loose the grip on my fire zirilium until a ball of blue flames sat in the palm of my hand. I could see the reflection of my flames in her icy blue eyes.

"While that isn't even remotely true, I don't need swords anymore. A lot has changed, Aurora. *I've* changed," I said icily.

A beat of silence passed between us, so I tried to mend the gap. "I'll make sure you can stay here. You'll be safe. But I have to go tell the others about all of this."

Aurora's hand reached out and gripped my arm tightly before I could even stand up to depart. "What happened to you?" she asked, her voice quiet and slightly fearful.

I gently broke free of her grasp, standing up as I responded, "I finally found where I belong."

***

"But why *do* all of this? We had finally agreed on peace," Byn asked, not for the first time.

The first thing I did after helping Aurora get dressed in some of my old clothes was find Byn. Fortunately, he had already gathered the Valwain, plus Laurence. He pulled us into one of the private wing's meeting rooms, and I just started explaining everything Aurora had told me.

"It's my fault—I didn't realize my father was using our marriage as part of a grander scheme. I really thought he was capable of change, but this simply proves he isn't. Now it makes sense why he dismissed everybody from the room when he made Teagan his proposition about Byn marrying me, why next to nobody was allowed to see me off, and why there was no one on my side who attended the wedding." Then, I shrugged and added, "Also, he's simply power hungry. He always has been. I think it runs in his blood at this point."

It'd been a half hour since I found Byn and the others, and we were still figuring out how to process this information. One thing that surprised me, though, was how easily Byn and the Valwain took my word to heart. They didn't question me, or second guess me in any way.

It left that warm feeling in my chest.

Byn sighed, pinching the bridge of his nose. "I honestly didn't think we would have to face battle again so soon."

The energy in the room shifted as everybody remembered what the last battle had cost Byn, his sisters, and the entirety of the South.

Their king and queen.

Byn cleared his throat, his kingly mask falling back into place as he straightened up, then turned to Teagan.

"I need you and Lychen to go ahead and scout out our side of the border. Find a place for us to set up the army's camp—somewhere in Wittuck Woods, where they won't spot us as easily from the sky," he said. Teagan nodded, placing a fist over her heart and holding it there.

Byn turned to Chess next, making eye contact as he addressed each member. "I need you to get all of the trokavs ready. As many as you can, from any town you can send word to in time. I have a feeling the North will be extra brutal, and we're going to need all hands on deck."

Following Teagan's lead, Chess nodded, then placed his fist over his heart.

Addressing Quinn, Byn said, "Get our armies ready to fight. Armor buffed, weapons sharpened, sun stones charged up—the whole ordeal. We'll discuss strategy when we arrive at the border." Quinn mimicked Teagan's and Chess's movements.

Turning to Ezra, Byn's look softened as he took in the male who was as close as a brother. "Ezra, I know you won't like this, but I need you to remain here. Somebody has to keep an eye on Margo in case... in case we don't all make it back. The South will need her." His voice cracked just a bit as he spoke, but he recovered quickly, clearing his throat.

Ezra opened his mouth to argue, but Byn held up a hand and said firmly, "This isn't up for debate. Besides, you're not trained for the front lines, brother. Leave this part to us." He offered Ezra a smile, which Ezra meekly returned.

"I'll guard her with my life," Ezra said finally, dipping his head, then placing his fist over his chest, just as the others had done.

Faster than I could process, Margo pushed herself into the room, obviously having been eavesdropping.

"I want to help! Byn, *please!*" she cried out, running to him and tugging on his hand.

Byn kneeled down to her level and took her gloved hands into his. The size difference was astonishing—she was so small for her age, yet she had such a big heart, wanting to help her family and friends in any way possible.

"Margo, you have a *special* mission, one only the best little sister on the continent can accomplish. While we're gone, I need you to make sure The Haven, Cairnyl, and all the people in it are safe and cared for, alright?" he asked, his voice soft and gentle. "Can you do that for me?"

She sniffled and wiped at her eyes before any tears could fall. She nodded, then leaned close to his ear and whispered something.

His face lit up as he listened, then he nodded at her encouragingly. "Go ahead," he said to her.

She suddenly looked sheepish as she stepped into the circle the Valwain had loosely made around the room. We'd all been too anxious to sit down.

Margo pulled the pouch on her hip open and walked up to each and every one of us that were leaving, even Laurence and I, handing us identical, small charms that she'd obviously crafted herself. The gems and beads were different shades of green, her family's color, and had a small clasp at the end of them so they could be hooked onto clothing or such.

I didn't let it go unnoticed how she didn't allow her gloved hands to make contact with anybody else's skin. I might've asked about it before now, but it seemed like something the Thorntier siblings specifically didn't talk about, so I hadn't pushed.

Once she handed them all out, she stood close to Byn, handing him his last. Ezra placed a hand on her shoulder, and they shared a loving look full of soft smiles. Ezra and Margo were the only two not to have received one—likely because they were staying behind. Plus, Margo already had beads hanging from various places on her person.

"They're good luck charms," she said quietly. "So that you all come back."

I could feel a sharp pang of sadness strike through my chest, and I knew it wasn't only Byn's emotions, but my own.

Margo had experienced so much more than any eight-year-old should have to shoulder. Tears threatened to well in my eyes at the simple thought.

Everybody gave her their sincere thanks, hooking the charms onto different pieces of clothing or on an earring. I made sure to secure mine onto the lobe of my left ear so it dangled freely.

Byn straightened, clearing his throat, then turned to address Drayven.

"We're going to need backup," Byn said to him, some silent understanding passing between the two of them. "Do you think you can get them to come to our aid?" he asked.

Rayven nodded, placing his fist over his heart as he said sternly, "Leave it to me."

Byn nodded, then said, "Take Willow, my mother's Titan Wolf. She'll get you there faster than any other mode of transportation."

Rayven's eyes softened just slightly, but it was there.

Next, Byn turned to me, to my surprise.

"Aviva," he said my name fondly, "I know you haven't known us all that long, but if you'll take on the task, I'd appreciate your help near the front lines. You know your father and brother best, what moves they're most likely to make. Will you help us?" he asked.

I nodded as I responded, "I will. And I know I haven't trained long, but I want to fight, if there's no greater need for me. It's time I faced my father."

Byn looked pleasantly stunned at my words, but didn't object, despite the anxiety I could feel radiating off of him at the thought.

I placed my fist over my heart.

Byn turned to Laurence next, then looked back at me. He nodded slightly, giving me the encouragement I needed to address him.

"Laurence," I said, turning to the older male, our eyes locking as I spoke. "I have a special request of you. But you can say no or back out at any time, without any judgement from any of us, alright?"

Laurence nodded once. "I will accept any and all tasks you ask of me, Your Majesty."

He placed a fist over his heart, and I mimicked him once again.

Teagan followed suit, then Quinn, and soon every member in the room had their hand over their heart, even Margo—a silent agreement, a promise, a vow.

We all took a moment to look around the room, all of us quietly acknowledging that this could be our last time all together if things went wrong. I didn't miss the longing look Ezra and Quinn shared as their fingertips brushed, or the terrified look Margo cast Teagan and Byn.

Byn dismissed everybody, each person scrambling to get their affairs in order, knowing we had no time to waste. But before I could exit the room, a large, calloused hand lightly gripped my arm and pulled me to the side.

Turning on my heel, I came face to face with Rayven.

His face betrayed no emotions, and I wondered if he was the first person I hadn't been able to read.

"We never had a chance to practice your shadow wielding," he stated, his voice rough. He placed a small, black leather journal into my hands. "I've written down everything you need to know about the zirilium itself, and how basic maneuvers work. Take the time to read them. Shadows can be life-saving," he said firmly, and I knew he meant every word.

I nodded, taking the journal from him and slipping it into one of my many pockets.

"Thank you. I wish we could have had time to practice, but I'll make sure to go over this as many times as I can before the battle," I said, my voice sincere.

He nodded, as though reassuring himself more than me.

"Good luck," he said, then slipped out of the room, starting out on whatever private mission he'd been sent on.

Chapter Twenty-Two

I anxiously clasped my hands in my lap to stop myself from fidgeting or picking at my skin as I sat around the war table in the giant tent.

The entire force of the South that had been stationed in Cairnyl, plus anybody who could get here in time from some of the smaller cities, had set up camp in this forest—Wittuck Woods. That was as close as we could get to the border without losing too much coverage from the trees, since Quinn and Byn wanted to make sure we couldn't be spotted easily from the sky.

Unfortunately, that meant instead of the battle happening at the border between territories, it'd happen just half a day's trek from Cairnyl, much farther into the heart of our territory than any of us had wanted. Quinn claimed the element of surprise was too important to lose, though, especially if my father was bringing the entire might of the North.

Fortunately, this meant the Northern fae would have had to fly farther, hopefully tiring them out to a degree before they arrived. It also meant the battle would happen closer to the morning, rather than the middle of the night, as we thought it would be when originally planning to fight at the border. We'd only have to stall them a few hours before the sun would come up, the strength of our sun stones rising with it.

Byn gently slid his hand over mine, likely sensing the anxiety welling in my chest, threatening to spill over.

"I believe that covers just about everything. Quinn, share all of this with your army captains, and make sure every single one of our soldiers are educated on the North's fighting style and army layouts. Chess, same goes for you—make sure the trokavs know what wounds they'll likely be facing, so they can be prepared," Byn said, squeezing my hand then releasing as he got to his feet. The others around the table—Teagan, Chess, Quinn, myself, and Laurence—all followed suit.

We'd been sitting in this tent for hours, ever since we arrived at the campsite, around this giant table that held a map of our entire continent and its islands. Laurence, though not an official member of the Valwain yet, had been a huge help in breaking down the North's armies and how they were organized. How they often used their weather wielders at the start of the larger battles to make it rain, sleet, and snow, so the rest of the wielders had unlimited ammunition to add to what they themselves could conjure. How they were some of the most protected of the army because of that, and how the air wielders were often on the front lines—deemed the most expendable yet also deadly.

On top of Laurence's insight on their armies, I was able to give the group a glimpse into their fighting style, with Quinn's captains being brought in at that point to study and pass on the information. Dimitri was taught by only the best of the North, and he taught me everything I knew. I used bows, rapiers, swords, daggers, and more, showing everybody what, exactly, I was taught. My body glided through the familiar motions, though my cheeks heated as all eyes settled on me, studying and analyzing, breaking down every movement.

After my demonstrations were finished and the Southern captains were dismissed, the Valwain finalized our army's movements and positions on the sprawling map atop the war table.

Weariness began creeping into my bones from the journey here and the hours spent preparing, but I knew there would be no time to rest, at least not anytime soon. There was still much to do.

Chess asked Byn a question I didn't hear as we all started to head for the tent's entrance, but spotting Laurence at the back of the group, I laid a hand on his shoulder, pausing him.

He turned to face me as I said, "Can I have a moment?"

He nodded, his eyebrows rising slightly—the only sign of his interest being piqued—and motioned for me to lead the way.

I stepped out of the large tent and turned right, heading around the side of the structure. My gaze snagged on Byn as I walked—like it always seemed to do these days—his head turned down talking quietly to Chess when our eyes met. He gave me a small, encouraging smile and a slight dip of his head before giving his attention to the trokav before him once again. My anxiety eased ever so slightly at the gesture, and I listened to Laurence's soft steps on the grass behind me as I walked. Just a few paces behind me had become his normal place the past few weeks, if not next to me, having taken on the role of my personal guard. It'd become a comfort I'd learned to appreciate.

My eyes adjusted to the dark quickly—a child of the sky, as well as of the night—as we strayed farther from the torches placed outside of the war tent's entrance, until a soft chirp rang through the air.

Laurence and I came to a stop before Eden and a servant named Cole, who'd been helping to take care of Eden since she arrived. Surprisingly enough, Cole even claimed that Atlas, Lychen, and Gaia had taken a liking to the griffin.

I gently took Eden's reins from Cole, dismissing him with a murmur of gratitude, and shifted to face Laurence.

I forced myself to stand a little straighter as I said to my guard and friend, "I want you to ride her during the battle."

Laurence, who had been admiring the griffin just a moment before, looked visibly stunned at my request, eyes snapping to meet mine.

"Majesty, I couldn't possibly. She's bonded to you, she's *your* mount," he said, beginning to shake his head.

I smiled slightly at his humility, but I didn't plan to take no for an answer.

"She is mine, and as such, I deem who is worthy enough to ride her. She may not be specifically trained for war, but she's agile, a fast flier, and tunes in very well to her rider's emotions and movements. She'll be a great asset to your fighting style tomorrow." Laurence parted his lips to argue, but I held up a hand and continued on. "You've never fought while grounded. I'd rather have you in the skies than on the ground where you're more vulnerable. You can take Eden with you tonight and get acquainted with her. Plus, this way you can watch my back up there," I said with a lazy grin.

Laurence swallowed thickly, emotion clouding his features.

"I never thought I'd see the day where I got to fly again," he said softly, his gaze on Eden. "Not in this life, at least."

His eyes met mine, tears threatening to spill over onto his cheeks as he said, "Thank you, my queen."

Before tears could spring up into my own eyes, I dropped Eden's reins and pulled the older gentlemale into a firm embrace.

As we pulled apart, neither of us bothered to mention the small spot on my shoulder where his tears landed.

A moment after introducing Laurence to Eden, she let out a sharp chirp and head-butted the guard's shoulder, nearly knocking him over with the force of it. I barked out a laugh, and the tightness in my stomach eased. The two of them would get along just fine after all.

After reassuring Laurence once again that I was sure of this arrangement, I hugged Eden and said my farewells. With a few parting words, Laurence led Eden off into the night.

I waved until I couldn't see the duo anymore, then loosened a breath. A small part of me felt guilty, asking Laurence to fight once again, but I knew he wouldn't have it any other way. The male had said so himself.

I smelled Byn before he made contact—rain and magnolia blossoms—and smiled to myself a heartbeat before his arms twined around my waist.

I leaned against Byn's firm chest behind me, still shocked that this was my reality. That I had come to trust him, somehow. Was even willing to go to war against my own people for his.

I was not the same female I was just a few months ago.

"I'm guessing that went as well as I told you it would?" Byn spoke quietly near my ear, intentionally getting close enough that when he spoke, his lips brushed my skin.

I had to suppress the shiver that ran along my skin at the contact.

I focused on my breathing as I nodded, then turned around in his arms to face him and laced my arms around his neck.

"It was... more emotional than I had expected," I responded, our eyes meeting.

"Given what he's been through, I'm not entirely surprised. He's a good male."

"So are you, you know," I added.

Byn smiled softly, but didn't respond. Instead, he dipped his head and softly pressed his lips to mine.

And it felt like coming home.

This kiss was gentle, tender, loving. Our feelings melted together in my chest until all I could feel was warmth as our lips danced together, perfectly in sync. My arms wrapped around his neck on instinct, pulling him closer to me.

Hidden by the dark of night, I lightly gasped as his lips left mine and found that sensitive spot below my ear.

"Ready to head to our tent for the night, my love?" Byn asked in between the trail of soft kisses that ran down my neck.

Intertwining my fingers in his hair, I fought all of the desires floating through my body in the moment as I responded, "I'm afraid I can't. I still have things to do before the North arrives."

It was with those words alone that I noticed the sudden weight on my chest—and that it wasn't originating with me.

Byn pulled back to look into my eyes as he slowly reached out to stroke the inside of my wing. He moved calmly enough that if I wanted to, I could move out of the way.

I chose not to.

"Are you sure I couldn't tempt you, wife?" he murmured, his voice carrying a teasing note to it.

I gritted my teeth together to hold back any embarrassing noises trying to surface as his fingers made contact. "You're going to be the death of me, Thorntier," I said through my teeth as the power in my body surged in response to him.

A soft, triumphant smile overcame his features, dimple popping, as he observed just how easily he could get to me.

Though, despite the welcome distraction, that heavy feeling hadn't left.

I looked up into Byn's face, trying to read him, when he leaned down and lightly planted a kiss on my lips.

Sparks raced inside my veins at the contact, and it took all of my self-control not to groan with disappointment when he pulled away just a heartbeat later.

"Be safe, alright? I'll see you soon," he said gently, voice full of emotion that I couldn't seem to place in the moment.

***

Kicking up a plume of dirt and huffing in frustration, I dropped to the forest floor, wings dragging. This small clearing was still covered overhead by the trees, and most importantly, was vacant of any soldiers or trokavs.

Since we left Cairnyl, any spare moment I had was spent attempting to use the booklet Rayven gifted me to shadow wield. What I didn't realize when I began, though, was that it was unlike any other zirilium I'd ever used.

I hadn't even come close yet, and I'd been here for hours.

Taking a deep breath and letting Rayven's written words flow over me once more, I turned my attention inward.

Shadow wielding isn't something you force, it has to choose to work with you.

Loosening another breath, I focused on the shadow of a branch that lay before me. I analyzed the shape of it, the small gaps where the leaves parted overhead. The dark color of it, where the shining light of the moon overhead had been blocked out.

You can't bend it to your will right away—you must bend to it just as much as it bends to you. Meet it in the middle.

I kept my full attention on the shadow, slowly feeling a light buzzing sensation overcome my outstretched arms, closest to the darkness. I summoned a dredge of my own energy with those words in mind, and shoved that surge towards the shadow.

With that, I felt a tether snap into place—like pieces of a puzzle fitting together at last. I gasped at the contact of energy, and flicked a single finger out of place.

The edges of the shadow moved in rhythm with the motion.

I let out a victorious laugh, hopping to my feet once again, making sure to not let go of that tether of energy.

To become *shadow, you have to surrender your entire being to it—nothing can hold you back.*

Taking another steadying breath, I attuned my mind to that connection before me. My fingers were still tingling, and I hoped to the Stars that was a good sign.

I rolled my shoulders back, slowly relaxing each muscle in my body. I let go of my anxieties about the war to come, about Aurora who I'd left in Cairnyl, and the brother I'd likely see during battle in a matter of hours.

Each deep breath I released, I let go of another anxiety. And with each breath, more of my body was overcome with that tingling sensation. First my hands and arms, then from my toes up my legs, and onward.

Another series of breaths, and I stopped worrying about if I'd have to face anybody I knew during this battle, if my friends would survive, if my father would come to lead his people himself. *My* people.

The sensation spread up my limbs and into my torso, up my spine. I knew if I looked at my hands, I'd likely see the beginnings of my body turning to shadow, but I didn't dare break my eyes away from the shadow before me and risk losing that focus.

Just as I went to take in another series of breaths, to hopefully succeed in this task, a crushing weight sucked the air right out of my lungs.

Gasping, I felt that tether between me and the surrounding shadows collapse, and I stumbled back a step at the loss of contact.

But the weight on my chest wasn't coming from me.

Byn.

As fast as my muscles would allow, I spread my wings—taking up the entire width of the small clearing—and used that pain and agony in my chest to guide me to him.

I followed that feeling deeper into the forest, farther away from the South's campsite. If Byn wasn't feeling his best, reconnecting with nature and grounding himself with it would have been one of the first things he attempted to do. I remembered him mentioning that during one of our late night talks while at the cabin.

I followed those emotions as if they, too, were a tether between us—between our very souls.

Soon, heart racing, I circled over the same small group of trees twice when I finally spotted him below the largest of them.

Drawing my wings in, I fell, only releasing them again when I was close enough to the ground to catch myself and elegantly land just a few feet away from my husband.

The sight before me left me feeling gutted.

Byn was kneeling, hands covering his face, and was violently hyperventilating. Tears streamed down his face, and his entire body shook with the sobs that wrecked his chest.

Flinging myself onto the ground before him, I gently grasped his hands in mine and pulled them free of his face.

"Byn," I said softly, my voice steady despite my racing heart and panic of my own blooming in my chest.

His eyes shot up to mine, darting around my face before landing on my eyes again. His breath was still coming quicker than I could count, but I could feel his agony ease just slightly at the sight of me before him.

Despite the small reprieve he seemed to have when I arrived, his hyperventilating resumed quickly, his hands leaving mine to reach up and grip his hair tightly.

"Byn, my love," I said, then flared my wings out and around the two of us. Letting him once again enter one of the only places in the world I'd ever felt truly safe, and hoping he'd feel the same.

"Byn, focus on the calm you feel in my chest—like I focused on yours back at the cabin. I'm here," I offered, hoping focusing on one steady emotion would help.

He shook his head side to side forcefully at the idea, but was unable in the moment to offer a further explanation.

Not knowing what else to do when that didn't ease his pain, I decided to do exactly what he did for me all those months ago when I first arrived.

Wrapping my arms around the male I had come to love more than life itself, I pulled him to me so his head rested on my shoulder, and began to hum.

I hummed that same tune that had weaved into my head and never left, though I'd only heard it once.

I began softly, a bit tentatively, but when he didn't pull away after a heartbeat, my courage grew, and the notes I made became stronger, though just as gentle and loving.

The tune itself was beautiful, though a bit on the sad side. It was something bittersweet.

I gingerly ran a hand up and down his spine—his shirt damp with sweat—as I continued to hum. With each passing note I released, his hyperventilating slowly ceased and his breaths deepened.

After a few more notes, the tune came to an end, but I continued to move my hand along his back until he was finally ready to lift his head on his own.

When he finally did and met my eyes, I could feel the love and gratitude radiating from him in place of that crushing weight—but the anxiety of his was still ever present.

"Tell me," I said gently, but firmly.

Byn began shaking his head, and a haunted look overcame his expression. Suddenly, I felt like I could actually see just how heavy his crown weighed upon him.

Cupping one side of his face, I turned his head to look at me once again.

"You can't deny something is wrong any longer. Tell me," I said quietly. "Please, my love."

His mouth set into a firm line, as though he was trying to stop his lip from trembling.

Then, as if a dam inside him had broken, he simply poured himself out before me.

"I've known I was to rule for years now, but that responsibility has never felt heavier than it does right now. The pressure to be perfect all the time, to always have the right answers. The weight of not only my sisters depending on me, but an entire kingdom..." He let out a shuddering breath. "The last time I planned a battle, strategies and all, as I did tonight, my parents died." His voice broke as tears once again welled in his eyes.

"Who is going to die because of my decisions this time? How many families will I have to face who loses somebody in this battle? Each and every person who dies on this battlefield is an additional weight on my soul, along with my parents' deaths." He paused, taking a steadying breath. "Sometimes I go over in my head how I could have positioned our army differently last time, in order to spare my mother and father. Sometimes, in the darkest hours of the night, I wish I could have traded my life for theirs." He said the last part so quietly it was hardly a whisper, tears escaping his eyes.

Hand still cupping his cheek, I tilted his head up to meet my eyes so he really heard me as I spoke.

"Your parents would have not changed a single thing, if it meant you got to keep living, Byn. *Not a single thing.* They loved you, and Margo, and Teagan with their entire beings, and if they could redo it, they wouldn't change a thing—I guarantee it. My love, they wouldn't wish this for you in the slightest, but I know that when their time came, they were confident their kingdom was in good hands with you as their heir. They had faith in you, *believed* in you, because they knew how courageous, loving, and brave you are," I said with confidence.

"Not only that, but you don't have to carry these burdens by yourself anymore. We're in this together now, and any decisions you and I make, we face the consequences together, alright?" I asked.

Byn, still looking slightly doubtful, nodded his head. But behind the doubt clouding his eyes, I saw something even brighter.

Hope.

"Why couldn't you focus on my calmness?" I asked him, my voice displaying only genuine curiosity.

At that, Byn paled slightly. He rubbed the back of his neck, obviously reluctant to share as he explained.

"Emotions can't... expand, or take over others, like I might have allowed you to believe. They still have to go somewhere. When you focused on my calmness and peace back in Echen Bay, and took it into your own chest, I took all of your panic and fear into myself. Essentially, we swapped emotions in that moment." He paused. "It was the only way I could think to help you at the time."

"Byn..." I started.

The tightness in my chest from Byn has ceased completely now, only slight guilt radiating from him now, but just as he opened his mouth to respond, we both heard it.

"Robyn!" The sound of somebody running through the brush. "*Aviva!*"

"That's Teagan," Byn breathed.

Him and I shared a single glance, then I was retracting my wings and we were both on our feet, following the sound of Teagan yelling our names.

Because of the darkness of the forest at this hour, I took the lead, my eyes adjusting better to the lack of light.

"Teagan!" I shouted into the forest.

"This way!" she responded, and I shifted our direction slightly to the right, when I finally saw her up ahead.

My feet carried me until we were upon her, Byn at my side and Teagan panting slightly.

"What is it?" Byn asked tightly, and I could tell without the feeling in my chest that his anxiety was rising once again—along with my own.

"They're here," she breathed, "the North. They're on the horizon as we speak."

Chapter Twenty-Three

T he roving hills at the base of the mountains, yet just beyond where the forest ended, was the perfect battlefield. There were no large bodies of water nearby, but the Southerners had the very earth beneath their feet to their advantage.

The entire host of the North was a blur on the near horizon, difficult to see by just the light of the moon above. Where the hills met the forest, I stood with Byn and Teagan, watching as they approached. Quinn was readying her soldiers—Laurence and Eden included—while Chess readied the trokavs. Atlas and Lychen stood, waiting, behind us—further in the trees to hide their large forms.

I still had no clue where Byn had sent Drayven, but I had come to trust him enough to know that wherever he sent the spy, it must have been worth not having him on the battlefield today.

Teagan, standing on the other side of Byn, was murmuring to herself, counting the rows of soldiers coming towards us. Between the ones marching on the earth below us, and the ones in the sky above, there must have been thousands. Tens of thousands, if the Stars were against us today.

One of the largest hosts the North had gathered in decades.

My stomach was leaden, my chest tight with worry radiating from the male standing next to me.

We didn't get to talk further once Teagan found us, but from his firm grip on my hand, I was hopeful that what I said got through to him. That we truly are a team, one unit.

And the extra ring on my right hand weighed as heavy as my crown. The ring, full of poison and housing a small spike, was my absolute final option if things didn't go our way today.

Today would be my father's last day, one way or another.

His rule could go on no longer.

"Our soldiers will be waiting for your signal," Teagan said to Byn, having finished counting—dread now clouding her soft yet strong features.

Byn shifted, his armor clinking quietly. The three of us sprinted back to the campsite to don our armor and weapons before heading here—to the edge of the forest. I had my usual dozen daggers, my sword Elaera, a bow and quiver of arrows, and my mother's dagger all strapped to various places on my body. I knew Byn and Teagan had just as many weapons on them, too—if not more.

The three of us were the first line of defense between our army and theirs.

"I know," Byn responded to Teagan solemnly.

We stood on that hill for what could have been minutes or hours, watching as the army of children of the sky marched and flew into Southern territory, some flying on the backs of their griffins.

Just when I could see the deadly expression of one male on the front lines, and the sweat beading his brow, Byn took a step forward.

Then another.

He walked until the trees barely provided him cover anymore, then paused.

That was when he made his move.

He leaped straight up into the air, then came crashing back down to the earth, falling into a crouch as his fist struck the rocks and dirt below.

And the earth *shuddered*.

Originating where his fist hit, a crack formed in the ground, spearing forward rapidly, straight toward the awaiting army.

The males before us paused as they heard the earth groan, crack growing.

Then the screams began, as the earth opened and began to swallow them whole.

They tried to scatter, to run, but the rip in the earth only grew. Some tried to fly, but then Teagan was there next to Byn, using the roots in the earth to wrap around their ankles or torsos, dragging them back into the depths of the sprawling chasm that was still rapidly spreading.

Each one who tried to escape was pulled deeper in, and their screams echoed as they fell.

Without warning, Byn lifted his fist, breaking his connection with the rip in the earth, and the ground once again groaned as it snapped shut, like the maw of a giant beast.

Crushing each and every male inside, now entombed in the ground below permanently.

And cleaving the Northern ground army right down the middle.

Slowly rising to his feet, Byn panted, then stumbled a step. I picked my jaw up, which had fallen due to the display of incredible power just displayed, and closed the distance between myself and my husband. He wrapped an arm around my shoulders, leaning into me as he steadied his breathing.

"That was... incredible," I murmured to them both.

Teagan shot me a proud look, while Byn smirked. Disentangling himself from me and standing on his own two feet again, he said, "Now the real fun begins."

***

After Byn's display of power—which had been the signal our army was waiting for—the battle horn was sounded, and the South ambushed the North in the dead of night. We most definitely took them by surprise, their shock and grief palpable in the air from Byn's strike, but to their credit, they didn't back down. They simply raised their shields row by row and braced themselves. They didn't bother trying to close their lines where Byn had split the earth, likely from fear of him doing it again.

So, as our army pushed forward, battle cries sounding the air, they speared toward that crack in the North's defenses. If we could get past the grunt men at the front and could reach the weather and lightning wielders closer to the middle and back, we'd have a better chance at besting them.

The clouds above were already being molded by the weather wielders, and I knew it wouldn't be long before we were all fighting in horrible conditions.

We positioned our fire wielders on the front lines to best combat the air wielders we were confident the North would place at their fronts. After all, they'd simply be fanning the flames.

As for me, we decided my main mission today was to get close enough to my father to take him down once and for all. When discussing what my role would be today, it was deemed I didn't have enough training yet to fight in the army itself. I'd been trained, yes, but to fight as an individual—not within the army lines. So, I was taking a different approach.

As for the topic of taking my father down, I advocated for Dimitri. That he'd be a better ruler—that he was more reasonable than our father, that he actually had a *heart*. That he was somebody we could negotiate peace with—for *true* peace this time.

Byn had objected to me taking this mission on, of course. But the Valwain functioned on votes, and he was overruled. I knew he just wanted to keep me safe, but the rest of the group seemed to understand that I was the only one who stood a chance at being successful.

Part of me wondered if I should feel worse than I did about plotting to end my own father's life. But if we were being honest, I was angry at him. I believed I had been for a long time. For never being a true parent to me, for never being what I needed him to be, for the neglect and different forms of abuse he had inflicted on everybody in his life.

I supposed I would simply have to hope that anger was enough to push me to follow through. And if not that, then the fact that Byn and everybody else was counting on me to do this would.

The result, we hoped, would be worth the pain I'd feel afterwards.

But one step at a time. First, the issue of Father and getting close enough to him to strike.

I flexed my wings wide, almost ready to take off and join the frenzy of war—which Teagan and Byn had already taken their places in—when I tilted my head to the side to glance at my wings again. It still startled me, seeing my white and silver wings covered in soot to look a drab gray.

We didn't light many fires while taking cover in the forest, but the one in the main war tent had been large enough to produce just enough soot and ash to coat my wings.

One thing about the Northern army was that their ground troops were always more organized than their aerial ones. It could be difficult with different wing spans to create concise, orderly rows and columns, so that was where we decided to plant me.

Though it was brought to the attention of the group that my wings by themselves might give me away, since Dimitri and I were some of the only ones with dual-colored wings in the

North—hence the soot. Now, my wings better resembled those of Aurora's.

Along with that, my bright, white hair was tightly braided back, easily hidden in the shadows of my oversized cloak so that it wouldn't give me away, either.

Just when the battle before me began to grow less organized, I pushed myself off of the ground and into the sky above. I had a bow in my hands already, so it was easy to blend right in with the group above that was firing arrows towards the Southerners below.

With my ability to see well in the dark, I could already see clouds forming a storm overhead—definitely courtesy of the weather wielders my father brought.

Unfortunately, I wasn't the only one who could see well in the dark—all of the North could.

I tried not to focus on the falling bodies on the ground below as I plucked an arrow from the quiver slung across my back. I stuck to the edge of the group of Northern archers, so it would be easier to slip away when the time came.

Using the opportunity that came with aiming at a target—which I always seemed to miss—I studied the battlefield below and around me, full of wielders, griffins, and Titan Wolves alike.

The winged males near me whooped and cheered every time they hit their target, and I couldn't stop the dread that pooled in my stomach each time. Did they hit anybody I knew?

I fired, continuing to intentionally miss, and readied another arrow as I continued to scan both the ground and air for specific movement.

I had fired six arrows, each one missing their mark, when I finally spotted what I'd been looking for.

The Northern army messenger, weaving between soldiers.

In the South, we simply used the corvids—the birds already flying about the field—but the North didn't have that option. They still used somebody—likely not a wielder, or at least a lower class one—to scatter back and forth across the battlefield, bringing official messages between the captains, general, and king, so they could all stay aware of what was going on.

I readied another arrow to maintain my facade, this time aiming for the messenger.

I waited until he got closer to the edge of the woods, his eyes flickering around the battlefield, likely searching for one of the army captains, when I loosened the arrow.

And it flew clean through his left wing.

I dove towards the earth before he could even fall, appearing like any other aerial soldier, landing to finish off his prey.

I landed next to the wounded messenger, who was groaning in pain and pressing a hand to the wound. Not so gently, due to our size difference, I did my best to drag him behind a nearby tree.

"This is going to sting," I said, picking up a rock the size of my hand, then swinging it to the side of his head. I silently thanked Quinn for showing me exactly which spot to hit back at Echen Bay.

He was unconscious before he could even register what was happening, and then I was stripping him of his outer garments that signified him to the North as their messenger. Fortunately, the North was accustomed to wearing layers, so I didn't have to leave the male in only his undergarments.

It was an outfit of steel blue, silver, and black accents, with a symbol of three circles overlapping—signifying the three groups of males they serve on the battlefield—over the wearer's heart. I made sure to snag his cloak to hide my hair, which had the same messenger symbol largely sprawled across the back.

With my new disguise, I ducked out from the forest and began making my way through the fray of soldiers, taking to the skies.

Nobody from the North paid me any mind, and the South was outnumbered, so they had more important things to worry about than the small figure breezing by just above them.

My wings carried me to about halfway through the battlefield without incident, staying closer to the edges so as not to get too caught up in the fighting. The night air reeked of iron from all the blood being spilled, and screams of the wounded rattled around in my skull.

Fortunately for the South, the dark sky was beginning to turn gray and brighter with every passing moment. Though, I could tell the downpour was going to start soon as thunder roared and lightning began to light up the clouds, occasionally striking the battlefield—and likely our soldiers.

I spotted Atlas and Lychen ahead of me, towering over their opponents and jumping into the air with snapping jaws, bringing down winged bodies with them.

Despite the time I'd lose walking instead of flying, I decided to land, so as to not become the wolves' next meal in my disguise.

Making sure my hood stayed in place, I began my trek through the teeming bodies once again.

That was when I heard it.

The footsteps of somebody charging.

And it sounded like they were heading straight for me.

Whirling around, I realized I noticed his presence too late. The Southern male with an angry face was barreling straight towards me. He obviously didn't seem to recognize his own queen, and he was now a meager six feet away with his sword raised, ready to slice me in half, when a streak of ginger flashed across my vision, intercepting the angry male.

Their swords clashed and slid, bouncing off of each other's, when Quinn yelled at him, "You idiot!"

The anger on his face shifted into confusion, but he didn't say anything to contradict his general.

"Dismissed, soldier. Find somewhere else to be," she said, her voice full of authority as she stood in front of me, shielding me partially from view.

The soldier, who was most definitely confused, didn't object and easily fell back into the fury of war.

The moment he was from earshot, Quinn turned on her heels to face me.

"What were you thinking? You have *got* to be more careful, for crying out loud! You're lucky I've stayed nearby to prevent incidents just like this." She shook her head as if she was in disbelief.

"I would have been fine, *General*. You worry too much," I bluffed, trying to downplay the situation and how close I was to being skewered. By one of our own soldiers, no less.

Quinn went to make a likely sarcastic retort, but I held up a hand to pause her as I stared back towards the edge of the forest I had just come from, movement snagging my attention.

At this point in the battle, all of the South's soldiers were on the battlefield. There shouldn't have been anybody else in or around the forest.

"What is it?" Quinn asked, squinting in the direction I was staring in and sheathing her sword.

The sun hadn't risen just yet, so I was still able to see better than Quinn could in the dim lighting.

And the sight unfolding before me from afar caused my breath to get stuck in my throat.

Peeking out from behind a wide tree, I spotted Margo's little face.

Panic laced through me like nothing I'd ever experienced before at the sight of her being here, in the middle of a battle, so close to the front lines.

"Quinn," I breathed, unable to express what I was seeing.

I watched as a large Northern male with light gray wings broke off from the main battle and began stalking towards Margo.

And she was looking the complete opposite way, totally oblivious to the fact that she was about to face her doom.

"*Margo!*" I screamed, then shot into the sky.

It wasn't until I was in the sky that I saw the blur of brown and white racing towards Margo, too.

I flapped as vigorously as possible, aware of Quinn somewhere below me racing to keep up.

I saw Quinn pause, but I didn't stop like her and the blur of brown and white did. I watched as they locked eyes, and Ezra smiled at Quinn—a smile full of sorrow, apology, and love.

Then I watched helplessly, flying as fast as the winds would carry me, as Ezra ran the final stretch between himself and Margo, then threw himself in front of the small child at the last possible second.

"Ezra! *NO!*" I heard Quinn scream from the ground, not too far behind me.

We were so close, but not close enough.

We both watched as the Northerner thrust his sword at an upward angle into Ezra's side, just below his ribs, and twisted.

Chapter Twenty-Four

I couldn't tell if I was screaming, or if I was hearing Quinn or Margo scream. We all watched as the Northerner yanked the sword out, causing Ezra to stumble back. His hand went over the wound, but still did his best to guard Margo with his crumpling form.

The panic in my chest ignited, turning into pure fury. I landed swiftly a heartbeat later, unfastening a dagger from my belt and plunging it into the main artery of the Northerner's thigh with no hesitation.

He bellowed, teetering backwards when Quinn appeared from the edges of the battlefield and finished the job with an efficient, clean slice across the male's throat.

It was a greater mercy than he deserved.

She didn't even wait for him to fall to the ground before running to Ezra, sliding to her knees to catch him as he finally fell.

I ripped the messenger's cloak off, balling it up and pressing it to his wound, which was pouring more and more blood with each second that passed. Quinn took over, pressing it firmly in place, when I finally turned back to Margo.

She was shaking from head to toe, her eyes full of tears, unable to tear her eyes away from Ezra. In an attempt to spare her from further pain, I stretched a wing out in front of her to block her view of Ezra and Quinn.

"I... I just wanted to come help," she said, her voice small and so unlike her usual giddiness, still staring at where she last saw Ezra. It was obvious she was falling into shock.

"I just wanted to help," she said again, a tear escaping and gliding down her cheek.

"Well, you didn't help, Margo. Not at all. You've just ruined *everything!*" Quinn screamed, tears cascading down her face as she continued to murmur to Ezra how everything would be alright.

I picked Margo up as she began to crumble, trying my best to keep it together myself as I watched Ezra grow paler from the blood loss quickly overtaking him.

My panic and fury must have alerted Byn that something was wrong, because I watched as Atlas and Lychen came barreling towards us.

Byn and Teagan leaped from the wolves' backs and broke out into a sprint, and I ran to meet them, a sobbing Margo in my arms.

"She's alright. Physically, at least," I reassured the two siblings quickly approaching, worry etched onto their features.

I handed Margo over to Teagan, who seemed eager to make sure my claims about her younger sister proved to be true for herself.

The moment Margo was taken from my arms, Byn cupped my face, tilting my head side to side and looking me up and down.

"You're alright? You're not injured?" he asked, his concern written across his face.

"I'm fine, Byn, but..." I trailed off, then turned and motioned towards where Ezra and Quinn remained on the ground thirty feet away.

Immediately upon seeing them, he broke into a sprint heading for the couple, and I did my best to stay hot on his heels while Teagan took Margo over to the wolves to calm her.

Coming to a stop, Byn and I both took up a side each next to Ezra, with Quinn cradling his head in her lap and Byn applying pressure to the wound now.

"It's going to be alright, Ezra. Just hang in there. We'll find Chess and he will fix it, you'll see," Quinn said through her tears, which she was desperately trying—and failing—to blink back. She moved to get to her feet, as though to go find Chess, when Ezra's hand flew up to stop her.

"Stay," Ezra said simply, *weakly*. When Quinn went to argue, Byn simply cleared his throat to interrupt.

"Congratulations, you two. I knew it was only a matter of time," he said with a voice thick with emotion, then motioned to Ezra's inner arm, where Quinn's family crest—a flaming crystal—was inked onto his skin. I was confident if Quinn removed her own armor, we'd see Ezra's crest marking her skin, too.

Sometime in the last couple days of preparation for this battle, they must have slipped away and gotten married.

My heart ached in my chest, and I knew for a fact that Byn was hurting, too. Even more so.

He had to watch his brother fade away.

And Quinn, her husband.

Ezra responded to Byn with a weak smile, but the motion looked pained, and it was obvious by the blood soaked cloak that he was fading fast.

Tears welled in my own eyes as I watched the interaction and the weight of it. Ezra was the first person to really try to make me feel more at home in the South. He made sure to continuously go out of his way for me to make me feel welcome. Without him, I wasn't sure I ever would have come around to feeling at home with Byn.

Byn reached out to Ezra and they gently clasped arms.

"Thank you," Byn's voice cracked. "You've been there for... *everything*. Ever since we were toddlers, you've been there. You're my brother, in every sense of the word. When I asked you to watch out for Margo, I never thought it would come to this." He looked away. "And I am *so* sorry."

"If I could do it all again, I wouldn't change a thing, Byn. You have to know that. You, Teagan, and Margo are my family, too, just as your parents were," Ezra said, his breaths wet and labored. "It's been the greatest honor I could have asked for, to watch you grow into the king you were always meant to be."

Tears escaped both males' eyes, and Byn quickly wiped them away, glancing towards me. Ezra did the same, offering a small smile.

"I knew you'd come around," he teased, despite the situation.

I chuckled, but it was a weighted sound.

"Thank you, Ezra. I wouldn't be here without you," I said thickly, knowing he'd understand what I meant.

He nodded, still smiling slightly as he grabbed my hand.

"My queen. My friend. My sister," he murmured with a final dip of his head to me.

I had to turn away as the tears rolled down my cheeks.

Byn and I slowly got to our feet and stepped away from Ezra, allowing him a moment with Quinn as she moved to take up Byn's place next to Ezra.

We'd accepted his fate, grateful that we got to say goodbye, and knew that he wouldn't last but another moment or two. It was obvious by his reaction to Quinn trying to leave that he knew he wasn't going to make it, and wanted to spend the time he had left with those he cared about, Quinn especially.

I doubted Quinn would accept his fate so easily.

"My gem," he said softly to Quinn, reaching an arm up to wipe the tears from her face. His blood smeared where his fingers touched her blanched skin, but she leaned into his touch anyways, as if savoring every touch, glance, and exchange she had left with him.

"Don't leave me," she replied, her face still resting in his hand.

"I can't hold on much longer, gem," he responded, speaking softer than I'd ever heard.

Quinn's shoulders shook from the effort of holding back her sobs, and fresh tears fell down her face.

"I never wanted to be the reason you cried," he said to her, his voice full of despair.

"It isn't fair. We didn't get enough time," Quinn said through her tears.

"Every moment with you was perfect. And if this was all the time we were permitted in this life, it was worth it. I'd rather have the time we did than go a lifetime not knowing you. Not loving you." His voice cracked at the end.

"I'll tear the Stars apart to find you again," Quinn responded, unrelenting even to the end.

Ezra smiled. Pure, and genuine, and full of unyielding love. "I know, gem. I'll be waiting for you."

And with that, Ezra's arm dropped from his wife's face. He closed his eyes, and did not open them again.

Quinn's screams cut through the air as she watched the life fade from her lover, a gut wrenching and heart aching sound.

The sun rose over the horizon, spreading its light like a gift upon us, as if our lives didn't just change forever. And in the same moment, the rain began.

***

Teagan, having left Margo safely with Lychen further in the forest, approached Byn and me moments later. The three of us looked on with tearful eyes as Quinn endearingly pushed Ezra's white streak of hair to the side, kissed his forehead one last time, then gently lowered him to the ground from where she had been holding him up.

Ever so slowly, she rose to her feet. Her armor and leathers were drenched in her husband's blood, which was still smeared across her face.

She walked over to where the three of us stood, but she looked as though her soul was weighing her down. Her eyes were empty, void of any emotion beyond pure fury.

I could feel Byn's own anger rising in my chest as he looked upon her, then back at Ezra's unmoving form. Not directed at his friends, his family, but at what had become of them.

She came to a stop in front of me, meeting my eyes.

The lack of emotion and life in them sent a chill down my spine.

"Let's finish our mission," Quinn said firmly, though her voice was rough from overexertion.

"Are you—" I started, but she quickly interrupted.

"His sacrifice will *not* be in vain."

I pressed my lips together, but nodded. "Let's regroup," I responded, turning to face Byn and Teagan, too.

That was when we all heard it.

Footsteps, coming from the west.

Hundreds of them, if not thousands.

Their steps sounded like the beat of a drum as they descended upon the battlefield, with one lone figure leading them.

Drayven, riding into battle atop Willow.

He actually did it. He brought them.

After decades of remaining neutral, he had convinced the Ocrein Isles to offer up their support in this war.

Chapter Twenty-Five

Teagan and Byn caused a variety of flowers and plants to sprout around Ezra's body—a small way to honor him until the battle was over and we could come back for him in order to give him a proper burial. So we could take him home, one last time.

We stood at the edge of the forest, upon a hill overlooking the battlefield, as we plotted our next moves.

Rayven had arrived at the perfect time.

Because we were losing.

The sheer number of soldiers the North had on us was starting to take its toll on our army, and not even the extra power of the sun coming up on the horizon was enough to turn the tides in our favor.

Teagan left after the revised plan was in place, both her and Byn refusing to let Margo be on her own for too long without one of them nearby, even if Lychen was a good enough protector on his own.

Quinn, Byn, and I all raced for Atlas, then charged across the field to meet Rayven after Teagan departed. The Islanders were already charging into battle, battle cries flooding the air as they descended into the fray. The Southerners, upon seeing that the Islanders weren't cutting them down but rather the Northerners, took up arms with them and began pushing the Northern army back, step by step.

It was difficult to tear my eyes away from the shadow wielders and warriors that joined the battle. I watched as one shadow wielder used the tiny spots of darkness clinging to one Northerner in the sky to make himself appear mid-air next to the soldier. Before the Northerner could even process he was under attack, he had lost his wings, and the Islander was already jumping away through shadows to his next victim.

I cringed internally as I watched the Northerner fall to the ground—wings separated from his body. I looked away before his too-still form touched the earth.

The sight replayed in my head, reminding me of Laurence. I sent a silent wish to the Stars that he and Eden were alright.

Before the three of us could slide off of Atlas' large form to meet Rayven, he appeared next to us on the wolf's back, having used his shadows. His expression was neutral as always, yet somehow still gave away the urgency he felt.

"Seems like we made it just in time," Rayven said, looking across the battlefield after quickly scanning the three of us for any fatal wounds.

I could feel Byn's relief at seeing Rayven unharmed, and it matched my own.

"Rayven..." Byn started, but was interrupted by Quinn's sudden scream of pain.

She fell to her knees atop Atlas' saddled back, and I was instantly there to catch her so she didn't fall further.

"Quinn? What is it?" I asked, anxiety once again pooling in my stomach.

"Something's wrong," she panted, clutching her chest with both of her hands, as though she could ease some sort of pain there.

She doubled over, groaning in agony, clawing at her chest as though she could physically remove whatever was ailing her.

Then, as though nothing ever happened, she ceased her sounds of pain and slowly sat up. She was still panting heavily as Byn, Rayven, and I looked between each other, obviously troubled. Byn leaned into Rayven's ear, likely telling him about Ezra by the look of grief and horror that passed over Rayven's usually guarded expression.

Pulling back from Rayven, Byn started, "Quinn—"

"I'm fine," Quinn said, forcing herself to her feet. "For the sake of the Stars, let's win this battle already."

With that to set the mood, we caught Rayven up on our plans, despite how reckless they might've been. While we were all curious how Rayven rallied our new ally, we didn't have time to get into the details.

Rayven shook his head, obviously not agreeing with our plan to put me in harm's way. Byn didn't either at first, but both males quickly seemed to realize how little options we had left, despite their wishes to keep me safe.

It had taken pulling Byn off to the side and reassuring him I'd be fine to get him to calm down. That he had to trust in my abilities, and that he couldn't protect me himself forever—I had to do that for myself, too.

Now that it was raining, the soot had been washed away from my wings. The same dual colored wings that would have easily given me away before I could get close enough to my father to do any real damage. This small detail in itself ruined our original plan, along with the fact that the messenger's cloak now covered Ezra's body, drenched in blood and rain.

So we reassessed.

Once we were all on the same page, Quinn mounted Willow, sitting behind Rayven but leaving obvious space between their forms. I remained on Atlas, gripping Byn as both wolves broke out into a run on the outskirts of the battlefield, away from the forest behind us.

And towards our enemy.

***

It was easy enough to run through—or over—the few soldiers in our path as we made our way to the far, northern side of the battle-field. From our original spot on the hills by the forest, the tents set up by my father's people looked like no more than specks in the distance. But now, with every step Atlas and Willow took, those tents grew larger, and the situation laid out before me became more and more real.

I was here to put a stop to my father.

No matter what it took.

Now that we were growing closer to their king, the winged soldiers were turning their attention to the two large wolves in their midst. Most had been stopped by Robyn's earth or fire and Quinn's crystals, but if any of the soldiers from above happened to shoot for us, I'd readied myself to use my ability to manipulate the air around us to make shields or to block any arrows.

As I formed one of those hard wind shields around myself and Byn, just in case, I couldn't help but wonder how I'd changed so much, so fast.

When I arrived in the South just a handful of months ago, I was untrusting. Skeptical. Rude, even. I kept to myself as much as possible, because I didn't *want* to trust those around me. It had always been me, Dimi, and Aurora against the world. Without them, who was I?

Then came in Byn. I was so sure in the beginning that it was all a trick. I mean, who wouldn't after being told a lifetime of lies about those who I was now surrounded by? But piece by piece, I saw that the South wasn't trying to trick me—I had already been lied to, *manipulated.*

Byn had been so patient, so caring, until I saw for myself that the South wasn't my enemy. I wouldn't be surprised if he truly had begun to fancy me that very first day when I pressed a dagger to his throat.

One Northerner dipped down from the sky, getting a little too close to Rayven and Quinn. Before he could do any damage, he fell victim to one of my rogue air currents that sent him crashing to the ground faster than he could right himself.

We were maybe two hundred feet away from the campsite now. Byn and Quinn were defending us brilliantly, Rayven even disappearing for a moment at a time to intercept a soldier or two with his shadows.

A sudden, bright light caught my eye to the right, likely only a hundred yards from our current position.

The light was something I had only read about in books, and pity washed over me at the sight.

I watched as the Northerner's light grew brighter, his form still swinging his sword at those who came too close. The light seemed to emit from *inside* of him, like a caged animal finally breaking free of its restraints.

Once he felled those around him, and those who remained realized what he was doing, it was too late.

He gave himself over to the Relenting.

Blinding, white light shone from where he stood, his form no longer visible, as he gave up every piece of himself in order to kill those around him—Northerner and Southerner alike.

The Relenting was a last-ditch effort—most fae never even witnessed it in their lifetimes. It was the act of surrendering yourself to the Stars—your zirilium, your energy, your entire *being*. And then—

The surrounding area of where the Northerner had stood *exploded*, originating from the light that had only grown brighter and brighter.

I shielded my eyes with my arm, forcing myself to look away as those who had been too close were reduced to ash.

The Relenting was considered a war crime—there was no safe way to enact it. The more powerful the person, the larger and more impactful the Relenting. It was an extremely painful way to go, for both the fae Relenting and those who fall victim to it.

"*Avi.*"

I wrenched my arm away from my face and forced myself to not look back at what I knew would simply be scorched earth and piles of ash.

Byn threw me a knowing look over his shoulder, then pointed to what was ahead of us.

A weight that felt like pure dread settled in my stomach at the site of the nearing tents, and what they meant.

I hadn't seen Father since the day I'd left the North. The day he forced me to leave everything I had ever known behind, including the only people I had loved—at the time. He used me like a pawn in his game—though I supposed that was all I ever was to him, anyways. Something to be used then discarded. Never cherished, never loved, not the way a daughter *should* be.

He only ever tended to me out of obligation, so he'd be seen a specific way. Like a loving father, a fair ruler. Little did his subjects know that the mask came off when the doors closed behind him. That he may wear a smile on his face, but his eyes matched his soul—void of any emotion beyond greed and selfishness.

I rarely saw him outside of our morning visits for my elixirs. Though I bet he spun some elaborate tale in front of others to make it seem like he simply visited each day because he enjoyed my company.

After so many years, I believe we both preferred it that way. Living separate lives within the same castle.

I always felt for Dimitri, though. Father never let him wander far, his leash kept short. Looking back on our situations now, I was selfishly grateful Dimitri was able to take the brunt of Father's attention on himself. At least I was still able to sneak away every once and a while. Dimi rarely had that luxury.

Part of me wondered if my twin was on the battlefield today, or if he was left to oversee things back at Gatlyn Castle. An even smaller part of me selfishly wished he were here, just so I could see him and reassure myself he was alright. Aurora made it sound like he had been falling apart since my departure, but he had always been the strongest person I knew. What was so horrible that he couldn't weather it alone?

Shaking my head slightly to clear the thoughts spiraling in my head, I rested my cheek against Byn's back as we neared the campsite.

Just one more moment to soak in the warmth and comfort of my husband. I just wanted *one more moment*.

Sooner than I had hoped, Atlas came to a slow stop, and Byn helped me off of the wolf's back. Sometimes I wondered if he forgot I could fly.

Before I could take more than a few steps towards the circle of Northern tents, a tender hand circled my wrist. I allowed Byn to turn me around and hold me at arm's length, hands resting on my shoulders.

"Listen, Aviva... I wouldn't ask this of you if I thought anybody else had even a slim chance of getting close enough to your father. You're in a unique position here, with all his subjects believing you were taken by force. They'll *want* you to reach him, maybe they'll even help you. But once you reach him, he'll know something is wrong. Play it smart, alright? Use every tool and ability you have. If we can cut the head off of this beast of an army, they should all fall back. With the Islanders here, we stand a chance, but the less that die on our side, the better," Byn said, his voice gentle and reassuring, but with the strength of a king.

I nodded and threw him a cocky smile. "I know, Byn. I can do this. Plus, if things go horribly wrong, I'll have backup," I reassured him, wiggling the ring sitting on my gloved hands. "And you didn't ask this of me, love," I added.

He reluctantly removed his hands from my shoulders, and I could feel the guilt settling in his chest anyways, simply because he knew this was putting me in harm's way.

Grasping at the leather and metal armor on his chest, I pulled him down to my level and pressed my lips to his.

He returned my kiss fervently, and through our intertwined souls, I could feel everything he wasn't able to voice aloud. The love, the guilt, the longing, the desperation, the pure *need*. The kiss sent small sparks running through my veins, and I wondered if it was even possible to ever grow tired of the male before me. I ingrained the feel of him into my mind, and dedicated the smell of him to memory—spring rain and magnolia tree blossoms.

I broke away a handful of heartbeats later, resting my forehead against his as I whispered reassurances to him one last time. "I can do this."

Quinn cleared her throat from behind Byn, Rayven next to her looking towards the tents not too far off now.

I looked to her without a hint of the anxiety I felt showing on my face, and gave her a dip of my chin. She returned it with a bow of her head. I appreciated the gesture, knowing that there would be no big speeches or grand reassurances from her, especially not after what just happened to Ezra.

I turned to look at Rayven, only to find him already scanning my expression, likely checking in on me like he did everybody else in the Valwain.

"Ready?" he asked, his voice rough and husky like always.

I nodded, shrugging off the remnants of the messenger's uniform. I tried not to cringe, thinking of him lying beneath a tree on the other side of the roving hills, unconscious. Our original plan hadn't even worked.

Without the uniform, I now stood in elegant, lightweight armor made of black leathers and gleaming metal. It was a mixture of the hard, almost impenetrable leathers the North wore—lightweight so as to still be able to fly—with some of the South's metal armor providing extra protection over more vital areas.

Rayven then handed me his gray cloak—worn in enough to look tattered, as though I had escaped the clutches of the South. That was the story I needed to make my father's people—*my* people—believe. I donned it without a second thought, covering the armor underneath completely.

I met Byn's eyes one last time, hoping he could read the emotions written in them as I began walking into enemy territory.

I heard the beat of the wolves' paws as they retreated, not wanting to bring any extra unwanted attention to my sudden appearance.

I ducked behind one of the smaller tents on the outer ring of the campsite, Rayven next to me.

"You won't see me, but if you pay close enough attention, you'll be able to feel me with your shadow wielding. Remember your training, and know that I'll be right there in case things go wrong," Rayven said, his dark chocolate eyes peering into mine.

"Thank you, Drayven," I replied, which he dipped his head to.

A male of few words.

Rayven suddenly dissipated into shadow, but I forced myself to be hyper-aware of any and all shadows around me. The unexpected might just be my greatest weapon yet.

I felt Rayven clinging to the long shadow I cast along the ground, courtesy of the rising sun, as I rubbed dirt across my face, in my hair, and along my wings.

I wished to the Stars it was enough to trick those I'd have to make my way past, or at least give them pause.

Then, I broke out into a run.

I ran as though my entire world depended on it. And in some ways, it did. I felt free for just a moment, like I didn't have the weight of a crown on my head, like two different nations weren't relying solely on me and my upcoming decisions to win this battle.

And after that, to win the war.

For once, I allowed my anxieties to overwhelm me. I let them fester in my chest, let them eat away at my stomach until it was nothing more than a growing pit in the center of my body.

I thought about Aurora and how much we seemed to have grown apart since I left the North. I brought to mind Dimitri and all of my worries I had revolving around him, and if he was truly going downhill or not. I pondered how alone I felt when I was first sent away to a strange place with strange fae.

I let it all eat at me until tears were streaming down my face as I ran. I let the hood of Rayven's cloak fall back as the wind whipped at my tears, leaving streaks running down my face through the dirt I smeared there.

As I got closer to the largest tent, right in the middle of the campsite, my brothers and sisters from the North began to murmur and gasp as I ran past, my booted feet carrying me as fast as one of my air currents.

The closer I got, the louder those murmurs became, until they began to shout.

It only made me run faster.

My chest was heaving by the time I reached the center tent, but as I rounded it to reach the front, I came face to face with six winged guards, each one covered head to toe in that near impenetrable leather and carrying a variety of weapons. Each male looked as though they were carrying their own personal armory.

"What—" a familiar voice started. "Wait. Princess Aviva?"

Looking up, I remembered to put on my best performance.

"Joel!" I sobbed, throwing myself into the young guard's arms and allowing the tears I had worked up to flow freely.

The gray eyed, dark haired guard had served my father for around six years now, and he often guarded Father's meetings with his advisors. He was one of the only guards who would break his stony mask to smile at me, or would sometimes even look the other way when he'd find me outside of my room when I shouldn't have been as a young teenager. Though he was only a handful of years older than me, he had worked hard to make his way from a servant in Gatlyn Castle to a member of the royal guard. And though I no longer served the North, I admired him for it.

"Princess, how-how are you here? What happened? We were all devastated when we heard you had been taken from us," Joel said, his voice laced with concern as he gently put space between the two of us when he noticed the way the five other guards were watching us. Each one had removed their hands from their swords though, which was a good sign. They didn't view me as a threat to them.

Yet.

I had to bite my tongue to keep from correcting him as I responded. *Queen*. No longer *Princess*.

But I knew they recognized me right away. Their eyes bounced around from my partially covered face, to my white hair, to my dual colored wings. They, at least, had not forgotten me so easily.

"The South has been trying to persuade me to join their side of the war for months. They've been trying to break me." I forced my voice to crack, reaching up to touch the eyepatch covering my green eye, hoping they'd believe it an injury. "I-I don't know why they chose me, but this battle was to be m-my first test. The moment they turned away for just a second, I ran. I knew I'd find my people here somewhere." I paused, sniffling, tears falling still. "Is... is Father here?" I made a show of looking around cluelessly, though I knew he'd be inside the tent Joel guarded.

Joel looked to the other guards around him, and though they seemed slightly skeptical, they also seemed to look on me with pity.

If only they knew.

When Joel hesitated, sharing weighted glances with his fellow guards, I pushed again. "He is, isn't he? I just want to see my family. I want to go *home*, Joel." I spoke with a voice full of raw emotion, my lip trembling and eyes watering all over again as I looked upon him and the other guards.

"Let her in, Joel. The King can't be upset that we let his stolen *daughter* in," one of the others said, the only part of his face not hidden by his helmet was his blue eyes.

For a split second, I wondered if it was weird that I had missed seeing other blue eyed people, just slightly. Even if I wasn't *fully* blue eyed anymore.

Not that these males seemed to know that, or even suspected anything was amiss.

Joel loosened a breath. "Alright, alright. Let's get you inside, Princess."

I forced myself to let out a sob of relief, thanking Joel repeatedly as I allowed him to lead me inside the giant tent.

It took everything in my power not to drop my act as I beheld who was inside.

Not only my father and his advisors and his top general—who, to his credit, looked as though he'd actually been called off of the battlefield—but also my brother. My twin.

Dimitri.

He was alive. And he was *here*.

My father's piercing gaze settling on me was enough to knock the air from my lungs and make my anxiety spike. I felt Rayven stir slightly in my shadow, now pooling closer to my feet with the torch-lit chandelier overhead. His presence eased that knot in my stomach just enough so I could breathe.

I continued to make myself look small, helpless, and scared as I looked back at the king sitting before me, only a few paces and a wooden war table between us.

Dimitri stood like a startled doe at our father's right hand. His jaw went slack at the sight of me, and I saw him take a step forward before Father cast a cruel looking warning glance at him that made Dimi freeze. It was like my arrival broke him of his trance—but Father didn't want it to be broken. He wanted to keep Dimi's leash as tight as possible.

My heart ached at the sight.

Father turned his attention back to those before him.

"Joel, I thought I told you not to let anybody inside this tent," Father said, though it sounded like a threat.

"Y-Yes, my king, but it's—"

"*Anybody.*"

I audibly heard Joel gulp, and suddenly I was reminded why my father was still in power.

Everybody feared him.

After a few tense heartbeats, Father sighed deeply, then waved a hand.

"Everybody but my children are dismissed. And Joel?"

The guard looked upon my father's face with pure fear.

"Don't let anybody else inside. At any cost," Father said, much too calm for somebody who was just reunited with their daughter after months apart.

Joel nodded, and without another word, ushered each person out, being the last person to leave. He cast me a worried glance before letting the tent flap fold shut behind him, leaving me alone with the only family I'd ever truly known.

Chapter Twenty-Six

The moment the tent was sealed off from the outside world, I corrected my posture, rolling back my shoulders and doing my best to no longer look so small and scared.

"Finally. I thought they'd never leave," I said nonchalantly.

Father's expression shifted slightly, while Dimi was still frozen in place. As though he couldn't quite believe his eyes.

I unclasped the cloak I wore and flung it over the back of a high-backed chair, specifically made for those with wings. Then, I walked over to the side of the tent where a basin of water sat. My heart pounded as I turned my back to my father, but I knew with my newfound connection to the earth, and the extra power of my sun stone adorned gloves in my pocket, I'd be able to feel him coming if he moved from his chair at the head of the war table.

I wanted to appear comfortable. As though Father didn't terrify the life out of me.

I wanted to look like the queen I truly was.

Using water wielding, I coated my hands in a layer of water, then ran them over my face, hair, and wings—slowly. Stroke by stroke, I removed the layers of dirt and grime I had put there in order to make it this far.

Once I had cleaned the dirt from myself, I wielded the water into a small bucket next to the basin, so as not to contaminate the clean water.

"Much better," I said calmly as I turned back to the two males, who hadn't moved a muscle. Though I couldn't help but notice the way Father's hands roughly gripped the arms of his chair, knuckles turning white.

He always hated being reminded of my abilities. He had forever wanted me to be powerless like Dimitri; he hated that *I* was his true heir and not his son. Reminding him of that, as well as my control over my wielding, would force him to break his composure, even if it was only slightly.

"And here I had thought I'd finally rid myself of you for good," Father said with only a hint of annoyance in his voice. "Seems as though I was mistaken."

I let his words roll off of me like the water I had just wielded, not taking anything he said to heart.

"I fear you can't get rid of me that easily, Father," I responded with a smirk that I knew Byn would be proud of.

I settled myself into the chair I had placed my cloak on, making myself at home and appearing as comfortable as I could, even crossing an ankle over my knee.

Father opened his mouth to speak, but I held up a hand to cut him off. The same way he had done to me and Dimi so many times before.

"This is how this is going to go. You're going to call back your soldiers, surrender to the South, and then we can come to an agreement between our two nations that will put an end to this war. Surely, we can be of more help to each other if we were to cease slaughtering one another," I said, making a show of examining my nails.

Father barked out a harsh laugh. "*Never*. Besides, why would I take your word for what the South will or won't do?"

"Because I am their queen, after all." I flicked my eyes up to meet his and smiled sweetly, shifting my arm to show off the tattoo inked there—the Thorntier family crest.

He looked stunned, as though he couldn't quite believe the marriage he arranged actually went through. And that I'd won them all over.

Then, his expression shifted into a sly smile.

"I've got to hand it to you, you've actually surprised me. I didn't imagine you'd actually win their respect. And in such a short amount of time, too," Father said. "But that changes nothing. I will never surrender to the likes of *you*, or your new people. *If* my army is to fall today, we would rather fight to the death."

Got him, I thought to myself.

"It's funny that you suggest fighting to the death," I said, lowering my hands onto the arms of my chair. "Because I'm still Northern born. And as such, I have certain rights. So, I'm evoking the right to challenge you, Father, to a veltik khan."

A veltik khan was an ancient Northern ritual where the two parties were forced to fight to the death. Rejecting the challenge of a veltik khan was a huge disgrace, and was seen as admitting weakness and known defeat. While breaking the rules of a veltik khan was looked down upon and branded as untrustworthy, that was nothing compared to simply rejecting the challenge. Additionally, only one weapon per party was allowed. Only the two party's bodies, one weapon each, and any zirilium they could wield.

Rejecting the veltik khan was something I knew for a fact the king before me would never do.

Both Father and Dimitri were stunned into a lapse of silence, but I didn't break it. I allowed them to mull over what I'd just proposed—let my father ponder over his limited options.

For the first time since I sat down, I cast a glance at Dimitri. I didn't want to show any indifference towards him in front of our father, in case he tried to use him against me somehow. But looking upon my brother now, I could read him like an open book. Like always.

Just by his eyes alone, I could tell he was begging me not to do this. He wholeheartedly believed I'd lose, that he was about to watch me die, and he wouldn't be able to do anything to stop it.

My heart ached for him, and I wished so badly that I could let him know it'd be alright.

That I wouldn't be losing today.

"Fine," Father said at last, rising to his feet to tower a good foot over me, making me feel like a child again, even with the table between us. "But you won't be fighting *me*," he said with an evil grin.

Father unclasped his widely known, black onyx crested sword, Tarrious, from around his waist and shoved it towards Dimitri.

"You'll be fighting him, instead, right here and now. I choose Prince Dimitri to represent me," our father said.

At those two sentences alone, my stomach plummeted.

I knew this was somewhat of a possibility, but I truly thought my father's pride would overtake him and he'd want to put me down himself.

I miscalculated.

And now I had to pay the price.

My eyes flickered to meet Dimitri's, and I saw the pure panic written in them. I saw the exact moment he came to the conclusion that only one of us would make it out of this tent alive. His eyes were full of sorrow, and I felt as though he was already grieving me. If I were in his shoes, I'd be doing the same thing. As far as Dimi knew, he'd taught me every maneuver and trick I knew.

Unfortunately for him, he didn't know I had a few new tricks up my sleeve.

I tried to silently reassure Dimi, casting him a weighted yet emotional glance. I let him see every emotion written on my face for just a split second, before letting my neutral mask fall back into place.

Getting to my feet, I felt Rayven stirring, as though in warning. It took all my effort not to call upon him for an ounce of comfort or courage.

Father led Dimi to the back of the large tent, murmuring to him fervently. He pulled a pair of fighting leathers out of a wooden chest, handing them to Dimi, who quickly donned them over his more casual clothes.

Leaving Dimi to prepare, Father swiftly shoved the war table to the side, closer to the water basin, to make a larger area for the veltik khan.

Standing closer to the center of the tent now, I unsheathed my own sword from across my back—the one Dimi had given me for my fourteenth birthday, that I had named Elaera. It was among my things back at Cairnyl, and I brought it out specifically for the possibility of this battle. Though I never expected to be using it against the person who gifted it to me in the first place.

After placing all other weapons on the war table, I made sure to specifically shift my mother's dagger to the bottom of the pile to hide it. I weighed my sword in my palm, looking down at the shimmering silvery blade, crested at the top with an array of bright blue sapphires. Originally, Dimi had said they matched my eyes.

If only he knew.

Cracking my knuckles, I watched as Father said a few final words to Dimitri, then they both turned to face me. Father backed up a few paces, while Dimi stepped forward.

"It didn't have to be this way," he said to me quietly.

I smiled at him sadly. "Yes, twin. It did."

And with that, I swung my sword in a high arc, aiming straight for his fighting shoulder.

Dimi quickly lifted Tarrious, blocking the blow, but the unexpected swing cost him a few feet as he yielded a couple steps backwards, obviously startled.

Our eyes met, and I could see the warrior instincts in him rising to the surface.

Good, I thought. *Let's put on a show.*

One thing about Dimi was that he had tells. The slight shift in his foot before he swung, the intake of breath before lunging forward. I had spent years studying people, but because he taught me to fight, I studied *him* more than anybody else.

Every move he made, I easily blocked, until we were both in a dance of swings, arcs, blows, and lunges, trying to knock the other person off balance. The only sounds filling the air was the sound our swords made when they met, and our heavy breathing.

Finally, I saw Dimi's patience beginning to thin ever so slightly. He threw himself into his next blow, aiming for a non-fatal spot in my lower side.

Taking the opportunity while I could, I side stepped swiftly and lowered my sword towards his shins so his legs hit the flat part of Elaera, causing no damage but still making him falter. He stumbled forward, and I kicked his back between his wings just hard enough to cause him to land on his knees. I placed the tip of my sword at the top of his spine, where his head could easily be severed from the rest of him. I pressed slightly, not breaking skin, but enough where he could feel the threat.

Almost too fast for me to keep up with, he turned on me, obviously enraged at having been bested by his own previous student, even briefly. He hammered his sword so hard into Elaera that she went flying, skittering to a stop at the far edge of the tent.

Because I had been looking at where my sword landed, I almost missed Dimitri advancing on me. My eyes flickered to meet his as he raised his sword, and there seemed to be nothing beyond pure rage in his eyes. Like everything he had been holding back his entire life was finally rearing its ugly head.

With no weapon left, and only a heartbeat left between me and what was likely certain death as Dimi's sword was coming down, I played the only card I had left.

Wielding.

I flung my energy out into the earth, searching. I used the sun stones in my pocket resting in my right glove to center me, instead of focusing on my panic or anxiety. Only a few feet to the left and about ten feet below, I felt a chunk of crystal. I solidified my connection to it, then yanked with everything I had.

The iridescent crystal came between Tarrious and I at the last possible second, and shattered it into a thousand different pieces on impact.

I threw my arm over my face as I fell backwards, shielding my unprotected eye. I heard, more than saw, Dimi also fall.

I could feel our father's eyes on me with a newfound interest, who now stood behind my brother, but Dimitri's rage had been temporarily interrupted.

"Viva... how?" he asked.

I cringed, wishing we were kids again when I had told him everything.

Well, almost everything.

"It seems I inherited more from Mother than just her good looks," I said boldly, although I didn't feel it, as I slid the eyepatch still sitting over my right eye off.

I looked up at him with both eyes for the first time since I walked in, then let my gaze flicker to Father's for a moment before looking back to Dimi.

Then, still holding the eyepatch in my palm, I called towards the fire in my veins, and the patch erupted into blue flames.

It burned until there was nothing but ash, then I gently let the ashes fall to the ground below.

I would hide no longer.

Father's expression was guarded, but Dimitri seemed awestruck for a moment as he watched the ash fall from my hand.

Then, his face shifted. Now, instead of awe and wonder, his usually handsome face was clouded by hurt, anger, and disgust.

"I always suspected you had Northern zirilium—it was the only thing that made sense as to why you were so secretive the older we got. Then Aurora more or less confirmed it after you left, and I felt so... *defeated*. My whole life has revolved around being heir, and the title isn't even rightfully *mine*." He began to shake with pent up anger. "Now you mean to tell me not only did you inherit Northern zirilium, but the Stars gifted you with zirilium from the South, too? What happened to us being equals?"

"Dimitri, it isn't like I chose this—" I started, but was interrupted.

"Stop. I don't want to hear it," he said, getting to his feet, brushing shards of crystal off of himself. "Let's get this over with, *twin*," he spat the last word like a curse, making my chest ache.

I quickly got to my feet before I could be bested again, but instead of shaking the crystals off, I used my zirilium to quickly shape them and those around me into another sword and a small arm shield.

Placing my feet apart to anchor myself to the ground, I faced Dimi once again.

But when I looked into his eyes, I noticed the jealousy there, fueling his rising rage.

So far, we hadn't actually hurt each other. It was like we both knew Father just wanted a show, an act. But looking into my brother's eyes now... for the first time, a whisper of doubt regarding my twin sang through my veins.

I didn't allow myself to focus on it long, though, as Dimitri threw himself forward, sword aiming for just below my ribs.

I sidestepped, though not as quickly as I should have, then twirled back around to face him. I was stunned at the amount of anger and frustration radiating off of him.

I felt Rayven stirring, but paid him no mind. I had already shown my hand—that I possessed Southern zirilium—but they didn't know the extent of which ones yet.

I sidestepped once again as his sword arched towards me, but not fast enough this time. I sucked in air through my teeth as Tarrious sliced my upper arm open, blood dripping onto the floor.

I looked up to meet my twin's eyes, shocked, both of us breathing heavily. I know I started this challenge, but I never intended on actually hurting *him*.

But looking back at me, I couldn't see even a sliver of the brother I once knew. The male before me now was a stranger.

A dangerous one.

I saw Dimitri's weight shift a second before he lunged, his aim fatal, as I quickly moved to the left to avoid him.

I noticed a heartbeat too late that it was a trick.

It seemed he didn't teach me *everything* he knew, after all.

Before I could right myself, Dimi tripped me, making me teeter forward, unbalanced. My crystal weapons went flying forward. It was a dirty move, but one I would've used, too, if I were desperate.

Though before I could fall flat on my face, Dimi's hand gripped the back of my armor between my wings and hauled me upright, pinning me against his chest. Then, Tarrious was at my throat, forcing me to still, though everything in me screamed to *fight, fight, fight.*

My stomach sunk.

This was it.

I could feel Dimi's heavy breathing, which matched my own. The blade sat against my throat—one powerful swipe and it'd be like I never existed at all.

Then, Father began slowly clapping as he moved to stand in front of us. I forced myself to stand as still as a statue, my eyes tracking his every movement.

"It was a valiant effort on your part, daughter. Truly, good try." He smirked, which I realized was such a different expression than the one Byn would wear. Where Byn's was warm and playful, Father's was cold and calculated.

I hated it.

Not daring to move a muscle in my current position, I stayed quiet.

Stalking forward, as though he wanted to soak in every detail of what was about to happen, Father instructed, "Finish this, Prince Dimitri. Then there will be nobody standing in the way of you and the title of rightful heir."

Rayven speared towards me through the shadows of the tent, but I made a small motion of flicking my wrist, and he stopped in his tracks. I could sense his hesitation and his urge to defend me, his queen and friend, but he obeyed anyways.

Father had been too busy staring at the blade against my throat to notice the slight movement.

I felt Dimitri's small pause, a beat of hesitation, and that alone was enough for me.

There was only one option left.

Just as I felt Dimitri beginning to move—to do what, I didn't know, but I wasn't taking any chances—I sprung.

I threw my energy forward, begging but also demanding a quick connection with the shadow Father's pitch black wings cast along the ground behind him.

Within the span of a heartbeat, the connection was solidified, the tingling working quickly this time, overtaking my entire body as though the shadows also realized how dire of a situation this was.

One second, Tarrious was pressing into my skin, my blood beginning to spill, then I was nothing.

I was nothing yet everything all at once. I could still see and hear, but it was as if my body was far away, disconnected. I became lighter than I'd ever imagined possible, and there was no restriction to any of my movements.

If I thought flying felt like freedom before, it was nothing compared to not having a physical body.

I could still feel the sting of my wounds, but somehow I knew in this form, they weren't something I had to worry about.

I speared forward, aiming straight for the shadow I had originally connected with, then loosened my grip on the connection that was holding me in this shadow form.

With that loosening, I materialized behind my father, and in the same heartbeat, flung my hand out, calling crystals to it. Once a large chunk of that iridescent crystal landed in the palm of my hand, I gripped it tightly, not allowing myself even a second to hesitate as I drove it home.

Straight through my father's back.

I shoved and twisted, an angry yet gut wrenching sob breaking free from my throat as the crystal shard struck home—straight through his wicked heart.

The crystal broke free of his chest, having gone all the way through him, completely impaling him.

A strangled sound came from deep in his throat as his hands reached up around the crystal.

Then I watched as he fell to his knees before me.

Dimitri's scream rung out through the air, dropping Tarrious and lunging forward to catch our father, gently lowering him to the ground as blood began to pool around them.

I watched, hands soaked in my own father's blood, as Dimi examined the crystal protruding from Father's chest, as though he could somehow fix it.

Dimitri continued to cry out, tears falling from his eyes, as he tried to bargain with Father to keep breathing. To stay alive.

My heart began to crack.

Father's breathing slowed as he reached up to place a hand on Dimi's shoulder.

With labored breathing, his attention solely on my twin, he said, "My boy. Carry on my legacy. Do everything I was unable to, do you understand me? *Conquer them all, Dimitri.*"

With those final words, Father's arm went limp, falling back to his side, and his last breath shuddered out of him.

Dimitri, hand shaking, reached up and closed Father's eyes, then tilted his head back and let out an agonizing scream, tears streaming.

I could vaguely feel my own tears rolling down my face, but I felt so far away from my body, I didn't even register the shadow pooling by my feet—a silent comfort.

After his scream cut off, Dimitri slowly turned his head to look at me, soaked in our father's blood.

"*You.*"

He pulled himself to his feet, but before he could charge, Rayven materialized in front of me and let out an animalistic snarl.

"The veltik khan is over," Rayven said by way of warning.

Dimitri gave pause at the sight of another shadow wielder in his midst, then slowly began to back up towards the tent entrance, Tarrious in his hand once again.

His eyes met mine, a cruel smile on his face. And for the first time in our lives, I couldn't help but think of how much he looked like Father.

The thought sent my heart shattering into more pieces than the crystals I had wielded.

I never wanted my brother to become my enemy.

"This is far from over, Viva."

"I know," I responded, my voice empty of any emotions, and moved to stand beside Rayven.

Dimi looked between the two of us, obviously seeing he was outnumbered, and continued to back up towards the exit.

Before he departed, he met my eyes once again, his smile somehow even more vicious as he said, "By the way, Mother wanted me to tell you *hello*. Too bad she'll never get to tell you, or *the other one*, herself."

With that, he tilted his head back and laughed wickedly. It was as though some sort of switch inside him had been hit—one that turned off any emotion that Father wouldn't have approved of.

My jaw went slack as I tried to process what he just said, but he simply smirked at my reaction, then flexed his wings and left the tent, taking to the skies.

Chapter Twenty-Seven

L ogically, I knew we needed to flee, but my body felt so far
away, like I was rooted to the spot.

I stared at the tent entrance where I'd last seen Dimitri, as though
in a trance.

Somewhere in the back of my mind, the thought floated around
that if I didn't move, if I didn't carry on, then this wouldn't be my
reality. That maybe this was just a nightmare, a bad dream, and I'd
wake up if I just stayed still.

"Majesty," Rayven said, stepping in front of my line of sight so
I could no longer see where Dimitri had departed from.

My gaze drifted to the side where my father's body lay, his form
much too still. The pool of blood around him was so dark it was
almost black, though it had stopped spreading before it could
touch my boots.

From what sounded like far away, I could hear the guards outside yelling after Dimitri, then arguing about entering the tent.

"Aviva," Rayven said softly, crouching down to peer right into
my eyes, "we have to go *now*."

Ever so slowly, I peeled my gaze away from Father's form, meeting Rayven's eyes.

My entire body felt numb, as though it wasn't really mine anymore. I've done so many horrible things with my body, with these hands...

From far away, I felt my limbs begin to shake.

"We're going to sneak out of here using the shadows, and we won't stop until we reach the others, alright? I'll lead the way, but I need you to hold onto me when we shift—can you do that?" he asked, still searching my eyes for any sign of emotion.

I blinked, the words *the others* standing out, clinging to the air around me. After a heartbeat of processing, I nodded.

"I can do that," I confirmed, my voice sounding so small compared to usual.

Rayven nodded, then used a shadow at the edge of the tent to wield, until he no longer stood in front of me. Not physically, anyways.

I took a deep, shaky breath. I could feel the incoming panic flooding my veins, but I did my best to block it out. With the panic, I could feel my zirilium surging, trying to overpower my control.

After quickly collecting Elaera and my mother's dagger, I turned back towards my father's form and slipped the ring off of my finger. I gently tossed it, the ring landing perfectly on his torso, near the crystal protruding from his chest.

Turned out the backup plan hadn't been necessary, after all.

Forcing myself to face the shadows again, I focused on my breathing. Then, I threw my energy out into the surrounding shadows until a connection was solidified between myself and a shadow not too far from Rayven.

Each time I shadow wielded, the tingling sensation and form shift came faster than the previous time. I tunneled all of the energy I could muster up into that connection, until I could no longer feel the blood dripping down my neck and arm, or any part of my body at all.

Rayven's shadow came closer, and I tethered my energy to his. I imagined it as though I was reaching out to take his hand in mine, as you would in a physical form, and the connection between us as friends and shadows filled in the gaps.

Once we were firm in our tether, he shot forward, slipping beneath the edges of the large tent and spearing towards the safety of the South.

I couldn't help but look back at my father one last time, the image of him, his blood, and the crystal through his heart burned into my mind.

I heard the panicked shouts begin behind us just as we slipped away.

The King was murdered.

King Horace Heartshire is dead.

***

Being tethered to Drayven, I didn't have to put much thought into where we were going, I simply held on and trusted him to get us back safely.

I allowed him to drag me along, making sure to keep pace with him as we soared across the battlefield, leaping from shadow to shadow.

A battlefield that was slowly growing emptier by the minute, as I watched more and more Northerners and griffins turn tail and run—or fly—the other way. Dimitri must have given out the signal, because soon the word *retreat* was all I could hear as Northerners yelled to those around them to flee.

Once it was obvious the children of the sky were giving up, cheers rang out across the hills, from both the Islanders and the South.

After the cheers died down, the reality of the situation seemed to overwhelm the surrounding soldiers.

We had won, but at what cost?

And what had made them retreat?

I was sure Byn and I would have to make a formal announcement explaining what happened, and that King Horace Heartshire of the North of Inphis was now deceased.

My father.

I... I actually did it.

I killed him.

The fact crashed into me like a typhoon. I may not be able to feel my body the same in this shadow form, but my emotions were definitely still present, and overwhelming.

The guilt, the sadness, the frustration, the hurt, the anger—all of this and more swirled around in what I imagined was the shadow equivalent of my chest, wrapping around my heart and squeezing until it ached.

As we moved, aiming for the trees we had set up camp in before the battle, I couldn't help but glimpse at each body we passed. I checked to see if it was somebody else I knew, if I had lost another friend. If I'd lost more of my family.

The guilt hit harder with each too-still form I saw, and my thoughts grew louder until I couldn't hear any of the soldiers we passed, whether they were cheering or crying.

If I had killed my father sooner, would these soldiers still be alive?

How many of these people have family, and are wishing to the Stars that they come home safely, not knowing they're already gone?

Does taking the life of my father cleanse my soul of all the soldiers that fell today?

The rise in my emotions sent me spiraling, and I couldn't even tell how long it had been since Rayven and I fled the scene. In the middle of my panic, I forced myself to focus on my surroundings for just a heartbeat. I quickly noticed that we were almost to the safety of the trees, and that it had begun to turn dusk.

The battle had lasted less than a full day.

Next to my own panic, I felt Byn's emotions rising in me once again, just as heavy as my own. He lost his brother today, and countless soldiers. The weight of which, I knew, would stick with him for the rest of his days.

Just as it would burden me, too.

That, and more.

Before I could even process where we were, Rayven severed the tether between us and materialized before a portion of the Valwain I recognized as Byn, Chess, Laurence, and Eden.

I remained in the shadows, though I noticed Byn and Laurence looking around for me. Rayven gave Byn a speedy report with vague details, just providing the main points. From far away, I heard Byn say that Teagan was at camp with Margo, and Quinn was with her soldiers, having taken up her place in the front lines after Rayven and I departed. He also mentioned that Quinn should be reporting to him soon, so they could go over body count, wounded, and discuss taking Ezra home.

The debriefing between the two took less than a minute, and then Rayven leaned into Byn's ear and murmured something I couldn't quite catch.

Byn began to scan the shadows, presumably for me.

Byn nodded to Rayven, the two males clasping forearms, then Rayven peeled away from the group, heading towards the Islanders.

"Aviva?" Byn called out softly, looking around once again.

I could almost *feel* him tugging on our connection, on the bond between us, and then his eyes snapped to the shadow of the tree where I was. How, exactly, he knew, I was unsure.

Byn looked to Chess and Laurence and asked if they could wait nearby, and they nodded before slipping away, farther into the trees, with Eden in tow.

He then came and sat right next to where he knew I was, loosening a breath.

"My love, you can come out now. It's just us." He paused. "We both know you can't hide from this. I can feel it, you know. The panic, the guilt. It's eating you alive. Please, come here."

Hearing him speak so gently and lovingly to me, after all that I'd done, cracked something inside of me.

I let go of the connection between myself and the shadows around me, and sat next to my husband, bringing my knees to my chest and wrapping my arms around them.

Byn went to wrap his arms around me, but I cringed away, making him pause.

"Please," I whispered, "don't touch me."

His expression fell, and it made me feel even worse—something I didn't realize was possible.

His disappointment was palpable, but he nodded his understanding. He shifted so he was sitting directly in front of me, close, but not touching. I wrapped my wings around the two of us, blocking us in from the outside world.

Feeling like I added to his burdens, a single tear slipped loose.

Then another.

I couldn't help but feel unworthy right now. I didn't deserve the love Byn was offering me, laying at my feet.

"Tell me what you're thinking, Avi," Byn said softly, trying to coax me back to reality instead of drowning in my own head.

I took a moment to ponder. Should I be honest? I knew we agreed to be open, but he hid his rising emotions from me until he physically couldn't anymore. Should I push him out, the same way he did me? Was it worth it? Part of me thought so, but an even larger part of me was begging to let him in.

Deciding to just go for it, I whispered, "I don't deserve this."

"I know, love. You deserve better than—" I shook my head, cutting him off.

"I don't deserve *this*." I motioned to the small space between us. "I'm unworthy of the love you offer me, Byn. My name will go down in history as *Kin-Slayer*, and nothing more. With my mother, it was an accident. I couldn't control it. But this time, I mean... I knew exactly what I was doing, and what would happen. *And I did it anyways*."

The tears flowed freely now, and my breathing came faster and harsher.

Byn reached up as if to cup my cheek, but paused, as though remembering my earlier request. Without hesitation, I tilted my head to meet his hand, pressing the side of my face into his warm palm. Selfishly, I wanted his comfort.

I just wanted *him*.

Byn's eyes flicked to my throat, where I suddenly realized I was still lightly bleeding from.

Before he could freak out on me, I said, "Byn, I'm fine, please don't make a fuss."

"I can go get Chess," he offered, still staring at the wound.

"I'm alright, I promise," I reassured him.

Despite the reassurance, he ripped a small strip from the bottom of his shirt and reached forward, lightly tying it around my throat like a choker.

"Thank you," I murmured, eyes flickering to where his shirt now exposed some of his tanned stomach.

"Can I hold you?" he asked quietly. "I... know what it's like, more or less. To lose a parent or two."

Tears welled in my eyes once more, heart aching for the male before me, who had been through so much.

"You deserve everything you think you're unworthy of and more, my love. I promise," he said gently, then opened his arms, motioning me forward.

I chewed on my lip a moment before giving in, despite my heavy heart. I crawled into his lap, repositioning my wings to fit around us tighter than before, and wrapped my limbs around him. Soaking in his warmth, his comfort, as he rubbed small circles on my back, I sighed shakily. His gentle strokes helped to ground me back into my body, slowly but surely. As if he understood exactly what I needed.

This is it, I realized.

This is *what home feels like.*

With that thought alone, the dam in my mind that was holding everything back finally broke.

And for just that moment, safe in the arms of my husband, I allowed myself to grieve.

***

After allowing myself to break down in a safe place—in Byn's arms, wrapped in my wings—we began walking farther into the forest to find the rest of our group.

Not but fifty feet in, we found Chess and Laurence, along with Eden.

The moment Eden saw me, she chirped happily and bounded over to me. I flung my arms around her neck in a warm embrace by way of greeting, and she rested her head on my shoulder.

"How are you, girl? Did you take care of Laurence for me?" I asked her sweetly.

"She most definitely did. If she wasn't so quick and agile, I'm not sure we would have made it out of some of the situations we found ourselves in," Laurence responded for Eden, making his way over.

Laurence gently stroked the griffin's head, then glanced my way. "Thank you. Being able to be in the sky again, especially at a time like this... that meant everything to me," he said thickly.

I smiled softly at him and nodded. "Anytime, Laurence. Truly. With all the duties I'm sure Byn and I will have when we arrive back at Cairnyl, she'll need somebody to check in on her more often than I'll be able to. Would you mind looking after her for me, when I can't?"

"But what about—" he started, but I interrupted.

"I can find a second guard, if it means Eden is being taken care of by somebody I trust."

The older male smiled at me, the emotion written there raw.

"It would be my pleasure," he said. "Looks like you're stuck with me a while longer, Eden." He stroked her head again.

Eden chirped sharply in response, causing us both to laugh.

Once our giggles died down, Laurence looked at me. *Really* looked at me.

"I heard what happened," he said softly. "Are you alright?"

I pondered the question a moment, then shook my head, smiling sadly. "No. But I will be," I said, unable to stop myself from looking towards Byn.

Laurence followed my gaze, then gave me a knowing look.

"I'm here if you need anything at all, my queen."

"Thank you, Laurence."

Byn and Chess broke apart, and Chess walked over, looking ready to examine me.

"I can give you a salve for that, you know," Chess said, examining the strip of fabric around my throat.

Without thinking, I reached up and lightly touched the fabric.

"I'll think about it," I responded.

Truthfully, I wanted a reminder of the events that transpired today. I never wanted to forget; today had shaped me.

Once Chess saw the deep cut on my arm, he insisted on going full trokav mode on me, sprouting some fancy plant and crushing its leaves to mix with water and rub on the wound. It sealed over quickly after, leaving nothing more than a thin, small scab. He said the wound on my neck wasn't deep, but due to the location, would likely leave a faint scar.

I decided I was alright with that.

Just as I saw Byn looking towards the battlefield, probably wondering why Quinn hadn't checked in yet, the general herself came barreling through the forest, straight towards us.

She stopped running once she got close enough, panting lightly. It wasn't until she stood closer that I saw the panic in her eyes, and the troubled expression covering her face.

"Ezra's gone," she declared, and I could tell even she was confused by it.

The group was quiet a moment, before Byn simply said, "Show me."

Laurence, Eden, and I took to the skies, flying directly over Byn, Quinn, and Chess as they sprinted in the direction of where we all last saw Ezra's body.

As we neared the area at the edge of the forest, I could see from the sky that Quinn was, in fact, right.

Ezra wasn't there.

We landed nearby, wings tucking in, as I walked to the edge of the plants we had sprouted earlier, reuniting with the group.

Now, each flower and plant had been trampled. It looked almost like a crime scene—semi-fresh blood had spilled on the greenery, then it looked like something, maybe Ezra himself, was dragged away.

At seeing the blood and ruined plants up close, Quinn fell to her knees, her breathing heavy as tears welled in her eyes.

"I lost him once, and now I've lost him again," she said quietly, eyes glued to the deep red blood before her.

"Maybe one of the carriages saw him and picked him up. For all we know, his body is already headed back to Cairnyl," Byn suggested, but I could feel his uncertainty.

Quinn shook her head, her shoulders drooping.

Before I could think better of it, I crouched down next to Quinn.

"Earlier, the random pain you felt. You and Ezra used the royal inks, didn't you? You weren't in pain yourself, you were feeling Ezra, right?" I said, somewhat quietly, as though divulging a secret.

Quinn stilled, then whispered, "Yes. I think so."

I could tell the entire group was stunned, troubled, and confused as I glanced to them. I felt it in Byn, and saw it in the firm set of Laurence's eyebrows, in the down-turned lips of Chess.

"Tell me about it," I said to Quinn, gently grabbing hold of her hand.

Quinn finally tore her eyes away from the bloody mess before us, looking to where our hands met. Then she looked up, searching my face, and the pure grief in her gaze made me want to look away.

"I felt the connection between us fade to almost nothing when he closed his eyes for the last time. But then when I was feeling his pain, it felt like... like being torn apart from the inside. As though my heart and lungs were on fire, or being lit up somehow. I didn't know what it was, but I realized it must have been coming from him when I saw he was missing. That's when I finally slowed down long enough to figure it out," she said, still peering into my eyes, looking frantic.

"Figured what out?" I asked.

"Ezra. He's still alive," she said, and finally saying it aloud seemed to take a small weight off of her shoulders. "I can still feel our bond, connecting me to him. It's faded, like he's still gravely hurt, or far away, but it's there. I don't know how, but he's not dead."

Yet, was the unspoken word that held in the air.

At that, I wasn't quite sure what to say. I looked up to Byn, hoping to find answers in his face, but he looked just as stunned as I felt.

"You're confident?" Byn asked her.

"Yes," she said simply, her hand unconsciously grazing the spot under her armor where her tattoo lay. If it were showing, the tattoo would reveal a hefty tree with branches of fire.

Byn ran a hand through his hair, contemplating, then nodded.

"We will do everything we can to find him," he promised her, "but right now, we need to think of our people. We need to re-group, follow the proper protocols, and assess the wounded. Ezra is strong—wherever he is, he'll be alright. Once we reassess, we'll start looking for leads. Deal?"

Quinn stared at him for a moment, as though contemplating leaving to find her husband this very second. Finally, she nodded.

"Thank you. For believing me. I know it sounds crazy," she said softly, rising to her feet.

"Your instincts have never led us astray before. I doubt they will now," Chess stated, Byn nodding his agreement. I looked hesitant-ly at Laurence, but his expression was guarded, troubled.

I considered questioning him when I felt Rayven's shadow en-ergy nearby, heading for us, along with two other new energies I was unfamiliar with.

"We have company," I said by way of warning.

Byn's eyebrows furrowed, confused, but then Rayven and two other people—one male and one female—materialized not but ten feet from us, stepping out of the shadows of a tree.

Byn, likely having felt when their physical forms touched the earth, whirled around to face them.

Then, a smile broke out across his face, despite the revelation just revealed moments before.

Fortunately, I had been studying him long enough now to be able to tell when he's truly happy or not. And right now, it was definitely just for show.

"It's good to see you again, Prince Callum and Princess Caelia. I heard how you both voted in the South's favor to send aid. Thank you for that. We're in your debt," Byn said, tipping his head to the royals in thanks, then clasping forearms with who I assumed was Prince Callum.

Both the princess and prince reminded me of Drayven—quickly reminding me that his family originates from the Ocrein Isles. The female, Caelia, had curly, black hair that reached her waist, and dark eyes to match—like two voids of light. Callum's eyes matched his sister's, but the coils of his hair were closely cropped to his head, and he had just a bit of a beard growing in, like he hadn't had time to properly shave in a while. The siblings' skin tone was darker than even Rayven's—something I was unaccustomed to seeing in the North. They reminded me of Maya, from The Haven's library. Though, unlike her, both were dressed in thick, dark metal armor from head to toe, and had various amounts of blood on them from the battle.

"Well, we couldn't allow you to have *all* the fun," Caelia responded with a smirk, placing her hand on her hip.

Callum nudged her in the side with his elbow, then looked back to Byn.

"It was the right thing to do," he said to Byn, dipping his chin.

"Stay a while, come with us back to Cairnyl. We can find arrangements for your soldiers," Byn offered.

Callum and Caelia shared a look, then Callum nodded to Byn. "Alright. It's time we catch up, anyways. And gives us time to figure out why there's a child of the sky standing with your group."

Feeling my cheeks heat up, I looked to Byn. He held a hand out to me and met my eyes, where I found silent encouragement waiting.

After taking his hand, I stepped up to his side as he told the siblings, "This is my wife and queen, Aviva of the North."

Both royals' eyes went wide as they looked me up and down—from my wounds, to my wings, and finally my eyes.

"Not solely Northern, though, huh?" Caelia said, the tone of her voice rubbing me the wrong way.

"My mother hailed from the South, but my Father was King Horace Heartshire," I responded, making sure to keep my chin held high.

At that, Caelia's expression faltered, as though simply hearing my father's name ignited fear in her.

After that, both royals' faces appeared much more guarded.

Byn cleared his throat after a second to break the silence—and tension.

Slinging an arm over my shoulders, he said, "Let's work on getting home."

Chapter Twenty-Eight

One Week Later

I turned to the next page in my current read, an old book of war records, breathing in the smell of leather and ink on paper surrounding me.

The royal library was quiet today—Laurence and I were some of the only ones inside, tucked away in our usual small pocket of the main room.

Today had been the first day since the battle that we were actually able to do some research of our own—and the first day I had felt up to doing so. Quinn, who normally wouldn't bother with books, had requested the library workers to bring her multiple manuscripts lately. She had specifically been looking into the ink the Southern royals use for marriage tattoos, to better understand the vague feelings she had been having lately.

Chester had been busy as ever, with The Haven's infirmary just now beginning to thin out some. He was not our only trokav in the castle, but he was the best we'd got, so he was often needed. Whether it be a newer trokav asking questions or a patient needing immediate help or simply making his rounds, he had his hands full.

Rayven had been doing his best to entertain the royal siblings from the Ocrein Isles, Byn sometimes joining him when he has a spare moment.

Apparently, Rayven's parents were quite close with the Prince and Princess' parents back when Rayven was young, before he relocated to the South. I didn't know the entire story, but since Rayven was the only one besides Byn they were familiar with, he had bitten the arrow and had been keeping them occupied.

Teagan, as our usual point of contact for the North, had been trying to get in contact with my brother, but had so far failed. It seemed Dimitri didn't want to be reached right now. So, in her spare time, she had been with Margo, trying to comfort the little one. Margo blamed herself for Ezra's... *death*. We decided not to tell her about Quinn's revelation, just in case we were only getting her hopes up to crush them again. She'd taken it really hard, but she was resilient. To get her mind off of it, Teagan has been training with her, trying to coax any zirilium Margo has out of her.

Byn and I have had back-to-back meetings almost each and every day with various groups—the nobles, the advisors, Quinn and her captains, the Islander royals and the points of contact for their army.

The day after we returned to Cairnyl, we made an announce-ment to all of Cairnyl that King Horace Heartshire of the North was dead, and the battle had been won—but not the war. It had been an awful feeling, hearing my new people cheer for the death of my father.

Byn had kept the details vague, but rumors spread anyways. Fortunately, I'd been so busy, I hadn't had the time to listen to all of the gossip.

When I'd had time outside of meetings, I'd been showing Au-rora around The Haven, and some of Cairnyl. One evening we took to the skies, and I gave her a tour from the sky, pointing out different landmarks and shops that Byn had once pointed out to me.

I made sure she knew she had a place here with me, but she still seemed like a shell of the female I used to consider as close as a sister.

"Hey, where'd you just go to?" Laurence asked quietly, a habit he held despite the library being mostly empty.

I sighed. "We've been so busy the past couple weeks, I've hardly had any time to process anything. I mean, can't we all just catch a break to catch our breath? Even for a moment?" I asked, frustrated.

"A crown is a heavy burden," he responded simply, as if that fixed my problems.

"Tell me about it," I mumbled.

Leaning forward against the table and resting my chin in my hand, I forced myself to actually process the words and numbers in the records book before me.

Slowly, my eyes widened with each statistic I read.

"Laurence," I said after a few moments.

"Hmm?"

"Am I reading this correctly?" I asked, sliding the book across the table over to him and pointing to a section of what I just read.

His eyes scanned the page, then did so again for a second and third time. His head snapped up and our eyes locked, his mouth hanging open slightly.

"Does this mean what I think it does?" I asked, keeping my voice quiet as I began to pick at my finger's cuticles.

Slowly, he nodded. "I think so. But how—"

"Aviva?" Teagan's voice called out through the library. Laurence's library habits obviously hadn't rubbed off on her just yet.

She sounded slightly panicked, so I quickly closed the book I had just slid to Laurence and scooped it up into my arms before heading out to the main portion of the library.

"I'm here. Teagan, what's wrong?" I asked, heading towards the entrance where she stood.

"There's somebody here to see you. I told her there was no way they were getting an audience with the queen alone, so Byn is already with her and her two companions, and I'm to escort you and be present," Teagan explained, hooking her arm through mine and beginning to lead me away. Though I could tell by how swiftly we were walking that she was stressed.

Laurence followed behind us without question; I'd grown used to the sound of his footsteps being nearby.

"We don't know who they are?" I asked her, allowing her to lead me across The Haven and towards one of the private meeting rooms that only the royals use.

"Oh, Byn and I know who the female's companions are—they're some of our nobles. But we don't know who *she* is, where she came from, or what she wants. She said she'll only explain everything with you present," Teagan responded. Somehow, she didn't seem to feel any nervousness about having a stranger in our home.

After another couple minutes of walking, Teagan stopped before a honey-colored wooden door with a golden handle. Without any warning, she opened the door and walked in, holding it open for me.

I looked back to Laurence, catching his eye. He nodded without me even having to speak, and took up position right outside of the door, already on guard. I patted his shoulder as I passed by in silent thanks.

Shutting the door behind me softly, I turned to face the strangers who dared to enter my home and practically demand an audience with me.

And came face to face with the female from the market. The same fae I had chased and who had seemingly disappeared.

I was so startled, I almost dropped the book in my arms.

"You," I said quietly to her, stunned.

"Me." Her mouth quirked to the side in a smirk.

A smirk that reminded me of Dimitri.

Her wavy hair had been cut even shorter than the last time I had seen her, now sitting just above her shoulders. Despite that, I instantly recognized her by her eyes—a striking ring of green surrounding a center of brown. A beautiful hazel that brought out her light, olive skin. She was wearing casual clothes under her open cloak, though they looked a little worn. Her hood was pulled back to show her face and ears, adorned by gold and a deep purple gem on each ear.

No running or hiding this time, I supposed.

Her two companions consisted of an older female with graying, dark hair and a nervous smile who stood alongside a brown-haired male, also graying at his temples, but with a much more guarded expression. They both looked like they had at least a little bit of Ocrein Isle heritage to them, but the striking green eyes of the female and the chocolate brown hair of the male made me think they were both more Southern than anything.

Regaining my composure, I crossed the room to where the female from the market sat in a chair next to the low-lying table. I listened to my boots gently click against the marble floor as I took up a spot next to Byn on the couch, Teagan moving to stand near her brother and king. The two older fae stood near the window, the female of the two still obviously nervous, though almost in an excited way.

"I'm assuming you have questions," the younger female said after I sat.

"Why did you run that day in the market?" I asked first.

She laughed, tilting her head back, before responding, "Don't you want to know my name? Or why I'm here?"

Grinding my teeth, I forced out, "What is your name, *stranger*?"

She smiled, as though she won some kind of game I didn't realize we were playing. "Matea. Nice to meet you, *Your Majesty*."

"Alright, Matea. Now, why did you run?" I said, my patience tired of being tested as of late.

"It's... sort of a long story," she said, showing a glimpse of nervousness for the first time since I walked in.

"I have time," was all I said.

"Well, you see, I've been hidden away my entire life, by my grandparents." She motioned to the two figures standing near the window. "It wasn't safe for me to let the world know I existed, at least not until recently. My grandparents even made sure my name wasn't jotted down in any family records. It's bittersweet, really." She smiled with a hint of sadness.

I didn't react, my face perfectly neutral.

"Anyways," she carried on, "that's why I ran in the market. Ever since I was little, I've been taught to be a wraith, a ghost. Nobody was supposed to catch me like you did that day." She paused. "You're the first one to truly *see* me."

"So, what changed? Why are you here now? It's been over a week since I chased you at the market," I questioned.

"You killed your father," she stated bluntly, shrugging lightly.

I flinched at the ease with which she said that sentence. As if the fact didn't haunt me in my nightmares.

Byn tilted his leg towards mine until our knees were touching—a silent support. A lifeline.

Matea didn't let the small movement go unnoticed.

"What does the death of King Horace have to do with *you*?" Byn asked, picking up the slack when I fell short.

"His wife, your mother—Queen Elore? I was... important to her. King Horace would have hunted me to the ends of the world if he knew I existed, simply so Queen Elore wouldn't have anything tying her back to the South." She paused. "I assume you've figured out that she was Southern by now?" she asked.

I nodded. "Why would my father have put in so much effort to hunt you?" I asked, wishing she'd just get to the point.

"Because... Queen Elore was my mother, too," Matea said, softer than she'd spoken before.

The statement felt like a punch to the gut.

That was why I felt like I recognized her that day at the market.

She looked *so* much like Mother. Her heart shaped face, the firm set of her jaw, her straight nose—even the green of her eyes matches the color of my own.

Both inherited by a female neither of us seemed to know.

"How—" I gasped. "How is this possible?" I finally managed to get out.

Matea sighed, as though she was already tiring of the conversation. "Elore grew up here, in the South. These," she motioned again to the two figures behind her, "are her parents, Billie and Geoff Ashford."

My eyes snapped up to the female's face—my grandmother's face—and I couldn't help but notice the tears welling in her eyes. In that moment, I wondered what she saw when she looked at me.

Suddenly, I remembered the records I studied when I first arrived at The Haven.

I looked back to Matea. "You're... not lying. I've seen the noble house records myself—they stop after Mother's name."

Matea gave me a smug smirk, then nodded.

"Elore wielded all five Southern zirilium—not unheard of in our noble houses—but she loved helping others more than anything else. She used her abilities to become a trokav for the Southern army when she was young. Back then, the Ocrein Isles hadn't closed their borders yet, and our two peoples mixed freely. She met my father, Ethan, on the battlefield, where she found him gravely injured and left for dead. She ended up nursing him back to health over the course of a few months, and during that time, they fell in love—hard and fast.

"They welcomed me to the world a little over a year after my father was back to full health, having carved out a small life for themselves here in Cairnyl. My father was going to take Elore's last name and become a member of the noble class, in order to be with her. Even though he was a loyal soldier, Elore didn't care about social status—she herself worked hard as a trokav in every battle that came and went. Until one battle, when... they didn't come back."

She took a deep breath, but didn't give herself time to think before barreling ahead.

"When I was just a few months old, The Ashfords, my—*our*—grandparents, were told that they had both been slaughtered in battle. It was an especially bad battle—we had been taken completely by surprise, and it was all hands-on deck. But when the battle ended, their bodies were never recovered. It was like they simply *vanished*."

A chill ran down my spine as I listened to what she was saying. There was no way she knew.

Right?

"But then, another eight months after the battle where they supposedly died, *Queen Elore* came into the picture in the North. When I was old enough to start piecing things together, I didn't think much of it at first. Just a coincidence, right?" She laughed under her breath.

"Well, after years of trying to figure out what happened to my parents, I decided to take matters into my own hands. I journeyed to the North," she shot Byn and Teagan a concerned look, likely because crossing into the North was forbidden, "and stayed in Hollis for a couple days, gathering clues. There—"

"How did you make it there and back without being caught?" Byn interrupted.

Matea looked as though she had to hold back an eye roll as she extended her hand.

Then melted into the shadow of her chair within the blink of an eye.

Byn pressed his lips together tightly.

Matea appeared again in the chair, then asked, "Make sense?"

Byn nodded, then motioned for her to carry on. I realized that must be how she *disappeared* that day at the market, too.

"As I was saying. You know what I found in Hollis?" she asked, looking in my direction.

I shook my head, still slightly skeptical.

"There was a small tavern on the outskirts—Tammy's Tavern—that had portraits of all the Northern royal couples. And the most recent one depicted the cold-hearted King Horace with his arm around my mother. There was no denying it—I had studied her portraits in Ashford House for my entire life. Her face is burned into my mind.

"It was at that point I knew she was alive. Or at least she hadn't died that day on the battlefield. I wondered what that meant for my father, but I'm still unsure, seeing as Elore obviously somehow became involved with *your* father, and I couldn't imagine she did so willingly," she said, and I could tell she must feel a certain way about that topic.

"So... if all of this is true, why are you telling me this now? That was years ago," I asked, unwilling to present my and Laurence's findings without her confirming her own theories first.

"I think they're still alive. I heard about that member of your Valwain—Ezra." She nodded to Byn, who went stiff upon hearing the name. "I believe he's still alive, too. And if my research is correct, there are more out there somewhere. *Alive.*"

My heart pounded as I slowly set the book in my lap onto the table before us, opening to the page I had showed to Laurence.

"I believe you. And your theories," I said after a moment.

Matea's eyes snapped to meet mine, as if searching for any signs I might be lying or pulling a cruel prank on her. But I simply held her gaze, letting her see how genuine I was being. Slowly, she nodded and looked down to the book between us.

In that moment, I decided to take a leap of faith and trust this female—my half-sister.

"Earlier, I found these records. And if they're accurate, then over the years, we've lost thousands of our soldiers and trokavs—ones who didn't make it home, dead *or* alive," I stated.

Byn scanned the pages, taking in each report and statistic, while Teagan rounded the couch and came to lean over Byn's shoulder to inspect it as well.

"Why hasn't this been brought to my attention before now?" Byn asked, and I could feel a new weight settling on his shoulders.

"We didn't know, Your Majesty. Think about it—if a Northern-er freezes a soldier in place, then shatters them, there isn't a body *to* recover. It's all just been brushed under the rug—until now," Matea answered without missing a beat. It was obvious she had given this a lot of thought.

I looked up to Billie and Geoff—my grandparents. "What do you two think about all of this?" I asked them.

The two looked at each other, then Geoff nodded slightly. Billie took a step forward.

"We agree with Matea's theories, though maybe not how she gathered her evidence." She sent a scowl towards Matea, who smiled cheekily in response. "Matea might be stubborn, brash, and sneaky, but she's not a liar. Plus, the records speak for themselves." She motioned towards the book on the table.

I nodded, and I found myself agreeing with them. I didn't know if Mother and Ethan were alive still, but I did know Quinn believed

Ezra was, and the records go back years, all showing the same results.

"So the North is taking our people. Not just our soldiers and trokavs, but even members of nobility and the Valwain now," Teagan stated, and I looked to Byn to gauge his thoughts. I could tell by the light in his eyes that this revelation, while adding a burden to his already heavy shoulders, had also brought him a sliver of hope. Our friend, his brother, might still be out there somewhere.

Matea nodded. "That's the theory here, Princess."

There was a moment of silence, where everybody simply processed the heavy revelation that had just been laid out before us.

Not only did my father hurt everybody he came in contact with, try to conquer the world as we knew it, forced me to hide who I truly was, and more—he also kidnapped Southerners for what I could only assume were his own selfish purposes.

A small portion of me began to feel less guilty about taking his life.

After all, sometimes you had to sacrifice those you love for the greater good.

A heartbeat later, I locked eyes with Matea—my sister—before finally responding.

"Let's go get our people back."

Epilogue

The snow battered the high, arched windows as the male paced up and down the stone corridors. His shoes sounded as he walked, *click, click, click*, with each step he took.

His thoughts were overflowing, attacking him from the inside. The North had lost the battle he was so sure they'd win, and the king was dead. Never again would he have to face the king, and he couldn't decide if he was happy about that fact or not.

But now, the weight on his shoulders—and head—only grew.

His body ached, his very veins hurting and straining. From what, he wasn't sure, but he didn't have time to worry about it. The meetings he was now required to attend and endure were never-ending, but he could hardly think straight anymore. He'd be of no use in another pointless meeting, so he'd dismissed everybody. They had argued, of course, but he did so despite their protests.

It was a temporary reprieve, but a reprieve, nonetheless.

He paced the long corridors for hours without let up, trying to ignore the throbbing of his veins, until finally he fell to his knees in agony.

And with that, he cracked at last.

The very ground beneath him shook and rippled. Darkness shifted to surround his kneeling form. He tilted his head towards the ceiling and let out a gut-wrenching scream of agony. And with that scream, a ring of fire blotted out the darkness around him, surrounding him in bright flames.

And there in that moment, within the cold of that dark corridor, the next king was formed.

About the Author

Photo by Jana Vaughan

Alaina Hope was born in Houston, Texas and was raised just north of the sprawling metropolis. She has two younger siblings who mean the world to her, and a cat she's had since she was seven, who also serves as her writing companion.

When she isn't writing or reading, she's hanging out with those dear to her, or traveling across the country to see some of her closest friends.

Most of all, she can't wait to provide you with the next installment of Aviva's story!